A RAE GREYSON MYSTERY

WHERE WOLVES WAIT

BW HOFF

Black Rose Writing | Texas

This is a work of fiction. Names, characters, businesses, places, events, and incidents are either the products of the author's imagination or used in a fictitious manner. Any resemblance to actual persons, living or dead, or actual events is purely coincidental.

ISBN: 978-1-68513-543-0
PUBLISHED BY BLACK ROSE WRITING
www.blackrosewriting.com

Printed in the United States of America
Suggested Retail Price (SRP) $23.95

Where Wolves Wait is printed in Baskerville

*As a planet-friendly publisher, Black Rose Writing does its best to eliminate unnecessary waste to reduce paper usage and energy costs, while never compromising the reading experience. As a result, the final word count vs. page count may not meet common expectations.

Cover by BW Hoff

For those ready for another twot plist...I mean, plot twist.

WHERE WOLVES WAIT

CHAPTER ONE

If Rae Greyson were a piece of laundry, she would be a fuzzy sock. Not a pair. Just the one fuzzy sock with a design on it, probably of a sloth. Rae believed that she and these reluctant animals had similar DNA and behaviors. For instance, like sloths, Rae moved faster in water than on land, starved to death on a full stomach and pooped a third of her body weight in just one visit to the bathroom. Unlike sloths, Rae couldn't sleep in a tree all day and, instead, worked as a graphic designer. At the moment, she slowly curled her auburn hair around her middle finger as her stormy gray eyes struggled to focus on whatever her boss was about to present during their mandatory three o'clock Monday meeting.

Travis was the Art Director, the owner of Graphics Inc. *and* the boss. In another life, he probably was a sterling silver tea set, always polished and stored in a glass case. He never had a five o'clock shadow and matched his socks to his tie. Rae suspected that he suffered from undiagnosed OCD. Genuinely feared, Travis reigned over the dreaded conference room B. Or towered. After all, he stood at six feet five inches. And since he seemed to be constantly burning hot under his collar, Rae nicknamed him The Torch behind his back.

Smelling of espresso beans and chocolate, The Torch stood in front of the Smartboard, holding a red interactive pen in one hand. The other gripped a twelve-inch high coffee cup. This enormously tall to-go cup had an orange band around its middle with the popular logo of a brown coffee cup on it. This was no ordinary brown coffee cup, however. This cup had blue flames following it, as though it ran at very high race-car speeds. Anyone with eyes recognized this logo as the stamp of the beloved Espresso Lane, a coffeehouse chain in Monroe that was known for executing coffee orders (and hot cocoa) very quickly.

As Travis gulped down more liquid, Rae said, "I've never seen an Espresso Lane cup that large before."

Travis swallowed before saying, "It's a new size called Sky High. It holds forty ounces. That's double the size of their Skyscraper."

Raising her eyebrows, Rae commented, "I always order the Stubby. Eight ounces of their hot cocoa is enough for me."

"You're the size of a pygmy marmoset. I'm surprised you can handle eight ounces. I always pictured you drinking the three-ounce Puny."

"Please." Rae raised her lip in disgust. "Stop picturing me. I don't like that."

"Back to business." Facing the Smartboard, Travis wrote a strange and scary word across the surface: TEAM-BUILDING. As he spoke, he prowled in front of the board like a snarling tiger. Rae and the three other graphic designers sat at the long rectangular table like defeated wild boars, awaiting their slaughter.

"This morning, I attended a seminar called *A Team That Gets Along Gets Work Done*." Travis then underlined the word on the Smartboard while saying, "It was all about team-building. And as I sat in that auditorium on this beautiful summer day, listening to the speaker and thinking about you clowns, I realized that my team needs building. A lot of it. I mean, just look at you limp biscuits." After setting the display pen down, Travis picked up a nearby round makeup mirror and made sure to place it in everybody's face. "Paaathetic," he said before taking his usual seat at the head of the table. He drained the rest of his coffee in five large gulps, slammed the cup on the table, and then glared at the group.

Chuck was the first designer to risk his life to speak. As the Multimedia Designer with spiky red hair and a mismatched black goatee, he reminded Rae of a Las Vegas magician without the confidence. She nicknamed him Chuckles, again behind his back, but he wasn't laughing at the moment. He was sweating. Chuck wiped his brow. "Will we have to put in extra time?"

Travis hissed at Chuck, which caused Chuck to sweat more.

Tonya ventured next. As the Layout Artist, she pictured herself as the Nefertiti of Graphics Inc. This confused Rae because Tonya had full thighs and an ordinary face. Although, sometimes Tonya had two faces. The first face had a wide smile and dancing hazel eyes. She saved that pleasant face for Travis. The second face was for everyone else. It had soul-sucking eyes and a sneer. Rae called her Two-face Tonya, but never to either of her faces. Presently, Tonya bubbled over with enthusiasm as she said to Travis, "How inspiring! I'm also for getting along and getting work done!"

"Put a cork in it, Tonya." Travis leaned back in his chair. "Once a month, we are going to have a team-building, team-*bonding* experience. And we're all going to like it. For this month, we, as a team, will be camping at a wonderful place. I have reserved a campground for two nights and will supply the tent. Expect an email with the details. All you have to bring is whatever your precious asses need. Remember, we are camping, not glamping. So, don't pack like a prima donna. Got it, Chuck?"

Air slowly escaped from Chuck's lungs as he nodded.

"Good." Travis looked at Rae. "Any questions?"

Rae raised her hand. "I have two. Is that your personal mirror from home? And is that how you groom your eyebrows so nicely?"

"Yes," Travis replied, "and you should think about buying one for yourself. And some tweezers." He looked around the group. "Any other questions?"

Kimmy, the Production Artist, blended into the beige chair. Her faded brown hair matched her eyebrows, eyelashes and skin. The only makeup that Rae ever witnessed Kimmy apply was the classic original chapstick. Rae secretly nicknamed her Klimpy, after soggy noodles. With wilted shoulders, Kimmy looked downright water-soaked and softly inquired, "When is this happening?"

"Tomorrow morning. Lasting through Thursday morning. We'll be back to work here on Thursday afternoon."

Tonya gasped, bringing her hands to her mouth. "That's not going to work for me. Tomorrow is my directorial debut at the premiere opening of my play. It's a satirical tragedy. I have evening shows all week."

Kimmy meekly added to the conversation. "I have a small conflict this week too. I'm supporting my sister at her AA meetings, which are every evening. I'm her sponsor." She half-heartedly raised her fist and pumped it twice. "She's two days strong. If she makes it to day seven, we both get magnets for our refrigerators."

Chuck's hands shook as he nervously unfastened the top button of his shirt. "I have kickball playoffs, starting tomorrow night and-"

Travis interrupted Chuck, scolding all of them. "Those are the weakest lies I've ever heard. Tonya, a directorial debut? What show? *Death of a Layout Artist*?" Tonya lowered her eyes as Travis turned to Chuck. "You can't raise your leg high enough to tie your shoe, much less kick a ball." Chuck nodded when Travis pointed at Kimmy. "And you don't even have a sister."

Kimmy sighed. "I know that, but I didn't think you did."

Travis now narrowed his eyes at Rae. "What's your lie?"

Rae shrugged. "I don't have one. But I have a real excuse, which is that I hate camping. Bad things always happen when I camp. Can we do something else? Like going out for pizza? Or how about a movie? Then nobody has to talk. That's a bonus. Otherwise, I vote for pizza."

Travis stood, placing his hands on the table in a threatening manner. "Now, listen to me closely because I'll only say this once.

The midwest pizza around here doesn't meet *my* New York standards. New York pizza was created by Leonardo DaVinci himself. He used New York tap water, which had been blessed by the Virgin Mary. Got it? Your Monroe pizza tastes like cardboard stuffed with Velveeta cheesy dust rags. And as for your tap water, I'd rather boil my pasta in horse piss." Returning to his seat, he continued, "Also, a quick FYI, if you all want a job to come back to on Thursday afternoon, then you all better come on our team-building, team-*bonding* retreat. Expect an email with the details." He adjusted the collar of his shirt. "Now, this is your last chance to ask any relevant questions."

Rae asked, "Are we driving together?"

With his elbows on the table, Travis folded his hands. "Hell no."

"Then are you going to pay for everyone's gas?"

The other designers nodded in unison until Travis rose to his feet again while extending his arm. As he pointed to the door, a vein pulsed in his neck. His voice boomed, "Out! Now!" Then he pointed at Rae and said, "You. Stay."

. . .

Stone Winters stood behind the counter of his bar called The Rail. Leaning against the wall with his ankles crossed, one arm hugged his middle while the other arm acted as a pillar for his resting head. Brown curls peeked from underneath his baseball cap while his electric blue eyes stared at the floor. The last paying customer from the lunch crowd left, thanking Stone in a mocking tone for the burnt sandwich, but Stone's eyes remained lowered.

The last ten days were as calming as the green rolling hills in the English countryside. He wasn't in England, though. He was in the busy city of Monroe. Still, Stone felt wonderfully undisturbed. His psychic ability took an unexpected hiatus, which actually alleviated his constant tension headache. For almost two weeks now, no tingly arms warned him of ghosts. For ten nights, no terrifying visions overtook his dreams. Still, he dared to say he felt normal because he knew he was anything but normal.

Normal, shnormal, Stone thought as he mentally switched to a more entertaining daydream of Rachel. He smiled at the thought of her. Rachel Greyson. Beautiful Rachel Greyson. Beautiful and spunky. Also sassy. And very stubborn. Not to mention aloof.

He frowned.

They were friends during childhood, acquaintances during high school and complete strangers on the second after throwing their caps into the air. What were they now? After a recent reconnection, an accurate description would be struggling flirts. Although, he feared he already messed things up. He just didn't know how. One thing was for sure. He felt her drifting, like a log down a river. No matter. He had a plan. The Fourth of July happened a few days ago and a more important date approached. This Friday, Rachel would celebrate her twenty-sixth birthday and Stone planned to win her over with a smashing gift.

He felt warm.

What should that smashing gift be? There were some obstacles, of course. First, he had no idea what to give the girl of his dreams who slugged him in the gut when he kissed her. They were eleven years old then, but his stomach still hurt from the recollection. Besides, she hadn't changed much.

He wiped his hand across his slick forehead.

Should he buy her something that showed his true feelings? Like a bracelet? Shaking his head, he knew that a bracelet would send her running toward an active volcano, full of lava and commitment. How about a case of diet soda? Or did she switch to regular soda? Was that a smashing gift? How about new swim goggles? Perhaps running socks? With arch support?

He crumbled like a buttery cracker.

Maybe he shouldn't buy her anything? Maybe he should just wrap up a box and put nothing in it, but space? While scratching his curly hair underneath his baseball cap, Stone groaned. If only there was someone who could help. He looked at the two people at the bar. One was Zalen, a new acquaintance and shoddy empath, and the other was Sally, a regular and older friend of Stone. Both were pretty solid as far as supporters go, but both gave shitty advice.

CHAPTER TWO

The team quickly abandoned Rae and scurried through the door without looking back. A few tense minutes passed between them and then Travis surprised her by removing a flask that was apparently taped to the underside of the table. He emptied it in four swigs and then tossed it over his shoulder. His flushed cheeks instantly drained of anger.

"This is new," Rae said while glancing at the corner that was now home to an empty flask. "What was in there?"

"Coping medicine."

"Oh, dear." Rae nodded. "You seem higher strung than normal. What's wrong with you?"

"I am now an instant father of a two-year-old. That's what's wrong with me."

Smiling, Rae said, "How is your son, Hu?"

"Hu was his Chinese name. We changed it to Mortimer." Rae scrunched up her face and Travis quickly explained, "Seth wanted to name him after his grandfather. I couldn't say no. My husband is my best half, after all." Travis raised one corner of his mouth into what almost looked like a smile. "Besides, I lost the penny toss."

Rae squinted at what she thought was a tear in Travis's eye. He quickly evaded her gape as his hands dropped underneath the table. She heard the ripping of tape again.

"Anyway," Travis continued, "Mortimer keeps breaking things. So far, he's shattered our mirror, our french doors, our glass console table *and* smashed our pool filter."

"How did he do all that?"

"With his tiny, two-year old hands."

Rae sighed. "You yelled at Mort, didn't you?"

"Of course, I yelled at Mortimer. Any good parent yells at their kid." Travis raised another flask to his lips and drained it. He then tossed this one over his shoulder too and it landed in the same corner.

Shaking her head, Rae asked, "How many of those do you have under there?"

Travis ignored her question and said, "I need to distance myself from parenthood, Rae, just for a few days."

"You've only been a parent for two weeks."

"Correction. It's been ten long days."

"So, you're making us camp because you can't handle parenthood?"

"You're asking a lot of questions, Rae."

"Here's another one. What does Seth have to say about you camping?"

"He's very supportive and offered to pack my bags."

"Well, his support of you is destroying me." Rae twirled a new strand of hair around her finger. "You do realize that taking your employees on a team-building camping trip is just another form of parenting."

"And you must realize that I don't care." A forlorn expression covered his face.

Rae gave him her best stink eye. "I'm not a fool. What's the *real* reason you want to camp with us instead of retreating to the nearest spa? What's *really* going on?"

Another tear formed in Travis's eye and Rae felt like she was spiraling down to the center of earth. Her boss never showed any emotion other than anger. What was happening?

He sighed. "Seth and I have been arguing ever since we brought Mortimer home. Seth says that I care about material items and cleanliness more than I care about our son. He says that I need to find my inner kindness and learn how to live among the mess or he's leaving me. So, today, when I went to that damn seminar in a heart-broken daze, I heard someone call out camping as an idea for a work retreat. And you know what I thought, Rae?"

"Unfortunately, I think I do."

"Camping is a perfect way to show Seth that I can change. I have two days to find a kinder, messier side of me and then I can go home and show him that I'm awesome, after all."

Aside from the time constraint, Rae instantly saw another loose thread in this sweater of a plan and debated whether or not she should pull it. In the end, she couldn't resist. "What if you don't have a kinder, messier side?"

Travis nodded. "I know what you mean. After much thought, I think I have the dignity and grace to find my kinder, messier side. And I'm starting with the messier side first. It'll be easier to prove to Seth that I actually have one."

"How?"

"With selfies. I'll just dirty myself up and send a snap. No big deal. Then I'll wash up."

"Oh, boy."

"It's finding the kinder side of me that has me worried."

"Yep."

Travis grinned. "But I have a plan."

"Is it foolproof?"

"If that's what you want to call yourself, then yes."

"Wait. What?"

"You got it, chica." Travis seemed excited. "*You* will teach *me* how to be kind."

Rae's stomach dropped. "Me? Why me?"

"Well, all kidding aside, you know I like you, Rae. You're a straight-talking, no-nonsense, sarcastic kindred spirit."

"I believe you've mentioned that before."

Travis talked over her. "Three weeks ago, I let you house-sit my manor. I just don't let anyone into my house and you know that. But I let you because we're such good acquaintances."

"You couldn't find anyone else to house-sit, so you bribed me, remember?"

"Oh, that's just a fun game that you and I like to play. You know and I know that I like your wit and, clearly, you don't care about your looks. I want to be more like y-" Travis cleared his throat. "I want to be more like y-"

"Are you trying to say *you?*"

Travis nodded. "See? You're already helping me. Th-" He rolled up a sleeve. "Th-"

Perturbed, Rae asked, "Are you now trying to say *thanks?*"

Travis winked. "You get me."

Rae's hands were now flat on the table, bracing herself. "I have a few questions."

"Of course you do."

"First, this is ridiculous."

"That's not a question, Rae."

"Second, why don't you and Seth just go to a marriage counselor? Surely, you have a little black book full of names of many therapists, right? Can't you call one? Or all of them?"

Rae knew she crossed a line when the whites in Travis's eyes turned red. He said, "Enough chit-chat. Thanks to your wonderfully snarky comments and prying questions, you are now The Team-Building Committee. Congrats. Your first assignment is to plan this retreat."

Rae booed. "Plan a retreat? For whom exactly? You and Seth or our team?"

Travis nodded. "Both."

"You know," Rae said while eying him skeptically, "I could just tell everyone right now we're really only camping to save your marriage, ending this retreat idea. What's stopping me?"

"Three things." Travis solemnly said. "One, you know that I need Seth and, in order to keep Seth, I need to camp."

Rae shrugged. "It sounds desperate and I don't really-"

"Two, you know that our team needs to bond and this camping retreat could lend the perfect environment for us to do so."

Rae shook her head. "Actually, I-"

He batted his eyelashes. "Three, I'll give you a paid week off whenever you want, if you lead this camping retreat *and* keep this between us."

Rae felt the devil appear on her left shoulder. Her right shoulder remained vacant, so it didn't take much for her to agree. She tried to sound put-off while mentally celebrating. "Fine. I suppose. Now, what did you mean by me being The Team-Building Committee?"

"First, I need you to find a campsite and then-"

Rae held up her hand. "Wait. You just told everyone that you reserved a campsite at a wonderful place."

"Well, I lied. Moving on."

Rae held up her other hand. "Wait. How am I supposed to find a campsite on such short notice?"

"I have the utmost confidence in you. Now, *moving on,* I then need you to figure out the cheapest budget, an agenda, get our team ready and email everyone with the info tonight, after I've approved it, of course."

"Am I reserving this hard-to-find-campsite-on-such-short-notice? If so, I'll need a company charge card."

"No. I'll reserve it after I approve it."

Rae sighed. "Just one more thing, what do you mean by an agenda?"

"Well, start with a goal. Come up with some activities. Blah, blah, blah." Travis shrugged. "I don't know. That's why I put you in charge. Look up how to plan an agenda on the internet, for Christ's sake. Come on, Rae, use your resources." He gave her a thumbs up. "It'll be fun. Oh, and to answer your earlier question, I'm not reimbursing you guys for gas."

"Hey!" Rae exclaimed. "Not so fast. Since I'm also in charge of teaching you how to be kinder, consider this your first lesson. This bunking bedlam was your idea, so you *must* pay for our gas." She could tell by the look in his eye that he wasn't convinced and Rae quickly added, "Pay for gas and I'll buy you another flask to tape underneath this table."

Travis said, "I have many flasks. What I need is a bigger table."

. . .

"You look like you've been hit by a car, Stone." Sally leaned over the counter and reached for the gin. "I was hit by a car once and it took me a week to recover in the hospital. Of course, by car, I mean a sixty-ounce bottle of gin. And, by hospital, I mean ditch."

Stone ignored Sally and chose to study Zalen. Somehow, he always found his way into Stone's bar, even if the doors were locked. And he only drank seltzer water with a lot of ice. A tall glass of the said seltzer water stood at attention in front of him; however, Zalen hadn't drunk a sip. Instead, he glanced over the edge of his puzzle book with a smile, which was in contrast to the concern filling his deep brown eyes. His deep brown *interesting* eyes. Although both were round, his left eye was larger by a smidge. While using his empathic ability, Zalen would widen that eye in order to do something empathic. Stone didn't really understand it, nor did he want to understand it. All Stone knew was, when his new acquaintance widened his left eye, like now, he was going to *feel* something.

"I *feel* your pain, my man." Beads of perspiration sprinkled Zalen's smooth head. Currently, his hand grasped a pencil while he studied the sudoku puzzle. He carefully drew a six in one of the little boxes and then immediately erased it. "How does Rae complete these in less than five minutes?"

Stone shrugged. "She's nuts."

Sally's choice of wig for the day was a glamorously long patriotic one with loose red, white and blue curls, sparkling with glitter. Some of the glitter fell into her gin, but she seemed not to notice and poured until the gin was level with the glass's edge. After hunching over her drink, she lowered her mouth to the glass and managed to fit her lips around the top of it without the use of her hands. She lifted the glass with her head. Her lips became suction cups and Sally tipped her gin up and back, guzzling the liquid in a matter of seconds.

Stone lifted his eyebrows. "I've never seen anyone do that with a regular glass before."

Sally licked her lips. "So, is Rae nuts or does she drive you nuts?"

Stone stated, "Both."

"I know what you can do for her birthday then." Sally untangled a fake blue eyelash as she talked, "Show up at her door, wearing nothing but shorts made out of clear wrap. That will drive her *nuts*. Get it?" While laughing, she excused herself to the ladies' room.

When they were alone, Zalen said, "Channel your inner psychic feelings for an idea."

Uncomfortable, Stone glanced around the bar and whispered, "I don't like speaking about anything *psychic* in public. Sally still doesn't know and I prefer it that way. Got it?"

"Sure." Zalen grinned. "I completely understand." He brought his fingers to the corner of his mouth and twisted the air, locking his lips. "You can count on me." Smiling wider, he nodded. "I *feel* you're doing yourself some harm by ignoring your ability."

"What did I just say, Zalen?"

"But, Stone, I left out the word *psychic*."

Sighing, Stone changed the subject. "I don't need to channel anything for a gift idea for Rachel. I'm going to call her late on her birthday and pretend that I forgot all about it. I know, deep down, that's what she wants."

Zalen shook his head. "I don't *feel* that's right. I *feel* that Rae would love some roses."

Now Stone shook his head. "She's allergic to flowers."

"I *feel* then," Zalen continued, "that Rae would like a new puzzle book."

"She has hundreds."

"A new pencil for her puzzle books?"

"Rachel uses medium point green marker pens."

Zalen's face became unusually serious. "Well, I don't get it right all the time."

"Yeah, I know." A small tension headache began to grow. Without any warning, Stone's forearms tingled furiously and he quickly rubbed them while shivering.

Zalen asked with concern, "Are you okay, my friend?"

Stone lied. "Yep, I'm fine." He checked the time on his watch. It was nearly half past three. "I just realized that I have a lot of work to do."

Zalen smiled. "Are you sure that's what's going on?"

Inching himself from Zalen, Stone shook his head. "I said I'm fine. Just need to get some things done. I'll be in my office."

He left, hurrying to the storage room where a folding table and metal chair awaited him. He opened the door and a damp smell immediately hit him in the face. A new world replaced the storage shelves and Stone quickly shut the door.

Desperate, he closed his eyes and whispered, "Look, psychic gods, just take my ability away. Someone else can have it." He counted to three. And then to six. When he opened his eyes, Stone turned the knob and entered his office. The pleading didn't work. In fact, it backfired. This vision was much more vivid than usual.

In the distance stood two identical monoliths, strong and erect, as the moon shone brightly above them. A roaming stream weaved toward a large body of water. Stone's nostrils filled with the stench of wet earth and fish. Suddenly, he felt an object move onto the toe of his shoe. It was a red lollipop with eight smaller legs and two large front claws, pinching annoyingly at his ankle. Kicking it away, the lollipop soared in the air toward the two animals. Both were huge and stood on their hind legs. They faced each other, snarling. Between them lay either a lifeless crumpled body or a big garbage bag that tipped over. While studying it, Stone noticed this garbage bag had a masculine build with broad shoulders and two long legs.

He sighed, shaking his head. For all the gin and tonic in the world, what was going on?

CHAPTER THREE

Internet? Use my resources? Rae rolled her eyes. The clock on the computer teased four fifty-nine. Hugging her backpack purse, she stared at the time while bouncing her knee and cursing the words *agenda* and *team*. Planning was not her strength. She could barely plan her breakfast. Plus, she wasn't exactly a team player either. Her favorite sports were running and swimming. Alone. Never in a relay. Regardless of these weaknesses, Rae had a plan. *Why use the internet when I have a better* living *resource?*As soon as the numbers changed to five on the dot, Rae exploded from her chair and sprinted out of Graphics Inc. to her two-door Toyota coupe.

After driving an hour in fourth gear, Rae arrived in the small town of Polk to not only pick up her dog, but also to see her living resource. The one organized person in her life. And this organizer was the head of the debate team for this coming school year, which was a team thing. Right?

"Hi, Emma!" Rae joined her blond niece, who stretched herself on a hammock in the backyard. Emma modeled a black one-piece with cut-outs all over it. Rae skeptically looked at Emma, aged fourteen, and asked, "What ate your swimsuit?"

Emma's face remained calm, but her tone reminded Rae of a perturbed viper. "Nothing."

"Your parents must not be home. Otherwise you'd be wrapped up in a blanket burrito."

"Dad's still working and Mom took Henry and Meg to the doctor for a shot or something. Don't know where Bash is, so don't ask."

A July sun in the midwest made things sizzle pretty quickly, and, as Rae pulled a patio chair across the grass to sit by her niece, perspiration trickled down Rae's back. She spied a water bottle on the ground next to the hammock and it wasn't boiling yet.

Rae asked, "May I have a drink of your water?"

Emma opened one eye and glanced at Rae. "Do you mean my *purified* water made from reverse osmosis?"

"I'll buy you something for the tiniest sip of that osmosis water."

Emma turned her head, looked straight at her aunt and asked, "Is this a bribe?"

"Yes. I learned today that bribes aren't such a bad thing."

"What are you bribing me with?"

Rae offered, "A whole swimsuit?"

Emma turned away, hiding a hint of a smile. "You can have *one* sip."

Rae stretched for the bottle, squirted some warm water into her mouth and then squirted one of Emma's bare spots on her stomach.

Emma laughed. "Hey! You're worse than my three younger siblings all put together." After being squirted again, Emma yelled, "Stop! For reals! Or I'll hurl myself off a bridge!"

"Or," Rae began, "you can set your drama aside and help me *organize*."

Emma's green eyes sparkled with excitement. "Did you say *organize?*"

Her niece loved all things relating to organization. The colors, the highlighters, the control. Emma organized her bottles of fingernail polish alphabetically and her scented candles by seasons. In contrast, Rae chewed off her fingernails and stored her candles in a drawer.

Rae explained, "I need help organizing a work retreat at a campground and it has to be good. I have a paid week off depending on it. I need to figure out a goal, an agenda and other stuff. I have no idea where to start."

"Got it." She hurried into the house, calling over her shoulder, "Be right back."

While waiting under the heat of the sun, loud barking and a boy's laughter interrupted her solitude. A very large dog (resembling an unsinkable ship) and a sweaty boy (reeking of onions) rounded the corner. Springing from her chair, Rae jogged to meet them and wrapped her arms around the dog's thick neck. With her only being five feet tall and her dog, Tiny, standing just under forty inches, she hardly bent to hug him. When she released, Tiny cocked his melon-sized head to the left, as if to say, "Why are you here?"

Rae crossed her arms. "Well, I missed you too." She then squinted at her nephew, Sebastian Greyson, who everyone called Bash. At five foot one, he was a little taller than she, and resembled his aunt in a few ways. He had the same blue-gray eyes as Rae and his dark hair with auburn highlights matched hers. Although his short hair rested in every direction on top of his head, whereas hers was much longer and a little tamer. Bash possessed dimples though, which she did not. And right now, his dimples deepened after a big smile spread across his face. He lifted a book that he held underneath his arm and showed her the cover. "I checked this out from the library a week ago. You should read it."

Rae read the title aloud, "*What's Bugging You: A Quick Study in Entomology.*" She gave him a questioning look and said, "I'll get on that."

Bash rolled his eyes. "No, you won't."

"You're right, I won't." Shrugging, Rae continued, "You know me, Bash. I enjoy working on word puzzles. Not reading about insects or the supernatural."

Bash now gave her a questioning look. "Sometimes I wonder if we're really related."

Rae changed the subject. "Did you have fun with Tiny this weekend?"

"We had a blast. Thank you for letting him stay over." Bash's saucer eyes pleaded with her. "Can I keep him? Forever?"

Not this again, Rae thought. "No."

"C'mon, Aunt Rae. A big Great Shepherd needs a big great yard to run around."

"No, and may I remind you that your parents also said no."

"If you agree to it, then they'll agree to it. Maybe? Anyway, please, Aunt Rae. I'll buy you something, if you let me keep Tiny."

"Is this a bribe?"

"Yes."

Amused at their similarities, Rae tapped her bottom lip with her pointer finger a few times. "What are you bribing me with?"

Bash raised his eyebrows and remained silent. His eyeballs then rolled upwards in thought and he pursed his lips together. Finally, he offered, "A cat?"

Tiny growled as Rae asked, "Seriously?" Her whole body spasmed at the thought of owning a cat. "I'm allergic."

Bash gave her a disbelieving look. "Really? Since when?"

"Since this conversation."

Tiny grinned and nodded.

"Aunt Rae, cats come with benefits. For instance, did you know that cats were beneficial companions to the Egyptians? Especially in the afterlife?" Bash smiled, mainly at himself.

Rae smiled too, but in a smug way. "And do you know cats are evil? There are studies proving cats are arrogant, manipulative beasts that suck out souls with their creepy yellow eyes."

Tiny arfed at Rae's declaration, raising his front paw as if he were saying, "I concur."

"See? Tiny knows. Plus, cats need special stuff, like little kitty cat food and little yummy cat milk and little prissy cat beds. No deal."

Bash's eyes sprung open. "Topic change. My mom just gave me some tarot cards that she found at a garage sale yesterday. Want me to give you a tarot card reading? I can give you insight about your past, present and future. I can also find out what kind of pet is perfect for you."

Rae laughed. "I've heard of this. Isn't there a death card or something like that?"

"Well, yes, but it doesn't necessarily mean death." He pulled out a small case from his back pocket. "These are tarot cards. They are used in telling people's fortune. According to Britannica, tarot decks have been around since the fourteen hundreds. They're Italian. There are seventy-eight cards divided between the major arcana and minor arcana and-"

Rae raised her palm to stop Bash from explaining. "You lost me at Britannica."

Bash quickly took the tarot cards out of the case and fanned them. "Here, Aunt Rae, just take one. For funsies."

"No."

Bash's shoulders dropped and Rae felt bad for the twelve-year old. "Fine," she said while picking one. She briefly viewed it. There was a moon between two castle-looking towers, a stream, a crayfish and two animals fighting with each other.

Bash peered over her hand and said, "That's the Moon card."

"Uh huh."

"It means illusion, deception-"

"Great."

"Danger, terror-"

"This is getting so much better."

"And something else." Bash pulled on his bottom lip before snapping his fingers and cheerfully exclaiming, "Occult forces!"

Fortunately, Rae heard the patio door slide open and she gave the Moon card back to Bash, ending this reading. She then turned to see Emma, bounding out the house with an oversized canvas bag. Slung over her shoulder, it was filled with office materials and weighed down her left side. When Emma approached, Rae spied six notebooks, four packs of colored marker pens, paperclips, two black binders and other supplies that gave Rae the heebie jeebies. She shivered under the hot sun.

Bash and Tiny, on the other hand, both looked curiously at the bag as they craned their necks toward it. Bash asked, "What do you have there?"

"Stuff." Emma plopped down on the grass, spreading all the supplies before her.

Pointing to one of the black binders, Rae asked Emma, "What's that?"

"Organizer."

Rae pointed to the other black binder. "Then what's that?"

"An organizer for my organizer."

"How many organizers do you have?"

Emma replied, "I have an even dozen. Now, let's start planning the agenda!"

Bash looked at Rae. "What agenda?"

"It's for work. My boss put me in charge of organizing a work retreat at a campground."

Lifting his eyebrows, Bash said, "That sounds like fun. Which campground?"

"I don't know. We need to find a place."

Alarmed, Emma looked up. "On such short notice? All of these places book up quickly."

Bash lifted his eyebrows even higher. "Can I help, Aunt Rae?"

"Of course, you can. The more, the merrier."

Bash quickly removed his cellphone from his back pocket. "Don't worry. I'll find something." His fingers rapidly tapped on his cellphone.

Rae then glanced at Emma who was in the process of selecting a teal blue marker pen. Emma then flipped open a notebook and positioned the marker for action. Without taking her eyes off the page, she began interrogating Rae, "How many people are going?"

"Five."

With great gusto, Emma wrote down the number. "How many nights?"

"Two."

The gusto didn't waiver. "Weeknights or weekends?"

"Weeknights. We're actually leaving tomorrow, which is Tuesday, and we're coming back on Thursday."

"Please keep your answers short, Aunt Rae."

Rae shrugged. "Sure." She turned to Bash. "Any luck?"

Bash nodded. "I found one place called Fun Warriors Ranch. It still has family campsites for six available. In fact, this whole section is open. It doesn't have electricity, though."

"That's horrible." Rae ran her fingers through her hair. "Keep looking for campsites with electricity."

Bash looked at her. "I did. The closest campsite with electricity is an eight-hour drive."

Rae groaned into her hands. "Fine. It'll just be for two days. For two long days in hell's heat with detestable coworkers and one soulless boss who-"

Interrupting Rae, Emma said to Bash, "Send me the info." She then checked her phone for his message and recorded the information. After capping the teal marker pen, Emma selected a red one. "Okay," Emma announced, "let's decide on a goal."

Bash now lay on the hammock and Tiny relaxed on the ground next to him. Holding his cellphone, Bash said, "On it." His fingers flew over the keypad. He soon found the information and began reading while stroking Tiny's head. "Here are four of the most common goals for work retreats. Reason one, to work on a project. Two, to come up with a company roadmap."

Rae interjected, "I don't even know what that means."

Tiny rolled his eyes.

"Reason three, to spend time brainstorming or, four, to boost morale for team-building."

Nodding, Rae replied, "Definitely the fourth one."

Tiny also nodded.

Emma already wrote *to boost morale* in red and chose a different marker. This one was burnt orange. "Budget?"

"Well," Rae began, "my boss told me to go the cheapest route."

"Got it. I'll be done in a sec." A sec to Rae meant an hour; a sec to Emma was apparently more like five minutes, which thrilled Rae. The agenda that her niece devised was a well-written, professional proposal for Travis to approve. It entailed four budgets with four different scenarios, depending on the generosity of her boss. Rae crossed her fingers for the third budget, which included a campsite, an admission sticker, food, refreshments and gas. She had a bad feeling, however, that the fourth budget of one paid meal, water, no admission sticker nor gas would be the winner.

Rae looked at Emma. "Let's remove the fourth budget."

Emma laughed. "Isn't that a little shady on your part?"

"Yep and we'll just keep that among ourselves."

Rae was genuinely impressed with Emma's ability to agendasize. She had the natural mind of a no-nonsense boss. She even wrote a sample day schedule and organized the events by days and times, down to the nearest minute. Rae noted that the wake-up time for every day was a rude 7:30, no later than 7:33. Other than that, the schedule was perfect. Talking to Emma, Rae said, "Now all we need to do is come up with team-building activities."

Bash's eyes sparkled with excitement. "According to the Fun Warriors Ranch website, *we* can hike, swim, canoe. And there are tons of wildlife to observe."

Rae spit out a fingernail and spoke to Emma, "What do you think about those activities?"

"That's your domain, Aunt Rae." Emma shrugged. "I don't know what your coworkers can do. Some may have physical restrictions. If I were there to see, then I could plan. But I won't be there, so I can't. And that's fine with me, Aunt Rae. Camping's not my jam."

Rae nodded while petting Tiny. *Camping's not my jam either.* Suddenly, her spirits instantly soared to the heavens when a brilliant thought entered her mind. Or it was Bash's slip of the tongue that gave her the idea. Regardless, Rae smiled at her sweet niece and said, "I'll buy you something, if you come with me. What do you say?"

.   .   .

After Bash heard his sister scream about wanting a ticket to see a hairy style that was coming to Monroe next year, he gaped in surprise. That wasn't the plan at all! He raised his hand in objection.

"I object," Bash stated strongly and Tiny whined. "First, why does *she* get to go with you? Second, camping *is* my jam. Third, I would never expect you to bribe me with some hairy *hairstyle* to go with you anywhere. I would go because I like hanging out with you. And Tiny."

"Overruled." Emma sounded like a strict judge. "And it's H-A-R-R-Y. As in Harry Styles, the singer."

Bash then did what any twelve-year old brother would do to his fourteen-year old sister in a disagreement. A natural gas bomb boomed from his rear end and he waved the smelly fumes toward Emma.

Tiny jumped onto all fours and barked at the polluted air. Then he sneezed and trotted toward the end of the yard where there was a small tree, creating small shade. He sat under it, looking content, even though the leaves tap danced on top of his head.

Emma also jumped to her feet, but not to seek shade. She clasped her hands over her mouth and started making retching sounds. Turning away, she bolted across the patio and took coverage inside the house.

Grinning at Aunt Rae, Bash explained, "My farts make her gag."

Aunt Rae pinched her nose, causing her voice to sound higher than normal. "I wonder why? And my god, what did you eat today?"

"Nothing out of the norm."

"Then maybe you should change your norm?"

Ignoring Aunt Rae's criticism, Bash impatiently asked again, "Please let me come too?"

Aunt Rae released her nostrils and her voice returned to normal. "I would, but there's one huge problem. My annoying boss, a.k.a. Travis, a.k.a. The Torch, will never allow the two of you to come. I'm not even sure if he'll allow Emma. You see, Bash, he's a monster. After all, it was his awful idea to take his designers on this stupid team-building camping trip under the guise of really saving his marriage. And he put me in charge! All because I asked a few questions-"

As Aunt Rae ranted about unwanted committee roles, Bash's mind drifted to Ma'iingan (my-ING-gun) Bluff. He knew all about it from his Social Studies class. It all started from a glacier that blocked both ends of a river's gorge with moraine many years ago. Fast forward to present day, quartzite bluffs now acted as stiff soldiers, standing at attention and rising 500 feet. He learned that many hiking trails weaved through these cliffs and around a lake called Wolves Lake, which was loosely shaped like a mile-long peanut and covered about 360 acres. The ancient lake and bluffs were almost as thrilling as the legend behind Ma'iingan Bluff's name.

Bash knew all about this too.

Two weeks ago, while perusing the shelves in the Village of Polk's local library, Bash stumbled upon a book called *Where Wolves Wait at Ma'iingan Bluff*. It jarred the memory of class, so he picked it up. After browsing the first chapter, he learned something that his teacher hadn't taught. The bluffs were homes to thousands of wolves. However, when humans populated the area, the wolves were hunted for various reasons. As Bash continued to read, the tone of the book gradually changed from mundane educational lessons to exciting new facts. This book wasn't just a book about wolf history. Oh, no sirree. In this writing masterpiece, the topic quickly shifted its meaning. Instead of it being about *where wolves* wait at Ma'iingan Bluff, it was actually about how *werewolves* wait at Ma'iingan Bluff. Werewolves! He checked out the book from the library immediately.

This summer was proving to be very stimulating indeed. First, he kinda caught a banshee in June and now he had a chance to hunt a werewolf in July, if he could talk his aunt into letting him come. He purposefully only gave the name of Fun Warriors Ranch to his aunt, which was the campground right next to the bluffs. His plan was near completion. He shivered from electrified goosebumps and hugged himself.

Then he noticed that his aunt was watching him very closely. She squinted her eyes and asked him, "What's going on?"

Bash gave her another overly-charming smile. "Nothing. Now hear me out. *I'll* buy *you* something, if you take me with you. What do you say?"

Before Aunt Rae answered, Tiny howled. To the untrained ear, the howl sounded like a normal dog sound that a normal dog made. To Bash, on the other hand, he thought he heard Tiny distinctly say, "Here we go again!"

CHAPTER FOUR

From Tiny's spot under the small tree, he watched as the nice boy named Bash rolled off the hammock and onto his feet. The next movements, involving Nice Bash's arms, intrigued Tiny. He never saw a human wiggle its arms in the air like that. Tiny believed that what he witnessed before him was what the humans called *flailing*.

Studying the angry lady named Rae, she gave Nice Bash the same look that she gave him when he needed to water a bush outside in the middle of the night. It didn't look good for Nice Bash and whatever he was trying to do. Then, when Nice Bash fell to his knees and clasped his hands together, Tiny sighed, knowing that the desperate move wouldn't help the boy.

Nice Bash whimpered. "Please, Aunt Rae, please! Take me with youuuuuuu!"

Tiny joined in the howling and Angry Rae yelled, "Enough! Both of you!" She then pointed to him and said, "Tiny, you stay out of this."

After being scolded, Tiny sheepishly lowered his eyes and rested his head on his paws. He watched silently as the scene quickly turned downright embarrassing for Nice Bash. Tiny wanted to look away, but couldn't. Instead, he watched as poor Nice Bash curled himself around Angry Rae's leg as she stood. As Angry Rae began to walk across the yard, Nice Bash hung onto her foot and she dragged him. Tiny quietly rooted for Nice Bash until the boy's shorts slid down the boy's legs. Regardless, Nice Bash held on to Angry Rae's foot. Tiny shook his head; after all, even he knew when to give up.

. . .

Damn, Stone thought as he wiped the bar's counter, listening to the buzz of the dinner crowd. After ten blissful days of normalcy, his psychic visions not only strenuously returned, but they also seemed more vivid as they tumbled inside his head, like a load of socks in a dryer. A few weeks ago, his vision of Rachel and Bash being in danger, came true. Then, unexpectedly and fortunately, all visions stopped. Until now. And this vision did not look like a real place. Everything had a black marker outline, like in a drawing.

While rinsing the cloth in the prep sink, Stone closed his eyes and pictured the two concrete monoliths. He knew that those foreboding structures were not from this area. The stream, leading to the lake, however, could be from here. Or anywhere, really. And what was with the two large animals? They looked bigger than dogs, even a dog like Tiny. And why a red lollipop with legs? Although, a lollipop was better than a banshee, like last time. The most jarring unanswered question was…who was the dead guy? It wasn't Rachel. That much he could tell and he quickly crossed his fingers, hoping he was right.

Stone opened his eyes and glanced at the vacant corner stool, Grandpa Ed's stool, behind the bar. Envisioning how his grandpa used to sit there allowed a melancholy mood to pour over Stone. Even though Stone and his grandpa rarely spoke before his death, Grandpa Ed left his bar, The Rail, to Stone. Since then, Stone felt closer to his grandpa. His grandpa's ghost even appeared to him recently when Stone needed him. Where was he now? Stone concentrated on the stool, wishing for the usual wobble or even a flip. There was nothing and, in frustration, Stone threw his cap to the floor.

"You dropped your hat."

Stone heard the sweet voice that always inflated his heart. Across from him were a pair of dark gray eyes, framed with long black eyelashes. The ceiling lights highlighted the random auburn streaks in her dark brown hair, which was pulled back into a messy bun. Next to her was a very large dog.

"Hi, Rachel."

"Hi, Stone." She bent down, picked up his hat and handed it to him with a warm smile. "I can't help but notice you're stressed. What's on your mind?"

Instead of wearing the hat, he gently slapped it on Tiny's head and said, "It looks way better on you." Then he turned to Rachel, clenched his jaw and lied. "The only thing on my mind is a birthday present for you."

Rachel eyed him and grabbed a handful of complimentary pretzel nuggets. "Goodness gracious. I don't want anything."

"Well." Stone cleared his throat. "I would like to give you something for your birthday."

"Why? Just save your money."

He cleared his throat again. "I have enough money. I want to buy you a gift because-"

Rachel held up her right hand and grabbed another handful of pretzels with her left. She shoved them into her mouth and said while crunching, "I really don't want a gift for my birthday. Especially a knick-knack. It's just another thing to dust. Plus, I don't like to get clothes. I'd rather pick out my own stuff. See? I'm difficult. Thanks anyway."

Stone's heart sank a little. Back in their adolescent days, Rachel kept to herself and thought dating was just plain silly. She hadn't changed much. Not that they were dating. Still, he felt a connection with her, especially when she literally fell back into his life a few weeks ago. And he knew that she felt it too. So, what was the problem then? Did she know about his fucked-up psychic ability? But how? Did someone tell her? The only person who would've spilled the beans was Zalen, but even with all of Zalen's peculiarities, Stone trusted him. Maybe the attraction between him and Rachel really was only on his part?

"Earth to Stone." Rachel grinned. "May I have a soda? It's been a day."

Returning quickly to the moment, Stone snatched a tall glass, shoveled ice into it and watched as the soda shot from the siphon. He then slid the glass across the counter toward Rachel and focused his attention on Tiny.

Tiny nodded at Stone. After twitching one ear, the Great Shepherd opened his mouth, causing his large tongue to flop out and hang off the side.

"Got it," Stone said to Tiny. He reached under the counter for a five-quart silver mixing bowl and filled it with water. After setting it on the floor, he quickly dodged Tiny's melon-sized head as the dog eagerly lapped up the water.

When Stone looked at Rachel, it startled him to see her deep gray eyes, watching him. Usually stormy, at this moment, they were more gracious. Even tender. Maybe even loving? Stone hoped that was it, but then shook that thought out of his head. "So, Rachel, why has it been a day?"

The loving look in her eyes melted like the ice in her drink, not terribly fast, but unavoidably as she remarked, "Do you remember when we were kids?"

In a joking manner, Stone replied, "Only when I'm forced."

"Well, we had nicknames for each other. You actually started it. Do you remember that?"

Stone refilled Tiny's water bowl and said, "Of course. The one I had for you still fits. And I believe the nickname you had for me was Stud Muffin."

"I never called you that."

Stone slyly smiled. "That's right. It was Rock Hard Abs."

"Only in your dreams."

"And then you changed it to Sweet Ass."

"Well," Rachel began, "ass should've been part of it. Anyway, my point is, I always liked the nickname you gave me."

Chuckling, Stone asked, "So, you want me to start calling you that again?"

"Well," Rachel began, "no, not now. I mean, it feels too contrived. Know what I mean?" She shoved more pretzels into her mouth while continuing, "Did I ever tell you the nickname I have for Tiny?" Without waiting for him to respond, she replied, "It's Trouble."

Stone raised his eyebrows. "I think that's a better nickname for you."

Rachel laughed and Tiny arfed, nodding along with Stone.

A patron at a nearby table shouted to them, "Hey! Is that a dog?" Stone looked to his left to see a middle-aged man, sitting among a sea of empty beer mugs. After the drunkard drained another one, he tried to steady his out-stretched arm and pointed to Tiny. "Dogs are taking over this world. They're in the banks, the grocery stores, the Walmarts." He shook his head. "They shouldn't be anywhere, but in their yards. They shit everywhere and no one picks it up." He belched. "Then I step in their shit." Speaking through another belch, he ranted while shaking his finger. "Shame on you for having a dog in this fine establishment. I should report you to the owner of this bar."

Stone said, "Well, as owner of this bar, I don't have a problem with it."

The man raised his lip in disgust. "You're breaking a health code violation."

Rachel seemed suddenly interested and asked, "Which one?"

After a few seconds, the man finally answered, "The one where dogs aren't allowed." He belched for a third time. "In bars."

Rachel gave the man an innocent look. "Why not?"

Rubbing his eyebrows, he said, "Because it's breaking a health code violation."

Squinting, Rachel looked at Stone and then at the man. "Which one?"

The man swayed a little on his stool. "The one where dogs aren't allowed in bars."

Rached asked innocently again, "Why not?"

At this point, Stone stopped the revolving conversation. "Okay, that's enough." After pouring a cup of coffee, he handed it to the drunkard. "Here, drink this and I'll take that."

As the drunkard toasted Stone with his coffee cup, he blinked a few times and then focused on Tiny, wearing the baseball cap. He yelled to them, "Hey! Is that a dog?"

Tiny shook his head and Stone replied, "Nope. That's my cousin."

"Ohhhh," said the drunkard while he stumbled over to Tiny, holding out his hand, "Nice to meet you."

Tiny lifted his paw and they shook. Happy, the drunkard returned to his table and resumed drinking the coffee.

Studying Rachel, Stone shook his head. "Why must you antagonize drunk people?"

She scoffed. "He started antagonizing you first. And my dog. I couldn't just sit here and watch. What kind of a slouch do you think I am?"

Stone laughed. "See? You are trouble." After snatching her soda, he topped it off for her. "So, are you going to tell me about your day or what?"

Nodding, Rachel said, "It was horrible at best. First, I was-"

Just then, Tiny interrupted, making Rachel roll her eyes. He stood on all fours, wagged his tail and bobbed his head. Through whines and growls, he told a happy tale, finishing his story with a strong yelp. Stone rewarded Tiny with a good scratch behind both ears.

"Now, it's your turn," Stone said to Rachel.

"My day wasn't as good as Tiny's." She sighed. "I was tormented by the team-building troll named Travis whose marriage could land at the bottom of some bluffs any day now." She then told Stone about the upcoming camping *execution* at Ma'iingan Bluff. "I mean, *excursion*. So, now, I'm not only supposed to help Travis find a messier and kinder side for Seth, I'm also The Team-Building Committee. I'm in charge of the agenda, the activities, the drama. And believe me, there will be drama."

"Ma'iingan Bluff?" In the past, Stone had been a regular rock climber there. The views at the top of the bluffs took his worries away. Even though it was his favorite place to climb, it had been awhile since his last visit. Now, strangely, at the mention of this place, his stomach twinged and all he could think to say was, "That's in the middle of nowhere."

"Technically, it's in the middle of bluffs."

The uneasiness left Stone like a passing coworker who was too busy to talk and, once again, he felt fine. Nodding, he said, "So, what are you going to do about the agenda?" He watched as Rachel's mouth turned into a wicked sneer. "Oh, no. What *did* you do?"

"Being the smart person I am, I drove to my brother's house and got Emma to handle it. Well, most of it. I still have to come up with some team activities. Anyway, she really did a remarkable job and has *Future CEO* stamped right across her forehead. I have no doubt that she is going to drive her employees nuts someday. My plan now is to get her to come. I just need Travis to approve it."

"Wait. You drove to Polk after work and then made it back here by seven o'clock? In two hours? If you obeyed the speed limit, that should've taken you three hours. At least."

"It only takes me about forty-five minutes to get to Polk from here by freeway."

"That's impressively scary."

"Stone, I'm a very good, fast and safe driver. A little fast. Mostly safe."

"I've driven with you, Rachel. You're a lot fast. You should try driving in the slow lane once. For some shits and giggles."

"I have many shits and many more giggles. Plus, my expert driving skills really aren't the point of this conversation. Getting back to my horrible day, as soon as I get some courage, I'm asking Travis to allow Emma to join me on this camping cataclysm. And Tiny. Wish me luck."

"So, you'll then have to drive back to Polk tomorrow to pick up Emma? That's a lot of driving. In the slow lane."

"What is wrong with you? I'm twenty-five years old going on twenty-six. That's what young people do. Drive places. In the fast lane. By the sound of it, you're twenty-six going on sixty-two. Maybe you should start taking the bus places? And a walker."

"Hey, *Stingray*, watch it. And for once in your life, try to enjoy driving in the slow lane. Take your time. Listen to those oldies that you like so much. Relax and live another day."

Rachel batted her eyelashes in surprise. Then she suddenly beamed. "You called me Stingray! And it didn't feel contrived. Oh, how I missed it!" She dabbed at her dry eyes and wiped away not only an invisible tear, but also her playful attitude. "As I was saying, *Stonehenge*, Polk is just a little out of the way and so what? I need Emma." Rachel added, "Having Emma with me will make my job as The Team-Building Committee a lot easier. So, I'll drive around the world for Emma's assistance, if I have to." Rachel wiggled in her barstool like a ragdoll, being used to clean off the wooden chair with its rear end. A big woohoo smile plastered itself on her face.

Stone snickered. "What in the hell are you doing?"

"My happy dance." She stopped her bottom bopping and exhaled contentedly. "Now, how was your day?"

"Almost as bad as your happy dance."

"Very funny. So, what made your day so bad?"

"Zalen was here again."

Rachel furrowed her eyebrows and then nodded to her immediate left. "Isn't Zalen still here, sitting next to me?"

"Yep, I am." Smiling at her, Zalen asked, "Do you have a nickname for me too?"

"Kind of. It's a long one."

"What is it?"

"Angrophobia."

"Isn't that the fear of anger?"

"Yes. I never see you without a smile on your face. But, for short, I just call you Zalen."

"How nice!" Zalen smiled wider and showed her the sudoku puzzle. "What number goes in this box? An eight? Or two?"

Rachel looked at Stone as he said, "Zalen's been here all day. Working on that puzzle. And not leaving. Maybe you can help him?"

Zalen handed her the book and pencil. "I'd be much obliged."

Using the eraser, it took her seconds to remove his wrong guesses. Then she switched the pencil with her green marker pen, forever tucked in her back pocket, and began to maniacally fill in the boxes with great speed. Less than a minute later, she handed the complete puzzle to Zalen.

At first, Zalen smiled from ear to ear; however, his expression abruptly changed to concern as he said to her, "I *feel* that you are going camping."

Stone tsked. "She just told us that."

Zalen cleared his throat. "I *feel* that there will be a storm. On Tuesday."

Rachel opened the weather app on her cellphone. "It looks clear."

Zalen guessed, "How about Wednesday?"

Rachel replied, "It's clear on that day too."

"How about Thursday?"

Stone interrupted Zalen. "Stop the madness."

With a grin, Zalen defended himself. "I told you that I don't get it right all the time." He stood, slipping the sudoku puzzle book underneath his arm. "Well, I should go. I have to buy an air mattress." He gave Rachel his biggest smile yet and placed his hand on her shoulder. "Be sure to take an umbrella. I *feel* you'll need it."

"Sure," Rachel said with a nod. "It'll be the first thing I pack." She then glanced at Stone. "And I should buy an air mattress too. That would make camping a lot more comfortable."

As Zalen reached the entrance doors, he turned and called to them, "Have a nice evening, guys! And I'll see you tomorrow, Stone!"

Rachel waved, Tiny barked and Stone said, "What?"

If that wasn't bad enough, a familiar voice sounded from a nearby bar table. "Hey!" It was the drunkard with the coffee cup, scratching his beard. He pointed at Tiny again and asked, "Is that a dog?"

CHAPTER FIVE

Upon returning home with her new air mattress, Rae received a long text from Travis, approving the third version of the agenda. However, there were amendments. He still agreed to pay for the campsite, but he refused to pay for food, refreshments and admission stickers. He also agreed to pay for one team meal and, surprisingly, for everyone's gas. *Hey, maybe he can change?* He also texted that he reserved the campsite at Fun Warriors Ranch and that he tried for a site with electricity, but there was none available. His last written word was an order for Rae to email the plan to the others, which she did right before bracing herself for their flippant responses. Curiously, no one replied.

Rae tapped her bottom lip in thought. She still needed to ask Travis if her niece could attend this team-building, save-a-marriage camping work retreat. She could text him, or she could just smash her kneecaps with a large hammer. After much debate, she texted Travis and waited for her cellphone to literally blow up from Travis shooting back a terse remark. Five minutes of fingernail biting passed with no response. Rae looked at Tiny who raised his eyebrows. "I agree, Tiny," Rae said while scratching his ears. "No news is good news."

Dropping to her knees, Rae reached underneath her bed and dragged an oversized duffel bag into view. She packed it with her clothes and essentials very quickly. In her haste, Rae still remembered some camping must-haves, a small metal shovel, bug spray, pain medications and lastly, her puzzle book with an extra green marker pen. She placed her bag next to the brand new air mattress still in the box. Wasn't there something else though? After racking her mind, the something else remained a mystery and she filled the rest of her bag with soda and chips. Throughout packing, however, she remained optimistic and convinced that Travis would come to his senses, probably around five in the morning.

Now reclined on her queen-sized bed with a cryptogram puzzle on her lap and Tiny next to her, Rae said, "I firmly believe that Travis, The Torch, will burn out by dawn, calling off this ridiculous two-day torture." Tiny, however, shook his head.

"Alright." Rae said to her beast of a bed companion, "Let's make a bet. If *I'm* right, then you have to start sleeping on the nice dog bed in the dining room."

Tiny sniffed and looked in the other direction.

"I know you don't like to sleep in the dining room, but your bed is too big to fit in here." She bit a fingernail. "How about this? If *you're* right, then you have to start sleeping on the nice dog bed in the dining room."

Tiny seemed unamused at her trickery and began barking incessantly.

Putting her finger to her lips, Rae quickly shushed him. "The landlord doesn't like barking, remember? So, calm down and let's talk this out. If you're right, what do you want?"

Tiny looked at her. Then, with one push of his smoky snout, he forcibly rolled her off the bed. Two thumps followed. The first one was Rae, landing on the hardwood floor. The second was the puzzle book, being thrown in anger.

As she sprung to her feet, her hands were already placed on her hips. She shrieked, "You've got to be kidding me!"

Tiny yawned, stretching his huge body over the entire bed. His long hind legs extended beyond the mattress and his paws stuck straight out. He wiggled his toes.

At that moment, Rae thought of the nice plush dog bed. She ordered the XXXXL to accommodate Tiny's size and she could easily fit on it. The spacious dining room would definitely fit her dresser and she would have space for a television too. The whole idea was a little unconventional, even preposterous, but some kind of an appeal formed. Without giving it more thought, Rae said, "Okay. New idea. If you're right, then we'll swap beds."

Tiny wagged his tail.

Rae extended her hand and they shook on it. With a severe expression, she looked him square in the eye and said, "Now, get off." She gestured with her hands. "This whole area is still mine. You try sleeping on the floor. For once."

With a low throat rumble, Tiny lumbered from his consecrated spot on Rae's bed to the barbaric carpeted floor. After circling a few times, he first scratched at the fibers and then stretched both legs, one at a time, as well as his forelimbs. He finally plunked down and looked at her with his eyes full of sorrow.

"You're a big ol' ham." After patting Tiny on the head, Rae crawled into bed and moved her fingers over her phone's screen, searching for soothing sounds to help calm her anxiety. Once she selected the hypnotic clicking of keystrokes, she turned off the light from her bedside lamp, clearing her thoughts of everything and everybody. Breathing deeply, her mind became a blank slate wiped clean. Turning onto her side, she exhaled and felt Tiny's hot breath on the back of her neck as he exhaled too. Not surprised at this regular bedtime move of his, Rae smiled. Truth be told, she acclimated to him climbing into her bed and there was nothing she could really do about it. He had an extra thirty pounds on her. So, she snuggled into her sheets, clearing her thoughts of everything again. No Travis. No Tiny. No team. No Stone.

Ugh, she thought. Now Stone was on her mind. *And* his sexy arms. They felt like a heated blanket wrapped around her, holding her tight. Well, she assumed his arms would feel that comforting, if she ever allowed him to hug her. How he made her feel safe! With or without his arms! And he made her feel irritated, just as easily. Catching the vibe that he was interested in her, she was torn like a piece of paper. On the one half, she was all for it. On the other half, she had some reluctance. All because of his clenched jaw, which was his tell. *He started lying to me again. Why?* She sighed. *Not to mention, the wall he built in high school is still there. And it's getting higher.* Turning up the volume on her phone, she listened to the keystrokes. *If he can't talk to me or trust me about what's bothering him, then we won't work. So, why date in the first place?* She bit a fingernail. *Plus, I don't typically date guys prettier than me.*

Tiny sighed and gently placed his enormous paw over her. The weight and warmth of it soothed her and she spit out the fingernail remnant. After inhaling deeply again and exhaling slowly, she flipped off her thoughts of stone walls and eventually slipped into a slumber.

Expectedly, around five in the morning, Rae awakened to the sound of her cellphone buzzing. She snatched it off her nightstand. Lo and behold, it was her boss.

Rae answered, "I knew you would call."

"There's been a change."

"Let me guess. You came to your senses and canceled our woodland tragedy in the making? I knew it and may I say that you made a good decision."

Travis sighed. "You talk too much in the morning, and no, I'm not canceling our woodland whatever. I've decided to *extend* our stay. We'll be camping from today through Friday. So, one extra night."

"Whoa, whoa, whoa. That'll be more money. Are you sure you want to do that? Can we do that? Is there availability for another night?"

"Rae, I know what you're trying to do and I really need you to stop embarrassing yourself over the phone. There is availability. Well, there wasn't and then there was. Long story. Just tell everyone asap."

"You're seriously being serious? Three nights? In a row?" The unexpected and dismal news caused Rae to punch the bed, which awakened Tiny. He barked.

Travis heard it. "Was that a dog? Do you have a dog? I thought you hated dogs."

"Well, Tiny's different."

"Your dog's name is Tiny? My dog's name is Tiny. Change your dog's name."

"No."

"What kind of dog is it?"

"A Great Shepherd, which is a Great Dane and German Shepherd mix."

Rae could sense Travis's disgust on the other end. He asked, "How big is that dog?"

"Tiny is around forty inches high, on all fours."

"That's taller than you. What possessed you to get a big dog? When did this happen?"

"First, I'm taller than forty inches, thank you very much. In fact, I'm five feet tall, which is sixty inches. Second, you could say I rescued him while house-sitting your manor three weeks ago." Rae chuckled. "Actually, he rescued me. You see, what happened was-"

"Nah, I don't care. Just change his name. We can't have two Tinys in the family."

"We're not family."

"On second thought, bring your dog. I want to meet my Tiny's namesake. And since I'm bringing my Tiny, he can teach your dog some class."

Rae bit her tongue and instead said, "Going back to that family remark, you never answered my earlier text about my niece."

"What niece?"

"The niece who I want to bring along. She's a great classy organizer."

"Good lord. How old?"

"Fourteen."

"That's awful. Is she emaciated-looking like you?"

"We're the same size, if that's what you're asking."

"So, she won't take up too much room. Or eat a lot. Still, she's a kid."

"You know, Travis, this is a fine time for lesson two on finding your kinder side. Especially toward *children*."

"Yeah, yeah, I got it." He mumbled something that Rae couldn't understand before saying, "Fine. Bring this niece of yours."

Rae smiled. "Thank you, Tra-"

Three beeps interrupted her sentence, bringing the conversation to an abrupt end. Travis hung up on her. After a few choice words, Rae emailed the others about their extended camping by one horrible day. On the surface, this news left her feeling like a worm where half of its body had been squished and the other living half couldn't squirm forward. Deep down, she felt much worse. Stuck at a camp for three nights and four days with The Torch, Two-face Tonya, Klimpy and Chuckles might possibly give her a raging case of shingles.

Flopping onto her stomach, Rae moaned into her pillow when a big paw nudged her shoulder. She turned her head and stared into Tiny's black eyes, suddenly remembering their bet. The bet that she just lost. When Rae opened her mouth to protest, his tongue lapped over his own nose before licking her from the bottom of her chin to the top of her forehead.

Rae gagged, knowing that being tongued by her dog was his way of rubbing it in.

.   .   .

Why did *she* get to go? That made no sense. Emma hated anything to do with leaving her bedroom, unless a hammock was involved.

Laying on his back in bed, Bash stared at the ceiling. According to Emma's agenda, which Bash intercepted, photographed and saved on his cellphone without anyone's knowledge, Aunt Rae would be arriving at eight o' clock to pick up his sister. Running out of time, he pressed his ear to the adjoining wall and listened anxiously to the conversation between his mother and Emma. They briefly bickered about something involving a thermometer. Once they said their goodbyes, he heard his mother's footsteps descend the stairs. She called to his dad, at which point they murmured to each other before she left through the front door. Bash remained on the edge of his bed, waiting for the sound of his mother's car engine roar to life. It did. Then, as he listened to that sweet varoom of her departure, his plan was set in motion like a marble run.

Sliding ever so silently off the bed, he tiptoed to his backpack, stuffed with a typical twelve-year old's essentials: underwear, swim trunks and one travel toothbrush. The rest of the space held Bash's essentials: one tarot card deck, his dad's utility flashlight, headlamp, one red spiral notebook, pencil, garlic bulbs in a Ziploc bag, a ball of string and three important library books about werewolves. He hoisted the backpack over his shoulder and slid his arms through the straps before grabbing his black case that kept his precious paranormal equipment. Feeling somewhat confident, he pulled on his lucky baseball cap for extra courage and crept to his bedroom door. He slowly turned the knob and peeked down the hallway.

Emma was in her room, curled on her bed in a fetal position. Thankfully, her eyes were closed. She wasn't the threat though. And neither was his two-year old sister, Meg. Bash could already hear Meg's delighted squeals from the kitchen below as his dad fed her favorite cereal to her, Bang Burst Boom, a puffed rice ball that packed a lot of sweet flavor. It also was fun to throw and he could hear his dad grumbling about the mess that Meg made.

With three of his family members occupied, Bash was almost across enemy lines, so to speak. However, his senses heightened. His real threat was nowhere to be seen or heard. Holding his breath, Bash quickly crept down the stairs, pausing at the bottom momentarily. No threatening visuals were detected in the foyer, so

Bash crouched. As quietly as he could with a hefty backpack and case in hand, he crawled to the family room. Thankfully, his dad and little sister were louder than his clamor and he found refuge behind the recliner. Holed up, Bash scanned the environment and only saw hundreds of plastic construction toys, scattered on the floor. This evidence warned Bash that his threat was nearby, but where?

Just then, Bash felt a wet finger in his ear. When he turned his head, his heart sank. Crouched next to him and sucking his thumb was the threat, his younger brother, Henry. He had rosy cheeks.

Henry, age four, was a xerox copy of Bash, except much noisier. He had the same dark hair with auburn highlights, the same big blue-gray eyes, the same dimples and the same habit of forming obsessions. The obsessions were different though. Bash obsessed about detective shows and the paranormal, whereas Henry obsessed about plastic construction toys and his thumb.

Henry greeted him with an exclamation. "Hi, Bwash!"

For a kid with a thumb permanently stuck in his mouth, Henry spoke pretty clearly. And loudly. Bash covered his brother's face with his hands, causing Henry to giggle. Shaking his head at Henry, his brother stopped giggling and starting sucking. Loudly.

Bash whispered in Henry's ear, "I need you to build me a tower with all of the bricks. Can you do that for me?"

Henry nodded and then emerged from the recliner. Sitting on his feet in the middle of the sea of toy bricks, he began snapping them together.

Bash took the opportunity to move. Waddling like a penguin, he squat-walked with his backpack and black case through the laundry room and out the door. Once hunched behind an overgrown evergreen bush, Bash blew out a sigh of relief. He succeeded at step one. Now, for step two, all he had to do was wait.

CHAPTER SIX

As Rae arrived to pick up Emma, Tiny shoved his large head between the front seats, hitting his head on the headliner. He tried to wag his tail, but it mashed against the rear window. Rae opened the door for him and he now stood on the driveway. "Well?" Rae said to her Great Shepherd, "Now's the time to move around." Tiny seemed to understand and began stretching his long legs, starting with his hind legs. He straightened each of the four as much as he could, arched his back and then went into a downward-facing dog pose. Once upright, he shook all over and lifted his snout. An evergreen bush, very overgrown, sat by the house and Rae noticed that, for some reason, it caught Tiny's attention. He trotted over to investigate, sticking his nose into the branches and leaves.

She waited, expecting him to empty his bladder on it. He didn't. He just stood next to the bush, staring at it. Impatient, Rae tapped her outer thigh for Tiny to follow. The two of them then entered the home, belonging to her older brother, Danny; his wife, Clare; and their four children, Emma, Bash, Henry and Meg. Tiny immediately trotted into the family room and laid down next to Henry. Rae wasn't as focused as Tiny and, after walking through the foyer, she turned the corner, almost tripping over Henry. She caught her balance to only then bump into a very tall plastic brick skyscraper. It wobbled. There were gasps. Somehow, Rae managed to steady it without destroying the building. As she slowly stepped away from it, she almost stepped on Henry again. He giggled. She reached down, smiling, and tapped his nose.

"Hello, Mr. Henry."

"Hewwo."

Rae popped his thumb out of his mouth. "Try that again."

Henry looked up at her. "Hello." Then he stuck his thumb back into his mouth and snapped more toy bricks together, using one hand and his knee.

"Hey, is your brother here?"

Shaking his head, Henry continued building.

"He's not? Where is he?"

Danny answered from the kitchen, "Sulking."

Rae crossed the room to stand at the kitchen island. She watched with amusement as Danny rinsed Meg's naked body in the sink with the faucet sprayer. "Should I ask?"

"Nope."

Scanning the ground, Rae found the evidence, leading to Meg's current state. In a pile by Danny's feet were Meg's clothes, smeared with various colors and textures. From what Rae detected, Meg enjoyed a breakfast of orange juice, puff cereal, scrambled eggs, grape jelly, possibly pancakes and, most likely, tater tots.

Rae gave her brother a quizzical look. "Meg likes orange juice now?"

"Nope."

Rae scrutinized Meg's clothing some more. "What's the brown gooey stuff?"

"Puke."

"Oh," said Rae. "Was it the orange juice?"

"Yep."

"Gross." Fanning her nose with her hands, Rae said, "The smell just hit me." She gagged and took one step back from them. "So, Bash is still mad at me?"

"Yep."

Now standing in the family room, away from puke fumes, Rae called to her brother. "Danny, as an EMT, how do you get by not saying more than one word at your job?"

Lifting Meg from the sink, Danny wrapped his two-year old daughter in clean dish towels and said, "Lucky."

"Why aren't you working today?"

Holding Meg on his hip, he looked at Rae. "Fever."

"You?"

"Henry."

"Oh." Rae glanced at Henry who was busy with building his skyscraper. "He seems fine."

Danny nodded. "Low-grade."

Rae raised her eyebrows. "Does anyone else have a fever?" In response to her question, she heard slow-moving thumps, descending the stairs. As Emma eventually crawled into the family room, she collapsed on the floor next to Henry's tower. Rae asked her, "Are you okay?"

Face-down on the carpet, Emma mumbled, "I possibly have a fever. And diarrhea."

Raising her eyebrows higher, Rae said, "Have you gone to the bathroom lately?"

"Yeah. It was explosive. And hot."

Rae turned to Danny who now looked more disheartened than a basset hound. Shrugging, she said to him, "Well, I can't take her camping with explosive hot diarrhea, so I guess I should go then. Good luck with all of this."

Danny raised Meg's hand and slowly waved it. "Bye."

As Rae walked through the family room, she stepped over her niece. Suddenly, she felt a hand squeeze her ankle, preventing Rae from leaving. She looked down to see Emma, desperately clinging to her.

"Take me. With. You." Barely able to lift her head, Emma slowly continued, "Harry. Styles. Tickets."

Rae solemnly shook her head at Emma and said, "Sorry, kid. No tickets since you can't go, but I will treat you to a movie for helping me with the agenda." With one finger, she patted her niece on the head. "It's not Harry, but it will be movie popcorn."

Emma gave her a half smile and her grip loosened enough for Rae to slip her foot from her niece's grasp. She then called to Danny, "Tell Bash I'll make it up to him when I get home!" Tapping her outer thigh, she alerted Tiny of their departure. As she passed Henry, she also patted him on the head and rushed outside with Tiny on her heels.

■　■　■

Stuffed into the backseat, Tiny looked like a pork brat that was way too big for the bun. He still panted happily though, waiting for the car to actually move. It was a very tight squeeze with Angry Rae's oversized lumpy bag underneath him. Not to mention, the lumpy bag on the floor kept squirming. No matter. And there were a pair of tennis shoes underneath the bag that wiggled. They smelled like onions mixed with dirty socks, reminding him of Nice Bash. How he would miss that deliciously smelly boy! Oh well. Hopefully, the wind in Tiny's face would make everything better.

Tiny watched as Angry Rae slid behind the wheel, rubbing her hands, face and forearms with some kind of liquid that had a powerful clean smell. She finally started the car and he whined at her. Facing forward, she spoke to him through the rearview mirror.

"Emma's sick and not coming with us," Angry Rae said. He watched as she moved a stick around to make the car move. She then continued, "So, it's you and me against the rest of the team. And what a team it is."

Tiny stared out the window when a song sounded from the radio. One of Tiny's favorites, it was a peppy little number about a dog working hard all day's night. Whatever that meant. He kept the beat with his tail.

"Here's a quick rundown on everyone, starting with Travis," Angry Rae said. "If the team were on a sinking island and there were five seats on a rescue plane, he'd take all five seats and leave the rest of us to tread water."

Tiny barked.

"I know. Then there's Tonya. I get the feeling that, if she had the chance, she would feed me to the wolves."

Tiny whined and flicked his ear.

"Yep, you got that right." Angry Rae shrugged. "Whatever. Now, Kimmy is quiet and has no backbone. I like her the most."

Licking his chops, Tiny yipped merrily.

"Yes, you'll like her too. And you'll like Chuck. He's very kind and oblivious to his surroundings. A true kindred spirit."

Tiny yawned at that and stuck his snout out the window, allowing the fast wind to caress his forehead, eyes and tongue. Somewhere off in the distance, the scent of grilled meat wafted through his nostrils. He closed his eyes, wondering if this was dog heaven.

The rest of the ride was peaceful and the feeling of serenity allowed Tiny to reflect. From what he understood, he was camping for the next few days. He learned that camping had something to do with being outside all the time and fed like wolves. What a thrill! Tiny sighed, though, at one sad thought. Poor Nice Bash was stuck at home. And he was going to miss the wolves.

CHAPTER SEVEN

During the three hour ride to Ma'iingan Bluff, Travis called four times. His first call came shortly after Rae left her brother's home. He needed to ensure that Rae was on her way. Then the second call came shortly after his first. Travis ordered her to make sure that the three others were on their way.

"I already did," Rae said. "I called them and they are driving up there as we speak."

Travis asked, "You're not lying to me, are you?"

Rae definitely lied. Her three nutso coworkers were the last people who she'd call. Ever. Rae answered, "Of course I'm not." That was her second lie.

"Okay, good. You're the only one who I almost trust." He hung up.

About an hour later, Rae followed Stone's advice and chugged merrily along the interstate in the slow lane, singing to her favorite song, "Happy Together" by The Turtles. And then Travis called her again. He ordered her to stop at a sporting goods store to buy a tent for their team.

Her smile slid into a frown. "What do you mean, I have to get the tent? You said you had the necessary materials."

"I did have the necessary materials yesterday. Six o'clock this morning, however, something opened the box and shredded the tent."

"A raccoon?"

"Not quite. It was Mort."

"Your son? Your two-year old son shredded the tent? How? And why?"

"With his hands again. Seth says that Mort is acting out because of me. I'm causing Mort stress. Can you believe that? He said that I need to learn how to communicate with our son. I reminded Seth that Mort and I do have a language barrier because Mort is Chinese and I'm from Manhattan. Seth didn't like that logic and told me to leave."

"Leave to go camping, or leave as in kicked out?"

"Not sure. He said that I can't come home until I completely change my negative attitude. What do you suppose he means?"

"Well, Mr. Manhattan, I think that's pretty clear." She rolled her eyes. "So, since you were kicked out at six this morning, what did you do? Where did you go?"

Sounding annoyed, Travis replied, "Duh, I got in my car and drove around to nowhere, like any other man, Rae."

"Then duh, you should've driven to a sporting goods store and bought another tent."

Travis sighed. "I walked right into that one. I'm horrible, aren't I?"

Without waiting a second, Rae agreed, "Yep."

Travis seemed unaffected by her honesty. "I blame the government. Anyway, you have a lot of work to do with fixing my marriage and buying a big tent."

Rae gripped the steering wheel. "Stop putting me in a lose-lose situation. It's stressing me out." Rae grinned. "I feel like shredding something with my bare hands."

Travis didn't laugh. "You're stressed out? I'm more stressed out, Rae. I can't have three failed marriages. I'll fall into a pit of emotional despair and make the office environment an even more god-forsaken place to work. That will be on you. Remember that while buying a big tent."

Yanking the wheel to the left, Rae propelled her little blue coupe into the middle lane. "No, it won't be my fault, and second, I don't have funds in my checking to buy a big tent."

Travis sounded puzzled. "How much are tents?"

"Two hundred. Probably."

"How much is in your checking?"

"As my boss, you're not allowed to ask me that."

After a short hesitation, Travis said, "I bet you have less than fifty bucks in your checking. Am I right?"

"It's none of your business." Her foot pressed the accelerator and she yanked the wheel to the left again, finding herself in the fast lane. The sudden jerking movement awakened Tiny. Her little blue coupe then lurched ahead and quickly approached an arrogant recreational vehicle in her lane, driving ten under the limit. This large and luxurious RV towed a small car, protected by a tailor-made car cover. Rae punched the horn and Tiny barked. The RV slowed even more.

Travis said, "Oh, I get it. You don't know how much is in your checking. Typical."

"Yes. I do."

"You don't strike me as someone who balances a checkbook."

After yanking the wheel to the right, Rae found herself in the middle lane again, grinding her teeth this time. Keeping her eyes on the road, she floored the accelerator and passed the silver monstrosity. When her bumper barely cleared, Rae yanked the wheel and she found herself in the fast lane again, leaving the rude RV behind her.

Her voice raised. "And you don't strike me as someone who's balanced!"

Travis chuckled. "Alright, take it easy. I'll let you win this argument. Do you have a credit card?"

"Yes!"

"Use that and I'll reimburse for it."

"I want a *full* reimbursement!"

"Stop shouting. Buy the cheapest tent that you can find for six people. Got it?"

"Travis, can I trust you to pay me back?"

"Rae, I'm probably the only person who you can trust. In any situation."

"If that's true, then I'm in deep shit." Sounding exasperated, Rae hinted, "Is that all?"

"Should there be more?"

"How about a thank you? That would be a kind thing for you to do."

"I thought I did already."

"Nope."

There was silence on Travis's end. "All. Right." He then said very slowly, "Tha-"

"Try again."

Rae heard him drink some water. Then he attempted, "Thannnnn-"

Sighing into the phone, Rae said, "We'll keep working on this. I'm hanging up now."

"Great. Just do me one last favor and pick up some toilet paper."

"Geez, Travis. Then you have to do me a favor and stop calling me."

"That's probably best. The drivers around here are crazy." He disconnected.

Tiny groaned from the backseat, followed by a short yip.

"I know he's nuts," she told him. "Listen, it's nine o'clock. After getting a tent and tp, we'll find a Pancakes Plus and eat our food at a rest stop. Or park. Or somewhere. Then it's just two more hours, okay?" Rae heard the thumping of Tiny's tail and knew that he happily agreed.

Three hours later, Rae and Tiny approached Ma'iingan Bluff with full stomachs and looks of wonderment. The five hundred foot cliffs loomed over the little blue coupe, loaded down with a large dog, sprawled in the back, and a larger tent, pressing down on the top. She soon arrived at Fun Warriors Ranch, parked her car and strolled through a luxurious main entrance building on the north end of the campground. It was manned by a young female with long dark hair. According to her nametag, her name was Casey. When learning that Rae was part of Travis's work retreat, Casey handed Rae a map and explained, "You are here." She pointed to a red dot and continued as Rae followed Casey's finger, "This is the north park office. You need to drive through the north campground, through the west campground, up a hill and then to the south park office, which is closer to your team's remote campsite at the south campground."

Rae nodded and really wanted to know only one thing. "How remote?"

Casey smiled. "Mare will help you find it. She'll be waiting for you on the porch and can direct you the rest of the way."

"Did you say her name's Mare?"

"Yes." Casey quickened her speech. "She's this little ol' lady who can be very stern, at times, but don't let her scare you and have a nice stay!" She then dismissed Rae by talking to the next customer.

Stuck on the word remote, Rae reluctantly found herself behind the steering wheel again, second-guessing herself. Again. And while driving on the white gravel road to the south park office, the scenic look comforted her inhibitions regarding Fun Warriors Ranch, comprising three campgrounds: north, west and south. The north campground, which looked more like spacious backyards of a wealthy subdivision, seemed homey. About a hundred flat grassy lots followed one right after the other with a toddler tree planted here and there. As Rae drove by each polished campsite, she noted all of the RVs. No tents. Just RVs. And the owners of these RVs were all adults. No children. Just adults. Men wore polo shirts and sandals; women rested on chaise lounges while sipping a rose chardonnay out of a large wine glass. Quiet voices were barely audible over the polite tittering and the meaty aroma of grilled steaks teased Rae's full stomach. It surprisingly growled again, as did Tiny's. They both sighed at the same time.

Just as the little blue coupe huffed around a curve, Rae spotted an RV, sneering at her. It was the same snobby silver monstrosity that she passed on the highway with the covered car, attached to the back. However, presently, the car was gone.

Great, she said to herself. *Something tells me that I'm going to run into this jerk a lot on this stupid camping trip.*

Tiny barked at the RV, seeming to show disgust for it too, and Rae nodded. "Yes, you can pee on that later."

Speaking of peeing, Rae thought as she then passed the posh concrete building with the word AMENITIES written on a fancy sign above the double glass entrance doors. *The bathrooms seem nice. No spiders would dare to live at the base of those toilets. Hopefully, the bathrooms for the remote campsite are just as nice.*

As Rae entered the west campground, she noticed a slight shift in the scenery, as well as the atmosphere. Still spacious, these hundred campsites boasted adolescent oak, maple and evergreen trees while maintaining well-manicured grassy areas for tents and wooden picnic tables. Smiling faces and hearty laughter slapped the apprehension right off Rae's face as she drove through this family-oriented area. Kids roasted marshmallows on sticks as teenagers threw footballs back and forth. Somewhere in the distance, the melody of "American Pie" swirled in the atmosphere and Rae's shoulders lowered a smidge. Maybe this really wouldn't be so bad after all? Another concrete building for showering and relieving oneself, just as nice as the other facility, marked the end of the west campground.

The little blue coupe marched up a hill and Rae first noticed that the white gravel road abruptly changed to plain brown dirt. Then the road narrowed into more of a path. And this path eventually led her to the rustic brown building where an older woman with a very stern glare waited on the porch for Rae.

Rae turned off her car's engine and unbuckled the seatbelt. She caressed Tiny's head, reassuring him of her quick return. As she emerged from her car, the older woman beckoned Rae to hurry and then entered the building. Now they both stood in the one room building with a counter between them. Rae politely smiled, but the older woman impatiently grumbled. Small in stature, she had a slim build, short gray hair and a mean mug, intimidating Rae not only with her dark defensive eyes, but also with her combative remarks. Even if they were true.

"You don't look like someone who can rough it," the older woman said.

Rae immediately agreed and then asked, "Is this the south park office?"

"Of course, it is. What else would it be?"

Rae glanced around the room and spied rakes, shovels, ropes, newspapers and a bag of garlic bulbs. "Capone's old storage shed?" Rae chuckled at her own joke, but Mare's lips were drawn in a straight line. Rae stopped laughing and asked, "Are you Mare?"

"Of course." Mare continued, "I already met your boss. Tell him he should learn to take no for an answer."

Puzzled, Rae asked, "What do you mean?"

"He didn't like it when I told him we were all booked, which we are in the two nicer campgrounds that you just drove through. He forced me into giving him one of the campsites out here. We don't normally open this area for the public. We're working on…fixing it."

Rae wondered aloud. "Did he bribe you too?"

"And threatened to call the BBB." Mare sniffed outwardly before slapping a map on the counter for Rae, highlighting a route to the campsite. That was it. Rae felt the end of the conversation and, after signing a check-in book, she bought an admissions sticker. While studying it, she felt Mare watching her. Rae politely smiled again and then received another glare, causing Rae to hurry through the creaky screen door.

In her haste, she collided into the stomach of a man on the steps. Feeling like she hit a brick wall, she bounced backwards, bracing herself for the ground, when he caught her shoulders with his bony, yet strong, hands. Rae squeaked in surprise while gaping into his eyes. Well, actually, she gaped in the general direction of his eyes, but couldn't see them through his thick brown dreadlocks.

A woman followed behind Dreadlocks Dude. She had very full lips and blond highlighted hair, pulled into a ponytail with teased bangs. "Oh my," she said to Rae. "Please excuse us."

"My bad," Rae said, sounding winded.

Ms. Full Lips and Dreadlocks Dude stared at Rae for a brief second before she asked Rae, "Are you part of that work retreat?" When Rae nodded, she asked, "So, you're staying for three nights now? All seven of you?"

Rae stopped her. "Actually, it's just five of us."

Ms. Full Lips stuck out her puffy bottom lip. "We have it down as seven people on two campsites next to each other."

"Oh," Rae said with an unsure tone. "Then I guess that's what it is."

Ms. Full Lips gave a look of contemplation. "Okay. Well, if you need anything, just let me know." She held out her hand. "My name's Jen and this is Matt, our maintenance man."

While shaking Jen's hand, Rae introduced herself. Matt, however, refused to shake Rae's hand. He did, however, walk around Rae, disappearing into the south park office.

Jen gave Rae an apologetic look. "Sorry. He's a little… rough around the edges."

Rae shrugged, smiling. "No worries. Nice meeting you." She then quickly retreated to her car to begin the last leg of the journey.

.   .   .

For lunchtime on a Tuesday, The Rail noisily buzzed with the many voices of a younger crowd and Sally mingled with all of them. In her element, her harsh laugh reminded Stone of a donkey's bray. She even looked like a donkey today. Her wig was long and brown, her outfit was a tan strapless polyester onesie and, every once in a while, she stamped her foot after she heard a good joke. Stone shook his head at her. For someone in her mid-fifties, she naturally fit in with twenty-year olds. He, on the other hand, was a man in a twenty-six year old body, but acted like a sixty-two year old, according to Rachel. Maybe he worked too much?

"You work too much!" Sally called to him over the crowd. "Go home! I'll handle the bar." She saluted him with a gin and tonic in her hand.

Stone was relieved that she did not knock herself out with the glass. "Are you sure?"

A young man hoisted Sally up on his shoulders. She could now touch the wooden beam on the ceiling and was holding onto it to keep her balance as her drunk base swayed. "Of course, I'm sure! I used to run this place with your grandpa, remember? I've had harder jobs, lying on my back, if you know what I mean!"

Stone did not want to know what she meant. Instead, he glanced at his watch. It was half past eleven and he felt that he was late for something. But what? Shaking off that anxious feeling, he checked for his wallet, car keys and his remaining sanity before leaving the bar. Once settled behind his steering wheel in his red Dodge, he closed his stinging eyes. *Just for a second,* he told himself. His tense shoulders slackened, his pursed lips softened and his eyes began to dart underneath the lids. Soon, his old pacifying reality morphed into a new unsettling one.

Standing on a dirt path, Stone was alone. The full moon glowed and hung low in the night sky. No stars twinkled. No night owls hooted. No cicadas trilled. The leaves on the trees, surrounding him, remained still. It was almost pleasant, except for the stench of death.

The power of the smell rushed over Stone like a linebacker. It reminded him of cow manure mixed with rotten eggs and expired meat. And stinky cheese. That wasn't the worst of it though. As he searched for the source of the pungent odor, bits and pieces of bone and flesh came into view. Ahead of him were limbs without hands and feet without legs. Skulls with their hollowed eyes and gaping mouths dotted the ground all around him.

Stone heard a horse neigh and he looked up to see a brilliant white stallion on the very top of a small hill, not far from him. Twenty yards, perhaps. Not far, at all. And next to the horse was a knight. Motionless. Just standing there and allowing his black armor to reflect the moon's light. As the knight faced him, Stone sensed the eyes behind the visor, intently staring at him.

For some unfortunate reason, Stone felt compelled to converse with this gallant. Many voices inside his head screamed at him to stay silent, but he did not listen as he said, "Hello there. Can you tell me where I am?"

There was no response from the mysterious horseman.

Clearing his throat, Stone again ignored the mental red flags, now shooting up like fireworks, and tried to strike up another conversation. "Do I know you?"

An eerie calmness pressed down on Stone and a dreadful, warm sensation flowed over him. It began to constrict his breathing. Feeling desperate, Stone needed to make this vision stop and he asked the nobleman, "What do you want from me?"

The man never moved and Stone's arms began to tingle. Rubbing his forearms, he instinctively knew what he had to do. Slowly, he stepped closer to the dark motionless shape. With each step, his chest tightened and the uncomfortable feeling intensified. Beads of sweat formed on his forehead, but his feet still propelled him forward. As Stone now stood inches from the stranger, he realized that the scent of death grew even heavier around this man.

Without any warning, the knight lifted the helmet and the bright moonlight exposed the face of a skeleton. The undead raised his bony arm and the shape of a sickle appeared against the moon. With a harsh, guttural tone, the phantom screamed, *"Run, Stone, run!"*

There was a crack of lightning and the horse loudly neighed in fright while springing onto his hind legs. Stone yelled at the top of his lungs as the sickle suddenly came down upon him, knocking on his head three times. Clang! Clang! Clang!

Stone opened his eyes with a start. The noon sun blinded him. Clutching his chest, he felt the thumping of his heart and the wetness of his t-shirt as it clung to his torso. Between gasps, he wiped the sweat from his face and then hugged his steering wheel. While slowly counting to ten, his breath became regulated while his hands steadied.

The calm didn't last long.

Again, the three knocks sounded, but on the roof of his car this time and not on his head. Thump. Thump. Thump. Out of the corner of his eye, he saw a dark shape, standing next to the driver's door. Stone gulped, closed his eyes and counted to ten again.

However, he only made it to four when he heard a familiar voice say, "Hey, dude."

Sure enough, it was Zalen, with his goofy smile stretched across his face. He wore a red bucket hat while his hand clutched a long umbrella. A fanny pack squeezed his waist. Scattered around his feet was a new air mattress box, backpack, cooler, toilet paper, a paper bag filled with snacks and a plant. He raised his eyebrows and said, "Do you have a tent?"

Confused, Stone asked, "Why do I need a tent?"

Zalen smiled wider. "Because I reserved a campsite for us at Fun Warriors Ranch. Now, let's go. We need to answer the bell, as they say."

Dazed, Stone's lips parted in surprise. *Answer the bell? A bell* sounded in his vision. Is Zalen somehow connected to his vision? Is he somehow connected to the knight? *Is Zalen the knight?* Stone mentally shook his head. Zalen could be the cotton candy on a paper cone or the melted butter on movie popcorn, but he never could be a chilling skeletal knight. Could he?

CHAPTER EIGHT

The last leg of the journey turned out to be a longer leg than Rae expected. The little blue coupe strained up hills and squeaked around tight curves as it maneuvered on dirt paths that thinned as quickly as an aged man's hairline. Rae slowed on these narrowing trails, carefully weaving through full-grown trees. Some looked more on the retiring end. Others had already passed.

There wasn't much sign of life. No manicured couples. No fun families. No nothing. Every campsite was vacant with overgrown trees and broken-down picnic tables. At one point, the little blue coupe seemed to put its foot down and stopped in front of a small dark brown wooden structure. It reminded Rae of Dracula's coffin, standing on end. However, a crescent moon shape decorated the slanted door and underneath the moon were the carved words PIT TOILET. As she debated about moving on, the sickening stench of rotten eggs penetrated through the glass window and overwhelmed her car's interior. This was enough to make the little coupe move up the last hill pretty much on its own.

Rae then slowly followed the gravel road, passing the vacant campsites. Bringing her thumbnail to her teeth, she nibbled. *Remote would be a welcoming description. This is more godforsaken, like a deserted village in the depths of the Grand Canyon.*

Isolation set in. While continuing to move from one unmanned campsite to the other, she noticed that the areas were near each other, but the hovering trees gave each site a strong sense of privacy. Finally, Rae arrived at her team's gathering and her little car relieved itself from the strenuous trip with an unexpected backfire.

Rae patted her dashboard in a caring manner while studying the scene before her. The only redeeming feature of her outdoor home for the next few days was the view. Being on higher ground, she could see spots of Wolves Lake through the trees that lined the hill's edge. Other than that, the campsite resembled the remains of a cabin fire that was poorly cleared. Black wood chips carpeted the small area. No grass. Just black wood chips. Dead logs rested in all positions and a metal lop-sided picnic table struggled to stay upright. Many tall trees loomed over the campsite, like scientists looking down on a team of microorganisms. In this case, however, it was a team of angry graphic designers. The center of the campsite flaunted a rusted fire ring that was surrounded by her team, all facing each other and readying themselves for a standoff. It caused a familiar oops feeling to form in Rae's gut. It was the same oops feeling that she felt every time she mistakenly opened an occupied bathroom stall door. She decided to stay in her car and watch.

In a pet carrier sling across Travis's chest rested his little Tiny, the snobby white Bichon Frise that Rae met ten days ago. Travis's face reddened with anger as he turned toward Two-face Tonya. She then positioned her pointer finger dangerously close to Chuckles' nose. He retaliated by turning his hands into duck bills and making quack-quack noises. Next to Chuckles was Klimpy who seemed calmly unhinged more than usual. Her mouth curved upward, but her eyes were frighteningly wide. Over and over, she tore a leaf until it resembled green confetti and then sprinkled the ground with it.

Turning around in her seat, Rae faced Tiny. "This team-building retreat is off to a rough start."

Tiny whined and glanced backward down the road. Following his gaze, Rae understood her dog's meaning and debated about shifting her car into reverse. California sounded nice. Unfortunately, Travis already spotted her and waved for her to join them.

She shook her head.

Travis glared and pushed Chuckles out of his way. As he marched to Rae's window, she locked her door.

He spoke through the glass, "It's about time you arrived. Why are you the last one?"

Rae replied, "I had to stop and buy *your* tent."

She saw the hot lava boil behind his eyes as Travis, The Torch, said, "Get out *now*."

Sighing, Rae conceded. "Fine."

After she slowly emerged, she released the lever to move her seat forward and Tiny exploded out of the car like a big iron ball out of a cannon. Chuckles screamed and Klimpy jumped on top of the picnic table, but that did not deter Tiny from searching for the nearest tree to mark. Two-face Tonya stood her ground, glaring at Rae and asking, "What's this?"

Rae calmly replied, "Well, Tonya, this is my dog, Tiny."

"That's no dog." Tonya scoffed, "That's a grizzly bear that mated with a musk ox."

Still reserved, Rae said, "Actually, Tiny is a Great Dane German Shepherd mix."

Tonya crossed her arms. "Leave it to Rae to make things harder." She spoke to Travis, "And how dare she copy your dog's name!"

Travis defended Rae. "Hey, come on, guys. It's not Rae's fault she's not original."

Ugh, Rae thought, *I knew I should've stayed on the highway.*

Travis continued, "Since The Team-Building Committee finally arrived, who can fill Rae in on our first team-building dilemma? Chuck?"

Chuck nodded. "There are only two parking spots for cars. So, whoever doesn't park here has to park in the lot by the south entrance."

Tonya said, "I think the fair thing to do is give it to me, since I was here first."

Chuck raised his voice. "No, I was here first."

Tonya raised her voice a little higher. "When I arrived, you were nowhere in sight!"

Chuck's voice now boomed. "I waved to you as I sat on the hood of my car! And you waved back!"

Ugh, Rae thought again. *I could've been on my way to California by now.*

Sitting cross-legged on the table, Klimpy raised her finger in a timid protest and gently said, "Excuse me, but I was actually here first. Or I would've been if Chuck hadn't run me off the road." Chuck opened his mouth to argue, but Klimpy quickly continued, "I know it wasn't intentional. You just didn't see me. Probably because my Prius is tan and tends to blend with the surroundings. I've been in four accidents in two months."

Travis rotated his pointer fingers around each other as he said, "Wrap it up, Kimmy."

Kimmy motioned behind her. "Well, my car is over there, down an embankment, and stuck between two trees."

Travis shrugged. "And?"

When Kimmy did not answer, he continued, "Moving on, let's see what The Team-Building Committee has to say about this parking dilemma. Rae?"

With all of the angry eyes on her, Rae licked her suddenly dry lips before saying, "Well, did anyone ask if we could park all of our cars here?"

Travis nodded. "I didn't have to. The old lady told me that we could only have two cars at this site." Then he gestured at all of the trees and the two small parking spaces. Plus, Rae, where would we fit all of our cars? Think next time, Rae. Think."

"Wait a minute." Rae remembered what Mare told her. "We have two sites. Why don't two cars park next door?"

Looking perplexed, Travis asked, "What are you talking about?"

"Mare said we have two reserved sites next to each other, so-"

Travis shook his head. "I didn't reserve two sites next to each other. Does that even make sense? Whoever told you that is wrong. Now, stop wasting time and figure out a solution already."

Clearing her throat, she said, "Then I *think* the fair thing to do is put our names in a hat and the two people whose names are picked can park their cars here."

Travis quickly corrected, "One name, one spot. I automatically get the first spot." He paused and then said, "Don't look at me like that, Rae. I have a Mercedes Roadster that costs thrice as much as your salary. Besides, I'm the boss, which makes me the leader, the chief, the number one, the head honcho. You could even say that I'm the ruler of this world."

Rae informed him, "That's in reference to Satan."

Travis nodded. "He's a blood relative."

Putting her hands on her hips, Rae said, "You put me in charge of this whole operation. Aren't *I* the head honcho?" Her voice cracked. "Shouldn't *I* get the one spot?"

Travis gave her a look of disgust. "No and no." He then said to the team, "I like Tonya's idea about using a hat."

Before Rae corrected Travis, Tonya said, "Thank you." She smiled when Rae muffled a groan.

"Who has a hat?" Travis asked impatiently.

The five of them inspected each other's hatless heads. Then they started searching the ground, themselves and the whole area for anything resembling a hat. Tiny, on the other hand, took it upon himself to groom. All was almost lost and the hat idea was about to become a crushed can when an unexpected voice sounded behind Rae.

"I have a hat."

Oh no. This can not *be.* Rae instantly recognized that voice. Spinning around, she plunked her hands on her head and squealed. "Where did you come from?"

.   .   .

After returning home, Stone called Sally to inform her of his unexpected camping trip to Fun Warriors Ranch. She was thrilled for him and, in the middle of an encouraging remark, the line was disconnected. *She accidentally hung up on herself again,* Stone thought. Sliding his cellphone into his back pocket, he now stood in his family room with his arms crossed. Also standing in his family room was Zalen. His arms weren't crossed, however, and hung loosely at his sides with his left hand still gripping the handle of a large umbrella. He sucked on a butterscotch and offered one to Stone.

"No, thanks," said Stone. The drive to his home was silent. He was too stunned by his vision to carry on a conversation with Zalen. His wits, however, now returned and he had questions while keeping his vision to himself. "I gotta ask, Zalen, what made you reserve a campsite at Fun Warriors Ranch? Is it because you heard Rachel mention yesterday that she's camping there and you *feel* compelled to bother her? With your umbrella?"

Zalen chuckled. "No. I only heard Rae say that she's camping at Ma'iingan Bluff. She never said which campground. But I did *feel* which campground this morning." Stone groaned as Zalen continued, "Sorry, but it's the truth. Being an empath, I've learned over the years to listen to my feelings, especially the strong ones. And I strongly *feel* that we need to be at Fun Warriors Ranch for Rachel. So, I called and made a reservation. I said we were part of Rae's work retreat."

Stone gasped. "You didn't."

"I did!" Zalen rocked back and forth on his heels in merriment. When Stone clasped his hand over his heart, Zalen quickly added,

"But don't worry, Stone, I know what you're thinking and we have our own campsite. They only allowed six people at each site, so we had to reserve another one."

Hearing his stressed heart beat in his ears, Stone said, "I don't want Rae to know we're there, Zalen."

"Like I said, don't worry. The whole campground is a large area, I'm told. Our campsites are probably far from each other. We probably won't run into her. That much. Maybe only a few times. After all, we have to save her life. So, we should run into her once, at least."

Stone sat down on his couch and held his head in the palms of his hands. "I can't run into her at all. She'll think I'm weirdly stalking her. I'm not going. I'm staying here."

"Don't be overdramatic, my friend. Now, have you ever been to Fun Warriors Ranch?"

Stone had been there many times. Beginning in his youth, he frequently camped at Fun Warriors Ranch with his dad, brother and Grandpa Ed. There were three campgrounds, but usually only two were in use. One was for RVs while the other was for tents. The third was always under some kind of construction. The campgrounds surrounded an hourglass lake called Wolves Lake, which had magnificent bluffs extending along the east side of the water. The RV campground strewn itself on the lake's north end and then the tent-only campground covered the west side. There was a small, but clean beach in the middle of the two. The south part of the lake was home to the third campground, which reeked spooky in Stone's opinion. It could've been a great setting for a film about a corpse hunting campers with a hatchet. The area was not a bluff, but it was on higher ground and full of trees. Stone shivered involuntarily and then replied to Zalen, "Nope."

Zalen narrowed his eyes and said nothing for a moment. Then he asked Stone, "I guess the real question is what do you *feel* your vision is about?"

Stone's still stance made him look like a statue carved from marble. Finally, he stated, "I'm not sure, but I *know* that my visions aren't about Rachel."

"Ah, you said visions. Now, we're getting somewhere." Zalen smiled. "How many have you had?"

"That's not important."

"Two?"

Stone mumbled, "Good guess."

Zalen smirked. "I didn't have to guess. Your tells give you away. You'll either rub your arms, excuse yourself to work in the storage room, have a pained expression or stare off into space."

"In my defense, most times, my pained expression is caused by bad headaches. And my office is in the storage room. That's where I work, Zalen."

"And hide. Yesterday afternoon, you stared off into space with a pained expression before excusing yourself to the storage room while rubbing your arms. You showed all four tells. And today, I just found you in the car, staring off into space with a pained-"

"Okay, I get it."

Zalen's grin turned into a very warm, very genuine smile. "Stone, you can trust me to help you. All you need to do is tell me about your visions."

With his arms still being crossed, Stone tightly gripped his own biceps while slowly admitting to himself that Zalen might be right. He blew out a loud sigh and began to surrender *some* of his secrets. "Yesterday, when I opened the storage door, I walked into another world. There were two very tall structures along with some type of water, like a lake or river. Then two large animals looked like they were about to attack each other and a red lollipop with legs appeared out of nowhere. It snapped at my ankle with its claws, so I kicked it away." He inexplicably felt compelled to keep the dead masculine body to himself. Besides, he was still holding out hope that it was really a bag of garbage. So what, if the bag had legs? "That was it. See? No connection to Rachel."

Zalen pursed his lips before saying, "Interesting."

Stone reluctantly asked, "How so?"

"I'm glad you asked. To me, this vision seems to be outdoors. Like at a campsite? Called Fun Warriors Ranch, perhaps?"

"Oh, no."

"Which is where Rae is. So, that's a connection."

"Don't start."

"Too late. Now, I bet there's some body of water at Fun Warriors Ranch, just like in the vision, right?"

Stone thought of Wolves Lake. It was the queen of the campground with the bluffs acting as protective guards. Stone swam in it. Many times. Not wanting to encourage Zalen's empathic thought process, he answered, "It's not jogging a memory."

Zalen shook his head in a non-believing way. He continued, "And those large animals? How large were they?"

"Well, I didn't have a ruler on me to measure."

"I *feel* they were bears-"

"Maybe. But I doubt it."

"Which makes sense to me because bears are everywhere in this state. One actually made it to the city of Monroe a few summers ago. It made the news, remember? It lounged in someone's inground pool and played with a beach ball. I *feel*-"

Shifting his weight, Stone interrupted Zalen's feelings. "What about the red lollipop? With claws? Or the two structures? How does that fit with Rachel and Fun Warriors Ranch?"

"To me, the red lollipop represents a crayfish."

"A crayfish?"

Nodding, Zalen said, "Sure. Crayfish have claws. And they're red. Ish. I'm sure there are many crayfish in the lake that's not jogging a memory."

Indeed, there were many red-ish crayfish in the shallow waters of Wolves Lake. Stone caught one once. Then he cooked it over a fire and ate it. He replied, "I believe all the crayfish left the lake to pursue other better lakes."

Chuckling, Zalen said, "You're funny."

Ignoring that comment, Stone asked, "Why is the crayfish a lollipop then? Tell me that."

"Oh, I have no idea. Unless, does Rae like lollipops?"

Stone grinned. "She actually doesn't. I know that for a fact because we used to trick-or-treat together, as kids. She would give me all of her lollipops in exchange for Reese's peanut butter cups."

Zalen politely smiled. "I don't understand the two tall structures though. Maybe they connect to the vision you just had while sitting in your car? Can you tell me about that one?"

Stone sighed, knowing that he wasn't going to escape this conversation any time soon. He mustered up any lingering patience and began, "There was a white horse and a knight in black armor. He knocked on my head three times with his sickle. Rachel wasn't in this one either. Just a white horse and a black knight. And there were no signs of camping. So, I'm sorry to tell you, but my psychic visions have nothing to do with Fun Warriors Ranch or Rachel."

A quiet moment passed and then Zalen asked, "The sickle is notable. And now I'm wondering about Bash. Was there any sign of him being there?"

Taken aback, Stone frowned. "No. Why?"

Zalen said, "I don't know. I just saw his sad face in my head. He was rubbing his shoulder. I *feel* like he's part of this."

Stone shook his head. "Bash isn't even with Rachel. He's at home."

Zalen suddenly smiled brightly. "Sure. You could be right. Or completely wrong. Well, let's be on our way!"

"Hold up." Stone narrowed his eyes. "Bash is at home. Okay?"

Zalen nodded and shrugged at the same time. "On another note, are you sure the knight held a sickle and not an umbrella?"

Stone's stomach dropped a little from that comment. Could the sickle symbolize an umbrella? He never thought of that. He did think of Zalen's comment about the bell again though. So far, Zalen used almost the same words as the knight and carried an umbrella that resembled the sickle. The tingling on his forearms surfaced. *Is Zalen the knight?* The tingling relaxed a tad. *Do I need to go with Zalen?* The tingling strengthened. *Well, this is interesting. And disheartening. Maybe leaving my bar in the hands of a tipsy bar matron to camp at Ma'iingan Bluff really is the right thing to do? Or,* he thought, *it's the worst decision of my life.* He rubbed his arms and noticed that Zalen was watching him very closely. "I believe," Stone told Zalen, "the knight held a sickle, not an umbrella." The tingling did not stop.

"Well, that's good, I guess," Zalen said with a twinkle in his eye. He raised his umbrella like a sword and announced, "Let us be off!"

As Zalen turned and marched toward the front door, Stone commented to his adventurous companion, "I'm surprised there were any sites left to reserve. Places like Fun Warriors Ranch are usually booked solid by now."

"I didn't have any trouble." Zalen shrugged. "Maybe the murder chased some campers away?"

CHAPTER NINE

"Rae, who's this kid?" Travis asked with an annoyed tone.

Aunt Rae's hands slid from the top of her head to the side of her cheeks. "This is my nephew, Bash." Now her hands found Bash's cheeks and she asked him, "How are you feeling? Are you sick?" When he shook his head, she said to her mischievous nephew, "What is your mother going to say?"

Miffed, Travis said, "Rae, you should be more concerned with what I'm going to say. You brought your nephew *and* your niece? I agreed to one kid, not two."

Aunt Rae shushed Travis. "My niece is sick, for crying out loud, and stayed home. Now, please, stop talking." She then turned on Bash. "Explain yourself."

After taking a deep breath, Bash sadly looked down at the ground and said, "I'm sorry for sneaking around, Aunt Rae. I came from the backseat of your car. I hid under your duffel bag and Tiny." He rubbed his shoulder. "I kinda got squished and hurt my shoulder, being on the floor and all."

Travis asked Bash, "How old are you?"

"Twelve."

"Good lord." Travis glared at Aunt Rae. "This kid looks like he eats."

"Travis," Aunt Rae scolded. "This isn't about you. Go on, Bash."

"Well, I must've fallen asleep. Or lost consciousness. I can't seem to remember the trip, except for eating a pb and j while you guys left to eat pancakes. Other than that, all I really know is that it wasn't very comfortable. And I'm still kinda hungry."

Travis mumbled, "Of course, he's hungry."

Bash continued, "But don't worry. It's really no big deal."

Aunt Rae's hands clasped the sides of her head. "Are you nuts?"

Travis shook his head. "Your whole family sounds nuts."

Ignoring Travis's comment, his aunt continued to scold Bash. "You snuck out of the house without your parents' permission. You took refuge in my car without my knowledge. Like a *stowaway*. There's a good chance that your brain experienced a loss of oxygen and you think none of this is a big deal?"

"Oh no, that's all pretty big. I was talking about my sore shoulder not being a big deal."

"You're *so* going to get grounded for this!"

With a sheepish look, Bash politely disagreed. "Technically, Aunt Rae, I'm *still* grounded from *last* time."

Aunt Rae pulled her cellphone from her back pocket and pointed it at him. "I'm calling your mom and dad and I don't know what's going to happen, but you better pray to the good lord above to keep us alive." As her fingers began to rapidly press the screen, she walked toward her car for what Bash assumed was privacy.

Watching Aunt Rae smooth things over with his parents was like watching her make a king-size bed with twin sheets. She was losing the battle. At one point, she set the phone on the hood of her car in order to remove a pack of gum from the front pocket of her shorts. She unwrapped two pieces and shoved them into her mouth. Bash knew his aunt's coping strategies for anxiety. She always chewed gum as the second to last resort. Her very last resort usually involved a bag of semi-sweet chocolate chips.

Bash sat down on a tree stump, covering his face with his hands. A wet nose pressed against his fingers and then a slimy tongue began licking his knuckles. Needing comfort, Bash lifted his head and wrapped his arms around the Great Shepherd's thick neck. "This might be it for me, Tiny. You may never see me again."

Tiny whined.

"I know. I'll miss you too. In the meantime-" Casting his arm into his backpack, Bash fished out one of his library books titled *A Simply Complicated Werewolf* by Beatrice Bones. He showed the cover to Tiny. "We still need to focus on our mission. In this book, written in 1977, the author knew a woman named Rose who married a werewolf without realizing he was a werewolf. Rose then started noticing strange things about her husband. One time, she followed him and watched him turn into a werewolf. From that point on, she took it upon herself to study him without his knowledge."

When Bash stopped talking, Tiny groaned at the end of his yawn.

"Okay," Bash said, "I'll keep reading. Rose noticed that her husband had bristles under his tongue and after he cut himself once, she saw fur underneath his skin."

Tiny licked his lips before lying down on his stomach.

Bash agreed with Tiny. "That's exactly what I was thinking. Rose never confronted her husband on being a werewolf or how he became a werewolf until their seventh wedding anniversary. He denied it and then the next day, he was gone, leaving her and their son."

Resting his head on his paws, Tiny sighed.

"Yeah, that is sad." Flipping to another section of the book, Bash continued, "According to Rose's research on her husband, werewolves are shapeshifters, which means that they can change from a human to a werewolf and vice-versa. And she believes that her husband was bitten as a kid because he had a scar on his leg that looked like bite marks. He told her that he was bitten by the neighbor's dog, but she thought he was really bitten by a werewolf." He pulled on his bottom lip and Tiny rolled to his side to pass gas. "That's a good question, but the author never states where this story takes place." He glanced at Tiny. "I personally think this sounds like something that would happen in the UK though, don't ya think?"

Bash closed the book and set it aside. As his arms sank into his backpack again, he said to his trusty dog, "I brought along two more library books to help us in our research." He pulled out his second book and looked at Tiny who now had one eye closed. "This one is called *Your Friendly Neighbor, the Werewolf,* and it also talks about how werewolves can shapeshift into humans. You could be living next door to a werewolf and not even know it."

While Tiny's ears began to droop, his other eye closed. He snorted sleepily.

"I know it seems far-fetched," Bash agreed, "but, honestly, so were banshees until we met them a few weeks ago, am I right?" Without waiting for Tiny's response, Bash grabbed his last book and showed it to the dog who was sound asleep. "Now this is the most interesting book of all and the reason as to why we're camping, Tiny. It's titled *Where Wolves Wait at Ma'iingan Bluff,* which is where we are right now. It talks about The *legendary* Ma'iingan Bluff Werewolf, who we are going to hunt and capture proof of its existence. Now, first, any good paranormal investigator learns the history surrounding its mark, so listen up." Bash gently nudged Tiny's shoulder and the Great Shepherd's head shot up at full attention. "As I was saying, according to this very factual book, The Ma'iingan Bluff Werewolf was first discovered here in 1937 when people saw a large wolf-man creature with red eyes around this area, running on two legs and chasing deer. Campers started having their cars scratched and food eaten. Animal mutilations became more and more common. And the animals would only be partially eaten with certain organs removed, like the liver and heart, of course. Then there's this interesting fact," Bash said to the now snoring Great Shepherd. "Ma'iingan means wolf in Ojibwe."

"Does it really?"

Bash looked up to see a man with broad shoulders, thin legs, a black goatee and red spiked hair. With a friendly smile, the man held out his hand and said, "I'm Chuck."

Bash placed his book on his backpack, cover side up, and rose to shake Chuck's hand. "I'm Bash."

"So, you're the nephew, eh?"

"Yep."

Chuck grinned. "Rae told me about how she somehow got you kicked out of summer camp last year, but she's vague on the details." Bash nodded along while Chuck continued, "She made it sound so mysterious. What happened?"

Glancing over both shoulders, Bash quietly said, "I'm not allowed to talk about it."

Chuck lowered his voice and leaned toward Bash. "Come on, I won't say anything."

Bash grinned and then whispered, "I can only tell you three things. It involved fireworks, duct tape and toads. Lots of toads. They weren't part of the original plan, though." Chuck raised his eyebrows and Bash could tell that he was impressed. "I'd tell you more," he added, "but I'm appearing in court soon."

Chuck gaped at him. "Really?"

Bash chuckled. "Nah, just kidding." Suddenly, a pink shimmer from Chuck's ear caught Bash's attention. Pierced in his left lobe was a sparkly pink gem, but his right was bare. Pointing to Chuck's head, Bash informed him, "You lost an earring."

Chuck shook his head. "I didn't lose it. I gave it to my ex fiancée."

"Your *ex*?" Bash quickly searched his mind for some supportive words regarding this sensitive subject, and said the first thing that came to mind. "Was it a cubic zirconia?"

"No, actually, it was a genuine pink diamond. Her favorite."

"Should've gone the cheap route. Can you ask for it back?"

"I did." Chuck nodded. "But she gave it to the guy she was seeing behind my back."

"Bummer, dude. Although, it sounds like you dodged a big bullet." Bash continued, trying to sound wise beyond his twelve years, "As the saying goes, there's other fish in the sea. Unless no one does anything to stop global warming. Then no sea, no fish. Why do you keep wearing the other earring?"

"For two reasons," Chuck answered. "First, to remind myself that love still exists. Second, to remind myself never to be fooled again."

Just then, behind Chuck, Bash watched as his aunt gave her cellphone an inquisitive look before sliding it into her back pocket. She then inhaled deeply and slowly walked over to him.

Bash used his most engaging tone. "Hey, Aunt Rae, what did my parents say?"

She didn't answer. Instead, his aunt looked at Chuck and asked, "Do you have cell service? My connection was horrible and then suddenly cut." She glanced at Bash. "Or else your parents just hung up on me. I couldn't tell." She blew a bubble with her gum.

Chuck checked his phone and then looked at her with a furrowed brow. "I have no bars."

With his cellphone in hand, Bash nodded. "Me too. No bars. No service."

"No bars?" Tonya sounded worried. "I need bars."

Kimmy quietly added, "I don't mind being off grid."

Tonya wrung her hands. "Travis, did you hear that? We have no cell service."

Travis held up his hands. "Guys, I'm sure that The Team-Building Committee has a back-up plan for this dilemma. Rae, take it away."

Aunt Rae opened her mouth, exhaled and the gum accidentally fell out of her mouth. Sadly, she said, "I don't have a back-up plan." Looking down at the chewed gum blob, she sadly added, "And that was my last piece."

Dismayed, Travis petted his Tiny's head while announcing to the team, "We'll address this later. For now, let's forget about Rae's little screwup and figure out the parking situation."

As the others engaged in that debate, Aunt Rae plopped on a tree stump next to Bash and Tiny. "My head hurts."

Bash placed his hand on Aunt Rae's shoulder and suggested, "Perhaps, we should discuss my parents later?"

Aunt Rae narrowed her eyes at him. "They are very upset."

"Did they even know I was gone?"

"No, but now that they know, they are very upset. And, incidentally, they can't come and pick you up. Before the call dropped, I heard the words *spraying vomit* and *sinking ship*. They have a lot on their hands. By the way, are you sure you're feeling okay?"

Nodding energetically, Bash said, "Yep."

Aunt Rae folded her arms over her knees and cradled her head. "Boy, I got an earful. I think. I heard every other word. But the tone your mom used. Wow. She sounded really mad, Bash."

"That's normal."

"Bash, I refuse to drive three hours back to your house today. Although," Aunt Rae continued absentmindedly, "a three-hour drive doesn't sound so bad right now."

"Please, Aunt Rae, think about what you're saying."

"You're right. Three hours away from this place isn't far enough. Travis would find me." She sighed. "Later, I'll get over to the main entrance and call your parents, if there's cell service. In the meantime, congratulations. Your plan worked. Now, where's your paranormal equipment?"

"What paranormal equipment?"

Aunt Rae straightened her back and rotated her neck, wincing. "The paranormal equipment that you take with you wherever you go."

"Oh, that paranormal equipment. Well, I have it in the car. It's no big deal."

She sternly looked him in the eye. "What are you up to?"

He mastered the same stern look and gave it right back to her. "Nothing. You just never know when you need a spirit box, an EMF meter, a digital camera, garlic and a brand new thermal camera on a camping trip, you know?"

"No, I don't know." Aunt Rae's eyes darted to the book nestled on top of Bash's backpack. She snatched it before Bash could. "*A Simply Complicated Werewolf?* Are you crazy?"

"Possibly."

Gasping, Aunt Rae's mouth fell open. "You sneaky little man. When you helped me find a campground yesterday, you picked this one because of some crazy werewolf, didn't you?"

"He's called The Ma'iingan Bluff Werewolf."

"That's why you desperately wanted to come along, isn't it, Bash? Are you seriously planning on staking out The Maccoboy Beef Werewolf?"

"Maybe. And it's The Ma'iingan Bluff-"

"I heard you and absolutely not. No three o'clock morning adventures for you. I'm keeping your equipment. With me. At all times."

"Come on, Aunt Rae. You're just being silly."

Suddenly, Travis approached with his fluffy dog still strapped to his chest and said to Aunt Rae, "Tonya won the eenie meenie, so you and Chuck will have to park in the lot by the entrance. Also, what activity do you have planned for breaking the ice tonight?"

Aunt Rae scrunched her face. "I don't have one."

"Jeez, Rae. First, no service. Then no ice-breaking activity. You need to man up and get one." He nodded to the team behind him. "Look at them. They have no direction. They're just standing around with their thumbs up their-"

"Hey, watch what you're going to say, Travis. Bash is only twelve."

"I know, Rae. I was only going to say asses, for shit's sake. Now, don't change the subject. As The Team-Building Committee, it's time you build this team."

Aunt Rae furrowed her brow. "I thought this whole retreat was about helping you find a messier and kinder side first and the team-building came second. It's starting to feel the other way around."

"Put it this way, Rae." Travis lowered his voice. "If you want that paid week off, you have to do both really well. In any order. So, again, it's time to man up." As he spoke, he bent down, rubbed his fingers on the ground and smeared the dirt across his forehead. Then he took a quick selfie, reached into his shirt pocket and removed a wet wipe from a travel pack. While cleaning his face, he said to her, "Thanks for the reminder. Seth is going to love this pic."

As Travis stalked off, Bash leaned closer to her and said, "Again, I apologize for being sneaky, Aunt Rae, and I'd like to make it up to you by helping you man up. In exchange for my paranormal equipment."

"Please, Bash, I'm not a push-over." Aunt Rae turned toward him and began biting a fingernail. "So? What did you have in mind?"

Bash suggested, "How about this? I brought along my tarot cards and can lead the ice breaker with a reading. I've been wanting to practice with real people anyway." Bash grinned, showing his dimples. "You just need to allow me to use my paranormal equipment later tonight and track a werewolf. No big deal."

"Werewolves don't exist, Bash."

"Then I guess it's a win-win for you." When he saw the struggle in her eyes, he added, "You won't have to say one word during the ice-breaker activity. I'll do all the talking."

Aunt Rae stopped biting her fingernail and studied his face. He held his breath. She finally half-smiled and presented her hand. "Since I have a feeling that you're going to track a werewolf with or without my permission, I'll accept this deal. Except, I must come with you tonight. It's part of being an aunt."

"Are you sure? It'll be early, like two-thirty in the morning. And I'll be werewolf hunting for a good hour. Are you up for that?"

"Absolutely not." Rae shrugged. "But I'll still go for you."

Shaking her hand, Bash beamed. "You're going to *love* hunting a werewolf. And don't worry, you'll be fine. By the way, you didn't happen to pack any bear spray, did you?"

．　　　．　　　．

Stone shifted through the gears of his red Dodge like a maniac. "Murder? Please tell me that you meant to say malt beer."

Zalen smiled. "Oh, no, my friend. I said murder. And I meant it."

"What murder?" Stone's mind went straight to the crumpled body in his first vision. Feeling discouraged, his grip tightened around the steering wheel. Why couldn't it be a bag of garbage? Perspiration instantly formed along his hairline. "I don't remember hearing about it in the news. Are you sure?"

"Oh, this is something I *feel*. But I'm not sure if the murder already happened or if the murder is going to happen. If the murder already happened, then I *feel* that the body hasn't been found. If the murder is going to happen, I *feel* that it will be soon."

Resembling a boy striking out at bat, Stone sadly said, "I should've packed murder." He quickly wiped the sweat trickling down his forehead. "I mean, malt beer."

Zalen chirped. "You're in luck! I brought some along!" With proud conviction, Zalen rolled his R's as he stated, "I have Remington Root Beer."

"Oh, no."

Zalen clapped his hands in merriment. "Oh, yes. It's really good. It's *more* than root beer. It's *time travel* back to the days of soda shops and confections." He suddenly returned to the somber subject of murder. "Now, in your visions, was there anything that might have suggested a murder? Anything at all? It could be the smallest detail."

No use in denying it anymore, Stone thought. "Well, there was one thing that seemed suspicious."

"Oh, good. What?"

"A dead body."

"Really?" Zalen asked. "That is suspicious. Was this in your first vision or second?"

"My first."

Slowly nodding, Zalen asked, "And you still *feel* that Rae is safe?"

Stone listened to his gut. "Absolutely. The dead body in my vision was a man."

"Do you remember anything else about this man?"

Tight-lipped, Stone flippantly replied, "Nope. Nothing. No detail."

Zalen said nothing. He just turned and faced the window while twiddling his thumbs and humming a soft unfamiliar melody. After a few minutes, he abruptly began, "You know, one Christmas, my ex-wife asked for ideas of what she could get for me and I told her that I would love only one present. It was a new release. Hot off the presses. By a big-named author. And I couldn't wait to read the 500 page masterpiece about mystery, secret codes and titillating adventure." He spoke slowly while staring out the window. "Then, on Christmas Day, she handed her present to me and it was the size of a card, about a half-inch thick. It turned out to be a small coffee table book about various artists." He paused to clear his throat. "I knew I should've been grateful, but I really wanted that other book. Know what I mean?" Stone didn't answer, but allowed Zalen to continue. "So, a couple days later, I took it to the bookstore and tried to return it without a receipt. I didn't tell my ex-wife. I didn't want her to know I was disappointed. Anyway, I was talking with the employee and she didn't recognize the book as belonging to this bookstore. When she looked it up on the computer, she discovered that the small coffee table book was actually out of print. The last time it had been printed was back in 1974. No bookstore carried that book." Stone kept his eyes on the road while listening to Zalen. "My ex-wife never shopped for me. She found the coffee table book in her parents' basement. So, after finding that out, I wanted to throw it away. Instead, I read it and I learned about a fascinating painter who developed an innovative style of painting called pointillism."

While keeping his eyes on the road, Stone said, "You're talking about Seurat."

"Yes! Isn't that wonderful?"

"He's Rachel's favorite artist."

"He is now mine, as well."

"That's great, but your story is still kinda shitty."

Zalen looked at Stone. "I can understand how being a psychic is like receiving an offensive Christmas present. A present that you immediately want to throw away, but you can't. You can't throw it away or return it or even hide it in your basement for someone else to find and regift. And do you know what, my dude?"

"What?"

"That's kinda shitty too." Zalen held up his hand. "Excuse my language. Anyway, I really just want you to know that I get it."

With a nod, Stone returned his focus to the road. For the duration of the ride, he remained silent while clutching the steering wheel and sitting with a steel spine and cement shoulders. He thought of Seurat, basements and bad Christmas presents. And he thought of Zalen and how he could easily be a sad Zalen instead of a happy one. Wanting to say something nice, Stone dug deep for any compassionate words to give and found none. He resorted to keeping his eyes on the road, following the flowing movement of the yellow center lines to Fun Warriors Ranch.

CHAPTER TEN

Rae hadn't packed any bear spray, but a more pressing matter arose. It was setting up camp. She realized that this chore would have sailed on smoothly, without more trouble, if only there hadn't been a tent. Or insufferable heat. The tent escalated the drama instantly and the heat kept the drama boiling. No one could agree on location. Tonya wanted it under a tree, Chuck wanted it near the campfire and Travis wanted it near his car. Kimmy remained the silent one, still sitting cross-legged on top of the picnic table. In the end, Rae chose to set up the tent on the flattest part of the ground. Unfortunately, there were many rocks. After ordering all of the adults to pick up the sharp stones, Rae was met with groaning, sneers and abusive language.

Irritated, Travis said, "This is a job for your mammoth dog. He's the size of a bulldozer. Can't he just open his mouth and walk across the ground to clear it?"

Rae said to Travis, "Or we can use your Tiny as a broom and brush the rocks away?"

Travis sucked in air through his teeth. "How *dare* you!"

Rae, however, didn't back down. "Look, you put me in charge and you told me to man up. Twice. So, guess what? Picking up stones is our first team-bonding activity. And let that teach you to never put me in charge of anything again!"

Surprisingly, the task of clearing the rocks became a quiet one. Angry moods seemed to soften, mainly because no one spoke. It was only when Rae assigned jobs that bad attitudes arose once more, beginning with Tonya.

With her thumb and forefinger, Tonya held Rae's shovel. "You want me to dig what?"

"The trench."

She asked testily, "What is the *trench?*"

Rae explained, "It's a shallow ditch around the tent."

Tonya protested, "You're just coming up with something awful for me to do because you're jealous of me."

"It's called tent trenching and it's a real thing. When I camped as a kid, my dad, who was a marine, would make me dig the trench. It prevents rain water from soaking the bottom of tents. It's important, if you want to stay dry."

Ignoring Tonya's groan, Rae continued giving out orders, starting with Kimmy. She told her to organize the supplies.

Kimmy saluted Rae. "I got this." She then slid off the table and laid on the ground, flat on her back.

Rae shook her head and then turned toward Chuck. "You and I will put up the tent."

His red spiked hair no longer stood straight on top of his head. The tips now drooped over from the heat. Without looking at Rae, he mumbled, "Great. Love putting up stupid tents."

Feeling more discouraged at everyone's outlooks, Rae said, "Come on, guys. We have to set up camp. The faster we do it, the faster we'll be done. Now, Travis, you can clean the grill."

Travis stared at her as though she had three eyes. "What grill?"

Pointing to the black rusty box covered with charcoal dust, bird poop and another suspicious red liquid, Rae said, "That grill."

Confused, Travis asked, "With what?"

"A grill brush or crumpled foil."

Travis motioned to his pressed casual dress pants. "Do you honestly think I have a grill brush or foil on me? Ask me when was the last time I grilled." When Rae didn't ask, Travis answered anyway. "It was never."

Chuck raised his hand. "I can drive to the main entrance and get something to clean the grill."

Using a mocking tone, Travis repeated what Chuck said and then called him an overachiever.

Studying Travis, Rae asked him, "What's wrong with you? He's helping you. You should *thank* him instead of teasing him."

Chuck protested. "It's not necessary."

Rae and Travis spoke simultaneously. "Shut up, Chuck."

At first, Travis merely stared at Rae while petting the top of his Tiny's little head. Then he rolled his eyes, took a breath and forced the *th* sound out of his mouth.

Rae nodded out of pity and said, "Hey, big guy, you can do this. Try again."

"It's really not necessary," Chuck repeated.

Ignoring Chuck, Travis kept his narrowed eyes on Rae. She wondered what emotion would follow. Anger? Complacency? But Travis surprised her by inhaling deeply, holding it for a moment and then blurting a loud, "THANK!"

Rae gave him a thumbs up. "Good. Next time, just remember the *s* at the end. And because you tried, how about you just clean off the picnic table? We won't worry about the grill right now."

Tonya stood up from trench digging and gave both Rae and Travis a quizzical look. "What's going on with you two?"

Quickly answering, Rae said, "Nothing." She turned to Bash and Tiny. "Now, you guys find kindling." She was met with their positive cheers and Rae smiled. At least they were happy with their jobs. Addressing the team, Rae continued, "Okay, to recap. Chuck and I are putting up the tent, Kimmy is handling the supplies, Tonya digs the trench, Bash and Tiny will find kindling and Travis will clean off the picnic table. Maybe you can even level it somehow?"

Petting his Tiny's head, Travis said, "Yeah, yeah, yeah."

"Okay." Rae smiled again and yelled, "Let's do this!"

At first, the team just stood there like wooden posts. However, eventually, they all began working and they even began working *together*. Rae patted herself *once* on the back for taking charge of her chief role as The Team-Building Committee. With her leadership abilities, she could steer any ship! Unfortunately, before Rae patted herself *twice* on the back, the team mutinied and the ship sank. It was a fast turnaround, led by Travis. The mutineers then quickly left the campsite, mumbling about unions and breaks, and piled into Tonya's SUV. The black Outback roared to life, spraying stones as it furiously sped from camp. The only loyalists to remain were Bash and Tiny.

As the three of them watched the team disappear into the horizon, Rae asked Bash, "What happened?"

He shrugged. "I dunno. I think they're taking a break." He turned toward her, saying, "Ah, let 'em go, Aunt Rae. We don't need 'em."

Tiny strung a few barks together and Rae agreed with him. "You can say that again."

Shaking his head, Bash commented, "It's hard to raise adults these days." He patted his thigh. "C'mon, Tiny. Let's find some sticks for kindling."

Tiny's ears stuck up as he danced what looked like an Irish Jig when Rae held up her hand. "Guys," she said, "I'm giving up a possible paid week off of work, but this is our chance to leave! Let's just get our things and go before they come back! *If* they come back, I mean."

"They'll come back, Aunt Rae. All of their stuff is still here."

"Bash, we need to save ourselves. On our way home, I'll find the best hamburger joint and we'll eat the greasiest cheeseburgers ever!" Rae rubbed her stomach. "Yum!"

Bash's shoulders slumped. "Aw, come on, Aunt Rae. I don't want to leave."

"If we head home now, I will take you to an amusement park."

"I always leave those places with extreme nausea. No thanks."

"I'll take you to a ball game then."

"Nope. Choked on a hotdog last time. Bad memories."

Sounding a little more hysterical, Rae said, "Let *me* bribe *you* with anything you want, Bash. More library books? A visit to the museum? Just tell me what you want."

Bash and Tiny looked at each other and seemed to communicate with their eyes. They then nodded before both facing Rae and wearing the most serious, desperate expressions.

"Aunt Rae," Bash began with a hint of sorrow, "we really just want to stay."

Rae whined. "You just want to stay for The Marshmallow Fluff Werewolf."

Tiny quivered his bottom lip as Bash corrected her. "It's The Ma'iingan Bluff Werewolf and I also want to stay for you. We have fun together, Aunt Rae. Besides, what do I have to look forward to, if we go home? A stomach virus, that's what. And despite your coworkers, *you* have *us* and I promise that we will make this a good time for you."

"You don't understand, Bash. Every time I camp, something terrible happens. And with this group, this trip could be fatal."

"We won't be camping long, Aunt Rae. Just three nights."

As they smiled at her, Rae saw the hope in their eyes dance around in a circle like happy children at a birthday party. She surrendered. "Fine. We'll stay under one condition. You both have to help me dig the trench."

Delighted, Bash agreed by saying, "Of course! Right after Tiny and I find some kindling." As the boy and the dog raced into the woods, Bash shouted over his shoulder, "And don't worry, Aunt Rae! I'll help you with the tent when we come back!"

Rae called after him, "Wait! We should put up the tent first!" She listened closely for her nephew's response, but only heard the rustling of leaves and the stomping of feet as they left the area. Bringing a fingernail to her teeth, she nibbled while studying the enormous crumpled pile of nylon and polyester. Aloud, she said to herself, "If only I had another pair of hands."

A voice interrupted her solitude. "I'd love to help you, Rae."

Turning around, Rae found herself staring into the face of a handsome man. Well, actually, it wasn't his face, but his rib cage. He stood at least a little over six feet. Not quite as tall as Travis, but taller than Stone. Wearing a large hat, he resembled Smokey the Bear. This guy, however, was thin, shaved and broad-shouldered, like Smokey the Bear's little brother who went to college.

Rae cautiously grinned. Perplexed at this guy for calling her by name, she ran her fingers through her hair and asked, "Who are you and how did you know my name?"

. . .

With his nose hungrily sniffing the damp soil and fresh air around him, Tiny inhaled all sorts of good things, like perfumed flowers, vanilla yellow foliage and a bouquet of bacon. Ah, bacon. The smoky aroma brought back many memories of Tiny's puppy days when he lived with the old woman and old man. Licking his lips, he remembered the tower of bacon strips placed on top of the sloppy stuff and how the warmth of the fried meat made the sloppy stuff taste better.

Angry Rae didn't cook bacon.

Tiny sighed. If only he could show Angry Rae how to use what he thought was called a frying pan.

Tiny sighed heavier.

If only Angry Rae had a frying pan.

Lifting his snout in the air, he followed the bacon aroma and quickly trotted deeper into the woods.

"Hey!" Tiny heard Bash holler behind him, but he did not stop. The bacon smell strengthened, encouraging Tiny to pick up the pace. Soon, however, the delicious fragrance took second seat to a new meat smell. He quickly changed direction.

He heard Bash yell from a distance behind him, "Now you're over there?"

Shaking his head, Tiny refused to wait for Bash and to explain the importance of eating meat in a timely manner. According to his experience, fresh-ish meat only lasted a day, tops, before it started to smell rank. Although he didn't mind eating rank meat, one of Angry Rae's neighbors told her that it was too gross. The nerve of that lady! Tiny raised his snout and the fumes told him that the fresh-ish meat time was fleeting. Instead of waiting for Bash, Tiny shifted his four long legs into third gear.

"Hey!" Bash yelled, even farther back. "Something stinks around here. Wait a minute. That couldn't be what I think it is. Tiny! Wait!"

As Tiny approached the meat source, it changed from fresh-ish to almost rank. He tentatively stepped toward an animal corpse and paused to appreciate the size of this tan furry animal with four stick legs. It was large. Larger than he was. And it had long dark brown branches growing out of its head. On the underside, there was a hole in the white fur, staining the area a deep red. Long thick noodles seemed to have crawled out of the hole of this animal, spilling onto the ground, and tinted the grass the same red color.

Flies invaded the kill. Stepping toward the dead animal, Tiny lowered his head and snapped at the flies. They didn't leave, so he shifted his attention to the questionable meat again. All he needed was one bite. Just one. Unfortunately, even before he could open his mouth, Bash lassoed Tiny's neck with his arms and pulled him from the special forest treat.

"You can't eat that!" Bash yelled, "It's evidence!"

Bash then faced Tiny and held his hand up, which commanded Tiny to sit. Tiny whined and stuck out his bottom lip, causing slobber to drip onto the ground.

"I know." Bash's chest heaved in and out as he breathlessly explained, "I need to take a picture of this deer. As soon as I smelled it, I hoped it would look like a werewolf attack. And I was right."

Tiny turned his head to view the innards and his mouth watered more.

Bash removed his cellphone from his back pocket and began taking a series of photographs. At one time, he picked up a stick and, to Tiny's dismay, he did not throw it. Instead, he poked the animal with it, moving it around the inside of the hole, and took more pictures. When he finished, he showed one to Tiny. "See this?"

Tiny licked Bash's phone.

"From what I can tell," Bash continued while using his shirt to clean the screen, "this deer has been dead about twenty-four hours. There are flies, but no maggots. You see, Tiny, according to *What's Bugging You: A Quick Study in Entomology*, flies can start laying eggs an hour after an animal dies and it takes a few days for the eggs to hatch. This deer is covered in flies, but I don't see any maggots. As I said earlier, the deer stinks, which also happens within a day of dying. So, I think it's been dead for *at least* a day. Maybe two."

Tiny woofed quietly. *At least* he could have one bite. Maybe two. Right?

"Also, I noticed that there are bite marks around the neck. And this animal bit clean through the deer's spine, which means this predator has very strong jaws."

Tiny yipped. He also had strong jaws that he used for eating. Anything.

"And the most interesting part," Bash continued, "is that the only organs missing are the liver and the heart." Bash smiled at Tiny. "Do you know what this means?"

Tiny knew what it meant. No snack for him. He brought his hind leg to his ear and vigorously scratched it.

"It means," Bash's eyes widened as he said, "The Ma'iingan Bluff Werewolf does exist! Now all we have to do is catch it."

Suddenly, Tiny jumped to all fours and raised his nose toward their campsite. All food cravings vanished. With his ears straight up, he began snarling.

In a hushed tone, Bash said, "Tiny. What is it?"

CHAPTER ELEVEN

"Hello, I'm Tom." Tall, dark and dashing, Tom held out his hand, which Rae didn't take. "I'm one of the park rangers."

"Hence the hat." Rae crossed her arms, scrutinizing the nametag on the park ranger's shirt. Indeed, his name was Tom. Thomas Miller, to be exact. She asked him, "How did you know my name?"

Tom batted his eyelashes and grinned. He spoke with a hint of arrogance, "Oh, that. Well, I overheard your conversation, just now."

Rae eyed him suspiciously. "Is eavesdropping a job requirement?"

"You'd be surprised at all the job requirements I have to meet." He touched the brim of his Stetson. "You could say that we wear many hats." Laughing at his own joke, Tom stopped when he saw Rae's serious face and his demeanor softened. "Look, I wasn't exactly eavesdropping. It was more like reconnaissance."

Rae grimaced. "You're not going to tell me that your reconnaissance involved finding out my name, are you?"

At first, Tom did nothing, but stood in front of Rae and stared at her. Then he shrugged. "Maybe?"

"Look, Tom, you'd have better luck flirting with a tree."

Tom chuckled. "Not really. I've tried that already." He rubbed his chin. "Look, my first impressions are as good as one-ply toilet paper, but I kill at second impressions. May I have another shot?"

After briefly mulling it over, Rae gestured for him to continue.

Smiling, Tom extended his hand. "Hello, stranger, my name is Tom."

Rae also smiled and, this time, she shook his hand. "Hi, Tom. I'm Rae."

"So, Rae, are you camping here with just your nephew?"

"No, I'm not that lucky," Rae said, "and it's kinda creepy that you already know that I have a nephew. But I'll let that slide, I guess. Anyway, I'm actually here with my coworkers for a work retreat. It's a long story. Fortunately, my nephew came along and my dog. So, that helps."

"Oh." The park ranger smiled. "I didn't see your dog. What kind is it?"

"You didn't see my dog?" Rae's mouth dropped open. "He's huge."

"I must've been blinded by your beauty."

Holding back a gag, Rae said, "My dog is a big Great Shepherd."

Tom gave her a disbelieving look. "Really? I figured you for a small purse-dog person."

That reminded her of something and, changing the subject, Rae asked, "So, just out of curiosity, can you arrest people? Like my nasty boss, for instance?"

Tom smirked. "Sadly, I don't have those police powers yet." He pointed toward his hips. "I can't even carry a gun. But I'm working on it."

"Oh," Rae said, "so, you weren't always a park ranger?"

"No. I've only been doing this for seven months. Before this, I worked in a corporate office for a few years."

"Replacing the indoors with the outdoors is a nice idea."

"That was my thought exactly. I desperately needed fresh air after working in a horrible place, filled with horrible people. My boss should've been arrested, just like yours. He was the most unfeeling man in the world and I left my career because of him." Tom smiled at her. "That's a long story too."

"I bet my boss is worse."

"Mine definitely was."

Rae challenged him. "Well, I'm not so sure. I've only had this job for nearly two months and barely know any of my coworkers, right? Well, get this. My boss is forcing me to camp with these people, including him, *and* share a tent with all of them. Can you beat that?"

Tom countered. "My old boss gave me crippling tension headaches that turned into migraines *and* the only cure for the pain and nausea involved an emergency room with shots in my ass. Excuse my language."

Rae nodded. "You're excused and you won."

He laughed and then said, "I could tell you some awful stories, but I don't suppose you're staying here for the next ten weeks, are you?"

Laughing, Rae said, "Thankfully, no. We're leaving on Friday."

"Too bad. In that case, we better get started on the tent."

With the help of a tall Park Ranger Tom, the process of pitching the tent was faster than Rae's process of showering. Granted, Rae loved taking long hot showers, so that probably wasn't a fair comparison. At any rate, with the tent chore completed, Rae's anxiety was now at a level five. Out of ten. Before Park Ranger Tom, her anxiety level reached fifteen. Still out of ten. As she breathed a small sigh of relief, Rae thanked the ranger while retrieving her metal hand shovel that Tonya chucked to the ground.

"You're very welcome, Rae," Park Ranger Tom said while his eyes slowly moved from her face to her feet and then back to her face. "You know, it's strange, but I feel like I've known you forever." Park Ranger Tom lowered his voice. "Maybe before Friday, we can get together? I know a hidden spot in the woods. We could meet after my shift tonight?" His gaze now lingered on her chest. "Just you and me and-"

Recognizing that hungry wolf look, Rae quickly interrupted him. "Nope." She now felt her anxiety rise again to level fifteen and she took a step backward.

Taking a step closer, Tom's expression changed as well as his voice. It was deeper and more intense. "You know, Rae." His height loomed over her. "A pretty girl like you shouldn't camp here all by herself. And you're so little. Anyone can grab you with no trouble."

Her pulse quickened and, suddenly, she felt very isolated. Very vulnerable. What happened? What switch did she flip in Tom to make him become dark? Not fully understanding the change, self-preservation set in and her grip on the shovel tightened. "Like I said earlier, I'm not by myself. So, you can be on your way." He took another step toward her and Rae firmly planted her feet. She switched her grip on the shovel and held it like a knife in front of her.

Tom froze, holding up his hands. "Whoa, wait a minute." His voice returned to a normal pitch. "There's no need to be *that* way. I thought you were giving me some signs, you know?"

Rae kept her tone even and calm. "I wasn't. Like I keep saying, I'm here camping with my coworkers, my nephew and my very large dog. No signs. No nothing."

Tom grinned while looking over his shoulder. "Yeah, I hear what you're saying, but you seem to be *alone* right *now*."

Rae swallowed hard. She adjusted her grip and began to mentally plan her exit strategy when she noticed the foliage behind Park Ranger Tom furiously jerk in all directions. In a quick second, Tiny thankfully flew from the woods and positioned himself between her and Tom. He barked loud and strong. Continuously.

Smiling, Rae remained behind Tiny and yelled over the thunderous woofs, "I'm never really alone! My dog is always nearby!"

Narrowing his eyes, Tom tilted his hat in a departing gesture and hollered over Tiny, "Yes, I get it! I apologize, Rae! I misread the signals!" He turned on his heel and, at the same moment, Bash stumbled from the woods, falling into Tom's arms.

Bash quickly straightened himself and, after noticing Tom's outfit, he spoke in a panicky fast way. "Oh, thank god, a park ranger. You must know about The Ma'iingan Bluff Werewolf, right? The legendary beast from around here? Right?"

Tom turned his head, gesturing it toward Tiny, who was still barking. He raised his voice. "I believe the beast is right there!" He then hurried down the path.

When the ranger was out of sight, Tiny stopped yapping and Rae scratched behind both ears. "Thank you, Tiny. I owe you one." Tiny licked her arms, making Rae screech, "Please no! Small steps, remember?"

Now suddenly calm, Bash slowly approached Rae with a thoughtful look on his face. Pulling on his bottom lip, he muttered, "It can't be."

"It can't be what?"

Looking straight into her eyes, Bash asked, "Didn't you notice his ear, Aunt Rae?"

.   .   .

Three quiet hours later, Stone and Zalen arrived at the main entrance of Fun Warriors Ranch. Zalen happily volunteered to stay in the car and Stone happily agreed. As he entered the building, he quickly saw that this main entrance was more like a super/deli/clothing/convenience store. It had everything from bundles of firewood to underwear. It even had three aisles of groceries, not including a refrigerated section. His stomach growled and he wasted no time, heading toward the packaged sandwiches in the wall chillers.

After carefully selecting two sandwiches, three containers of various pasta salads and two brownies, Stone carried the lunch items to the front counter where a dark brunette waited behind the counter. Five multi-colored bracelets wrapped themselves around her wrist; she couldn't have been older than eighteen. After telling her of his campsite reservation, she looked up his information and told him to drive to the rustic park office where someone named Mare would direct him the rest of the way. He then paid, hurried to his car and handed the bags of food to Zalen who opened the bag, exclaiming, "Hey, hey, hey! Turkey and swiss on rye. One of my favorites!"

Stone started the engine and backed out of the parking spot. "They didn't have your other favorite of spinach, artichoke and mushroom, but I felt that you liked turkey and swiss on rye."

Gasping, Zalen sounded like he just won the lottery. "This is a great step forward, Stone! You listened to your feelings! That's fantastic news!"

Stone shook his head. "Let's not get too crazy. It's just a sandwich."

By now, Zalen dug through the bag and pulled out potato salad. He squealed, "How did you know I love potato salad? Did you *feel* that too?"

"Not at all." Stone lied though. As soon as he saw the potato salad with the egg slices resting on top of it, an image of Zalen's happy face overtook Stone's senses. He had to buy the damn salad.

"Oh my golly! *And* a brownie, Stone! *Woowie!*" Zalen brought it closer to his eyes. "It has chocolate chips!"

While Zalen celebrated the anticipated lunch, Stone maneuvered his red Dodge through the campgrounds and along the winding roads to the rustic park office in search of Mare. Right as he arrived, he noticed an old lady standing on the porch and waving for him to hurry.

Stone said to Zalen, "Does she look like a Mare to you?"

"I don't know." Zalen hugged the food bags on his lap and said, "She reminds me of my second grade teacher who gave me a low grade for not showing enough enthusiasm in class. I'll wait here."

The old lady turned and walked inside the office. Stone then emerged from the driver's seat and bounded up the porch steps, knocking his crown on the hanging dinner bell. Rubbing his head, he hustled through the screen door and entered the building. It banged shut behind him, causing him to jump a little.

The old lady stood behind the counter and grunted at him. Stone skirted around a scruffy man who was sweeping the floor. A striking character, the man was taller than Stone, had strong arms attached to shoulders as wide as the condor's wingspan, and piled long dreadlocks on top of his head. Stone nodded to him, but Dreadlocks didn't return it. He just continued slowly dragging the broom bristles across the floor while keeping his dark eyes on Stone.

As Stone approached the counter, the old lady wore a no-nonsense expression. "My name's Mare." She asked gruffly, "Why are you here?"

Taken aback, Stone stammered. "I…I have a reservation here to camp." He shrugged. "That's all."

Mare eyed him closely. "Yes, I know. You're here with that work retreat. But why are you here?"

"In all honesty, I don't really know."

"Hmmph." Mare pushed a book toward him, removing the pen that rested behind her ear. "I don't do computers. Fill this in."

"Yes, ma'am." Stone followed the order and when he finished, the little old lady presented him with a map to his campsite. She even highlighted the route for him. Stone smiled and thanked her, but she remained stiff and stoic.

She asked him, "Do you have a vehicle admission sticker?"

"No." The look in Mare's eye made Stone feel like a five-year old who didn't know how to tie his shoe.

"Then you need one. It's ten bucks." She grumbled, opened a drawer and slapped the sticker on the counter. "Put this on your windshield. Otherwise, you'll get fined."

"Thanks." After he paid, he picked up the sticker and a brochure that he spied. As he walked toward the screen door, he paused. A strange feeling tickled the back of his neck. He turned around and noticed that both Dreadlocks and Mare stood motionless, facing him with the same straight expressions and the same thin lips stretched into a severe line. Mare, however, was very short whereas Dreadlocks was tall and had broad shoulders. Very tall and very broad. Squinting, Stone scrutinized those broad shoulders and long legs before quickly leaving the building.

CHAPTER TWELVE

Rae wrinkled her nose. "So? Who cares if Park Ranger Tom has a pink diamond earring?"

"Well, as a matter of fact, Aunt Rae, Chuck would care." Bash then told her all about Chuck's backstory, involving his ex fiancée and the infamous pink diamond earring. "What are the chances that he's the guy who's having the affair with Chuck's ex?"

"Zero to none. Come on, Bash. There's no way."

Shaking his head, Bash said, "I can't believe you didn't notice the pink earring."

"I typically don't notice a guy's earlobe." Rae bit her fingernail. "I never noticed Chuck's pink diamond earring either." She spit out the piece of bitten fingernail. "I did notice, though, that Dark Ranger Tom isn't right. He gives me the creeps."

"I see what you did there. Instead of *Park* Ranger Tom, you nicknamed him *Dark* Ranger Tom." Bash nodded. "I like it."

"I don't like Dark Ranger Tom, Bash."

"Me neither. Dark Ranger Tom stole Chuck's fiancée."

Rae shivered. "The last thing I was trying to do was look at any part of him. And I definitely didn't give him any signals, despite what he thinks."

"Chuck and Dark Ranger Tom had the same earring, Aunt Rae. The same pink diamond earring, Aunt Rae. That's not a coincidence."

"One minute, Dark Ranger Tom helped me with the tent and, the next second, he turned into a predator." Biting another fingernail, she asked her nephew and Tiny, "Do you think I should report him?"

Bash asked, "Did you say predator?"

Tiny, however, answered her question by nodding.

Bash quickly asked another question, "As in a *werewolf* predator?"

"No, not a werewolf predator. Just a predator. Again, werewolves don't exist."

"Yes, they do." Disappointed, Bash added, "I bet he marked you."

"Stop it."

"The Legendary Ma'iingan Bluff Werewolf, dressed as a park ranger, marked you with his scent and now you're doomed." Bash sadly shook his head.

Rae spit out a fingernail remnant. "Three weeks ago, you warned me about being doomed by The Legendary Birch Grove Banshee."

"The question is how did he mark you?"

"You were wrong about the banshee."

Bash was taken aback. "How can you say that?" He raised his finger and pointed it at her. "Oh, I see what you're doing. You're trying to get me off track. Well, it won't work, Aunt Rae. Now, stand still. Tiny needs to pee on you."

Incredulous, Rae screeched, "What?" Tiny lifted a hind leg and Rae jumped to the side, out of his pee range.

"Listen," Bash begged. "Tiny needs to scent mark you to cover up The Ma'iingan Bluff Werewolf's scent *now*. We're trying to save your life here!"

"Dark Ranger Tom didn't pee on me! He didn't mark anything on me!" Rae then stepped around her nephew and marched to the firepit. Tiny obediently followed and stood next to her, raising his hind leg again. She sternly said to him, "Don't even think about it."

He lowered his hind leg and sat down, sighing.

"Bash," Rae began, "Tom is no more of a werewolf than I am a patient aunt." Her eyes searched the firepit. "Did you find any kindling?"

Surprised, Bash looked at her and said, "Funny story."

"Is the punchline something about finding kindling?"

"No, but interestingly enough, we found a dead deer that was killed by The Ma'iingan Bluff Werewolf. Within the last day or so. I'm pretty sure."

Rae's stomach growled loudly and she clutched it. "Well, I'm pretty sure that I need to stress eat. You didn't, by chance, find a steak dinner out there next to the dead deer, did you?"

"No." Both he and Tiny raised their noses and sniffed the air. Bash then said, "But I suddenly smell barbecue." He sniffed again. "And apple pie."

The crunching of footsteps on the gravel road behind Rae caused her to turn around and a smile spread across her face. She instantly forgot about werewolves, banshees, predators and her team's rotten attitude because of what The Torch held in his hands. Take-out boxes and a plastic pie container. Curiously, the group was walking, not driving. Tonya's SUV was nowhere in sight.

Travis spoke first. "While sitting around a clean, level table inside an air-conditioned restaurant, we realized that we may have failed at our first team-building challenge. So, we brought you and Bash some barbecue sandwiches from BBQ Hanks and apple pie from the store inside the main entrance." While passing the food to her, he said, "This is our way of saying that we were wro. I mean, wron." He cleared his throat. "What I'm trying to say is that we were wronk."

Rae helped him. "Wrong."

Travis nodded. "We talked and decided to really try as a team to make this a fun adventure and strengthen our bond."

Chuck asked while patting himself down, "By the way, has anyone seen my wallet?"

In a scolding tone, Travis said, "Jesus, Chuck. Can you spell unmindful?"

"Travis." Rae narrowed her eyes at him. "Be *kind.*"

Travis heavily sighed. "Fine." He glanced at Chuck and said, "I'm sorbet."

"I think you mean *sorry*, right?" Rae raised her eyebrows at Travis.

"Of course. Let's move on." Travis continued, "And just so you know, Rae, I found out that there is cell service at the main entrance as well as charging stations. Also, Tonya has unselfishly given her parking spot to you."

Rae noticed that Tonya's lips curled like an angry raccoon and, deep into her eyes, Rae thought she saw villages burning.

After thanking Tonya, Rae made eye-contact with Kimmy who softly said, "My car is still stuck between two trees."

Chuck suddenly exclaimed, "Found my wallet! It was in my side pocket."

Travis raised both arms like a boxing champion and announced with a booming voice, "Let's start this team-bonding retreat!" He clapped once, which startled his Tiny who still sat in the doggie carrier sling across Travis's chest. "We're behind schedule, so chop-chop! The first thing on the agenda is the Ice Breaker Activity given by The Team-Building Committee." He pointed to Rae. "Take over."

All eyes settled on her. "Alright. Well, Bash brought along his tarot cards." Bash smiled and Rae continued, "So, for our Ice Breaker Activity, he will give you a tarot card reading."

Tonya's hand shot toward the sky, like a rocket. "Isn't this the devil's work? Like playing with the Ouija board? Or reading Mark Twain?"

Incredulous, Rae retorted, "Mark Twain isn't the devil's work. He was a progressive thinker who tackled controversial issues in his books."

Travis raised his voice. "I'm already losing my patience, people! No time to tackle Mark Twain or the damn devil. Stay on track! Now, who's going first in this Terror card thingy?"

Rae pointed to Travis. "You."

"And it's called Tarot," Bash added while gesturing to the picnic table.

*   *   *

When Stone slid into his car, he quickly started the engine and peeled away from the south park office. Zalen gripped the grab handle with one hand while holding onto the food bags with the other. Glancing at Zalen, Stone said with a hint of stress in his voice, "There is something I need to tell you about the crumpled body."

"Oh, good. I'm listening."

"He had broad shoulders. And long legs."

"So, he's tall then?"

"Yeah. Anyways, I feel that he is, or was, tall."

Zalen gasped delightedly. "What else do you *feel*?"

Stone sternly looked at Zalen. "Nothing, but I just saw a very tall guy in the park office, sweeping the floor. He's a worker here."

"And you think he might be the dead guy in your vision?"

"He fits the vague description."

"Hmm." Zalen raised his eyebrows. "So, what are you going to do about it?"

Panicked, Stone asked, "What do you think I should do?"

At first, Zalen remained silent. Then he said, "I *feel* you shouldn't approach a guy you just met and tell him that he might die. I *feel* that we should mull it over while relaxing and eating our delicious lunch." He nodded while licking his lips. "Yes, that is what I *feel*."

After inhaling, Stone slowly exhaled and fell into agreement with his carpool buddy. Then, with a couple neck stretches and a mental pep talk, Stone refocused his attention on the map and easily found their base after driving past many empty campsites. It was a typical small site. No electrical outlets. Larger rocks outlined the circular firepit and off to the side slouched an old and unused grill, covered in bird poop. Their crude dwelling didn't stop them from ferociously enjoying their fare at the picnic table, which was now adorned with the plant that Zalen brought. Feeling better, Stone regarded the plant. It was taller than a ruler, having long stems and wide palm-shaped leaves.

Confused at the centerpiece, Stone asked, "Why did you bring that?"

"Well, I had another plant like this, but the poor thing died. So, I bought this one and read that plants live longer if you talk to them and make them feel loved. I couldn't in good conscience leave this little lady at home and decided to bring her along."

"Little lady?"

"Yes. Her name is Doris. Isn't she lovely?"

"She looks a little droopy."

While Zalen examined the leaves, Stone left the table to set up their area. As he did all of the heavy lifting, Zalen talked to Doris in soothing tones. At one point, while Stone struggled with the four-man tent, he heard Zalen tell Doris that Stone was a true frontiersman. Then Stone heard a snap, closely followed by explosive fizz, as Zalen opened a soda can. While he drank his refreshment, he watered Doris. Stone rolled his eyes and busied himself with the final tent touches. A few minutes later, Zalen strolled over to him, one hand in his pocket while the other swung loosely at his side.

"Hey, Stone," he said, "I'm going to use that pit toilet. And why don't you stop for a moment? You look like you need a break."

As Zalen ambled down the gravel road, the sweat running down Stone's back agreed with the break idea. He walked over to the cooler and bent over it, scrounging under the many water bottles. Just as he found a cold can of Remington Root Beer, a voice from behind startled him. High-pitched and energetic, it immediately zapped the energy from the overheated Stone.

"Hello, I'm Priscilla," the mousey voice said. "But you can call me Prissy."

The day was too hot for this kind of civil conversation and Stone prepared himself to pour ice on it to cool it down. Quickly. As he stood, he turned to face Priscilla and awkwardly stifled a gulp. Standing an inch taller than himself, Priscilla looked like a linebacker with big biceps and spiky blond hair. She wore a gray short-sleeved shirt, green trousers and a Stetson hat.

Smiling, Prissy said, "I'm one of the park rangers. Well, actually, I'm the superintendent. I was just promoted and still can't quite get used to the new title." She spoke fast and didn't allow time for Stone to add to the conversation. "I saw you arrive and thought I would introduce myself." After he told her his name, her continued stare made him feel very uncomfortable. "If you need anything, you just let Prissy know. I can get you anything, like charcoal, lighter fluid, brats or hamburgers."

"It's okay. We're good."

Prissy began to slowly walk backwards. "Well, it was a pleasure meeting you, Stone. I must be going, but will look forward to seeing you. Around." Then after a salute, Prissy marched onto a trail leading into the woods.

Stone spoke aloud, "That was the quickest conversation I've ever had with anyone." He suddenly shivered as Zalen reappeared.

Still adjusting his zipper, Zalen said, "I couldn't make it to the pit toilet. I did make it to a beautiful thick bush that looked thirsty, though. I feel bad about that." He furrowed his eyebrows. "You seem rattled. What did I miss?"

Turning to Zalen, Stone replied, "No, I'm not rattled, just kinda dizzy. A very tall park ranger named Prissy just came by. She was very eager and strange. And she offered me hamburgers and brats."

"Did you say tall?"

"Very. Taller than me."

"And did she have broad shoulders?"

"Yeah." Stone gave him a side eye. "You're not thinking what I think you're thinking, are you?"

Zalen shrugged. "Well, are you thinking what I think you're thinking, but you don't want to say out loud?"

"Most likely. What are you thinking?"

"That she also fits the crumpled body description, even though she is a she."

"Damn. That's what I'm thinking."

"Right." Smiling, Zalen said, "So, the crumpled body in your vision may not be a man, right?" Stone's stomach dropped, which prevented him from answering, and Zalen continued, "Don't worry. It's no big deal. Let's just say that it could either be a man or woman, and we'll just add her to the list. Now, about the brats. Did I ever tell you the story regarding the best brats I've ever eaten?"

"Nope." Then Stone removed his earbuds from his front pocket, inserting them into his ears. He wasn't trying to be rude, but Zalen's revelation unsettled him. After selecting a song from his favorite funk rock playlist, he raised the volume and continued setting up the campsite while thinking about the crumpled body. Maybe it wasn't a man? And if he was wrong about that, what else was he wrong about?

CHAPTER THIRTEEN

Bash couldn't believe his luck. He waited for this exact moment ever since he received his tarot cards, two days ago. Glancing at Tiny, curled up on the grass and snoozing in the early afternoon sun, he knew that his dog was equally as excited. Standing before him were five people. Actual people! And they agreed to have him, little ol' Bash, guide them on their first tarot card journey. As pride filled his soul, he smiled and secretly congratulated himself. Now, being an expert at reading the room, Bash decided to use the three card spread, feeling that his audience couldn't handle more than three card interpretations.

With the whole deck in his hands, Bash looked up and said to the team, "The three cards will represent different things. The first card is about the present situation. The second one is about possible challenges that may come up. And the third is about resolution and what you need to do to solve the issue. You are each supposed to shuffle the deck while asking a question. But the question shouldn't be a yes or no question. For example, don't ask, will I win the lottery? Instead, you should ask, what can I do to make more money? Also, don't ask about when you're gonna die. Tarot readings can't predict that." Bash looked at Travis. "I'm ready when you are."

Travis joined Bash at the lopsided picnic table and sat opposite of him. "Do I have to voice my question? Can I just ask it in my head while shuffling?"

"I'm pretty sure you're supposed to say it out loud since tarot card readings were originally like story-tell-"

"I'm not saying my question out loud, Bash." Travis separated the deck into two. "How many times do I shuffle?"

"Um, as many times as you want. And then separate the deck into three piles."

Travis shuffled once. Then he slapped the deck on the picnic table and crossed his arms over his dog, still in the pet sling.

"You forgot to separate into three piles."

"Did I?"

Travis's intimidating nature caused Bash to gulp. However, for the sake of tarot cards, he soldiered on. "And then you have to turn over the top card in each pile."

Travis rolled his eyes. "Please."

"I'll just make the three piles then. Traditionally, the card readers used their left hand to pick the cards, so, I guess, that's what I'll do for you."

Slouching in a chair around the firepit, Chuck asked, "Why the left hand?"

Bash shrugged. "I think it has something to do with receptive energy."

In another chair next to Chuck, Tonya seemed bored as she pressed a cold can of soda to her forehead. "It sounds like we're in great hands."

Nearby, on a small grassy area under some shade were Kimmy and Aunt Rae. Kimmy hugged her knees and thoughtfully stared at nothing. Aunt Rae, on the other hand, busied herself by alternating between stress-eating her sandwich and blowing up her air mattress with her lungs. After Tonya's comment, she paused the blowing to say, "Please don't trash talk my nephew."

"Hey, guys," Travis barked. "This is *my* turn. You can all talk during *your* turns."

Bash inhaled and exhaled slowly. Then, after summoning his courage, he separated the cards into three piles, using his left hand the entire time. Tingles rippled through Bash's body as he said, "We will now begin." He turned over the first card of the pile on his left. It showed a man, alone on a mountain top. On the ground before him were three cups. A fourth cup, floating near him, came to him on beams of sunlight as an offering; however, the man did not notice it. Instead, he looked down at his feet with crossed arms. "Your first card about your current situation is the upright four of cups."

"Upright? What does that mean?"

"It just means that the card is facing you. It's not upside down to you."

Travis nodded. "Go on."

"The card suggests that you are feeling discouraged. Unmotivated. You feel there is no good solution for your situation. It suggests that you do a self-evaluation to improve your attitude and help you get out of the rut. Also, the four of-"

"Next," Travis ordered.

With barbecue sauce smeared on her cheek, Rae called from her shady spot, "Hey, maybe you should listen to this? You know what I mean?"

He glared very hard at her. So hard, it looked like his eyes were about to pop out of his head. He sneered, "I said *next*, Rae. Do you know what *I* mean?" Travis returned his attention to Bash. "Well? What are you waiting for?"

Bash gulped again. "Okay." After flipping over the top card of the middle pile, Bash squeaked in alarm. This card showed a skeleton, wearing black armor and wielding a sickle. It stood next to a grand white horse, and many skulls and bones surrounded them on the ground. "This is the upright Death card," Bash began. "It doesn't mean actual *death*. It just means that there will be an end to something. So, since the second card is about possible challenges for you in the near future, I guess your challenge will be facing some kind of an end."

Travis curiously remained quiet, so Bash took the opportunity to flip over the top card in the third pile on the right. "Oh, this isn't a bad one." He breathed a little easier. "I actually pulled this one for my own reading yesterday. It's the upright Three of Pentacles." On the face, there were three figures. Bash first pointed to the middle person. "This guy is an apprentice. The one on his right is a priest and the other guy is a nobleman. And behind them is a cathedral."

"If you're going to tell me that I have to build a cathedral in order to evade death, I'll throw you into the lake."

Bash nervously chuckled. "No, this card is about coming together with others to build something together."

"What a bunch of crock. Rae, you're next." Travis rose from the table, hugging his dog. With a worried expression, he anxiously searched the campsite while exclaiming, "Where is the damn beer? And why don't we have a fire going, for Christ's sake? Don't campers have fires? Hey, I've got an idea." He gestured to Chuck, Tonya and Kimmy. "Why don't the Three of Pentacles work together and build a fire?"

Chuck said, "It's ninety-five degrees right now."

Travis raged. "And I could make it a lot hotter, Chuck!"

Tonya jumped up from her chair and searched for matches while Chuck organized the logs in a pyramid fashion. Kimmy hopped to it by breaking off small branches from nearby trees and laying them on top. During this mad scramble, Aunt Rae plugged in her air mattress, popped the last sandwich bite into her mouth and sauntered to the picnic table. She sat across from Bash and spoke with her mouth full. "Be nice in what you say about me."

Bash corrected his aunt. "It's not what *I* have to say, but what the *tarot cards* have to say." He then handed her the deck, which she shuffled three times. With a smile, she told him that her question would also be private and she then separated the cards into three piles. Her reading began after she flipped over the first card.

"Ooooo," Bash cooed.

"What?" Aunt Rae leaned over the card, studying it. She suddenly sat upright with a disgusted look on her face. "Are those two naked people?"

Bash shyly grinned. "Your first card is the upright Lovers card." He paused for a moment to bob his eyebrows and his aunt groaned. "This card is all about your current situation and your current situation is all about your soul-mate."

"Oh lord."

"And his name is-"

"Just stop."

"Stone."

"It doesn't say that." Aunt Rae turned over the second card. "Moving on."

Laughing at his aunt, Bash then looked down at the new card and the laughter stopped. He quickly looked at his aunt again. Wearing a curious expression, she stared at the familiar depiction.

Aunt Rae pointed at it. "Isn't that the Death card that Travis picked?"

"Yeah, and it's upright," Bash said to his aunt. "How strange. This doesn't happen very often. I mean, there are seventy-eight cards in the whole deck. So, the chances are pretty slim."

"One in seventy-eight, I believe." Aunt Rae smiled. "Well, I know about this card already. Moving on again." She flipped over the last card.

They both looked at each other quizzically. It was the Three of Pentacles.

Bash leaned over the card. "This is even stranger. I mean, I kinda got the creeps."

Not seeming to be too affected, Aunt Rae nodded, frowned and then shrugged. "Maybe I didn't shuffle well?" However, she brought a fingernail to her teeth, alerting Bash of her anxiety. While nibbling, she turned to the group and asked, "Who wants to go next?"

Tonya answered, "Rae looks a little upset. This might be fun, after all. I'll go."

While Tonya shuffled the deck four times, she also kept her question private. She then arranged the cards into three piles and flipped over the first card. It showed a blindfolded woman who held two swords.

Pleased, Bash explained, "This is the Two of Swords. See how the card looks upside down to you?" Tonya nodded and he continued, "That means it's reversed. So, your current situation is about being caught between a rock and a hard place. I guess you're in a difficult position and you don't know what the right answer is."

Tonya's eyes widened. "I actually am. What else does it mean?"

"Well, the blindfolded woman means that you might be blind to other solutions and you might be overwhelmed with information, so listen to your gut." He smiled at her. "Not bad."

Tonya returned the smile. "This is kind of fun." She happily squirmed in her seat as she flipped over the second card.

Bash couldn't believe his eyes. Once again, the upright Death card appeared. Bash didn't say anything. Instead, he asked Tonya to flip over the third card, which she did without question. Lo and behold, it was the Three of Pentacles. What was happening? He quickly grabbed all the cards, gathered them into a pile, tapped on the top card three times to cleanse them and yelled, "Next!"

"But weren't those the same cards again?" Tonya asked. "What does this mean?"

Bash tried to sound nonchalant, but his voice cracked. "There must be a glitch in one of the time dimensions." He looked around Tonya. "Who's next?"

Chuck approached, fanning himself with a leaf. "I guess I'll go, if I have to. I also would like to keep my question to myself." He sat down as Tonya stood, hovering nearby.

Bash nodded, giving the tarot cards to Chuck. "Don't worry. I cleansed the cards, so we should be good."

"Cleansed?" Chuck began shuffling the deck.

"Never mind. When you're finished shuffling, make three piles and then flip over the top card from the pile on my left, your right."

Chuck followed the directions and was about to turn over the first card when Bash stopped him. Needing a mental moment to chase away any bad energy, Bash took a deep breath and then nodded to Chuck to continue. Chuck flipped over the card and so far, so good. It was the upright Tower card.

Bash still felt like he was in a tarot card pickle, caught between third plate and home. To ease the building tension, Bash began Chuck's reading by suggesting that they quicken the pace. "The upright Tower card represents destruction and upheaval, like a death of a loved one, health issues, losing your job or life, yadda yadda yadda. You get the idea." Before Chuck uttered a word, Bash overturned the second card, using his left hand. He paused. He gasped. His mouth hung open as he then hastily flipped the third card. The two same cards surfaced again. Bash struck out, after all.

Chuck seemed worried too. "So, let me get this straight. The Tower card says that my current situation is about some horrible personal disaster. The second card, which is the Death card, is about how some upcoming challenge will mark an end. For me and, well, for the others too. And the third card about how to overcome this challenge is the Three of Pentacles, which means what again?"

"Teamwork."

"Right." Chuck slowly rose. "I'm screwed."

Tonya commented, "We're all screwed, by the sound of it."

By now, the whole group gathered around Bash and Chuck. However, they all looked at Bash. Travis and Tonya seemed angry as they both had squinty eyes. Aunt Rae furrowed her eyebrows while biting another fingernail. Chuck's spiky red hair sagged and Kimmy picked up more blades of grass to shred.

Aunt Rae asked, "Why are we all getting the same second and third card?"

Bash shrugged, wearing his most innocent expression.

Travis demanded, "Are you stacking the deck?"

Bash raised his eyebrows. "What does that mean?"

Tonya hissed. "It means you're tricking us."

Immediately looking at his aunt for support, Bash said, "I'm not doing anything."

Everyone faced Aunt Rae as she stood next to Chuck. She spit out a bitten fingernail remnant. "My nephew doesn't play tricks like this."

Travis said, "Well, this is a horrible ice breaker." He drank the rest of his beer. "There's only one thing to do." He pointed to Kimmy. "You're next."

"What?" Tonya yelped. "Don't make her do this. We're inviting the devil to camp with us. I'm out." However, Tonya did not budge from her position next to Travis.

Petting his Tiny's head vigorously, Travis said to Kimmy, "We'll all watch Bash closely. I'm sure he's just trying to drive us nuts. That's what kids do these days."

Bash shook his head. "I'm not. I'm just reading the cards like anyone else."

Travis slyly smiled at Bash. "Hey, kid, you just gave me an idea. Tonya, you're going to shuffle, deal and read for Kimmy."

Surprised, Bash looked at his aunt. "She can't deal the cards. I'm the dealer. I'm the reader. Aunt Rae, do something."

While biting her third fingernail, Aunt Rae said to Travis, "I'll read Kimmy's cards."

Travis shook his head. "Oh, no. Not you. I've seen how close you two are. He probably learned his card sharpness from you."

"Oh, please," Aunt Rae scoffed. "Then, how about Chuck? He's a little more open-minded than Tonya."

Tonya sneered at Aunt Rae, but Chuck perked up at the mention of his name. However, his shoulders slouched when Travis said,

"No. My ninety-year old mother has a keener sense of her whereabouts than Chuck does. And her arteries hardened twenty years ago." He gestured at Bash. "Move, so Tonya can sit there."

In desperation, Bash reached for his aunt. "Tell him that not anyone can read cards. It takes practice."

Nodding, Aunt Rae defended Bash. "That's true. It took Bash two years to learn this."

Travis tsked at Aunt Rae. "You're lying." He nodded toward Bash. "How long did it really take you?"

Bash looked away and replied, "Two weeks."

Narrowing his eyes, Travis demanded of Bash. "Be honest."

Sighing, Bash mumbled, "Two days." He then faced Travis and begged. "But these are *my* tarot cards."

Travis tsked again. "And this is *my* team." He turned toward Kimmy. "Come on, let's go. It's not like I'm forcing you to do acid."

Tonya said, "I don't want to read these evil cards. Why can't we just stop this activity?"

Travis groaned. "To prove a point, Tonya. To prove that Bash was playing a trick on us, okay? And you have to read the cards because you're the only competent one in this group."

Tonya's face brightened as she raised her nose in the air at Aunt Rae. "Okay. I'll do it." Using her hip to scoot Bash out of the way, Tonya sat in his spot, poised and confident. She held out her hand for the deck of tarot cards and, before giving them to her, Bash tapped on them three times again for cleansing purposes.

Kimmy hesitantly sat opposite Tonya who mixed up the cards before giving them to Kimmy. Then Kimmy also shuffled the cards seven times, under Travis's order, and separated them into three piles in the same manner as the others.

Bash asked Kimmy, "Did you ask yourself a question?"

Tonya shushed him. Then she addressed Kimmy. "Did you ask yourself a question?"

Kimmy timidly nodded.

The next question spilled out of Bash's mouth like a waterfall, fast and with some spray. "Do you want to ask the question out loud or keep it private?"

Travis scolded Bash. "That's enough."

Kimmy looked at Travis, then at Bash and finally at Tonya. "Private."

Bash couldn't help himself and he blurted, "Okay, let's begin!"

Travis warned him. "I will throw you in that lake, if this continues."

Aunt Rae then warned Travis. "Then I'll make sure your Tiny follows."

Tonya raised her voice. "Stop it, you two. I want this over as soon as possible." Both Travis and Aunt Rae nodded, allowing Tonya to gesture for Kimmy to continue.

With a trembling hand, Kimmy flipped over the first card. It was an image of a man, carrying five swords in his arms and leaving behind two other swords. She expectantly looked at Tonya who then looked at Travis.

"I'm going to need some help here," Tonya said to him. "All I see is abstract art with wonderful line variations."

Travis huffed. "Fine. Whatever. Bash, don't touch the cards. Just tell us what this card means. Quickly."

Delighted, Bash rushed his explanation. "This is the upright Seven of Swords. It means you're keeping a deep dark secret."

Kimmy's eyes widened. "It says that?"

"Yeah." He shrugged. "You just need to forgive yourself."

Sounding impatient, Travis ordered Kimmy to flip over the second and third cards. Together. At the same time.

Bash argued, "That's not the correct way. Hey!"

It was too late. Travis grabbed the two cards and looked at them. Then, with an accusing alarm in his eye, he slapped them down on the table for everyone to see. Staring back at the team were none other than the Death card *and* the teasing Three of Pentacles.

. . .

Tiny awakened, opening one eye to survey the loud racket. He did not understand the raised voices, but he did understand the tone. They were all mad at somebody. He had a sneaky suspicion who caused the offense and, lifting his head, he searched for Nice Bash. Not able to find him, Tiny pointed his nose upward, sniffing the air. He caught the mixed scent of onions and sweaty hair, which was Nice Bash's brand, so Tiny knew that the boy was near. Then Tiny heard Nice Bash's voice, rising from somewhere in the middle of where the taller people gathered.

"I didn't mess with the cards! How could I? I didn't even touch them this time!" Nice Bash pleaded.

This brought another round of raised voices and Tiny felt antsy. He shifted his body, debating if he should stay under the tree in his cool relaxing spot, or if he should stand and bark. As he weighed the pros and cons, he heard Angry Rae speak.

"Guys, listen," she said, "I think we're all just tired and hot. Someone needs to put out that stupid fire." The guy with red hair poured water on the flames as Angry Rae continued, "Now, you all know that saying about breaking bread. Well, we don't have bread, but we do have apple pie. So, let's break that instead and build a sense of brotherhood."

Tiny licked his lips. That sounded like a winner. Unfortunately, no one moved toward the box with the apple pie in it. Instead, there was more hollering. Tiny glanced at the pie, which sat all alone on top of what people called the cooler. Tiny knew then that he had to help. Rising to all fours, he trotted over to the pie, sat down and yipped. But alas, the group continued raising their voices at each other.

Angry Rae waved her arms. "Hey, hey, hey!" The voices quieted and she continued, "Maybe we all had the same question? I asked, if I was going to survive this camping fiasco, how? Anyone else ask that?"

Shaking their heads, the group remained silent. The only sound heard, according to Tiny, was his own rumbling stomach. He sniffed the box and cinnamon apple vapors teased him.

"Okay," Angry Rae said. "Well, maybe our questions have something in common. What did you all ask?"

No one spoke.

An idea sprang to Tiny's mind. He slowly raised his paw and quietly placed it on top of the box. With a look of boredom, he glanced to his left and waited patiently for his chance.

"Come on, guys," Angry Rae pleaded, sounding annoyed. "What did you ask?"

Raised voices erupted again and Tiny casually swiped with his paw, knocking the pie onto the ground. Luck was on his side as the box lid sprung open.

"You know," Angry Rae continued over everyone's protests, "this is why our team sucks." The group stopped talking and Angry Rae put her hands on her hips. As Tiny filled his mouth with buttery crust and sugary apples, he knew that she now meant business. "We don't open up to each other. We don't trust each other. How is our team going to bond if we can't share our silly questions to a silly game? And may I remind you that this is just a silly game?"

Nice Bash disagreed. "It's not *all* that silly."

Angry Rae spoke over him. "My twelve-year old nephew just wanted to do something fun tonight with you all. He was really doing me a favor because I didn't have an ice-breaker activity in mind. And my nephew is a good, trust-worthy person. He would never trick us or anyone. I'm embarrassed of how you are all treating him."

The whole group now lowered their eyes and stared at the ground. Tiny also lowered his eyes and stared at the last half of the apple pie. He gobbled it up.

Angry Rae still spoke. "I think you owe my nephew an apology."

Her words seemed to work in Nice Bash's favor. The group smiled at him and the shorter male patted Nice Bash's back while the tall man with that snippy dog ruffled Nice Bash's hair. Then the tall man took a picture of himself with the group as he stuck up his thumb.

As Tiny methodically pressed his tongue on the apple bits, stuck on the bottom of the pie plate, he watched the group and felt the tension leave, like an army of fleas after a warm soapy bath. All seemed peaceful again and Tiny sunk onto his full stomach, feeling satisfied for Nice Bash.

Angry Rae suddenly clapped her hands and said, "Good job, everyone! I think we just had our first successful team bonding moment! This was a good ice breaker, after all! We really broke some ice between us!" She clapped again, saying, "Let's celebrate and eat that apple pie!"

Upon hearing the word pie, Tiny lifted his head again and his tongue fell out of his mouth. Pie would be a great snack. Especially apple pie. Now, where was it?

CHAPTER FOURTEEN

When it was discovered that there was no apple pie left, an uproar of voices erupted again. Rae's shoulders slumped as she moped her way over to Tiny. He slowly pushed himself onto his haunches and sheepishly looked into her eyes. Suddenly, the humor hit her.

She laughed. "Come on, Tiny. Let's go for a walk."

"I'm coming too, Aunt Rae." Bash velcroed himself to her side. "This crowd is getting rough."

Without a word, the three of them left the arguing team to their own devices. The only time Rae looked back was when Tonya grabbed her upper arm and spun her around.

"Wait a minute, Rae." Tonya thrust the empty pie plate into Rae's ribs. "You can *at least* throw your dog's trash away." Abruptly turning on her heels, Tonya then stomped toward the tent, throwing the screen opening into the air before disappearing from view.

Rae looked at Bash and shrugged. She lowered her voice and said to him, "Let's go to the nice main entrance and see if they have any more pie. For *us.* I'm no longer in the sharing mood."

Bash beamed and they knuckle-bumped. Easily removing the brochure from his back pocket, he tapped it while saying, "The map on the back shows a shortcut. There are tons of hiking paths through the woods that we can take, cutting the time by half. If we walk on the gravel road, it could take a half hour or more. I vote for the hiking paths."

Rae smiled. "I second that vote. We'll be in the shade of the forest trees then."

Tiny wagged his tail.

"Good point." Bash studied Tiny. "Aunt Rae, does he need his leash?"

Rae shook her head. "Nah. He's a good dog. Aren't you, Tiny?"

Upon hearing his name, Tiny rose on his hind legs and draped his front paws over Rae's shoulders. He was now taller, which enabled him to rest his chin on the top of her head. Just for a moment. And then he effortlessly lowered himself back to all four legs.

"Thanks for the hug," Rae said and the three began their forest shortcut. Bash led with Tiny closely following. Rae was last in line, fanning herself with the foil pie plate and anticipating an uneventful stroll, which wasn't, of course.

. . .

Despite wearing earbuds, Stone heard the yelling from a nearby campsite. He finished piling the wood in the firepit for later use and his eyes darted through the woods that separated the sites. He couldn't see anyone, but the people sounded like an angry group of wasps. The words were unintelligible, but the buzz between them sounded highly irritable. Of all the campsites that Stone had to be assigned, it had to be next to this one. Raising the volume of his music to block out the neighbors' bickering, Stone wondered where Rachel's group was located when, suddenly, he felt dread. An image of Bash flashed through his mind. Then he smelled apple pie and he felt a shoulder tap. Looking over his shoulder, he expected to see Rachel. It wasn't.

Stone lowered the volume. "Yes, Zalen. What is it?"

"Well, my friend, it looks like you have everything handled here real well. And this day will never come around again. And that sun, well, it will never shine on this day at this moment, ever again."

"What are you getting at?"

"Oh." Zalen seemed surprised. "I thought it was obvious. I'm going to the beach."

Stone scanned Zalen from his head to his feet. He wore his red bucket hat and a blue collared polo shirt with tan khaki shorts. In one hand, he held a puzzle book with a green marker, fastened to the cover by its clip. In the other hand was the large closed umbrella. The only thing that looked beach-worthy were his black sliders with three white stripes, stretching across the wide strap.

Stone asked, "You're not going to swim?"

"Well, I'd rather just sit on the beach today. Enjoy the sound of the waves while working on a puzzle under the cool shade of an umbrella."

Pointing to the umbrella, Stone said, "I thought you brought that for Rachel."

"I did. I have a *feeling* that I'll run into her on my way to the beach. I *feel* like she's nearby."

Stone immediately turned off his music and removed the earbuds. "Don't say that. She can't be nearby. I won't have her nearby. I refuse to have her nearby. That's not going to work, Zalen. We can't run into her so soon. We haven't figured out our excuse for why we're here."

"Excuse? Aren't we just going to tell her the truth?"

"Which truth? The one where you feel she needs an umbrella for some stupid reason? Or the one where I'm having visions because I'm a stupid psychic? Or do you mean the one where both of us think something stupid is going to happen at this stupid campground, but we have no stupid idea what?"

"Well, I personally think that none of those truths are stupid."

"Look." Stone frowned. "If we say anything about psychics, visions or empaths, I *know* she will think we're stupid nuts and will never speak to us again."

Zalen chuckled. "I *feel* you're being overdramatic."

"Zalen," Stone spoke very seriously, "I have known Rachel for all of my youth. I know how she thinks. She doesn't believe in ghosts or aliens or anything paranormal. She believes in right, left, up and down. She believes in going to bed early and waking up late. She believes in hot summers, cold winters and, most of all, Cary Grant."

"He was the perfect leading man. He could do it all. Comedy, romance, action and- "

Crossing his arms, Stone interrupted Zalen. "We have to come up with a good, believable reason for why we are here. And, if that doesn't work, I may have another idea."

CHAPTER FIFTEEN

So many to choose, Bash thought after noticing many apple pies in the sea of baked goods, displayed on the table near the deli. He snatched one and held it close to his chest. Searching for his aunt in the grocery aisles, he found her, hugging a variety of large chip bags and four two-liter bottles of soda. Two were his favorite; the others were hers.

He raised the pie over his head in triumph and said, "It's a dutch apple."

They both smiled at each other and headed to the counter.

A woman stood at the cash register with a big smile on her face, accentuating her crow's feet. As Bash and Aunt Rae placed their staples on the counter, she said to his aunt, "Oh, hello again. Now, don't tell me. Your name is Rae, right? You're with the work retreat." Aunt Rae nodded and Jen turned to Bash. "Stocking up on some goodies, eh?" Bash smiled and she continued, "You picked our best seller. Everyone around here likes Rosemary's Homemade Pies. You'll have to tell me what you two think."

Aunt Rae replied, "I can already tell you my dog loved the first one. Now, it's our turn to sample this one."

The woman laughed. "I'll have to let Rosemary know that dogs like her pies too. She'll love hearing that." Glancing at Bash, her heart seemed to burst out of her chest. "You look a little too young and way too cute to be part of a work retreat."

Beaming, Bash showed his dimples. "I'm twelve and just came along to help my aunt as well as catch The Ma'iingan Bluff Werewolf." He glanced at Aunt Rae who rolled her eyes.

Jen bumbled a two-liter bottle, but managed to keep it from falling off the counter. "Werewolf?" She chuckled. "Around here? I don't know anything about that, but we do have a nice beach and hiking trails." While placing the contents in plastic bags, she glanced at him. "I have a son. You remind me of him when he was your age. He's now thirty-three and a bigger pain in my neck." She winked at Aunt Rae. "But I still love him."

Astounded at the news of her son's age, Bash blurted, "You don't look old." He cleared his throat. "I mean, to have a kid who's thirty-three."

Jen laughed loudly. It caused other shoppers to stop in their tracks and briefly look at her. "Well, thank you, young man," she said to Bash with an air of playful conceit. "I'm proud to say that I am old enough."

"You must've started young," Bash said, followed by a prompt shush from his aunt.

Jen didn't seem to mind the comment and offered, "Not that young. I was twenty-two." She then handed the two plastic bags to Bash and said to both of them, "Well, if you need more pie, come and see me. It won't be any trouble." This time, Jen winked at him and then waved good-bye at both of them.

Once outside, Aunt Rae gave him a disapproving look, but chuckled.

"What?" Bash innocently shrugged. "You were wondering the same thing."

With a quick eye-roll, Aunt Rae patted the side of her leg, signaling Tiny to join them. As the Great Shepherd left his shaded spot on the porch, she said to Bash while holding the pie like a trophy, "Let's find a picnic table and eat and drink and be merry."

Bash peered inside the plastic bags. "We forgot the forks."

"Well, we still have our hands." Aunt Rae shrugged. "We're related, so who cares?"

"What about the cups for our soda?"

Aunt Rae searched the area for a vacant picnic table. "Haven't you ever drunk out of a two-liter bottle before with your mouth?" After he shook his head at his aunt, she smiled and said, "Well, today is your lucky day." She pointed to the right. "There's a table over there. By the trees. Let's grab it."

Bash spotted the lonely table at the edge of the forest. As he leaned forward, readying his legs to sprint over to it, her hand wrapped around his forearm, stopping him. She stared straight ahead with her lips parted. He followed her gaze and saw Dark Ranger Tom walking toward them. He was in company with another park ranger. She had cropped blonde hair and a thin, but strong, frame. Suddenly, Bash felt pressure on his entire left side as his aunt pushed him behind the nearest pine tree. She made him squat, as well as Tiny.

As the two drew nearer, Aunt Rae stared at Bash and when he started to speak, she placed her finger against her lips. He shrugged at her and she whispered, "We're hiding." Shaking his head at his aunt's behavior, he soon heard the voices as they approached.

"I know," said Dark Ranger Tom. "It doesn't make sense to me either."

The female park ranger asked, "So, that's it? Gone without any explanation?"

"Yes. She quit and left immediately, leaving the rest of us in a bind."

"But that doesn't sound like something she would do at all. She loved this job."

They walked by the pine tree, never noticing its temporary purpose of concealing Bash, his aunt and Tiny. Aunt Rae exhaled, placing her hand on her chest. She looked at Bash and said, "Let's just take the shortcut back to our campsite and eat our pie there."

Bash grinned while squinting his eyes. "Why are we hiding from Tom? Is it because he's The Ma'iingan Bluff Werewolf and you know it, but you don't want to admit it?"

"Of course not. You know I don't believe in that stuff. I just think he's a creepy guy. Come on, let's go." Still holding the pie, now with both hands, she rose halfway. Then, hunched over, Aunt Rae jogged toward the woods. She entered between two trees and the whole forest swiftly swallowed her.

Tiny followed with Bash being the last, carrying both bags. He hustled along the weaving footpath, but struggled to keep pace with his aunt and Tiny. A couple of times, tree roots caught him off guard, causing him to trip. He always regained his balance, though, and never fell or dropped the bags. Eventually, he found his rhythm and began to gain speed. Just as he shortened the distance between him and Tiny, he heard a thump and a shriek ahead of him. He then heard his aunt say, "Oh, no. Not again."

Bash rounded the curve and stopped at the sight of Aunt Rae, standing with her hands covering her mouth. On the ground was the pie, flipped over and smashed inside the plastic container. Tiny sat next to it, staring at Bash. When they made eye contact, Tiny shook his head. The Great Shepherd then nodded toward a body, curled and lifeless on its side, in the middle of the trail. It was a lean man with long knotty locks of brown hair.

Dropping the bags, Bash scolded his aunt. "Why do you have to trip over dead bodies all the time? I mean, seriously, Aunt Rae. My mom says this is a problem of yours and I'm starting to agree with her."

Aunt Rae's eyes were very wide. Her hands remained over her mouth as she softly spoke, "Bash, I know this guy. I mean, I just saw this guy when I arrived here. I ran into him. I think his name is Matt."

Just then, Matt stirred and his aunt squeaked. Bash watched as Matt's body first twitched in various parts before he blinked his eyes open.

Aunt Rae gasped and said to Matt, "Oh my god, are you okay?"

Without answering, Matt closed his eyes again and licked his lips, smacking them a few times. He slowly rolled onto his belly, eventually rising to his hands and knees.

Tentatively stepping closer to Matt, Aunt Rae gently said, "I used to be a lifeguard and had first aid certification. Do you need medical attention? Were you electrocuted?"

Baffled, Bash asked, "Electrocuted?"

Aunt Rae looked at him and shrugged. Her voice still sounded panicky. "That's one of the questions you're supposed to ask. You'd be surprised at how many people are electrocuted. And-" She pointed to his feet. "He's barefoot. Without shoes, he could've stepped on a power line of some sort and zapped himself." She shrugged again.

Sure enough. Bash glanced at Matt's feet and they were sockless and shoeless. "Huh. Maybe he was electrocuted?"

Matt suddenly shook his head vigorously, his knotty locks whipping around his head like ropes.

Aunt Rae said to Bash, "I think that's a no."

Matt then stretched in the most peculiar way. He started with one leg, straightening it out as much as he could. Then he stretched the other leg in the same manner before moving to his arms. Still on his hands and knees, he arched his back, like a scared cat, and then he finished in a downward-facing dog pose. His stretching reminded Bash of how Tiny stretched in the morning. Once upright, Matt looked around his surroundings and noticed his audience for the first time since this unusual meeting. He nodded to Aunt Rae, petted the top of Tiny's head and stepped around Bash, saying, "Hey, little bro."

"H-hey," Bash stuttered and watched Matt as he loped down the path toward the office.

Aunt Rae furrowed her eyebrows. "That was so strange. And why was he barefoot? In the woods?"

Bash raised his eyebrows. "Did you see how he stretched? It was like a dog. Or a wolf." He raised his eyebrows higher. "Or a *werewolf*."

Aunt Rae brought her thumbnail to her teeth and nibbled. "No. I missed that similarity."

"And, Aunt Rae, did you see his toenails? They were long and sharp. Like claws. Like a *werewolf*."

"Stop it." She spit out the bitten piece of thumbnail. "Apparently, I don't notice stretching movements, toenails or ear lobes. Just bare and dirty feet."

Pulling on his lip, Bash remained silent. Then he sighed and said to his aunt, "We have a mystery here, Aunt Rae."

"Do you mean the mystery of will we ever be able to eat an apple pie?"

Bash said, "I mean the mystery of The Ma'iingan Bluff Werewolf. Both Dark Ranger Tom and Matt act the part."

Aunt Rae huffed and picked up the pie. Turning abruptly, she quickly trudged down the path and called over her shoulder, "I'm not listening to that! I'm more upset about the pie!"

Tiny whined and Bash said to him, "Don't worry. We'll make her a believer." He smiled slyly. "It all starts with the werewolf hunt."

· · ·

Stone's voice was soft and low as he explained his plan to Zalen while sitting across from him at the picnic table. "I swear it's a good idea." Stone leaned over the table and lowered his voice even more. "Who says we have to be with her? We don't. And she doesn't even have to know that we're here. I mean, I don't particularly want to see her. She'll ask me all sorts of questions that I don't want to answer. So, I propose that we'll camp here. Not tell her that we're here. And keep an eye on her from afar."

Stone gave Zalen a thumbs up and Zalen asked in a normal-volumed voice, "I'm just wondering when do we step in to save her life? If it's at the end, that may be cutting it too close."

Stone whispered, "Maybe there won't be a need to save her life?"

"What about the crumpled body? It could be a man or woman. And Rae is a woman."

Stone stopped whispering and straightened up. "But the crumpled body is tall. Rachel isn't tall, which I've said many times. Aren't you listening to anything I say?"

"Yes, but I admit that my mind drifts sometimes." Zalen caressed the leaves on his plant. "If we're supposed to watch Rae from afar, how am I supposed to give her the umbrella?"

"Let's just leave it at her campsite, once we find the campsite. We'll put a note on it with her name, saying she won it in some drawing." Stone shrugged. "I don't know. Maybe she really doesn't need the umbrella? Maybe the umbrella is a red herring?"

Zalen smiled while shaking his head. "I doubt it. Anyway, what you're telling me is that we're strictly here to figure out who the crumpled body is."

"You got it."

"And it could be a guy or gal?"

"Yep."

"And it's not Rae."

"Indeed, it's not."

For a full minute, Zalen said nothing. He just sat opposite of Stone, now holding the umbrella, and staring at Stone with one wide eye. "So, what do we say to Rae, if we see her?"

Stone twinkled. "Well, I *feel* that we won't see her at all. So, don't worry about it."

Zalen's eyes twinkled. "Well, I *feel* that you are wrong."

Just then, Stone felt a familiar tap on his back. Looking over his shoulder, he met two vexed gray-blue eyes, resembling an afternoon sky just before a torrential storm. It was Rachel.

In her hands was a decrepit apple pie in a cracked plastic container. Stone cleared his throat. "Oh, hi, cupcake. What a surprise." He pointed to the pie. "Is that for me?"

CHAPTER SIXTEEN

"Don't call me cupcake and what are you doing here?" Rae scrutinized Stone's stoic face.

Stone adjusted his cap. "How long were you standing behind me?"

"Long enough to hear you tell Zalen not to worry about seeing me, or something like that." She leaned closer. "So? Why are you here? You're following me, aren't you? And trying to keep it a secret? Is that it? Why?" Then, somewhere in the depths of his lightning blue irises, she found the answer and gasped. "You don't think I can handle camping, do you?"

Stone blinked in surprise. "Ah, what?"

Across the gravel road, Bash stumbled out of the woods with Tiny at his side. Rae turned toward them and yelled in exasperation, "I'm over here! Look who I found!"

Pure elation filled Bash's expression as he spotted Stone. Tiny also seemed delighted at Stone's arrival and took three energetic leaps across the road with the fourth one landing on him. They greeted each other like past troops who were bunk mates. They playfully wrestled, gave each other noogies and then Tiny jumped onto his hind legs to lick Stone's chin.

Rae scolded, "Enough already. You just saw each other yesterday, crying out loud."

By now, Bash joined, still holding the two plastic bags. "Hey, Stone, what are you doing here?"

Stone seemed to pale. "Me? What are you doing here? You're not Emma at all."

"No, I am not, thank god," Bash returned.

Rae explained, still with some audible annoyance, "Emma's sick, so Bash snuck into my car and hid under my duffel bag, in order to be part of this wonderful expedition."

Bash laughed and then saw Zalen. "Hey! You're here, too? This is great!"

Grinning from ear to ear, Zalen nodded to Stone before approaching Bash who set the bags on the ground. Then they both extended their right hands, gently smacked them together on both sides before making fists and bopped them together a few times. In awe, Rae watched this secret handshake as they hooked thumbs, pulled on each other's ears and wiggled their fingers before snapping them multiple times.

While that greeting carried on, Rae returned her attention to Stone. "I can't believe you took off work, reserved a site under the guise of being with this work retreat and followed me here."

Growing up together, Rae knew that Stone mastered how to look like a blank piece of paper. And he was doing a great job at it right now as he replied, "I don't know what you're talking about. I'm here because Zalen has never camped and, after hearing you mention it, he asked me to show him the ropes."

Rae noticed he clenched his jaw, which meant he was a big, good-looking liar. She shook her head. "You're here because you know that every time I camp, something bad happens to me. So, stop lying. I hate it when people lie. And I hate it more when they lie to me."

Stone stared at her with a tight-lipped grin and then jovially shrugged. "You got me."

Pointing at him, Rae scoffed, "I knew it."

Stone now stood and slid his hands into his pockets. He took a step closer to her, grinning. "Remember all those times we camped as kids with our families? I loved it, even with your many, many disasters." His grin disappeared. "So, I'm sorry for lying to you, but I just want to make sure you're alright."

Rae noticed that he didn't clench his jaw this time. Well, it wasn't clenched completely. She rolled her eyes and said, "Whatever."

Stone continued, "Don't be grumpy. It was fun then and it will be fun now. Remember lake swimming at night? Maybe we can do that here? And remember telling ghost stories around the fire? We can tell Bash the one about the lady with the golden arm. Just please don't end up in the emergency room, like usual."

"That only happened once."

"Now, who's lying? You ended up in the emergency room every single time." Shaking his head, Stone added, "I still don't know how you tripped and split your knee open on a rock. Blood poured down your leg. It was horrific."

"So, I needed stitches. No big deal. I was more upset that I dropped all of the hotdogs."

"And remember when we all stayed at Camp Akicita for a week? You were almost trampled to death while horseback riding."

"It wasn't that bad."

"Rachel, I saw you, hanging on to the side of the saddle, as your horse sprinted across the field. And then, when it jumped the fence, I knew you'd lose your grip and fall off." He squinted in thought. "What did you break from the fall? Your arm? Or was it your ankle?"

"Neither. It was just my wrist, Stone. Again, no big deal."

"I never heard your mother scream that loud. And remember our last camping trip? Our dads thought it would be fun to learn archery?"

Rae nodded. "I admit that I still lose feeling in my foot from time to time."

Stone reached for her and pulled her close to his chest, crushing the plastic pie container a little more. Rae didn't mind, however. His arms felt warm and comfortable around her. She then heard him say, "I can't let anything bad happen to you, Rachel."

With her face pressed against his chest, her muffled reply was quiet. "I'm not a princess, Stone."

"I'm aware."

"I camped my whole childhood life."

"We just reminisced about that."

"I never died once."

"You've come close, though."

"You know that I'm a very capable camper, Stone."

"I never said you weren't, Rachel, but I will go on record, saying you have lousy luck, at times."

"Lousy luck aside, I can roll up a sleeping bag faster than you can say I'm a dumbass."

"I don't know what that has to do with anything, but okay. I'm a dumbass."

"You're damn right."

Rae gently pushed herself from Stone, keeping some space between them. For the past few days, she noticed that his eyes began to spill over even more with enamored affections and she began experiencing runny stools. Feeling his warm gaze trickle down her spine, she knew that looking into his face could be disastrous because her vulnerability was at an all-time high and the closest bathroom was the pit toilet. Instead, Rae maintained her focus on the cartoon character, decorating his classic t-shirt. Her focus took a turn, though, as it shifted to how the dark gray shirt accentuated his pecs nicely. She mentally smacked herself and then pivoted back to the cartoon character.

"Hey," she said, "isn't that Underdog?"

Stone grinned. "*There's no need to fear. Underdog is here.*"

"That was my favorite cartoon growing up. All three seasons."

"I know."

She now looked into his face, allowing herself to fall into the depths of his lightning blue eyes. And when she allowed herself to peek into their future, she saw the rest of her happy life. With him. Again, she mentally smacked herself. *I can't go there. He's not ready for a relationship with all of his lies and I'm not ready for a relationship with all of my many insecurities.* "Well," Rae said as she stepped away from Stone, "we should return to the group." She turned to Bash. "Let's go."

"Really?" Bash asked. "Do we have to? I don't want to leave." He spoke to Stone and Zalen. "Her coworkers are bonkers."

"Bash," Rae said, "we're right next door. I'm sure you can come over here whenever you need a break. Right, guys?"

Zalen nodded while petting Tiny's whole body and Stone asked, "You're next door?"

Scrutinizing the cluster of trees that separated the campsites, Rae said, "If you look very carefully, you can see our tent. It's blue." Facing him, she skeptically asked, "You seriously didn't know that we were next door? I'm supposed to believe that?"

"How would I know you were next door?"

Rae gave him her best stink eye. "I don't know, but I get the feeling that you somehow made sure to get the campsite right next door to us."

Stone crossed his arms and shook his head. "Honestly, Rachel, the only thing I made sure of was bringing a tent. Mine's orange. So, I guess it was weird luck."

Zalen interjected, "Or it was fate."

Rae scoffed. "Fate shmate." Nodding to Bash, she said, "Let's go."

As Bash picked up the bags, he loudly moaned. "Ugh, this is horrible."

Tiny mimicked Bash's moan and Rae snapped her fingers at him to stop. She then said to Bash, "Then you shouldn't have snuck into my car this morning. Consider this a lesson."

"Lesson learned, Aunt Rae. Lesson definitely learned."

"Wait a minute, Rae." Zalen gestured toward the picnic table. "I have something for you." He jogged to the table, picked up a long umbrella and quickly returned, giving it to her.

Narrowing her eyes, she smirked. "How did you know that I forgot to pack one?"

Zalen replied, "I *feel* things, remember?"

Rae shrugged. "In my defense, you only correctly *feel* things half the time."

"Aw, stop picking on him, Aunt Rae. He's correct a little more than half." Bash looked hopefully at Zalen. "Just out of curiosity, do you feel anything else at the moment?"

Zalen put his hand on Bash's shoulder and opened his one wide eye wider, staring into Bash. "I *feel* John Donne."

Confused, Rae asked, "The poet? What are you talking about?"

Zalen's eye grew rounder as he thoughtfully said to Bash, "And I quote, 'Therefore, never send to know for whom the bell tolls'."

Suddenly, Travis's booming voice calling her name jolted Rae when it erupted over the atmosphere. She dropped the apple pie again. *I'm pretty sure Travis is tolling the bell for me,* Rae thought while slowly bending to pick up the battered plastic container. As The Torch shouted another beckoning distress call, frightened birds abandoned their nests, and Rae's cheeks flushed with rage.

"Well, Stone, Zalen," Rae began as her blood boiled, "we have to go to our camping site where nightmares are born. See you later."

Stone sighed and Zalen cheerfully waved his hand while saying, "And we're going to the beach where the sun is shining brightly!"

Bash raised his eyebrows. "That's quite a hike from here. I suggest you take the trails through the woods. There might be a shortcut. Do you have a map?"

While Bash discussed various shortcuts with Stone and Zalen, Rae turned on her heels and stomped the thirty yards down the road with Tiny following. She burst onto the campsite like Old Faithful. Enraged, she slam-dunked the pie on the ground. No one reacted to her loud entrance, except for Tiny. He pounced on the pie, causing the lid to pop open. As he devoured his second pastry,

Rae sighed at his gluttony. Then she faced her team, raised the umbrella like a sword and pointed it at Travis. "What do you want?"

Seeming to be oblivious of her mood, Travis said, "There you are. We've been waiting here for The Team-Building Committee to cool down and come back to us. Where were you?"

"The north park office, if you *must* know."

Kimmy tentatively raised her hand. "I saw you talking to a very good-looking guy next door, Rae. Who is he?"

Feeling overprotective, Rae vaguely answered, "My good friend. He's camping here with his friend."

"Oh." Kimmy strained her neck as if she were a giraffe looking over the tops of the trees. "He was *very* good-looking. What's his name?"

Travis testily interjected, "May I remind you that you're married."

"I know." Kimmy immediately stopped stretching her neck. "I was thinking about my younger cousin."

"You say he's good-looking?" Tonya asked as she joined Kimmy's side. "I have a younger sister who just got out of a relationship. Rae, what did you say is his name? What does he do?"

"I didn't and I don't know."

"His name is Stone," Bash answered as he now joined the group. "He runs a bar, but he's taken. Now, Zalen, his friend, is free as a bird and really cool."

"Zalen's a neat-sounding name." Tonya queried, "What does he do for a living?"

Bash cheerily said, "He's a teacher and an empath."

The conversation died at that point.

Travis eagerly rubbed his hands together. "So, what's next, Rae? What do you have planned for our next team-building activity? No offense, Rae, but you're kinda slacking and troops are getting restless."

Surprised, Rae replied, "Seriously? You want to do another activity even after the tarot hell *now*? Together? *As a team?* My god, you're all sorts of nuts."

Travis kissed the top of his Tiny's head. "Your sarcasm, although admired, is not what we need right now. I take it that you don't have anything planned again?"

Dumbfounded, Rae replied, "No."

Travis tsked. "Well, then, think of something. Quickly."

"I have an idea," Rae said through gritted teeth, "let's just do *one* good activity a day."

"Or," Tonya said, "instead of doing two mediocre team-building activities a day, let's just focus on doing one really well."

Rae shook her head and looked at Bash. "I just said that," she said to him.

"Just shrug it off, Aunt Rae," Bash said quietly to her as she pursed her lips together.

"We can't shrug it off," Travis began. "We didn't have one good activity today. So, if you want to do one good activity a day, we're still in need of such an activity. So, no shrugging it off." Travis glanced at his watch. "Now, come on, guys. It's barely two-thirty. Rae, what's next?"

Biting her fingernail, Rae knew she was in a lose-lose situation and the quickest way to escape it was to think of another activity. She glanced at Tiny who finished eating the last chunk of pie. No inspiration there. She then stared at Bash as he pulled on his bottom lip. He caught her eye and shrugged. Unexpectedly, an idea stirred in her mind. And, surprisingly, the team-building activity that popped into her head had nothing to do with throwing Travis and Tonya over the bluff. She smiled at her team, saying, "I think I know what we can do."

．　．　．

Bash wasn't pumped. He was jazzed! Even giddy! For two reasons. First, he was jazzed about going on a scavenger hunt and, second, he was *super* jazzed about going with Tiny. He read the list that his aunt texted to him for this wonderful activity. There were five items that he and Tiny had to find *and* then take a picture of them, using his phone. Everyone had five items, but they all differed. How exciting!

Elated, Bash said to his aunt, "You gave me all of my favorites! I mean, I get to find a walking stick insect, something slimy, a white oak tree, a Purple Martin and some kind of whole pie, uncrushed. I've already seen all of these today. This is gonna be easy!" He knuckle-bumped Tiny. "We got this."

Chuck read his list aloud. "And I have to find a dragonfly, something spiky, a Blue Spruce, a Red-Headed Woodpecker and Chuffles Cheesy Puffles. Then what do I do?"

Aunt Rae replied, "Take a picture of your items. You'll have an hour to find as many as possible. After the hour is up, or, if you find all of your items within the hour, then head to the main entrance store. We'll all meet there to compare our hunting trophies. The person who finds the most items on their list will win."

Tonya hummed. "I've heard that one before. I won a parking spot and then lost it."

Travis discarded Tonya's comment, looking disgusted. "What the hell, Rae? How am I supposed to take a picture of a moving wasp? And what do you mean by something sharp? Like something in nature that's sharp or something man made? And what the hell does a tall milkweed look like? Or an American Coot?" He shook his head. "The only thing that looks achievable on my list is the seedless strawberry jam. I'm surprised, though, that you didn't name some obscure brand." Swearing, he placed his hands on his hips and raised his nose high in the air.

Tonya hummed again, louder. "What interesting lists, Rae." She pointed at Kimmy. "What items do you have?"

"Well," Kimmy began, speaking softly, "I have a moth. Something gray. Meadow-rue. A wood duck. And white bread."

Now glaring at Aunt Rae, Tonya scoffed. "Oh, for heaven's sake. Your lists are characteristics of our personalities." She aimed her cellphone at Aunt Rae while saying, "I'm deeply offended, Rae. *Deeply* offended."

Bash noticed the smallest suggestion of a smile forming on his aunt's lips. She said, "That's not true, Tonya. Not at all."

Chuck asked, "What's on your list, Tonya?"

"I'm not going to give Rae the pleasure of reading it."

Travis nodded at Aunt Rae. "Just tell us what you put on it."

"Fine!" Tonya yelled, "I'll read it! A black widow spider, something sour, wild sarsaparilla, a turkey vulture and chunky peanut butter!" Her loud volume caused a baby to cry in the distance.

Bash barked with laughter. "I see what you're doing with the food items, Aunt Rae. You're building a peanut butter and jelly sandwich with Chuffles on the side." He explained to the team, "That's my aunt's favorite lunch."

Nodding, Chuck said, "Oh, yeah. I see you eat that every day." He winked at Aunt Rae. "That's kinda clever."

Tonya scoffed louder. "That's not clever! She's ripping on all of us! Don't you get that?"

Chuck shrugged. "I actually like woodpeckers." He read his list again. "I actually like all of this stuff."

Kimmy added, "My favorite thing to eat is plain white bread. I also like-"

Travis interrupted, "Rae, is that why you put *tall* milkweed on my list?" He then narrowed his eyes. "And American *Coot*?"

Tonya puffed out her chest and stiffly announced, "I am not putting my life in danger and taking a picture of a black widow spider."

Chuck laughed. "Just zoom in on it with your phone. You don't have to get close."

Miffed, Tonya gestured to Travis. "Aren't you scared to get near a wasp?"

Travis rolled his eyes. "Well, Tonya, I'm not going to kiss it. You sure like to make a mountain out of a molehill." He turned to Rae. "Now, back to the coot comment."

Wanting to save his aunt from abomination, Bash quickly asked her, "Can we start?"

"Sure." Aunt Rae quickly checked the time on her phone. "It's quarter to three. We'll meet at the main entrance in one hour. Sound good, everyone?"

Tonya raised the corner of her upper lip. "This activity sounds lame. It's not even a team-building activity, especially since we have to work *alone* and *risk* our *lives*."

Shrugging, Aunt Rae clarified. "You don't have to do this alone or risk anything. Just get the peanut butter or whatever. And, as far as working alone, you don't have to do that either. You can work with Travis, Kimmy or Chuck." She beamed. "Or me."

As Travis, Kimmy and Chuck shook their heads, Tonya rolled her eyes. "I'll work alone."

Chuck raised his hand. "I have a question. Will the winner get a reward?"

Caught off-guard by his question, Rae motioned for Travis to answer. He said, "It sounds like the reward for everyone will be a second lunch full of preservatives, sugar and fat."

"Can we start, Aunt Rae?" Practically in a crouch starting position, Bash waited for his aunt to say *go*. Once she did, Bash burst into the wooded shortcut with Tiny at his side.

CHAPTER SEVENTEEN

Bash raised his camera phone, stepped closer to the branch, crouched a little and then carefully aimed at the walking stick insect when a small hard object struck the back of his head, interrupting his shot. He looked behind him and saw no one. He craned his neck upward at the sky and scrutinized the tiny seeds connected to the many leaves above him.

Bash said to Tiny, "A seed must've fallen."

Tiny, however, cocked his head to the side. With both ears sticking straight up, he kept his attention on the evergreens behind Bash.

As Bash returned to the walking stick, he repeated the sequence of his actions, ending them by carefully aiming his camera phone at the specimen when, again, another hard object struck nearly the same spot as before.

Tiny growled and Bash asked him, "What did you see? What's out there?"

Without shifting his gaze from the trees, Tiny pointed at an acorn on the ground with his right paw.

Bash bent down and picked it up. "Is this what hit me?"

Tiny answered by flicking his ear.

Squatting, Bash leaned toward Tiny and whispered, "Do you see someone out there?"

Tiny shook his head, causing the metal T on his collar to jingle. He then lifted his nose and huffed.

"Do you smell someone out there?" Bash also lifted his nose and inhaled, but all he smelled was the earthy musk all around him.

As quick as a finger snap, Tiny's behavior changed. No longer stiff and cautious, he began bouncing up and down on his front paws while howling. When his tail wagged in excitement, unintentionally whipping Bash in the back, Bash straightened, perturbed, and said to Tiny, "I see what's going on." He dropped the acorn as he hollered into the trees, "Aunt Rae, we know it's you, so you can come out now."

Bash recognized his aunt's mischievous cackle as it drew near. The branches soon parted and his aunt stumbled out of the trees and onto the trail.

With a big grin, she said, "Hi, Bash." After releasing her handful of acorns, she brushed the dirt from her hands and continued, "I've been following you this whole time. I'm surprised you didn't know."

"I was focused on my scavenger list. It was Tiny's job to look out for goofballs, such as yourself." When Bash glanced at Tiny, however, he was disappointed to see the Great Shepherd nosing a weed rather than keeping watch.

His aunt chuckled and then asked, "How are you doing on your list?"

"I just have to find a walking stick and then get the pie." Bash raised his camera phone, leaned toward a tree in front of them and pressed the button. "Now I just need the pie. How about you? Are you almost finished with your list?"

"I finished my list before I started." Aunt Rae winked at him.

Bash narrowed his eyes. "You never gave yourself a list, did you?"

Aunt Rae shook her head. "Nope." Suddenly, she threw her arms around his shoulders. "I would never send you into these woods on a scavenger hunt alone. You could easily get hurt or eaten or hurt. So, I followed you."

"And threw acorns at my head."

"Only at the end."

"I had Tiny with me. I'm pretty sure I was safe."

Aunt Rae released Bash and they both looked at Tiny. No longer interested in the weed, Tiny now found a tent caterpillar to terrorize with his paws.

Bash shrugged. "Well, I'm sure if you had been a real threat, Tiny would've barked or something." He eyed his aunt. "You've always been good at sneaking up on people."

Aunt Rae nodded. "Oh, I know. It's a strength of mine."

"A definite skill."

"Thank you for noticing."

"Remember when you snuck up on my dad when he was trimming around the yard?"

"Yeah. That was poor timing on my part."

"He almost lost a toe."

"Moving on." Aunt Rae threaded her arm through his and they began to walk on the trail. "I just want you to know that I always have your back."

"I know that."

"And that I'm really glad you're my nephew."

"Thanks. Where is this conversation going?"

"Nowhere. I just feel bad that my coworkers are jerks and you're stuck with them."

"Well, I could stay with Stone and Zalen at their campsite."

Aunt Rae stopped. Without looking at him, she said, "Yes, you could. But, selfishly speaking, I don't want you to."

"Because you promised my parents that you won't let me out of your sight?"

Aunt Rae now faced him. "No. It's because I love having you with me. You can do no wrong in my book."

Bash thought for a brief second before asking, "Even when I sneak into your car like a stowaway?"

"Bash," Aunt Rae said warmly, "you can sneak into my car any day, anytime. Just sit in the front seat next time. I don't want you to lose consciousness anymore. It's dangerous."

They stared at each other for a moment and then both exploded in laughter, which caused Tiny to happily howl along. And, as the three of them strolled down the path with Bash in the middle of his aunt and Tiny, he said, "You know, Aunt Rae, your coworkers aren't that bad. I just think the tarot cards were a little too much for them to handle."

"You can say that again."

"Speaking of, what do you think is Kimmy's deep dark secret?"

"Oh, lord, who knows? It could be anything from cheating on her taxes to being the mafia godfather." Aunt Rae shrugged. "I wouldn't know where to begin my thinking on that."

"So, you think it's bad? Like criminal bad?"

"I think it's bad enough for her eyes to pop out of her head the way they did."

They were approaching the main entrance when a familiar voice ahead of them stopped their conversation. Bash saw Tonya around the small bend, talking on her cellphone. A cluster of trees acted as a veil, but he could clearly see her through the branches. Aunt Rae's hand lightly gripped his forearm and when he looked at her, she placed a finger against her lips. They both, as well as Tiny, remained motionless on the trail and listened.

"This connection is awful." Tonya then groaned. "No, I said con-nec-tion! Now, listen to me. I don't have much time. No, I said time!" She groaned again. "Hon, I know it's not ideal, but it's way better than my current situation!"

Aunt Rae's grip tightened as she quietly led Bash and Tiny to a nearby bush off the trail, still within eavesdropping distance. As Tonya turned toward them, the three of them quickly ducked behind the thick foliage, just in time to conceal themselves from Tonya's view.

"Hon," Tonya loudly continued, "I can't work for him anymore. I've tried to get on his good side, but he has none. And now he put this nitwit Rae in charge and she's worse than he is. You should see the scavenger list that she has for me, which I refuse to do." She groaned for the third time. "Sca-ven-ger!"

Bash looked at his aunt as she bit a fingernail. Tonya then grunted, causing Bash to refocus his attention on her.

"Are you there?" Tonya hollered into her phone. "Can you hear me? Look, I recently realized I'm tired of being stuck in a hard place. So, I'm going to accept it, even with the pay cut." There was a pause before she yelled, "No! I said stuck!" Tonya tilted her head back in despair. "Fine. I won't do anything until I come home and we talk. But this offer isn't going to be around forever." After she disconnected, Tonya strangled her cellphone and stomped past them.

When the coast was clear, Bash said to his aunt, "Hey. I don't want to brag or anything, but it sounds like the tarot cards were right again. Her first card said that she was stuck between a rock and hard place. And see? She is."

Aunt Rae spit out a bitten piece of her fingernail. "Am I really worse than Travis?"

Bash placed his hand on her shoulder in comfort. "Aunt Rae, what she thinks doesn't matter. What *really* matters is that the tarot cards were right." He patted her once and then said, "I'm tired of hiding in foliage. This is the second time today that we did this, Aunt Rae."

Aunt Rae did not rise from her squatting position, however. She actually sat down on the dirt and leaves, nibbling a new fingernail. "I don't want to go," she mumbled. "I want to stay behind the bush."

"Why? Are you pouting about something?"

She spit out a fingernail remnant. "Am I a mean person, Bash?"

"No, of course not. If anything, you're *snarky*. Not all the time, though. Now, let's go. I'm sure there's another apple pie at the main entrance store. I'll take a picture of it and then we can eat it." Aunt Rae glared at him, provoking him to ask, "Why are you looking at me like that? Tons of other people have called you snarky. My mom, my dad. Even Grandma and Grandpa."

"It's the way you said *snarky*. It sounded like an autoimmune disorder."

"I didn't mean it to be. I still love you. Now, let's go."

As Bash began to rise, Aunt Rae grabbed his arm and pulled him down, saying, "I love you more. Now, listen, I gotta know. Am I mean snarky?"

"No, you're not mean snarky. Just snarky. And sometimes judgmental."

"Whoa." Her gray eyes clouded. "What did you say?"

Heavy footsteps sounded, saving Bash from walking this shaky plank of a conversation. Unfortunately, it also meant remaining behind the bush. As Bash peered around the large shrub, he saw Matt carrying a dead deer over his shoulders. Bash scooted closer to his aunt and placed his finger to his lips, signaling for her silence. She gave him a quizzical look, so he mouthed the word *werewolf* to her. She rolled her eyes, so he mouthed another word to her: *judgmental.* This caused his aunt to inhale and purse her lips together. She was about to stand when Jen's voice called to Matt.

"Is that a fresh one?"

"No. It's already been gutted."

"Dammit. You know what this means."

"Yep."

"Well, take it to the-"

"I know, Ma. This isn't my first rodeo."

Bash nudged his aunt in her ribs, whispering, "Hey, Matt is Jen's son. That's interesting."

Aunt Rae returned both the nudge and the whisper. "What's more interesting is why isn't carrying a dead deer Matt's first rodeo?"

Bash replied, "Maybe keeping the campground dead-deer free is part of his job?"

New voices rose above them on the trail. Both Bash and Aunt Rae leaned over to see who approached, but Bash saw nothing. He peered behind him at Tiny who remained laying on the ground with his head up, but his eyes were closed. He seemed happy enough, panting and drooling in the cool shade of the forest. Bash then heard Jen speak.

"Oh, great. Tom's coming. Quick. Go that way. And don't let him see you."

Bash and Aunt Rae stared at each other as Matt fled down another trail while Jen retreated from wherever she came.

Bash whispered, "We have a window here. Let's follow Matt. He's up to something."

His aunt held onto his arm and shook her head. "No. I'm not following anyone."

"Fine. We won't follow Matt. But we gotta go anyway. The hour for the scavenger hunt is almost up and I need the pie. Let's go."

"I'm staying. I don't want to run into creepy Dark Ranger Tom."

"Aunt Rae, your ears must be plugged. I said pie."

It was too late. Dark Ranger Tom entered the scene with a young brunette by his side. She had the figure of a yoga instructor and hung onto every single one of Tom's words.

Tom spoke smoothly to her as they passed the bush. "I know we just kind of met, but I feel like I've known you forever."

Miss Yoga giggled. "I bet you say that to all the new campers."

Tom laughed. "Just the pretty ones."

She playfully slugged him and cooed, "I'm looking forward to seeing you tonight."

Drawing her closer, he said, "You bring yourself and I'll bring the red wine, chocolate sauce and whip cream."

"That sounds delicious," she said as they both laughed while descending the trail.

Bash nudged his aunt. "That sounds like your kind of dessert."

Aunt Rae was in the process of gagging. "Not anymore."

Checking the time, Bash had five minutes to find an uncrushed pie in order to check off all of the items on his scavenger list. He quickly stood and Tiny sprang to his feet, eyes wide open now. Bash said to Aunt Rae, "There are a lot of shenanigans happening in these woods today." He offered his hand to her. "Now, please, let's go and get some pie."

·   ·   ·

It was a thirty-minute hike along the lake-side footpath that led from their campsite on the south end of Wolves Lake to the beach, which was on the north-west part of the lake. More north than west. And the shortcut on the map was too rough of terrain for Zalen in his sandals, causing a mild frustration to rise inside of Stone. Deep down, though, Stone knew his frustration stemmed from something other than Zalen's footwear. Now reclining on the plastic white rungs of a chaise lounge chair, Stone draped his left arm over his face, moaning. The oppressive looming bluffs on the east side of the lake seemed to be judging him about how he was handling Rachel. And he felt that they were judging him very harshly. He could sense it and moaned again.

The moaning wasn't helping him cool off and neither were his jeans, even though the bottoms were now rolled up to his knees and his tennis shoes now rested on the sand. One sock was almost off his entire foot while the other discarded sock was on his overturned shoe. Stone wiggled his bare toes while complaining, "Why does the sun have to be so hot?"

"Well, my friend," Zalen began as he stared at the sudoku puzzle in his hand, "it's July and it's quarter to three, which is usually the hottest part of the day."

"It was a rhetorical question." He shot a disappointed look at Zalen who also reclined on a chaise lounge chair that he first covered with a beach towel. "Where did you get that drink?"

Sipping from a tall plastic glass, filled with ice and topped with a lemon wedge, Zalen replied, "From the beach hut. It's right over there." Using his green marker pen as a pointer, he motioned over his shoulder.

Stone looked behind him and saw a small blue building with a flat lighter blue roof. There was a large sign on top, advertising merchandise anywhere from sunscreen to first aid supplies. Tons of red plastic buckets ordained the front of the hut and were filled with a variety of floats and sand toys. Beach umbrellas in all different colors and sizes leaned against the side of the hut. On the other side were two large windows, rectangularly-shaped. One window served food and drinks while the other window served customers buying some form of a commodity.

Stone glanced at Zalen. He not only had a drink, but also a large beach umbrella that he stuck in the sand. It created a nice shade to shield him from the harsh sun. And only him.

"When did you get the umbrella?"

"When I got my drink."

"Well, when did you get your drink?"

"About ten minutes ago. You were moaning when I left and when I returned."

"I didn't moan that whole time."

"Yes, you did. It reminded me of a nature show I watched the other night. There was a distressed deer stuck in a barbed wire fence." Zalen smiled and filled in a sudoku box with a number, using his green marker pen. Then he quickly crossed it out.

Stone muttered, "You have so many green marks on that page, why don't you just color the whole thing in?"

Zalen ignored the comment and said, "I know why you were moaning, Stone, and you can't keep lying to Rae. You need to tell her about your-"

Stone loudly shushed him. "Leave me alone."

"So, you want me to leave or you want me to stop bothering you?"

Stone shot him another disappointed look. "Stop bothering me."

"Then you should say *let* me alone."

Draping his arm over his face again, Stone said, "I change my mind. Leave me alone."

Zalen chuckled. "Okay, my friend, I'll see you later."

As Zalen shifted in his chair, Stone grabbed his arm. "Just sit your ass down."

Zalen happily obeyed. "Look, Stone, I know you're scared of your ability."

"She'll never understand it."

"Give her a chance."

"I did. It didn't turn out well."

"Really? When was this?"

Sitting straight up, Stone turned his cap around so the bill shielded his face. He then swung his legs over the side of the chair and took a deep breath. On the exhale, he said to Zalen, "Never. I'm lying. To your face. I was just hoping it would stop you from talking."

Zalen smiled widely. "Lying to Rae isn't going to solve anything."

"Telling her the truth isn't going to solve anything either. It'll just make things even more murky. It'll be like treading water in quicksand."

Zalen nodded. "With weights tied around your ankles."

Stone raised his hands to the heavens. "Exactly! Now you get it! Now you see why I can't be with her." He shook his head. "I can't. She deserves someone who can protect her, not someone who has weird visions that feel like they are getting stronger."

Zalen wore the most serious facial expression that Stone ever saw. "Stone," he said, "that path has been well traveled. It's time to move on."

"What do you mean?"

"You thought you'd bring danger to her three weeks ago and you actually saved her."

"I didn't save her. I arrived late, Zalen. She would've died, if it hadn't been for-"

"No, my friend, you misunderstand. You saved her way before that." Zalen looked at the puzzle and wrote the number nine in a box. "So, don't start thinking that being with Rae will put her in danger again. That's not true at all. Don't drag this out. It gets old after a while." He changed the nine to an eight. "Now, if you'll excuse me, I'll leave you alone." Zalen rocked and rolled himself off the chaise lounge chair.

"Where are you going? You're not seriously leaving me alone, are you?"

Zalen said, "I'm just going to the bathroom." Chuckling, he shook his finger at Stone. "You're starting to become a clingy friend, my friend."

As Zalen ambled from the beach, Stone thought about the words that his shoddy empathic friend just said about Rachel and him. And he wondered how much of it was shoddy? How much of it was accurate? And did Zalen just call him clingy?

CHAPTER EIGHTEEN

When Rae, Bash and Tiny arrived at the north park office, the rest of the team was waiting for them at a picnic table near the entrance. All of them except for Tonya. Rae, feeling responsible for Tonya's absence, audibly sighed and Bash seemed to have understood the meaning behind that sigh. He swung his arm around her shoulder and began his pep talk.

"You can't win them all, Aunt Rae." He smiled at her. "Four out of five isn't bad. That's eighty percent. A passing grade." Tiny yipped in agreement as Bash continued, "And look at these guys. They all found the food items, at least."

Indeed, they all did. In fact, they also had paper plates, napkins and cold cans of soda. Rae, Bash and Tiny were greeted with plates holding a peanut butter and jelly sandwich with Chuffles on the side.

Confused, Rae asked, "Who bought all this stuff? Who bought the peanut butter?"

Chuck raised his hand. "I bought peanut butter. I ran into Tonya who made it clear to me that she wasn't participating in the scavenger hunt." Chuck shrugged. "I remembered that she had peanut butter on her list and you can't have a pb and j without the pb. So, I bought it. Travis bought the plates, napkins and soda."

Blinking in surprise, Rae looked at Travis who had dirt splotches on both cheeks. He was in the process of taking a selfie.

Then he futzed with his cellphone and Rae assumed that he sent that picture to Seth. Afterward, Travis cleaned his face with a wet wipe that appeared in his hand like a magician's trick. When Rae shook her head at him, he asked defensively, "What? I'm doing my best, Rae."

"I know and I appreciate it. Thanks for chipping in for the plates and soda."

"And napkins," Travis added. "Why are you looking at me like that?"

Rae replied, "I'm trying to figure out where you're keeping the wet wipes."

"I have travel packets in all of my pockets. Jealous?"

Rae shook her head. "Not at all. I was just thinking that a *kind* thing for you to do would be to share your wet wipes with everyone." She smiled at him as he intently stared at her.

"Fine." Travis relinquished a small packet from his back pocket and tossed it on the picnic table. "Have at it." While the group passed the wet wipes around their circle, Travis said, "I didn't find one item on my list, other than the jam. And I tried, Rae. I tried."

"Really?" she asked doubtfully. "How long did you try?"

"Five minutes, if you must know. And it was five minutes of pure torture."

Kimmy meekly raised her hand. "I found three items on my list. A moth, a gray car, which was my something gray, and white bread." She beamed. "That was fun."

Chuck raised his hand. "I also found three things. A dragonfly, a Blue Spruce and Chuffles. And I agree with Kimmy. It was fun."

"Well, isn't that special?" Travis spoke with an edge to his tone.

With peanut butter stuck to his cheeks, Bash excitedly said, "I found all five!"

Wagging his tail, Tiny celebrated with Bash, but Travis tsked. "Really? Weren't you supposed to find a pie? Cuz I don't see the pie."

Bash paused and then looked at Rae. She defended her nephew to Travis. "Okay, nitpicker, so he has four items. He still won."

Bash pointed to the north park office. "I could still run and get it, if everyone still wants some?"

The group agreed that pie would be a great addition to the early supper and, just as Bash took off, Travis stopped him, calling him back. After retrieving his wallet, Travis handed Bash a five dollar bill while saying, "You're going to need this to pay for the pie. Now, Rae, take a picture of me giving your nephew my money."

As Travis posed with a big smile plastered on his face, Bash looked a little confused and Rae snapped the picture on her phone. "Perfect," she said to Travis. "It looks like you're paying him to be your friend."

"Just send me the pic." Travis then nodded at Bash. "I want the change." Bash saluted, turned on his heels and sprinted to the north park office with Tiny at his side.

Chuck suggested to the group, "Hey, maybe we should take a picture of all of us?"

Travis replied, "Why?" He looked at Rae and sighed. "It's another failed activity, Rae. The winner of this scavenger hunt was your nephew and he's not even an employee of my company. Plus, we lost Tonya. What's next, Rae? Walking on hot lava? Should we take a picture of that?"

"Oh, come on," Rae said, "be nice."

"We're not *really* having another team activity today, are we?" Chuck wiped the sweat from his brow. "I thought we agreed to one activity per day."

Travis scowled. "One *good* activity. However, I'm changing it to two *good* activities per day. Right now, we are oh for two."

Before Rae could speak, Kimmy meekly raised her hand again and said, "I think we should spend the rest of the day doing an independent self-reflection activity."

Travis straightened and placed his hands on his hips. "That's actually a great idea, Kimmy. I should've made you The Team Building Committee."

While eating her sandwich, Rae jumped at the chance and spoke with a mouthful, "She can have it!"

Shaking his head, Travis said to Rae, "Nope." He turned to Chuck and Kimmy. "Now, if you'll excuse me, I'm starting my independent whatever right now." As he walked away, he called over his shoulder, "Hey, Rae, tell Bash that he can give me my change later."

"What about the pie?" Chuck asked Travis. "Don't you want any?" When Travis didn't respond, Chuck looked at Rae and asked, "Why do I bother?"

Rae shrugged. "I don't know."

Kimmy brightened the mood by saying, "That'll just be more pie for us."

At that moment, they all heard the park office door open and watched as Bash bounded from the building with the pie resting in his outstretched hands. Tiny, who waited patiently outside the office, joined Bash and they ran happily across the grass to the picnic table. Unfortunately, neither Bash nor Tiny saw the tree root breaching the ground like a whale in the ocean. Before Rae could say *yikes*, Bash tripped and hurdled Tiny who also tripped and they both somersaulted over the pie, obliterating it.

Rae sighed. She apologetically looked at Chuck and then at Kimmy. "I don't have any cash for another pie."

Chuck smiled. "I don't either."

Instead of cash, Kimmy offered her wisdom. "Maybe this is God's way of saying none of us need pie?"

"I'm okay!" Bash hollered as he slowly stood. Tiny began eating the bits of apple pie on the ground as Bash added, "Sorry about that!"

Rae gave her nephew a thumbs up and told Chuck and Kimmy to leave the clean-up for them. Her two coworkers gratefully, quickly departed and Rae sauntered over to Bash to help him pick up the pie scraps. It was hard with Tiny's tongue always being in the way, but they managed. And when they began gathering the dinner trash, Bash said a curious thing.

"Aunt Rae," he began, "it just dawned on me. Where was Tiny?"

Rae shoved the used paper plates into the trash receptacle. "What do you mean? He's right there, trying to eat the peanut butter container. You tripped over him, remember?"

"No, not our Tiny. I mean Travis's Tiny. He wasn't strapped to Travis's chest."

Rae froze in thought. She looked at Bash, narrowing her eyes. "That is a good question. His Tiny has always been strapped to his chest, as of late."

Bash shoved a handful of Chuffles into his mouth and spoke while crunching on them, "Maybe he left his Tiny at the campsite?"

"I don't think he would leave his precious Tiny unattended in the middle of nowhere, which means…" Rae crossed her arms. "He's the one who's up to something."

∎   ∎   ∎

Tiny thoroughly enjoyed spending the rest of the afternoon with his two favorite people in the whole wide world. And he could tell that Angry Rae and Nice Bash thoroughly enjoyed spending their time with him too, as they not only bought a brand new can of tennis balls, but also threw the new balls to him all afternoon. Every once in a while, they stopped to take a long walk and then Angry Rae would look around like she lost something. Nice Bash would take out a large piece of paper that he kept folded in his back pocket. Whatever that paper was, it always helped them find their way to another area where a good game of fetch awaited.

When the sun lowered, Angry Rae and Nice Bash began their long, tired trek back to the campsite, but first stopped at the north park office. Angry Rae entered the building while Nice Bash sat on the steps with Tiny, giving him a much needed ear scratching. Tiny leaned into Nice Bash and was soon relaxing across the boy's lap. Nice Bash didn't mind though. He never did.

When Angry Rae emerged from the north park office, she carried a bag full of sweet-smelling goodies. He stuck his nose inside the bag for a better whiff and Angry Rae lifted the bag over her head, preventing his drool from dripping on the food.

"Hey," Angry Rae scolded, "this isn't for you. Chocolate isn't good for dogs."

Nice Bash patted Tiny's head as they walked the trail along the water's edge, following the beam of Angry Rae's flashlight. "Sorry, buddy," he said. "You had a lot of pie today. You really don't need to eat any s'more." Nice Bash laughed, which Tiny didn't appreciate. He always had room for s'more, as the boy put it.

CHAPTER NINETEEN

When Rae, Bash and Tiny returned to the campsite, two of them began building a fire while the third one licked himself. As Bash configured the firewood in the pit, Rae lit the fire and they both roasted their marshmallows on some sticks. Soon, the team members arrived, one by one, like ants to a crumb. First, Chuck arrived. Then Kimmy. Eventually Tonya. And, finally, Travis. This time, his Tiny was strapped to his chest - a detail that wasn't lost on Rae.

"Hey, Travis," Rae began, "I couldn't help, but notice that your cute little Tiny wasn't with us at our pb and j gathering after the scavenger hunt. How I missed him so." She and Travis exchanged a scrutinizing eye and the conversation turned into a tense verbal tennis match. Rae served first. "Where was he?"

Travis returned. "He took a nap."

Rae gave an effortless forehand. "Where?"

Flippant, Travis made a backhanded comment. "I didn't know you had such an inquisitive mind, Rae. Tiny was in the tent."

Lobbing over an easy question, Rae asked, "All by himself?"

Travis nailed the overhead. "Everyone needs a break from certain *snarky* behavior. Can't you understand that?"

Rae pursed her lips. Then she said, "Interesting word choice."

Travis showed no emotion. "Sound travels in the woods. So, be careful, Rae." His eyes suddenly brightened and his tone changed to cheer as he addressed the team, "Who wants a marshmallow?"

Rae caught the marshmallow that Travis tossed to her and she stuck it on the end of her stick, wondering what Travis exactly heard and what did she and Bash exactly say? Did he listen to Tonya's phone conversation too? Her eyes flashed to Tonya who stacked her s'more with extra chocolate bars. Rae replayed what Tonya said about her. Was Rae really worse than Travis? Some sorry part of Rae awakened and she decided to mend this fence, wanting to prove to her coworker and to herself that she was nothing like Travis.

With a warm smile, Rae handed the marshmallow bag to Tonya who gave a stiff head shake. Rae then offered her another graham cracker and Tonya rolled her eyes. *No matter,* Rae thought. *I will keep killing her with kindness during this retreat. That'll show her. For now, however, I'll enjoy* my *treat.* She turned to Bash and gave him a loving look. *And I'll enjoy being with Bash.*

As everyone sat around the fire in folding chairs, eating and enjoying the quiet night, peace finally found the team. There was something about the popping snaps and the soft underlying whoosh of a campfire that instantly calmed people's anxiety and induced sleep, including dogs. Tiny snored at Bash's feet. The others were awake, but barely. As they sat under the dark night sky, the team seemed to be resisting the urge to close their eyelids. The relaxed mood felt like a welcoming grandmother with the most comforting hug. No one spoke and Rae relished the harmony, knowing that the tarot card catastrophe and the scavenger hunt were all in the past.

Sighing, Rae enjoyed being in the audience while the dancing flames took center stage. They twisted, twirled and arched gracefully around the pyramid of blazing wood. Envy set in Rae's heart. How she wished to be so free! Free to speak her mind more or free to do something for herself. Even to be free of her own inhibitions. Free like fire. Rae brought her knees up, hugging them to her chest.

She said to the group, "If you guys could do or be anything, what would you do?"

Initially, the team maintained their gazes on the mesmerizing campfire. Bash broke the trance by raising his hand. "Teachers always ask this question on the first day of school and my answer has always been the same since kindergarten."

"Let me guess," Travis said. "You want to be a fireman."

Bash shook his head. "A medical examiner. Plan B is a paranormal investigator."

To Rae's surprise, no one made a snide comment. Instead, they all nodded approvingly.

"Being a medical examiner sounds fascinating." Tonya crossed her leg. "I, too, had an interest in crime when I was younger. I wanted to be a lawyer and then eventually a judge on the Supreme Court."

Again, snide remarks remained unspoken and Chuck ventured next. "Painting has also interested me."

Rae asked, "Which artist inspires you? Monet? Seurat?"

Chuck replied, "Benjamin Moore. I love painting houses. The exterior. For one summer in college, I did that. It was awesome. I was outside, no pressure, no drama. Just me and the paint sprayer, moving back and forth, back and forth. Very therapeutic."

Rae agreed. "Sounds nice."

Chuck asked her, "What would you do?"

Grinning, Rae answered, "Well, when I was a kid, I loved detective shows. Then, in college, watching people mix drinks fascinated me. So, I'd be a part-time private eye and a part-time bartender."

Tonya smirked. "But you don't like alcohol."

Travis reasoned, "That's why she'd make a good bartender. She wouldn't drink the inventory."

Kimmy then spoke. "If I could do anything and get away with it, I'd raid Fort Knox and live out my days on the island of St. Helena."

Excited, Bash said, "Hey! Fun fact. The oldest living land animal lives there. It's a Seychelles giant tortoise and he's 185 years old. His name is Jonathon."

Kimmy added, "I also have a fun fact. Napoleon was exiled to St. Helena and died there at the age of fifty-one. It's still one of the most remote places on earth. It's only accessible by water." Her eyes glistened as she said wistfully, "No in-laws. Pure heaven."

As they all nodded in unison, Bash asked Travis, "What about you?"

Squinting his eyes, Travis stroked his Tiny's head. He proudly lifted his chin and said, "Broadway." Slowly nodding, he softly repeated, "Broadway."

"Like, you'd live there?"

"No, Bash, I would be *on* Broadway. I would have my own musical called *Travis* and it would be the longest running, most successful Broadway musical in history."

"Wow!" Kimmy exclaimed. "Do you sing and dance?"

"No." Travis kissed the top of his Tiny's head. "I don't have one musical bone in my body. And I can't keep a beat."

A voice unexpectedly sounded from the darkness. "Travis, if you had a musical on Broadway, it would be called *I'm a Pompous Ass and I'll Ruin Your Life*."

The team turned their heads toward the mysterious visitor. As Rae scrutinized the blackness, searching for the source, the peaceful tone of the evening dissolved like sugar in water. From the shadows, a figure formed as it stepped into the firelight. First, it was just a silhouette of long legs, a torso and an oddly-shaped head. As Rae's eyes adjusted, she frowned from recognizing the man with the deformed head. Only, his head was fine. It was the Stetson hat that bothered her.

"Well, I'll be damned," said Travis as he remained sitting, stroking his Tiny's head.

"Funny." Tom smiled. "I have damned you countless times. *Countless*. Really, it's been too many to count."

Travis narrowed his eyes. "Got it." Casually crossing his legs, he said, "I see you're still pissed off."

"Wouldn't you be?"

Rae bit her fingernail as Travis chuckled. "I'm always pissed off."

"Oh, that's right." Tom sneered. "You're always pissed off because, instead of having a heart, you have a sump pump, pushing diseased boiling sludge through your conceited veins."

Travis sounded smug. "Something like that."

Tom's gaze strayed from Travis and settled on Rae. "Is Travis the boss who you wanted me to arrest?"

Arching his eyebrows, Travis turned to Rae. "*You* wanted *me* arrested? When was this?"

Shifting in her seat, she shrugged while explaining, "Earlier today after I met Tom. It was a joke."

Travis tsked. "It wasn't a very funny one."

Disagreeing, Tom shook his head and said, "I think it is hilarious."

"Well, you would." Chuck startled Rae by speaking. "You always laughed at other people's misfortunes." Chuck's brown eyes turned a dangerous dark brown that Rae had never seen in her coworker.

Tom squinted. "Wow. I didn't recognize you, Chuck. Did you lose weight?"

Glaring at Tom was Chuck's response.

"Huh." Tom seemed impressed. "Look, I want to apologize about how things went down with us, Chuck. I should never have gotten involved with your fiancèe." Rae bit another fingernail as Tom continued, "I'll tell you what, we actually broke up, so you can have her back."

Ugh, that was harsh, Rae thought. Her stomach twisted as she looked at her nephew. She could tell he was faring as well as she since his raised eyebrows now reached his hairline.

With a disgusted tone, Tonya said to Tom, "You haven't changed at all."

Tom's eyes popped open. "Well, you have, Tonya! Did you put on all the weight that Chuck lost?"

Tonya snapped. "Screw you."

"Oh, no." Tom shook his head, raising his voice. "Screw all of you! You each had a hand in ruining my career *and* my life *and* you all know it!"

Rae noticed that everyone lowered their eyes to the ground when Tom said that, except for Travis. He calmly watched Tom's tirade.

"Tonya," Tom raged. "You didn't forget how you stole my design and passed it off as your own, which earned you The National Design Award, did you? I sure didn't. And you, Chuck," Tom pointed at him while saying, "before I messed around with your personal life, you messed around with my work life by intercepting a scheduled meeting with my biggest client and then stealing that account." He then searched the darkness. "And where's little Kimmy? I know she's here. I can feel her staring at me with those cunning eyes." He found her. "Hi, Kimmy. What you did was downright illegal. You're just lucky I couldn't prove it."

"That's enough, Tom." Travis sounded bored. "Leave my team alone."

Ignoring Travis, Tom spoke to Rae. "Kimmy tried to kill me. With her car. She tried to run me down in a parking lot. She succeeded in running over my feet."

Kimmy softly objected. "I forgave myself. Recently." Kimmy glanced at Bash who was staring at Rae.

Tom laughed. "You're all so nuts! But you." He shook his finger at Travis. "You're the worst one."

Travis offhandedly said to Rae, "He thinks I'm responsible for defamation of his character. He never worked in the graphic design field again and he blames me."

Rae looked at Tom who grinded his teeth. He raised his clenched fists and said, "One day, Travis, you'll get yours. I just hope I'm there to see it."

Fortunately for the team, Tom's walkie talkie sprang to life and a female voice on the other end spoke, requesting his help with a raccoon. Raising the device to his mouth, Tom replied, "Be right there, Jen. I just finished dealing with some trash." Before leaving, Tom gave Rae a stern look and warned her. "Watch your back with this group. They're all psychopaths."

When Tom was gone, Rae felt everyone's mood drop to a new low. She had four fingers in her mouth and chewed on all of them. In the end, she chuckled. Not because she thought it was funny. She laughed because she felt so uncomfortable that she really didn't know what else to do. Things had been going so well and now everyone seemed to have lost the ability to show emotion. They were on a good path. Now, they all just stared at the fire with blank eyes. It was Travis who ended up breaking the icy silence and turned to her while asking, "I suppose you want to know what that was all about?"

At first, Rae nodded and then ended up shaking her head. Then she shrugged. Speaking with her fingers still in her mouth, she said, "I don't know. Do I?"

Tonya spoke first. "Kimmy wasn't trying to run him over with her car, Rae. We had a bet to see how close she could come to running him down. That's all."

Incredulous, Rae asked, "That's all?"

Kimmy meekly explained, "It was after a Christmas party. The four of us were at a bar and he hit on me."

Tonya explained in more depth. "It was Kimmy, Chuck, Tom and myself. Tom was disgusting and very drunk." She paused. "Well, we all kinda were drunk. But he wouldn't take no for an answer. I tried to stop him and he pushed me, making me fall over a stool."

Kimmy said, "If it hadn't been for Chuck, who knows what would've happened."

Rae looked at Chuck who said, "I got him out of the building and threatened to call the cops. He quickly left."

Tonya shook her head. "Or so we thought. After things died down, Chuck went home and Kimmy and I were by our cars when we saw Tom walking toward us in the parking lot. Kimmy bet me ten bucks to see how close she could come to hitting him with her car. I joked and told her to go for it. Next thing I knew, she was inside her car, driving right for him. He moved out of the way and Kimmy never stopped."

Bash raised his hand. "I'm confused about the bet."

Kimmy shook her head. "Don't be. It really wasn't a bet. It was a dare."

By now, Rae's mouth hung so open that it almost hit the ground. She looked at Travis. "Did you know about this?"

Travis nodded. "I did. I found out the next day when Tonya told me everything. I didn't like how Tom acted toward Kimmy. His actions were so bad that it made Kimmy desperate enough to want to hit him with her car, which is unlike Kimmy. I debated about calling the police, but Kimmy didn't want that. She just wanted space from him. So, in the end, I thought the easiest way to get Tom out of everyone's lives was to fire him."

Bash raised his hand again and asked Kimmy, "Why didn't you want to call the police?"

Kimmy answered, "I tried to run over Tom and was afraid of being arrested."

"But he forced himself on you, Kimmy." Rae reasoned. "That's worse than running his toe over with your car."

"Well, he just kissed me. Twice. It was gross. I was trying to push him off and Tonya stepped in to help."

Rae countered, "That's still wrong." She then gestured to Tonya. "And he pushed you down? I would've called the police."

Tonya rubbed her hands together. "The problem was we were all drunk. As far as Tom pushing me down, he really just nudged me and I lost my balance, which made me fall on my rear end. If I had been sober, I probably wouldn't have moved. So, it wasn't like a brutal attack or anything. Besides, it doesn't really matter anymore."

"Yeah, but-" Rae began.

"Drop it, Rae." Travis ordered. "None of us want to talk about Tom anymore."

As the team nodded, Rae blew out a loud sigh. And then she picked up the conversation from right where she dropped it. "Tonya, did you really steal Tom's design to win an award for yourself?"

Tonya spoke sternly. "Absolutely not. We were supposed to work together on it, but he only critiqued what I would do. He didn't come up with anything other than the color scheme. Big deal."

"I see," said Rae. She turned to Chuck. "Did you really take Tom's best client?"

Surprisingly, Travis replied on behalf of Chuck. "I told Chuck to take Tom's client because Tom was late to the meeting. Very late. It was either have Chuck step in or lose the deal. Chuck did nothing wrong. But Tom wanted to blame Chuck, even though I told him that I was the one who made the decision."

Rae crossed her arms. "So, Tom blamed Chuck for client theft and Tom gets back at Chuck by stealing the fiancèe."

"Yep," Chuck said. "After Tom was fired, I thought he was long gone until I came home a couple months later and found him with her."

Tonya interjected, "I'm sure Tom had planned that the whole time."

Rae glanced at Bash whose eyes pretty much bulged out of their sockets at this point. She then studied Travis.

Without looking at her, he asked, "What?"

"Did you really defame his character?"

Travis shook his head. "His character was already defamed. He did that himself. The only thing I did was make a few calls to ensure everyone in the business knew his true character." He now looked straight into her eyes. "Got a problem with that?"

Rae swallowed hard and slowly shook her head. "Nope. Not at all." And she really didn't have a problem with Travis's choice to ruin Tom's career. It was beyond the scope of her job's responsibility. She did have a problem though. It was knowing that there was an angry park ranger out there in the dark, probably wishing bad things on everyone at this particular campsite. The other only problem she had was not knowing if Tom thought she was guilty by association and, therefore, a horrible person like her team. Not that she cared whether or not Tom thought she was bad. She cared because she wasn't sure what he would do to her, if he did.

■　　■　　■

Bash pulled on his bottom lip. Feeling a little anxious and somewhat stressed or maybe sad at the turn of events, he really thought that what everyone needed now was a fun game. In his house, whenever someone was a little blue, his mom would bring out a game and that instantly cheered everyone up. So, courageously, Bash made the suggestion of playing a campfire game. It was called Two Truths and a Lie.

"So," he explained, "we each have to tell two truths about ourselves and one lie and then the rest of us have to guess which is the lie. Okay?"

Travis blurted, "I'm straight. Tom and I are best buds. I love playing stupid games while camping."

While biting a fingernail, Aunt Rae said, "Those are all lies."

"Okay, how about this?" Travis stood. "I hate Tom. I'm going to bed. I'll see all of you in the morning."

Aunt Rae said, "Those are all truths."

By now, Travis approached the tent, briefly fought with the zipper and then entered. The other three coworkers followed their leader into the tent, even wearing the same sore expression.

Bash whispered to his aunt, "So, when Kimmy tried to run down Tom with her car, that was premeditated murder, right?"

Aunt Rae replied, also in a whisper, "I honestly don't know. Maybe?" She leaned over the arm of her chair. "Let this be a lesson to you and never get drunk. People do stupid stuff when they're drunk."

"More interesting, Aunt Rae, is that you were right about Kimmy's deep dark secret being an act of crime."

"I'll pat myself on the back later." She returned to her previous slouch.

"That's two for two."

"What?"

"Well, two of the tarot card readings have been accurate. Tonya is caught between a rock and hard place and Kimmy has, or rather had, a deep dark secret. Just like their cards said."

"Oh, boy."

"Which makes me worried for Chuck. His card was about a personal disaster."

"Let's change the subject."

"I wonder if his personal disaster has anything to do with poor Tom."

Still whispering, Aunt Rae shot back. "*Poor* Tom? Why do you think he deserves compassion?" Bash shrugged and she continued, "He's no martyr. I mean, this team isn't perfect by any means, but Tom gives me the chills. And not the good chills."

As she returned her attention to the fire, Bash listened to the others, rummaging inside the tent. He could hear them talking very quietly to each other, but he couldn't make out the words.

"Psst." Bash nodded to his aunt. "What are they talking about in there?"

"I don't know and I don't want to know."

Now Bash leaned over the arm of his chair. "I was right about Tom stealing Chuck's fiancèe. And, not to unnerve you even more, but Travis pulled the Death card."

While keeping her head facing the fire, Aunt Rae shifted her eyes to Bash. She then leaned over the arm of her chair again and said, "We seriously need a topic change."

"Fine. Let's go see what Stone and Zalen are up to. I want to tell them about this."

Aunt Rae shot him a surprised look mixed with resentment. "No. I don't want to tell them about any of this. Number one, it's late."

"It's only around ten."

"And number two, Stone already thinks I'm accident prone around campsites. The nerve. I don't want to give him any reason to think I'm in more turmoil. He'll never leave my side then and I don't need anyone spying on me."

"I don't think Stone would spy *on* you. Maybe spy *after* you?"

Sitting back in her chair, Aunt Rae said, "We need another topic change. What activity should I have for this team tomorrow morning? I got nothing."

Bash pushed himself back into his chair and pulled on his lip. Then he remembered. "Let me check the map. I noticed that on the back, there was a list of activities." He reached into his back pocket and scanned the information, saying, "There's beach volleyball and tennis. You can have partners play against each other? Or there's hiking the bluffs, swimming in the lake or maybe even kayaking?" His face lit up. "Oh, I know! There's a cool obstacle course somewhere near Fun Warriors Ranch. It's just a short drive from here. We could do that. You know, relay teams of three. Chuck can be on our team."

Nibbling on a fingernail, his aunt remained thoughtful before finally saying, "You just gave me an idea."

"Obstacle course?"

"Nope. Something more daring."

"What is it?"

With a sly look, Aunt Rae teased, "You'll find out after breakfast."

"Well, that sounds both exhilarating and ominous. Speaking of," Bash said, "our hunt for The Ma'iingan Bluff Werewolf will begin at two-thirty in the morning."

"What do you mean *in the morning?* I'm pretty sure I didn't agree to that, especially since I don't think clearly between the twilight hours and noon."

Bash ignored her complaints. "So, be ready."

"You know, Bash, the deal should be off because your tarot card ice-breaker reading was disastrous."

"And you know, Aunt Rae, that our deal had nothing to do with the success of the readings. The deal was that I would handle the ice-breaker in exchange for my paranormal equipment. It was your idea to accompany me on the hunt. There was nothing stated about the tarot card activity having to be successful. And we already agreed on the time of two-thirty *in the morning.* If you don't remember, go back and reread that section."

. . .

Tiny awoke to the sound of dirt hitting the ground. He opened one eye to observe both Angry Rae and Nice Bash bending over, scooping up dirt with their hands and throwing the dirt on the flames. He huffed. Humans and the strange things that they do! He stood, placing himself alongside the fire. After lifting his hind leg, he released himself and the fire was doused in a matter of seconds. The flames stopped dancing and darkness invaded.

Vigorously scratching Tiny's ears, Nice Bash said, "Good job, Tiny."

Angry Rae held a light beam in her hand. "I must confess, Bash, I'm actually looking forward to the hunt. It sounds kind of interesting."

"Catching a werewolf sounds interesting to *you*?"

"Oh, no," Angry Rae scoffed. "That sounds preposterous because werewolves don't exist. I think the equipment sounds interesting. I'm looking forward to seeing how all of it works."

Tiny whimpered and Nice Bash said to him, "Don't worry, big guy, you can come too." This caused Tiny's tail to happily wag.

Angry Rae aimed the light at them. "Let's go to the nice bathroom in the family campground and get ready for bed. If we have to get up early, I want to go to bed sooner than later."

Pointing toward the tent where the muffled voices still were audible, Nice Bash asked, "What about them? Should we ask if they want to come with us? You know, in keeping with the team theme?"

Angry Rae's shoulders dropped. "Yeah, I suppose."

Tiny's ears straightened as he watched her creep toward the tent and quietly unzip the opening. Her head poked into the space and disappeared, which made Tiny nervous. He pranced on his two front paws, concerned that she no longer had a head. When Tiny heard Angry Rae clear her throat, though, he knew that she was still alive and he stopped moving his feet.

The soft conversation from within the tent ended as Angry Rae told them of the bedtime plans. The others declined her offer of driving to the nice bathroom in the west campground, which relieved Tiny. Even he knew that there wasn't enough room in her car for all of them. After that, he, Nice Bash and Angry Rae were soon on their way in the little blue coupe.

Tiny filled the backseat with his enormous body. The only way he fit in the space was to lay his backend on the seat, tucking his hind legs underneath his tush, and then to crouch on his front paws behind the front seats. Angry Rae kept the back window rolled down so that his tail could wave freely in the wind. This was very much appreciated. Tiny knew his tail needed a good airing-out from time to time. As for his head, the only thing he could do was stick it between the front seats, invading the space in the front of the car. He could easily lick the dashboard, but Angry Rae scolded him every time he tried.

"So," Nice Bash said while sitting on the right side of Tiny's snout. "Did you catch anything that they were talking about?"

As Angry Rae drove carefully on the curvy road, Tiny listened to the sound of crunching gravel underneath the tires. It was one of his favorite sounds. He then stretched his tongue toward the dashboard and Angry Rae nudged him with her shoulder. Tiny knew that this was her way of telling him to stop.

Nice Bash spoke again. "Aunt Rae, did you interrupt anything important?"

Tiny glanced at Angry Rae who seemed to be deep in thought. After a few moments, she finally replied, "I don't know what they were talking about, but I definitely interrupted them. There was a feeling in that tent. A strange feeling that I can't quite explain."

"Really? That's interesting. A strange feeling? Like what?"

Angry Rae shifted her position in the driver seat as she explained, "Well, I walked in and saw the four of them huddled together and talking like old friends. Only the topic was serious." She cranked the wheel around a tight corner. "It reminded me of high school when my friends would talk about me behind my back. They would stand close together and speak with hushed voices. It made me feel like I was on the outs, which I was."

Nice Bash lifted his chin, looking over Tiny's nose to face Angry Rae. "I don't think the team was talking about you. If anything, they were talking about Tom."

"Oh, I know," said Angry Rae. "I just realized at that moment that the four of them have a history that I'm not a part of. And that's fine. What bothers me, I guess, is realizing that I really am not part of this team. I know that I'm the new person in this group, but I just don't see how I'm ever going to fit in." She pulled into the parking lot by the nice bathroom in the west campground and parked her car. While unbuckling her seatbelt, she continued, "Why did Travis put me as team leader anyway? Even if I want to fit in with my team, it's clear that they don't want me to. I get the feeling that they like their group of four. That's what I interrupted."

"Maybe that's why Travis put you as team leader? To help you fit in better. I'm surprised at you, Aunt Rae." Bash leaned forward and peered under Tiny's chin at Angry Rae. "I never thought you would care about fitting in with this team."

"Me neither." Angry Rae opened the car door.

Tiny sensed that Angry Rae felt sad as they all emerged from the car with their bathroom kits. As she left the two of them and walked in the opposite direction, Tiny whined. She turned around and said off-handedly to him, "Don't worry about me, Tiny. Stay with Bash. I'll meet you both back at the car after I shower."

Tiny pranced on his two front paws, quietly huffing and puffing, until Nice Bash patted his back. He looked at the boy who said to him, "She's good. Now, come on. I desperately need to pee. And then I need to shower, brush my teeth and go to bed." Tiny noticed a growing twinkle in Nice Bash's eye as he bent down to whisper in Tiny's ear. "And then it'll be time to find The Ma'iingan Bluff Werewolf."

With a small bag in his hand, full of clean-smelling objects, Nice Bash quickly turned and marched toward the building. Tiny took a step to follow and then abruptly stopped. His ears shot straight up after hearing familiar voices. When he looked behind him, his keen eyesight saw Stone and Zalen hurrying past the bathroom and into the dark shadows of the night.

CHAPTER TWENTY

Stone had a good view of the north park office's entrance. This was where the guy with dreadlocks led them. Goosebumps formed on his arms as he glanced at the time on his cellphone. It was twenty minutes past ten. Then he glanced at his stakeout partner across the picnic table. Zalen's face shone in the glow of the lantern between them. He continued to work on the same sudoku puzzle as before. He had the same green marker pen poised in the same erect position. The only difference was Zalen wore a new hat.

Swatting insects from his face, Stone asked, "Now, when did you get that mosquito net hat?"

With his eyes lowered, Zalen focused on his puzzle as he spoke softly, "Not this again." He slowly wrote the number three in a box and then looked over the top edge of his page. "You're not the observant sort, are you? After I went into the north park office to use the bathroom, I found a nice selection of all types of hats." He lowered his eyes and furrowed his eyebrows before turning the three into an eight.

"I didn't see you wearing it when you got back." Stone then noticed the object leaning against the end of the table. "Did you buy another umbrella for Rae too?" Zalen nodded, prompting Stone to comment, "This one is bigger than the one you gave her before."

Zalen smiled while keeping his eyes on the puzzle. "You can never know how big the storm may get, my friend. Has there been any movement?"

"None whatsoever. You didn't happen to see him in the store?"

Shaking his head, Zalen replied, "No one that matches your description of being really tall, really thin and having long hair in dreadlocks. Although, I had a very nice conversation with the cashier. Her name is-"

"Jen. You told me this already."

"And she runs the place with her-"

"Mother-in-law and son."

Zalen lowered the book. "I told you about that too?" Stone nodded and Zalen said, "I don't remember saying any of that to you."

Grinning, Stone asked, "You're not the conscious sort, are you?"

Zalen capped his green marker pen before removing a new one from his breast pocket. "Anyway, once we find our target, are we going to warn him that he might be in danger?"

"Of course not. We've been over this, Zalen. We're just watching him and getting a better understanding of who he is." Stone shrugged. "I don't even know if he is the victim. He's just one of two possibilities. So, pay attention to your feelings when you see him. Got it?"

"Got it!" Zalen smiled, raising the book. He turned the page.

Stone asked him, "Did you finally finish the puzzle?"

"Nope, I'm starting a new one." He saluted with his pen. "With a new green marker."

Stone had a quip ready on his tongue, but his forearms tingled and his attention shifted to the sound of fast-approaching, dragging feet. Prissy appeared from the darkness with a look of intent. She trotted past them, rushing toward the north park office. Drumming his fingers on the table, Stone said, "I wonder what her emergency is?"

"Who?"

"Prissy."

"Oh, is she here?"

"She just ran by us. Maybe you should put that puzzle down and start paying attention?"

Zalen looked over the top edge of his book again. "How fast did she run?"

"What?" Annoyed, Stone raised his eyebrows. "How am I supposed to know how fast? She's not a car. She doesn't have a speedometer."

"I didn't hear her at all. Are you sure she ran?"

Stone massaged his eyes and forehead. "Fine. It was more like a shuffled jog. The point is she looked worried. Or stressed."

Closing his book, Zalen set it on the table with the pen resting on top. "I sure hope Rae's alright."

Now confused, Stone asked, "Why wouldn't she be? Do you feel something?"

"No." Zalen's smile widened. "Do you? Your tells are showing."

Stone looked down and realized he was rubbing his forearms. And he did feel strange, but it was a different strange. Not his normal ghost strange. He crossed his arms, stiffly replying, "Just bug bites."

Zalen picked up the puzzle book again. "They sell bug repellant in the north park office."

"No thanks." Stone felt the darkness of the night settle down on him. An eeriness always accompanied darkness for Stone. He shivered and said, "This is taking forever."

"Stakeouts usually do, my friend."

"Oh, I didn't know you were a stakeout expert. How many stakeouts have you been on?"

Zalen chuckled. "You make me laugh, my dude. I haven't been on one, but I've watched many on television. And every stakeout

I've watched, it's the people who are on the stakeout that always end up being watched instead."

Stone scoffed. "That's absurd." It wasn't absurd, though, and Stone knew it. His forearms tingled a little stronger and he peered into the blackness. He stood. For a minute. Or so. Just staring into the dark atmosphere around the lantern's warm light. There was a spot by the trees that captured Stone's attention. He couldn't really see the trees and he definitely couldn't see any form or outline, but he felt a presence. He knew someone was there. More unsettling, he kinda figured that someone was staring at him. "Someone's there."

Zalen said, "I don't see anyone."

As Zalen spoke, Stone continued to stare at the spot. He snatched his cellphone from the table and activated the flashlight. He pointed the beam at the spot. There was no one there; however, he heard retreating footsteps. Stone swept the beam and found the source of the feet. Striding toward the rear end of the park office was the tall, lanky guy with most of his dreadlocks pulled into a man bun. And in his grip was a styrofoam cooler leisurely swinging at his side.

Stone motioned to Zalen. "There. Now do you see him?" As Zalen squinted, he shook his head and Stone didn't wait any longer. "Come on, let's follow him." Stone quickly crept across the grass, following Dreadlocks to the back of the building. As he approached, Stone backed up to the siding and peeked around the corner. A back outdoor light shone brightly and Stone did not need to lean on his cellphone flashlight for any aid in visibility. His eyes darted in every direction, but they were only met with trees and a parking space, which was empty. A shoulder tap prompted Stone to look behind him. It was Zalen with the puzzle book tucked under his arm.

"Well, Stone, what happened?"

"What happened?" Stone snapped. "You were no help, that's what happened."

"So, you lost him?" Zalen smiled. "I didn't even see the guy. Of course, I don't see well in the dark." He rocked back on his heels. "Oh well, better luck next time, I guess."

Frustrated, Stone thrust his phone in his back pocket, signaling his agreement to Zalen that the stakeout was over, even though he momentarily stared in the direction of where he saw Dreadlocks. Zalen's words echoed in his head. *Oh well, better luck next time.* As they began their trek back to their campsite along the lake-side footpath, Stone quietly deliberated about Dreadlocks, and two questions surfaced, resting on his brain like lily pads on water. First, how long was Dreadlocks watching them and, second, was Dreadlocks a ghost?

. . .

Upon their return to the site, Bash felt refreshed and smelled a lot better. His aunt said so. And as he trailed after her into the tent with Tiny at his heels, Bash clutched his black case containing his paranormal equipment and glanced at the others as they lay awake inside their sleeping bags. Except for Travis, Bash noticed. He was on top of his sleeping bag, wearing satin pajamas.

When Bash tiptoed around the group, Tiny mimicked how Bash gingerly walked on his toes and even followed the same path, which was over Travis, around Chuck and between Tonya and Kimmy. He found some space in the back of the tent next to his aunt. After Bash unrolled his bag and squirmed into it, he watched as Tiny circled a small, but open area in the middle of the tent a few times before dropping to the ground. Tiny curled himself into a donut shape and rested his melon head on his paws. Tonya complained of Tiny's expansive body in their *person* tent, but Travis, surprisingly, shushed her and she quieted.

Bash snickered to himself and glanced at his aunt who was buried inside her bag, resembling a ball with a pillow on top of her head. He was about to say good night when Chuck spoke to him.

"Hey, Bash, what's in the black case?"

At first, Bash felt bewildered that someone not only took notice, but also cared enough to ask him about his treasured equipment. So bewildered, that he was speechless. Then Tiny raised his head and huffed at him, as if to say, "Don't blow it, kid. This is your chance."

Bash straightened up and eagerly explained in great detail what exactly was in the black case. When all was said and done, everyone, except Aunt Rae, had their eyes on Bash, and Travis asked, "Why on God's green earth did you bring all of that?"

"I brought it in the name of the Science of the Paranormal." Bash heard his aunt whimper from inside her sleeping bag.

Kimmy commented, "How interesting! Are you trying to find ghosts here?"

"My god, Rae," Tonya scoffed. "Tarot cards and ghosts. Your nephew needs some faith, for Christ's sake."

Aunt Rae now grunted and Bash addressed Kimmy. "I'm not hunting ghosts. I'm actually hunting werewolves. Legend has it that they've been living here since 1937. The most famous one is The Ma'iingan Bluff Werewolf. What's spectacular about him, in particular, is his size. They say he's as tall as an RV."

Travis barked with laughter. "So, he's thirteen feet tall? Impossible."

"Well." Bash squinted in thought. "He's more like ten feet tall."

Aunt Rae's muffled voice sounded as she asked Travis, "How do you know that RVs are thirteen feet tall?"

"Everyone knows that, Rae. It's common knowledge."

Aunt Rae lifted the pillow and said, "I don't think it's common-"

"I've heard enough. RVs and werewolves don't interest me." Tonya inserted earplugs and turned onto her side away from all of them.

Chuck, on the other hand, seemed very interested in the werewolf and now sat up. He asked Bash, "Where has he been living, exactly?"

"Around the bluffs and inside the woods."

"*These* bluffs? *These* woods?"

"Oooo," Kimmy gushed. "This is better than a campfire ghost story!"

Nodding, Bash continued, "Tiny, my aunt and I are going on a little expedition this morning to try to gather evidence of his existence. If you guys want to come, you're welcome."

Travis barked out laughter and incredulously said, "Your aunt must really love you." He grinned. "To put up with your batshit crazy ambitions."

Aunt Rae suddenly threw off her cover and pillow, glaring at Travis. "I do really love my nephew and putting up with batshit crazy ambitions is what people do for the ones they love." She then returned to her hibernating state and mumbled audibly, "Watch your mouth. He's only twelve."

Bash cleared his throat and redirected the conversation back to the werewolf hunt. "We're leaving at two-thirty this morning in order to get settled before three o'clock. That's the witching hour when paranormal activity is at its peak. I want to be ready by then."

Kimmy nodded enthusiastically, but declined. "Maybe another time, Bash? It does sound exciting though." She then zipped up her sleeping bag, slipped a purple sleep mask over her eyes and rested on her back with her hands clasped across her chest.

Still chuckling, Travis rolled onto his side on top of his standard sleeping bag with his Tiny snuggled underneath one arm. He bent his other arm under his head to be used as a pillow. "You can definitely count us out."

Chuck shrugged, saying, "You can count me in. The Ma'iingan Bluff Werewolf sounds cool." With that, he shifted himself around, laid on his side and wrapped a pillow around the back of his head, making sure to cover his ears.

Bash's heart was about to explode with warm acceptance. He whispered to his aunt, "This is going to be fun. See you soon." She humphed and he checked on Tiny who was already snoring. With a content sigh, Bash squirmed and nestled, all snug in his bed, while visions of werewolves danced in his head.

CHAPTER TWENTY ONE

The second that Rae fell asleep was the exact second that Bash roused her for the hunt. And she now found herself in the company of Bash, Tiny and Chuck, sitting in the rodent territory of the forest among garlic fumes. After rubbing her eyes, she studied her surroundings.

To Rae, the woodlands in the early hours felt like another world in another dimension. There was something unseen that made the cascading moonlight magical and spine-tingling all at once. And, in this realm of spectral lights and twisted trees, that same something unseen awakened the creatures of the night. If quiet, trespassers might hear the soft vibrations of an innocent luna moth. Or they might hear something more eerie, like the woeful weeping of a forgotten soul.

Presently, however, the trespasser would hear neither vibrations nor weeping. What would be heard, however, were the snores of a Great Shepherd, the frequent questions of a tag-along, and the testy whispers between an annoyed aunt and her engrossed nephew. Crouched off the beaten path, the aunt quarreled with the nephew about the paranormal den that he chose. It was surrounded by bushes, oak trees, slugs, possibly panthers, possibly a supernova.

"Supernova, Aunt Rae? Be serious." Wearing a headlamp and a necklace of garlic, Bash returned his attention to some type of small object, resting in his hand.

Lifting the string of garlic around his neck, Chuck asked in a hushed voice, "Why do we need garlic? I thought that was to ward off vampires, not werewolves."

"According to my research," Bash began, "which is ongoing, European folklore states that garlic can be used to ward off vampires, devils and werewolves."

Chuck raised his eyebrows. "There's more than one devil?"

Rae nodded while yawning and then said, "If you believe in that stuff."

Astonished, Chuck asked her, "You *don't* believe in The Devil?"

"Only if his name is Travis."

Bash shushed them. "Come on, guys. It's two-fifty. It'll be the witching hour in ten minutes. We have to be quiet now. Werewolves have a keen sense of hearing, especially The Ma'iingan Bluff Werewolf."

Chuck asked in a very quiet whisper, "What will happen to us if he finds us?"

"He'll eat us."

"Aunt Rae, that's not true. *All* werewolves, including The Ma'iingan Bluff Werewolf, are misunderstood and practically harmless creatures. I've read that they're curious by nature. They only eat humans if they feel threatened by us."

"You're talking about chimpanzees."

"No, I'm not, Aunt Rae."

"My dear nephew, if all werewolves are practically harmless, then why did you make us loop garlic around our throats?"

"Safety always comes first. Whether you're a cook, air traffic controller or paranormal investigator, you have certain safety guidelines to follow and wearing garlic for protection against werewolves is a safety guideline. That and not moving, if you meet a werewolf. They may mistake you for a deer and then eat your liver. Or heart. Now, let's get serious, okay? As my mom always says, I need a helper, not a hinderer."

Chuck saluted Bash and Rae chuckled to herself. Then she scanned the ground with her cellphone flashlight. Rae saw the various paranormal gadgets, positioned in front of Bash. Zeroing in on something that resembled a walkie-talkie next to her nephew's knee, she reached for it.

Bash verbally stopped her. "Don't touch that."

Her hand indignantly retreated back to her lap. "You said you needed a helper and I wanted to learn about this equipment." When Bash remained quiet, she added, "And may I remind you that I'm the adult here. I'm twenty-five for one more day and you'll be twelve for another nine months. I can touch whatever I want to." She placed her hand on top of his head.

Bash removed her hand. "Aunt Rae, I have everything just so. I'll teach you about the equipment another time. Right now, I can't risk you or Chuck messing stuff up." He leaned forward and spoke around her to address Chuck. "No disrespect. It's just that too much is at stake tonight."

Chuck also leaned forward to talk around Rae. "I understand, dude, and I'm not trying to be difficult, but how can we help, if we can't touch anything? No disrespect."

Bash nodded. "None taken. I just need you to listen and tell me if you hear anything out of the ordinary or see-"

"Well," Rae interrupted, "I *feel* something out of the ordinary, crawling all over me." A tickle ran up Rae's leg and she smacked her outer thigh. She examined her leg and saw some nicks from reckless shaving and two old mosquito bites. Nothing new.

"You're fine. Besides, we can't move. Our base has to be hidden, so that we can observe without being seen."

"Some things." Her flashlight swept the ground all around her.

"What?" Bash sounded perturbed.

"I feel some *things* crawling all over me." Rae steadied her phone flashlight. "Bash, our base is on an anthill."

"Shhh." Chuck straightened his back. "Something's moving out there."

Bash whispered an order. "Guys, turn off your lights." Quickly reaching for the power button on his headlamp, he turned his light off first.

Rae asked Bash, "Why?" When he didn't answer, she begrudgingly obeyed, turned off her flashlight and listened to what sounded like hushed voices.

Chuck asked Rae and Bash, "Who do you think is out there?"

"I don't know," Bash replied.

"I don't like sitting in the dark, Bash."

"Aunt Rae, we don't want to attract any unnecessary attention."

Feeling vulnerable as well as protective, Rae squirmed closer to Bash. "Did any of your ghost contraptions pick up on anything?"

He studied a handheld device with a small square screen. "I see two figures. One seems to be really tall and the other one is really short."

"Figures?" She leaned over his shoulder.

"Like people?" Chuck leaned over Rae's shoulder.

Rae pointed to the device, asking Bash, "Is this your EMF recorder?"

"Absolutely not, Aunt Rae. This is my thermal camera. It's designed to pick up on the surface temperature of objects."

Still whispering, Rae asked, "What do all the colors mean?"

Tilting the screen in her direction, Bash explained, "The reds, oranges and yellows signify the warmer body temperatures while the purples and blues indicate cooler temperatures."

Rae could see the human figures very clearly now. Well, she could see the red and orange human figures very clearly. They briefly stood close together before embracing each other in some kind of animal lust. "Oh, dear," Rae said to Bash. "If they start taking their clothes off, we're out of here."

"No, Aunt Rae, we were here first."

"But Bash-"

"This is a prime location for werewolf hunting, Aunt Rae. I'm not leaving."

Chuck agreed. "I'm not leaving either."

Rae gasped. "My god, they're taking their clothes off." She gasped again. "I bet that's Tom and that giggly girl. They were going to have a rendezvous, remember? Come on, let's go. We'll do this tomorrow."

Bash and Chuck said in unison, "No."

Rae hissed. "Yes."

Bash held up his hand and raised the thermal camera with his other hand. "Wait, Aunt Rae. Someone else just came."

Rae leaned into the small screen. There were now three figures and the third person was tall too. There were some gestures accompanied with some inaudible talking. The first two figures quickly dressed, after which the short one exited to the right. The two tall figures, however, remained and began pushing each other. Fearful of a fight ensuing, Rae picked up a rock and threw it at the figures. After the rock hit a tree, the knocking sound ended the scuffle and the two figures left the scene in opposite directions.

Bash turned on his headlamp and said to her, "That was smart thinking, Aunt Rae."

Rae breathed a sigh of relief. "Is it time to go?"

"It's not even three yet. We have to stay until then, Aunt Rae. That's the time when the supernatural-"

"Is at its peak. I know. How much longer till then?"

"Five minutes." Bash grinned at her and turned off his headlamp. "I can't wait."

Nothing happened at the wicked three o'clock hour and Rae never saw her nephew look so dejected before this moment. Nor Chuck. She felt bad for her nephew, though, and allowed him to talk her into staying another thirty minutes. Chuck seemed to be just as excited as Bash at the prospects of hunting longer, but his excitement waned after fifteen minutes. Chuck ended his werewolf pursuit in a reclined position with his head resting on Tiny's stomach. They now both snored in their peaceful slumbers.

Rae sat cross-legged on the ground for the entire thirty minutes. Her feet felt like pin cushions with a million needles poking into each foot. As for her toes, all ten were past numb. Wiggling them was harder than finding a fictional werewolf. Needing to wake up her feet, Rae stood and stamped her legs while saying to Bash, "It's three-thirty. Time to go."

Bash jerked his head to look at her. "Aw, not now. Nothing happened. If we quit now, this whole evening was a bust. Please, Aunt Rae, just five more minutes?"

With her hands on her hips, Rae stared at her sweet nephew with the strange obsessions. "Only if you promise me something."

"What's that, Aunt Rae?"

"For tomorrow, I want you to forget about werewolves and find a new obsession, like hunting different kinds of tree leaves or trapping cotton balls. Something like that." Bash chuckled and opened his mouth to respond when Rae suddenly heard a clang of metal on metal in the distance. She turned her head toward the sound and when she did, she heard another clang. Two clangs? Bash stood up which caused Chuck to awaken.

Confused, Chuck asked, "What's happening? Are we done?"

Before Rae could reply, a third clang rang in the night. By now, Rae determined that the bell was coming from the direction of the south park office. What Rae wanted to know was who was ringing the bell so early in the morning and why? She turned to Bash and just as she did, the ground began to vibrate. At first, it was a subtle shake that quickly strengthened into a rhythmic quake. Now standing, Bash grabbed her hand and Chuck moved up to his knees when a whoosh of air rushed past them, blowing Rae's hair across her face.

She immediately kneeled down, pulling Bash down with her. "What was th-" Before Rae finished her question, the ground convulsed again and a stronger blast of air blew past them, pushing her onto her rear end.

When the ground steadied and the wind relaxed to its normal stale summer weight, Bash turned on his headlamp. "There were two huge whooshes, Aunt Rae. Two!" Like a mad scientist in a laboratory, Bash now scoured over every piece of his equipment. "My EMF gauge didn't pick up on anything. Nothing spiked!"

Rae swallowed hard. "My fear spiked."

"I ditto that," Chuck said.

"How curious," Bash now softly spoke. "Everything is on, but I got nothing. Can The Ma'iingan Bluff Werewolves evade detection?"

Rae heard Chuck gulp. He asked, "Did you say *werewolves*?"

Bash enthusiastically nodded. "There were two whooshes of air. To me, that's proof that there are two Ma'iingan Bluff Werewolves."

"Well, I think," Rae began with a shaky voice, "that they were two big bears. Or madmen."

He looked at her. "And did you hear that bell, Aunt Rae?"

Chuck answered instead, "I heard it. It sounded like an old-timey dinner bell. Like on a ranch in an old western."

Bash nudged her arm. "You know, Aunt Rae, to me, it sounded like-"

"A bell tolling."

Bash beamed brighter than his headlamp. "*Exactly*. Remember what Zalen told us? 'Therefore, never send to know for whom the bell tolls'. This can't be coincidental."

"I knew you were headed in that direction, Bash. And all I know is that it's time to get back to bed before more bells toll, banshees shrill or my wits blast to kingdom come." Feeling unnerved, Rae woke up her snoring Great Shepherd who missed all of the action.

With a furrowed brow, Chuck asked, "What are you guys talking about? Is Zalen the empath you mentioned earlier? He knew about the bell?"

Bash enthusiastically replied, "Yes! He warned us about a bell tolling."

Chuck now sounded just as enthusiastic. "*Really?* That is so cool. Can I meet Zalen? I always wanted to meet an empath. My aunt says she can see ghosts and-"

"Look, you two," Rae interrupted, "I'm heading back to camp with my dog." She tapped her thigh and Tiny stood. "I suggest you follow."

Upon standing, Chuck asked, "But shouldn't we talk about what happened? I mean, something did happen, right?"

"Definitely," Bash said. "And I think we should come back here again tomorrow and investigate further. And before you say no, Aunt Rae-"

Rae interrupted, "No. I don't feel safe being out here with bears. Or madmen. So, no, I'm not coming back tomorrow." She shrugged. "And you're not either. End of discussion."

Bash and Chuck looked at each other, saying nothing. Then Bash caught Rae's glaring eye and he quickly gathered the equipment with Chuck's help. Soon, the four of them trudged through the foliage to the wooded trail. They hiked the ten minutes back to their campsite and headed straight into the tent. While crawling into his sleeping bag, Chuck whispered a thank you for an exciting time while Tiny circled his spot, eventually plopping down on the ground. Bash squirmed into his bag, hugging his black case. With a relieved smile, Rae shone her phone flashlight on him to make sure he was settled when she noticed something very peculiar. The beam moved from Bash to Travis and his spot. Her smile vanished. The sleeping bag was there, but Travis wasn't.

. . .

Stone knew he was no longer in reality. He couldn't move a finger or open an eye. No matter how hard he tried. Was it a dream? Or was it a vision? In the black space all around him, he couldn't tell where he was. He only felt like he was upright because of the pressure on the bottoms of his feet.

Dread suddenly filled his chest. Heavy dread that made it hard to breathe. He was completely alone and a fear began to grow. Would he always be alone? No, of course not. He shook his head, trying to knock that thought out of it. It didn't leave. The thought crowded him even more and he was being squeezed. Slowly. Like he was in a tightening MRI machine.

Stone heard a voice in the darkness in front of him. *Just breathe, Stone.* It sounded familiar. And, then again, it didn't. His eyes widened, trying to see, but failing. A searing pain in his chest formed and his heart beat loudly in his ears. *Just breathe, Stone.* That voice. There was something familiar about that voice. Was it Zalen? Or Rae? *Just breathe, Stone.* No, it wasn't either of them. But he knew that voice. Didn't he? His face instantly flushed with perspiration as the air left his lungs.

The tightening strengthened on his arms. They were pinned against his side. The rough walls cut into his skin and he struggled to make the slightest movement. *Just breathe, Stone.*

Panic set in.

He couldn't see anything. He couldn't hear anything. Not even his own heartbeat.

Just breathe, Stone.

He closed his eyes. He counted to three. And then he slowly breathed in through his nose until he felt the air inflate his lungs. He pictured his lungs filling. They were now large and round, like two tires on a bicycle. He held that air. He counted to three. Then to six. And then he slowly exhaled through his mouth.

When he opened his eyes, he could see again. And what he saw was familiar to him. There was the same crumpled body on the ground in the woods with its back to him. Beyond the body were two ferocious beasts on hind legs, growling at each other. On either side of him were two tall structures that transformed into trees and they still held him captive. Looking down at his feet, he saw the red lollipop with legs crawling toward him. Stone squirmed, but he was stuck and he didn't know what to do.

The crumpled body stirred. Stone watched as it slowly, painfully rolled onto its back. It rested for a brief moment before the head laggardly turned to face him. The features were blurred, but Stone could see the mouth begin to open with much effort. And when the mouth was finally agape, it screamed for him.

Help me!

CHAPTER TWENTY TWO

Around eight o'clock on Wednesday morning, Rae announced where the team activity would take place, but kept the other details to herself. She didn't want to risk any cheeky responses. Then soon after breakfast cleanup, the team gathered at the beach, dressed in various styles of swimsuits. Rae wore her red racer, Bash modeled trendy blue shorts with large pineapples all over it, Tonya hid her figure under what looked like a nylon tent with a skirt, Kimmy's baggy bikini showed off her flat chest and protruding ribs, Chuck looked normal, wearing long green board shorts, and Travis, well, he sported shorty tighty square trunks that bore a remarkable resemblance to designer underwear.

Sipping from a twelve-inch high coffee cup, Travis explained, "I don't want tan lines." That was a strange thing to say since he had two black straps criss-crossing over his chest.

Rae's attention shifted from his swim trunks to his hand when Tonya demanded from Travis. "Where did you get that Sky High?"

Travis retorted, "Mind your own business."

Rae scolded Travis. "Be nice." She gave him her stink eye.

"Fine." Travis took a deep breath. "I'm sorbet. I mean, soiree."

Chuck asked, "Do you mean sorry?"

Travis nodded and Kimmy softly said, "Isn't the nearest Espresso Lane an hour away?"

Travis grunted. "For Christ's sake, this is a reusable cup that I brought from home and filled with coffee at the north park office. Move on, people."

A reusable cup? Rae stood on the shoreline in contemplation while the waves reached her feet from time to time, licking the back of her heels. As relaxing as that felt, she was tense. Her empty hands found her hips as she studied Travis. Still perplexed about his whereabouts in the early morning hours, she couldn't comprehend where he went for an hour. Or more. She really wasn't sure. And she knew he was gone for at least an hour because she watched the clock. Until she fell asleep. When was that? She couldn't recall. And when did he return? She couldn't recall that either. In fact, she couldn't recall anything past five.

"Well, Rae?" Travis asked in an impatient tone, "What are we doing for the activity? Staring at each other on the beach won't cut it."

Taking a deep breath, she placed those thoughts on the back burner and decided to interrogate The Torch later. One on one. After she had a caffeinated soda. For now, she mustered all her strength for her team-building idea.

Exhaling, Rae glanced at the line of tandem kayaks that Matt helped her drag over to this spot. Last night, she felt excited about this activity. Now, however, Rae yearned to end it. The werewolf hunt stole crucial sleeping hours and she now heard the distant beckoning of her sleeping bag for her prompt return. "Okay, guys," Rae began as she surveyed this circus troupe, "our first team activity-" She stopped herself from talking as her eyes rested on Bash. He was the only one facing the other direction. "Hey, Bash, you good?"

He stared into the woods. "Yeah. Good," he said while keeping his eyes on the trees.

He's obsessing about that bell, Rae thought. *That stupid bell and its stupid clanging or tolling or whatever. He's instantly obsessed with potential reasons for its tolling or clanging or whatever.* She shook her head. *Just look at him. His hair is matted in spots and sticking straight up in other spots. Not to mention his bloodshot eyes. Clearly, he never slept because of that werewolf nonsense.*

Travis also seemed interested in Bash's appearance as he said to him, "Well, you look like hell."

Tonya agreed. "You should've stayed in bed instead of looking for trouble in the middle of the night."

Kimmy asked, "Oh, that's right. Did you guys see any werewolves?"

Bash's response was to remain silent and to not break his sightline into the continuous shadows of the trunks and branches, so Chuck replied by shaking his head while yawning. He then said, "No werewolf, but a loud bell woke me up. And then there was this wind that…"

Exasperated, Travis scolded Chuck, "Don't you start. Now, can we analyze Bash's poor sleep behaviors and strange interests later?" He addressed the group, "By show of hands, who wants to start the activity instead of talking about Bash and bells?"

Everyone raised their hands, including Bash.

"Fine, I get it." Rae surrendered. "Let's get started. Now, I'm just making sure again, everyone can swim, right?" The team nodded and Rae continued, gesturing to the kayaks. "Here's our morning challenge."

Tonya observed, "I don't see any paddles."

"That's correct," Rae said. "Teams of two will paddle with their hands to that swim float, switch spots without using the swim float or getting into the water and then paddle back here. If you tip over or fall in, your team is out."

Chuck asked, "Can we pick our own partners?"

"No," Rae replied and everyone moaned like disappointed third-graders. "Chuck, you're with Tonya. Travis, you're with Bash. Kimmy, you're with me."

Surprisingly, the first objection didn't come from the coworkers. It came from Bash. "What about Tiny? Who's his partner?"

Rae glanced at her dog who found some shade under a nearby tree and was busy licking himself again. "He seems fine."

Travis tsked at Bash. "Too bad that your dog isn't small like mine. You could've strapped him to your back, like I did. Then he could've joined you."

Rae peered around Travis, noticing the little Bichon Frise. The little dog panted happily with his little pink tongue poking out. "Oh," she said while catching Travis's eye, "so that's where you put him. I was wondering." She briefly held his gaze before he looked away from her.

Tonya raised her hand and faced Travis. "What do the winners get? And I really think that they should get a *nice* reward and not a threat."

After cursing, Travis replied, "Why do the winners have to win something anyway? Our societal thinking about rewarding people for the smallest successes is out of control." His tone switched from frustrating to mocking. "How about a participation ribbon?"

Tonya stiffened her back. "How about if the winners get a free lunch?"

Chuck offered, "Or a day off?"

"I could use some help with my car," Kimmy said in a hopeful tone.

Travis answered, "No, no, and call a tow truck."

"How about this?" Rae gripped the sides of her head. "The winners can sit out the next team-building activity."

A rousing applause erupted and, with brightened moods, the activity began. As each team helped each other lift their kayak, Kimmy surprised Rae by lifting theirs by herself and setting it in the water. When each pair was ready, Rae said, "Ready, set, go!" The mad arm-paddling initiated and the other teams clambered toward the swim float. Kimmy's toothpick arms, however, sculled them through the water as fast as eight rowers, propelling them into the lead. They reached the swim float first. Rae turned around to face Kimmy and said, "Now we have to switch spots."

As she carefully moved to a squatting position, Rae heard Tonya and Chuck, slowly, but steadily, approaching. Tonya sat behind Chuck and barked orders. Chuck's red face and wide twitchy eyes made him seem maniacal. Rae then spied Travis and Bash. Actually, she only saw Travis. He was waist-deep in the water with his Tiny still strapped to his back. They both looked dry while Travis dragged the kayak back to shore. Bash then exploded from underneath the water's surface with a big smile on his face and locked eyes with her. He gave her a thumbs up, calling to her, "We're out! I'm heading over to Tiny!"

Rae chuckled as she watched Travis lower his Tiny to the sandy beach. The little dog instantly took the opportunity to scramble out of his confinement and ran to share the shade with her Tiny.

"Hey," Rae said to Kimmy, "We can win this! Since you're thinner than I am, stand up and step over me when I slide into your seat."

Kimmy nodded. As she stood, Rae crouched, readying herself to slide over to Kimmy's seat. Kimmy raised one leg. So far, so good.

Tonya and Chuck suddenly arrived. *No matter,* Rae thought. *We got this.* As those two opponents began switching places, Rae slid on her stomach too forcibly and accidentally bumped into Kimmy's standing leg. Her knee buckled. Rae tried to grab Kimmy's spinning arms, but couldn't lasso either one. The next thing she knew, fishy-smelling water gave her a cold hard slap across her face as she unintentionally rolled off the kayak and into the lake. Striking the surface with her fists, Rae then treaded water and watched helplessly as Tonya and Chuck somehow successfully switched spots and approached the shore, raising their arms in triumph.

.   .   .

Yawning wide, Tiny's big tongue flopped out of his mouth. As he reclined on his side, he panted easily under the shady tree. And even though the little white dog rested right next to him, taking some of the shade, Tiny didn't mind that much. After all, the little shit smelled like spicy pumpkin pie. Yum.

His attention shifted to Nice Bash when he ambled across the beach toward him. The boy dropped to his knees and he vigorously scratched Tiny's entire body. Just when Tiny thought life couldn't be any better, a gentle breeze brushed by, bringing a glorious meaty fragrance to his attention. It overwhelmed Tiny's olfactory senses, causing him to drool. Being outdoors was a wondrous thing!

Springing up onto all four paws, Tiny lifted his nose.

Nice Bash also lifted his nose and then spoke with enthusiasm, "Hey, Tiny, you got something, don't you? What is it? Show me."

Upon quickly standing, Tiny took three large steps toward the treeline. A small yip stopped him, however. He looked back and saw little Tiny now standing on all four paws, staring at him hopefully. Tiny doubled back, lowered his head like the claw in the arcade machine, and picked up little Tiny by the scruff of his neck. He then trotted to the woods with little Tiny in his chops and Nice Bash behind him.

Fortunately, the meat treat wasn't too far into the woods. The Great Shepherd dropped the little Bichon Frise on the ground. He squeaked. Tiny paid no attention and stepped over the little Tiny. He wagged his tail while scanning the long length of the dead animal. Nice Bash called this kind of animal a deer. And just like the other one, its innards spilled from the stomach like noodles out of a pot.

What luck!

Licking his chops, there was only one thing left to do. He readied himself for his tasty morning munch when, unfortunately, Nice Bash wrapped his arms around Tiny's neck once again.

"No, Tiny!" Nice Bash pulled to restrain him. "Don't destroy the evidence!"

As Tiny reluctantly followed Nice Bash's order to sit down next to little Tiny, the boy began examining the meat treat. "This is just like that other deer from yesterday. Its heart and liver have been removed. I'm positive it was The Ma'iingan Bluff Werewolf. I mean, what other beast could do such a thing like this?"

Tiny heard forceful footsteps quickly stomping their way. Before he could stand to growl, a bush parted and a different kind of beast stood before them. This tall beast was capable of stomping on people's hearts, according to Angry Rae, but right now, he looked pretty silly in his underwear swim trunks.

CHAPTER TWENTY THREE

While Tonya and Chuck celebrated their win by dancing on the beach and throwing sand like confetti, Rae and Kimmy swam their overturned kayak back to shore. Breathing heavily, Rae rolled onto her back and rested on the beach face, allowing the rolling swash to lap her legs. Breathing normally, Kimmy dragged the kayak completely out of the water before continuing her march to her towel. As Rae remained on her back, her eyes eventually drifted to the tree where she had seen Tiny, but he was now gone. And so was Bash. Of course. Alarmed about their unknown whereabouts, she rolled onto her side, then onto all fours before raising her rear end into the air. Rae took a deep breath and pushed herself into a standing position. With the help of her out-stretched arms, she steadied her legs and then began to search the area for both of them.

Rae first spotted Travis emerging from the woods about fifty yards away. His glare bore into her soul. Weaving around beach towels, coolers and people, Travis bee-lined toward her, holding his Tiny in one hand and his coffee cup in the other. His glare then turned into a scowl. Actually, his face was all fuzzy at this distance, but she pictured him with a scowl. Was that unfair of her? Meh. Probably.

His facial features became crisper with every approaching yard. He indeed wore that vexed expression with his lips etched into a straight line and his brows crinkled like foil. As he approached, he shook his head while saying, "First, your dog chewed up my Tiny and then spit him out like used tobacco."

"I highly doubt that."

"Second, your nephew had the audacity to yelp when he saw me and then apologized for thinking I was, and I quote, *a feral werewolf.*"

"That, I believe. Where is he?"

Travis thrusted his Tiny's head in Rae's face. "Look. On the back of his head."

Rae squinted and saw white fluffy fur. Shrugging, she said, "I don't see anything."

"Well, I'm surprised you can't smell the offense. His fur is soaked from your dog's putrid slobber."

Again, Rae shrugged. "It could've been another dog's stinky spit."

"Tell your dog to stop eating mine. And brush your dog's teeth!"

"Oh, stop it," Rae scolded. "Where were you this morning anyway? When we came back to bed around quarter to four, you were gone. So, fess up already."

Travis straightened his back. "Fess up? To what?" Before Rae could reply, he continued, "To nothing, that's what. We weren't gone, Rae. I took my Tiny outside to potty. It's strange you don't remember this because I saw you walk right past me when you returned. I even thought we made eye-contact." He shrugged. "After Tiny relieved himself, I cleaned him up with his wet puppy wipes and then we came back to bed. By then, you were already sawing logs, as they say."

Rae honestly couldn't remember when she had fallen back to sleep and, more importantly, she couldn't remember anyone ever telling her that she snored. "I was?"

"Yes. Quite loudly, I might add." He and his Tiny both raised their noses in the air. "The nerve," Travis said and thrusted his empty coffee cup into her hands. "Throw this away for me and then, maybe, I'll forgive you."

As he stormed off, Rae called after him, "Hey, wait a minute. Where's Bash?"

"I'm over here, Aunt Rae!"

Spinning around, she faced the direction of her nephew's voice. Waving his arms, he beckoned for her to follow him as he disappeared into the woods. Tiny then appeared and sat down to wait for her. He cocked his head to this side and barked at her to hurry.

Rae half-heartedly hustled over to Tiny and when they both joined Bash in the secluded area of bushes and trees, her heart instantly sank. Plugging her nose with her free hand, she peered at the carcass and remarked in a disdained tone, "You made me rush over here for this? It's a dead deer." She surveyed the bottom of her feet. "I should've worn shoes. Ugh. You're not wearing shoes either. We're going to get splinters and cuts. Or worse. We'll step on spiders."

Bash's eyes brightened with excitement. "Forget about splinters and spiders, Aunt Rae. This is way more exciting. What we have is not just a dead deer. It's the *second* dead deer *victim*."

"Oh, no."

"Oh, yes! We found the first one yesterday when searching for kindling, remember? Near our campsite? I tried to tell you, but you shushed me or rolled your eyes or something. Anyway, what you need to notice is that these corpses are identical."

"Got it."

"See how the heart and liver are missing?"

"No."

"That can only mean one thing."

"Turkey vultures."

"No, Aunt Rae. Please remember that when we are dealing with the science of the paranormal, all common sense flies out the window. These two dead deer victims prove that we are dealing with something way more serious and way more dangerous than turkey vultures."

A dim flicker of a nauseating realization quickly grew. "You honestly don't think the two deer were killed by The Moroccan-"

"Ma'iingan."

"Whiff-"

"Bluff."

"Werewolf, do you?"

"*Werewolves* and yes, I do, Aunt Rae. Both were sliced once down the middle and only had their hearts and livers eaten. Werewolves love hearts and livers." As he inspected the carcass, he added, "I'm showing this to you so that you're aware of how awesome this experience is turning out to be."

Rae inhaled and held her breath. As she exhaled through her mouth, she crossed her arms, still holding the coffee cup, and gave up. Talking sense to Bash was like her figuring out a problem in geometry. Impossible. Shifting her attention to Tiny, she asked him, "Well, what do you have to say?"

Tiny cleared his throat.

"Yeah? And what about Travis's dog? Did you really drool all over it?"

Cocking his head to the other side, he gave her a quizzical look and howled something that sounded suspiciously like, "Who me?"

Smirking, Rae told Tiny, "Next time you feel the need to put that dog in your mouth, don't drool on it. Just swallow the whole damn thing." She raised Travis's coffee cup and said to Bash, "Come on, let's go. I need to find a trash can."

Bash briefly scrutinized the writing on the outside of the plastic cup and pointed at it. "Look at that, Aunt Rae."

Rotating the cup, she read Travis's order. "It just says Choca Mocha, extra hot. Why?"

Bash seemed confused. "Didn't he say that was his used cup? Didn't he refill it this morning with the coffee from here?" Rae nodded and Bash asked, "Then why is today's date written on that cup, just below Choca Mocha?"

After bringing the cup closer to her face, Rae blinked in surprise. Sure enough, Bash was right. In true Espresso Lane's fashion, today's date was indeed written on the cup, just under the order. It was the usual thing for the baristas to do. They always wrote the order and date on the cup. Rae pursed her lips together as two facts imbedded themselves into her brain. The first fact pertained to Bash who was, thankfully, very observant. The second fact regarded Travis who was, horrifyingly, a very big *and* a very convincing liar.

·   ·   ·

Dried, dressed and perched at the picnic table, Bash pored over his book as his aunt brushed Tiny's short tan hair. The others dispersed a while ago to who knew where. Bash didn't care. He was onto something important.

He glanced at her over the edge of the page. "Aunt Rae, this is important. I'm telling you, we've got two legendary werewolves on the loose."

He heard her say, "Ugh."

"My thoughts exactly. Now, here is some information that you need to know in order to protect yourself. For starters, do you know that werewolves can shapeshift?"

"I put that together a while ago."

"I didn't think so. They can shapeshift, Aunt Rae, which means a werewolf can change into a person and then back into a werewolf. Do you know what that's called?"

"Lycanthropy."

"It's called lycanthropy and this ability to change happens during a full moon."

"But you don't believe that."

"Between you and me, Aunt Rae, I don't believe that. I think werewolves have the ability to transform whenever they like."

"Day or night."

"Day or night. So, we could have already met the two Ma'iingan Bluff Werewolves in human form. I'm talking about Dark Ranger Tom and Matt. Now, I've been re-rereading this book." He lifted the book and turned the front cover to face her. "*Where Wolves Wait at Ma'iingan Bluff.*"

"Bash."

He opened the book again and swiftly flipped to a page. "In chapter three-"

"Bash."

"It talks about a pack of werewolves, living on these bluffs-"

"Stop."

"Now, last night we felt two whooshes of air-"

"I'm going on a long walk-"

"But there could be many more werewolves around us who can shapeshift. Anytime."

"To charge my phone. It's at two percent. It'll probably take forever. Wanna come?"

Lifting his chin, Bash peered over the page. With her hands in her pockets, Aunt Rae stood next to a panting Tiny.

"But Aunt Rae," Bash began, "aren't you listening to me?" His eyes returned to the page.

"Yes, but you're not listening to me. It's about nine-thirty and I'm in desperate need to charge my phone. At the north park office. We're talking hours of charging. Do you want to come with us?"

With his nose back in the book, Bash asked, "What?"

"Bash!" Aunt Rae crossed her arms. "I said it's about nine-"

Chuckling, Bash said, "I heard you. North park office. Charging your phone. Thanks, but I'll stay here and do some more research."

He heard her sigh in frustration and then she asked, "Does your phone need charging?"

"Nah, it's good."

"Are you pos-"

"I'm positive."

There was another audible sigh. "Well, then call your mother this morning. I'm sure she would like you to check in."

Nodding, Bash listened to the sound of fading footsteps while opening his red spiral notebook. As he continued perusing the book, he feverishly scribbled down more clues in it. A furrowed brow formed as confusion set in. And then, thankfully, he turned the page to chapter twenty-four.

CHAPTER TWENTY FOUR

Tiny slowly loped down the gravel road as Angry Rae trotted to keep up. With his nose tilted upward, he knew exactly where they were headed. The beachy cologne scent in the air gave it away. And seeing Stone meant more belly rubs for him. He increased his loping speed and found his way in the center of Stone's campsite. Tiny sniffed again and followed Stone's scent to the tent. There, inside, was Stone on his back next to the Zalen man. A screen prevented Tiny from entering.

As Angry Rae approached, she whispered, "Shhh. Don't wake them."

At first, Tiny and Angry Rae stood on the outside, looking at Stone. Angry Rae then softly tapped her thigh, signaling Tiny to leave; however, she remained, looking at Stone. Then she did a curious thing. Angry Rae squatted and quietly raised the zipper to make a small opening. And, just as quietly, she crept through the small screen opening. Tiny pushed his head through the screen to follow, but Angry Rae pushed his head out of it and then held up her hand, which meant that he was to stay put. Tiny flicked his ear in frustration and now watched as she carefully crawled toward Stone. Her face hovered over his for a brief moment before she slowly lowered her lips to his forehead. After the soft kiss, she carefully crept backwards and out of the screen. Soon, the screen was quietly zipped shut and Angry Rae tapped the side of her leg again.

Tiny cocked his head to the left.

Angry Rae looked at him. "Come on," she whispered, "let's go."

Tiny didn't move.

Angry Rae put her hands on her hips. "What?"

Tiny cocked his head to the right.

"I don't know what you're saying."

Tiny pawed at the ground.

Angry Rae continued to whisper, "This is no time for a dance. We need to go."

Tiny flicked his ear and shook his head.

Angry Rae nodded. "I don't have time for this. They're going to wake up and find us standing here, looking creepy. Let's go."

Tiny woofed. He lowered his chin and pushed his forehead toward her.

"Oh," Angry Rae said softly, "I see." She bent slightly at the waist and Tiny felt her warm kiss land on the nice spot on the very top of his head. He raised his chin and she smiled. "There," she whispered, "are you ready now, or do you want a party thrown in your honor?"

Tiny wagged his tail. Sure, he was always ready for an adventure with Angry Rae. She didn't give the good belly rubs like Stone, but she gave great kisses. And he loved her.

■   ■   ■

In chapter twenty-four, Bash read an interesting passage, regarding a short eye-witness account. This woman, named Beatrice (no last name given), lived *here* her whole life and had a deep connection with a werewolf from the Ma'iingan pack. She spoke of how he could shapeshift, had black fingernails and toenails, had fur underneath his skin and had bristles underneath his tongue. *This sounds familiar,* Bash thought, and continued to read. One interesting fact that Beatrice learned about werewolves was they could pass this curse onto their offspring. After she confronted him about being a werewolf, he vanished. Neither she nor their son ever saw him again.

"Wait a minute," Bash said aloud, pulling on his bottom lip. The *aha* moment then flared like a firework and he quickly reached for his other book, *A Simply Complicated Werewolf.* He gasped at the connection. He was right! This book was written by a woman named Beatrice Bones. Same first name. "Is that a coincidence?" Bash asked himself. "In mysteries, there are no coincidences. Just facts." He pulled his bottom lip. "Or is it that there are no chances, just facts?" He shrugged. *Not really important*, he thought. *Or is it important? Can't chances and coincidences also be facts?*

Bash studied both covers of the two books. In *The Simply Complicated Werewolf,* Beatrice Bones wrote about a woman named Rose who unknowingly married a werewolf and began to notice strange characteristics about him. Where that story took place was never told. In *Where Wolves Wait at Ma'iingan Bluff,* a woman named Beatrice spoke about her personal experiences with a werewolf in this area and the stories were similar, if not the same.

Drumming his fingers on the cover, his mind bridged all this information together faster than any civil engineer. *Let's say that Beatrice Bones who wrote* The Simply Complicated Werewolf *is the same Beatrice in* Where Wolves Wait at Ma'iingan Bluff. *If so, when Beatrice wrote about a woman named Rose, she really wrote about herself. That would mean Beatrice Bones married a werewolf from Ma'iingan Bluff. And that would mean that she lived here and may also still live here! Now, the million-dollar question is how do I find Beatrice Bones?*

Grabbing his books, there was only one place that came to Bash's mind. He hurried down the forest's trail to begin his interrogation.

CHAPTER TWENTY FIVE

As Stone awoke in the morning, the same thoughts that interrupted his slumber now interrupted his consciousness, running around inside his head. Like a wild group of three-year olds. All hopped up on sugar sticks and cupcakes. And these thoughts were all about the two beasts, the lollipop and the crumpled body screaming for help. As far as Stone knew, there were two people at this campground, vying for the crumpled body role. Dreadlocks and Prissy. They were both tall and broad-shouldered. Dreadlocks, however, gave Stone a strange feeling last night during the stakeout that clearly ended with Dreadlocks watching him and Zalen instead. Was Dreadlocks a ghost? He had to find out.

Stone checked the time. Almost nine-fifty. With a deep breath, Stone glanced at the sleeping Zalen. He then slid out of the sleeping bag and tent without making a sound. Needing solitude, exercise and fresh air, he hoped to not interrupt Zalen's snores and he was successful. After all, a hurricane was quieter than Zalen's snoring. This first task proved easier than popping bread into a toaster. Two more tasks to go.

Before tackling the second one, he peeked on Rachel at her campsite. Everyone was gone. Feeling relieved and crushed at the same time, he wondered where his two God-given balls had gone. *My god,* he thought, *grow a new pair.* He then resituated his baseball cap and entered the woods by way of the trail, heading straight for the north park office where the second task awaited for him. It was in the shape of a large cup of fresh coffee. He licked his lips in anticipation. He hoped his coffee would give him the brain strength needed to find his third task of finding Dreadlocks. And once he found him, he just needed to follow him. To make sure that Dreadlocks wasn't a ghost.

Stone quickened his pace down the wooded trail and, as luck would have it, he bumped into his third task. Dreadlocks stepped out of the trees and onto the trail, just as Stone rounded the bend. It was a near collision. Surprised, Dreadlocks raised the styrofoam cooler like a shield, but Stone stopped momentum, resulting in no physical contact. It was just another awkward meeting.

Dreadlocks looked well worn. Cheeks sunken. Deep forehead creases. And the shade under his eyes was darker than a new moon. He grumbled at Stone.

The grumble didn't bother Stone though. It was the hair on the back of Stone's neck that irked him. That was a new unwanted sensation. Headaches were a regular psychic occurrence. And so were the tingling forearms. But this? The prickly little neck hairs were new.

Standing his ground, Stone maintained strong eye contact and said, "Hey."

Dreadlocks also maintained strong eye contact, but then turned away without returning the greeting. Stone watched as he leisurely strolled down the trail in the direction of the north park office while nonchalantly swinging the styrofoam cooler. And as the distance between them lengthened, Stone's forearms began the familiar tingling sensation. *Ah, there it is.* Then a sinking feeling abruptly hit him in the gut. Something was off about the cavalier Dreadlocks dude. Something that he couldn't figure out for the life of him. He took a step in the same direction as his subject in question when a female voice surprised him from behind by saying, "Well, hello there."

Stone spun around on the trail and found Prissy behind him. They were eye to eye, nose to nose. Wearing her park ranger uniform, she appeared very professional, very straight-faced, except for her warm smile. She spoke jovially and fast. "So, are you enjoying one of our many special hiking trails? They're all so beautiful. I try to walk them whenever I can. They're great shortcuts to take instead of walking along the gravel road. Do you have a map? Where are you headed?"

Stone answered, "No, I don't have a map, but I've walked this trail before. I'm headed to the north park office. I need some coffee."

Prissy brightened. "You're headed in the right direction. Just follow the wonderful aroma of Folgers. And be sure to pick up a map at the counter. It has all the trails marked."

Stone nodded. "I will."

As he half-turned to continue his way, she spoke again, "If you need anything else, just let me know. My name is Prissy."

Stone paused, studying her face. Then he said, "Yeah, I remember. We met yesterday."

Prissy wrinkled her brow and frowned. "We did? Yesterday? That's strange. I don't remember." She then suddenly laughed. "I'm sorry. I meet a lot of people." Sadness, however, eclipsed her irises.

"That's okay," Stone said and then he introduced himself again. He noticed the embarrassed look in her eye did not leave and he empathized with her. There was nothing more humiliating than being found out, whether it was from something as easy as forgetting a name or something stranger like being a psychic. Wanting to cheer her up as well as himself, he asked, "So, how long have you been a park ranger here?"

"For ten years, one month and thirteen days." She glanced at him and the sadness left. "I love this job. It's the best job." She beamed now. "I get to be out in nature all the time and meet many different people in all walks of life. The world needs more parks and less concrete or landfills. Is this your first time here?"

Stone shook his head. "I camped here a few times with my grandpa when I was younger." He thought briefly before saying, "I was ten the last time I was here." He smiled. "Time flies."

Prissy added, "When you're having fun!"

Chuckling, Stone nodded. He tilted his head as an idea struck. He wanted information about Dreadlocks and who was better to ask than a park ranger like Prissy? "I have an odd question for you."

"You bet. I always have time for questions, odd or not."

"Well," Stone began, "I was wondering if there is a guy working around here. He's tall and has dreadlocks."

"Oh." Prissy laughed. "That's Matt."

"Matt? So, he's real?" Stone forced a chuckle. "Not a ghost?"

Confused, Prissy shook her head. "No, he's not a ghost. He's the son and grandson of the two women who run this place. He's a good guy. Matt does all sorts of odd jobs around this place. Looks rough, but has a good heart." Her expression abruptly changed from relaxed to concerned. "Why are you asking? Has he done something?"

Shaking his head, Stone replied, "Oh, no. I was…I mean, I just wanted…No, it's nothing."

"Are you sure? Because I can talk to him about whatever. It's actually my job to address any issues with anyone who works here and I-"

"Oh, no." Stone interrupted her, raising his palms. "Please, don't. He's done nothing. It's all good."

Prissy shrugged. "Okay, then. Let me know if you change your mind. We run a tight ship at Fun Warriors Ranch and I will handle any issues with our campers." Smiling, she touched the brim of her Stetson hat. "Well, it was a pleasure meeting you, Stone. I must be going, but will look forward to seeing you. Around." Then after a salute, Prissy turned and continued marching down the trail.

. . .

When Rae arrived at the north park office, she found Jen sweeping the front porch and they greeted each other with a smile and a wave. Tiny offered his head for Jen to pet, which she did enthusiastically. He then left them to sit under the shade of a nearby tree.

Holding the broom upright, Jen said, "You have a very good dog. And very big. How old is he?"

"About two years."

"What breed?"

"He's a Great Shepherd, which is a Great Dane, German Shepherd mix. His name is Tiny."

Laughing, Jen raised her eyebrows. "So, you like big dogs?"

Rae smiled. "I do now. Hey, I don't mean to bother you, but I have to charge my phone. Can I bring my dog inside while I charge it? I don't want to leave him out here all alone."

"Unfortunately, you can't unless your dog is a service dog." When Rae shook her head, Jen suggested, "If you want, I'll watch your phone and you can sit out here with Tiny."

"Really?" Rae was surprised at Jen's friendly suggestion. "Don't you have a lot of work to do? I mean, my phone is nearly dead. It could take two hours. Or more."

"No, I don't mind. I'm in the store all the time anyway. I'll be here til five or six or seven. Eternity. You get the idea."

Delighted, Rae exclaimed, "Thanks so much!" With that last salutation, Rae wasted no time and bounded into the park office, searching for the charging station. After pulling her charger and cord from her back pocket, she plugged her phone into the outlet. As she headed toward the door, she spied a puzzle book at the checkout counter. She snatched it as well as a dog bone and a magazine, advertising closet organizers. She paid for the items and then left to find her shady spot on the ground next to Tiny. Tiny didn't stand when she approached with the bone, but he emphatically wagged his tail.

Within minutes, Jen approached her with a blanket. "Here," Jen said. "Sit on this. It'll be a little more comfortable than the ground."

Taken aback by the generosity, Rae stuttered, "Are…are you sure?"

"Of course. It's just a blanket that I keep with me in the store. It gets cold in the fall." Jen shrugged. "Tiny can sit on it too." She then chuckled. "Or some of him can. He might be bigger than the blanket."

"Well, thank you. I'm not used to such kindness."

Jen gave her a serious look. "Maybe you're hanging out with the wrong people?"

Rae smiled. "I don't call them people. I call them coworkers."

This caused Jen to explode in laughter. Briefly. Then she said, "I don't work with people or coworkers. I work with my family. So, I don't really know what's the best and what's the worst."

Rae learned that juicy tidbit of family information yesterday while hiding in the bushes with Bash. Matt was Jen's son. Jen was Matt's mom. And, after Rae said it to herself, it wasn't all that juicy. Still, Rae didn't want to confess to Jen that she eavesdropped on them among a bed of shrubs. It was time to play dumb, which came naturally to Rae.

"Rae, are you okay?"

Startled out of her thoughts, Rae blinked at Jen who waited patiently for a response. "You work with your family? What family? Cousins? Parents? Husband? All of the above?"

Jen replied with a smile, "My son and mother-in-law. Her name is Mare. I believe you met her yesterday while checking in at the south park office. And my son is Matt, the guy who bumped into you."

"Yes, I remember Matt very well."

"He's a hard one to forget. I've tried to get him to cut his hair, but he likes dreadlocks. What can I say? He's thirty-three, after all.

It's his life, his head." As Rae nodded, Jen continued, "You must've liked the apple pie yesterday since I sold another to Bash shortly after you bought the first one. They are good, aren't they?"

Rae sighed, giving Tiny the side eye. "I wouldn't know, to be honest. The first pie was dropped and ruined. Tiny ate it. The second was tripped on and smashed. Tiny ate that one too."

Tiny scratched behind his ear as if this story was a tad boring.

Jen bent and stroked Tiny's back. "Well, a big dog like you needs two pies."

Tiny raised his head, leaning into her arms, and Jen caressed his head. When his tongue lazily dropped out of his mouth, Rae knew that he was thoroughly enjoying himself. She rolled her eyes and said, "He really doesn't need two pies. Or any pie, for that matter. Or ham." Both Jen and Tiny looked at her with confused expressions, so Rae explained, "Because he's already a big ol' ham."

Upon standing, Jen chuckled and then graciously excused herself. She jogged back to the park office, leaving Rae and Tiny alone under the tree in the shade. Now on a blanket. Well, mostly. Tiny's big body stretched across the material with a small patch remaining for Rae's partial bottom and one leg. He gave Rae the side eye.

Shaking her head, she said to him, "It's true. You are a very big ham. So, no more pie." Tiny groaned and Rae grinned, nudging him in the shoulder. "Stop feeling sorry for yourself. Now, listen, we need to figure out what Travis is up to because I know he's up to something. I personally think-"

"Hello, Rae."

Rae flinched at the sound of a man's happy voice.

CHAPTER TWENTY SIX

Now standing alone on the trail, Stone felt conflicted. After learning that Dreadlocks wasn't a ghost, Stone also learned that Dreadlocks had a name. It was Matt. And he also had a mother and a grandma who ran this place. His mind immediately thought of Mare and her white hair. She looked like a grandma. Did she run this place? Did it really matter? Stone shook his head. All that really mattered was that Dreadlocks, correction, Matt was back to being a candidate for the crumpled body role. Since he was alive. For now. And so was Prissy. So, who should he follow? While pondering his next move, Stone felt a new presence approaching and he knew who it was way before the finger-tap on his left shoulder. "Hi, Zalen."

"Hey, my man." Zalen smiled from ear to ear. "I had a *feeling* you were headed this way. Going to get some coffee?"

"I was." Stone crossed his arms and leaned toward Zalen. He lowered his voice. "Guess what?" Stone didn't wait for an answer. "Dreadlocks isn't a ghost and he has a name."

"Matt?"

This surprised Stone. "How did you know that?"

"The same way I knew your name when we first met a few weeks ago in the frozen food section of the grocery store. It just hit me."

"Right." Stone sternly looked into Zalen's eyes. "You told me then that if a name hits you like that, it means you're supposed to get to know that person."

Happily rocking back on his heels, Zalen said, "That is correct, my dude. I'm glad you listen to me from time to-"

Stone interrupted, "Well, then, I need you to get to know Dreadlocks. I mean, Matt."

Zalen nodded. "Okay. Will do. Should I tell him that his life may be in danger, or are we still keeping that a secret?"

"Come on, Zalen. What do you think?"

"I'm just making sure that we're on the same page."

Stone pointed down the trail. "Matt just walked that way toward the north park office. Look for a guy in his late twenties or early thirties who is very tall and has brown dreadlocks."

"Got it."

"Go catch up and watch him from a distance. I want to know more about him."

"From a distance?"

Stone's hand dropped and he sighed. "I guess." After resituating his cap, he confided in his friend. "To be honest, Zalen, I don't know what I'm doing. I normally don't follow people."

Zalen smiled while walking around Stone to follow the trail. "Don't worry. This will be easy peasy. You have fun following Prissy."

Impressed, Stone crossed his arms again and said, "You're really dialed into your empathic ability this morning."

Zalen proudly nodded. "I know. It's all about trusting your *feelings.*" He then tripped over his own foot, but caught his balance before wandering down the path with a jolly whistle on his lips.

Stone turned to pursue Prissy, but was quickly met with another park ranger who had very noticeable and very alarming characteristics. He was tall and, as luck would have it, he had broad shoulders. He held a walkie-talkie near his mouth and walked with a redhead wearing a tank. The park ranger couldn't keep his eyes off her chest. As the couple passed Stone, the park ranger spoke into the device. "Yes, Casey, I'm working my way over." Then he disconnected and put his arm around the redhead who snuggled into it.

"So, Tom," said the redhead, "you like to hike?"

"Oh, I like a lot of things." Tom brought her closer and they giggled down the path.

Stone instantly became intrigued. Again, something felt off. Not with his arms because they didn't tingle. And he didn't have a headache. Nor were the little hairs on his neck standing up. He just *felt* like he ate four dozen eggs. He mentally replayed the last thing Zalen said to him. *It's all about trusting your feelings.* And right now, Stone felt that there was a new candidate for the crumpled body position. And his name was Tom.

▪   ▪   ▪

Rae was startled for two reasons. First, Zalen seemed to have materialized out of thin air and, second, his usual amble looked unnaturally determined. As he quickly approached her, she asked, "Where did you come from?"

He walked right by while replying, "I can't talk right now. I'm doing reconnaissance."

She watched him pass the north park office and walk the length of the grassy area, only to disappear on another trail in the direction of the beach.

Just then, a spectacular development occurred. Matt entered the scene, sauntering across the grassy area from the other direction. That, however, wasn't anything spectacular. It was that darn kid, walking just ahead of Matt and carrying two big library books. It was Bash and he glanced at her before quickly looking away.

As Rae watched her nephew enter the north park office, she nudged Tiny in the back and said, "So, I'm at a loss here. Should I let him do his thing, or do I intervene?" Tiny answered by covering his snout with one paw, leaving Rae to debate the issue by herself when her attention shifted to Dark Ranger Tom appearing from the trail in the woods. He had a new young camper hanging on his arm today. This one had shorty shorts, a tank and curly red hair bouncing loosely around her shoulders. As they walked by, Rae heard the same pickup line he used on her. The one about feeling like he'd known her forever even though they just met. Rae shook her head and began biting a fingernail. Just as she spit out the remnant, she turned her head toward Tiny and saw Stone appear from the same trail as Tom in the woods. *Stone's checking up on me again. What the hell, man?* Although, as Stone approached her, she noticed that he wasn't looking at her. He was staring at the back of Dark Ranger Tom's head. And he was walking gingerly on his tiptoes. When he passed her without a word of acknowledgement, this baffled Rae. *Why is he following Tom? Does he know Tom? Did I tell Stone about Tom?* She racked her brain, regarding the last conversation she had with Stone. *I don't think I said anything about Tom to Stone. So, why is he interested in Tom? Huh, how strange.*

After debating whether or not to go after Stone, she decided to remain on her corner of the blanket and leaned against Tiny. Number one, it was too hot to get up. Number two, the humidity felt like it was 1,000%. And number three, she had a sudoku puzzle to conquer. The record for completing one of these puzzles was fifty-four seconds and she was close with just under two minutes. She steadied her green marker pen, took a deep breath and forlornly watched Stone as he entered the woods on another path.

Rae mentally smacked herself and capped her pen. After closing the book, Rae thought about not thinking about Stone and then heard an approaching group of familiar voices on the other side of the tree. She leaned over Tiny for a better view. Discreetly peering around the tree, she discovered three of her coworkers huddled together a few yards away. Tonya, Chuck and Kimmy stood very close together, like football players on the field. Their arms weren't wrapped around each other, but their heads were bent down. Their quiet mutterings were almost inaudible. Chuck caught Rae's eye and he elbowed the other two, nodding in her direction.

Rae ducked behind Tiny's head and turned to face forward, just as Travis entered the scene from her left. He marched across the area, heading to the north park office. He held his Tiny in one hand and talked on the phone with the other. His furrowed eyebrows made him look upset. As he passed Rae, he also didn't acknowledge her, which she expected. What she didn't expect was his about-face. He changed direction and, instead of heading toward the lake path that led to the south campground, he headed toward the RV campground.

Once Travis was out of view, Rae leaned over Tiny again, checking on her huddled coworkers. They had broken up their summit and dispersed in different directions. Her eyes followed Chuck because he kept looking over his shoulder at her as he walked past the front porch of the north park office. When he was out of view, Rae nudged Tiny, who was drifting off to sleep. He opened one eye and she whispered to him, "As Shakespeare once wrote, the game is afoot. Now, as far as what game this is, I have no idea."

CHAPTER TWENTY SEVEN

Bash held two books under one arm while opening the door with his free hand. He waited for Matt who was behind him. As Matt approached, he nodded while saying, "Thanks, little bro." Bash smiled and followed the lanky man who had to duck under the top of the door frame.

Matt's attire interested Bash, especially on this hot day. He wore black jeans, a black t-shirt, two silver chains around his neck and work gloves. His long brown hair looked like a hundred tarantula legs grew out of his skull. They were all knotty and furry. And looked heavy. *He looks like The Ma'iingan Bluff Werewolf to me,* Bash thought. *One of them, that is.* As Matt strolled to the counter, an old lady with a sour expression waited for him.

The old lady lifted her chin and said to Matt, "You're needed in the back."

"Alright," Matt said before grabbing a new packet of gum. "I'll pay you back later."

While Matt walked to the back and through another door, the old lady called to him, "If you or Casey hear from Prissy, let me know. Why that girl went MIA is beyond me." Her eyes then settled on Bash.

Feeling the weight of the old lady's stare, he inhaled deeply and stepped forward. *Batter up,* he told himself. Bash forced a jovial tone. "Excuse me, ma'am. I'm looking for Jen. I have a very important question for her."

She scowled at him with sharp eyes and lips that tightened into a thin line. "She's busy. You'll have to ask me instead."

Drat. Maybe she can call Matt back? Bash cleared his throat. "Can I talk to Matt?"

The old lady's sharp eyes turned even sharper and Bash felt his soul easily slice in half, like in those commercials with the sharp knives and tomatoes. Bash's soul was the tomato and her eyes were the knife. And now he was dead inside.

She grumbled, "What is this all about?"

Resuscitating his courage, he lifted his two books for her to see. "I was wondering if Jen read these." While evading her glare, Bash continued, "This one is titled *The Simply Complicated Werewolf* and this one is *Where Wolves-*"

Using the flattest of tones, the old lady interrupted, "I can read the titles. I'm not illiterate."

"Oh, good. Well, ma'am, the reason why I'm asking is-"

"Don't call me ma'am. My name's Mare. And I'm pretty sure Jen has never read those books." Her demeanor was as warm as ice.

Bash stuttered, "O-okay, M-M-Mare." He cleared his throat again when a new thought struck. He gathered his last ounce of valor and asked, "Have you read either of these or heard about Beatrice Bones?" As he spoke, he nodded to the appropriate book. "She's the author of this book and, *I think*, was an eyewitness in this book."

Mare narrowed her eyes at him and said, "Beatrice Bones? Why in God's name are you interested in her? I thought kids your age only played video games."

By now, Bash's slick palms had a nice layer of nervous sweat on them and one of the books slipped. Using his knee, he managed to stop it from falling to the ground while saying, "I don't have any video games to play. We had a PlayStation 5 once, but my older sister and I wouldn't share it with each other. So, my parents sold it and then gave us a library card."

One corner of Mare's mouth rose briefly. "Smart parents."

"They like to think so." Bash smiled and showed his dimples, which could charm a cobra out of a woven basket.

There was a quick transformation. Mare now wore a wide grin and even chuckled. Reaching over the counter, she took the books from Bash and set them down on the surface.

I swung and hit a single, he thought. *Keep going.* "I'm interested in her because I believe in what she was saying about her husband."

Mare studied both covers. "And what was that?"

"That he was a werewolf." Bash heard footsteps coming from the back of the store and, out of the corner of his eye, he saw Matt appear. As Mare glanced over Bash's head, he felt Matt brush past him. Bash turned his head and spotted a rag and window cleaner in Matt's hands. He approached the storefront door and began cleaning the glass. Bash noted how slowly Matt wiped across the surface and he continued talking to Mare, "To make a long story short, Beatrice Bones wrote a story about a woman named Rose who married a werewolf. Only I believe that Beatrice Bones was really writing about herself."

"So, you think Rose and Beatrice Bones are the same person? Where does it say that?"

"Nowhere. It's just a hunch that I have. I was hoping to ask Beatrice if I'm right." When Mare showed no reaction to understanding Bash, he pointed to *Where Wolves Wait at Ma'iingan Bluff* and began to explain. "I read in this book that a woman named Beatrice had the exact same experiences with her werewolf husband that a woman interviewed by Beatrice Bones had with her werewolf husband in *The Simply Complicated Werewolf*. To make a long story short, I strongly believe that the two Beatrices are the same person. If I'm right, then Beatrice Bones might still live in this area."

She eyed him closely. "What's your name?"

"Sebastian Connor Greyson. Everyone calls me Bash."

The hint of a smile returned and Mare said, "Well, Bash, you're a smart kid, but you got that wrong."

Bash's resolution deflated a tad. "Really? How off am I?"

"She doesn't do much living these days."

Bash swallowed hard. "Is she dead?"

Mare heartily laughed and eventually explained, "No, she's a recluse. She doesn't talk to people."

Excitement rose in his voice. "Do you know her? Or where can I find her?"

More footsteps from the back of the store interrupted their conversation. Mare locked eyes with Jen as she approached the two of them. She held another apple pie in a plastic container.

"Hello, Bash," Jen said.

"Hi, Jen." Bash pointed to the books. "I was just asking about Beatrice-"

Jen interrupted him, "I saved another apple pie for you and your aunt. It's on the house." She placed it on top of his books.

"Oh." Bash paused, staring at the pie. "Thanks." He then looked at Jen and continued, "Beatrice Bones is-"

Jen interrupted him again. "I heard that Tiny ate the other two." She smiled with a strange look in her eye.

At first, Bash didn't know what to say. For some reason, he felt like he was the fire and Jen was the water, trying to douse out his investigative flame. He finally managed to say, "Yeah, Tiny loves to eat pies."

"Well, make sure he shares this one. Now, you go and get outta here. Swim or something. The day's too nice to be inside, asking questions about writers." Jen slowly turned and retreated to the back room.

As Bash watched Jen retreat, he felt a hand land on his shoulder. It was Mare and she was now leaning over the books on the counter.

Mare lowered her voice. "Beatrice never talks about her book or those experiences anymore. It cost her everything she had, including her reputation. It'll be a waste of your time."

"But-"

Mare spoke over Bash. "People claimed she was an unfit mother and they tried to take her son from her."

"But if I could just-"

"She doesn't want to be bothered by anyone, Bash. She doesn't want to talk about her family's curse."

"How about her son? Could I talk to him?"

"Nope." Mare shook her head. "The son's long gone. And the grandson wants no part of this. Sorry, but you're out of luck. Stick to reading and forget about hunting." She walked around the counter, saying, "Now, if you'll excuse me, my back is starting to ache. I need to sit down for a while." She hobbled toward the back of the store. "Don't forget your books."

As he picked up his library treasures and tucked them underneath his arm, Bash heard the entrance door open. No one entered, however Matt held it open and impatiently gestured for Bash to walk through it.

. . .

Although Tiny's eyes were closed, his nostrils were wide open. A scrumptious smell approached. Onions and apple pie. Fully awake, he lifted his head and quickly rose to his feet, wagging his tail. Sure enough, Nice Bash walked his way.

Angry Rae set her book next to her on the ground. "Hey, you. Is that another apple pie on a platter of books? What's going on? Or should I not ask?"

Nice Bash sat down next to Tiny. Reaching around Tiny's head, he handed the pie to Angry Rae and Tiny watched the transaction with great attention. Then Nice Bash set his books on the ground in front of them and pulled on his lip, saying nothing. Tiny sniffed the boy's hands, gave him a quick lick on the knuckles and resumed chewing on his bone.

Tapping the top of Nice Bash's head with the spine of her book, Angry Rae said, "Hello? Is somebody home?"

Nice Bash sighed. "Yeah. I'm home. I'm just bothered, that's all."

Tiny was bothered too. This bone could use some apple pie on it.

"Why?" Angry Rae spoke to Nice Bash. "What happened in there? Did they tell you that The Macadamia Bailiff Werewolf doesn't really exist?"

"Aunt Rae, I know you're intentionally mispronouncing the name on purpose and I can play that game forever. It's The *Ma'iingan Bluff* Werewolf and I'll correct you every single time. It won't bother me." As Angry Rae chuckled, Nice Bash continued, "I talked to the older lady behind the counter. Her name is Mare and she knows Beatrice Bones."

Tiny stopped chewing on his bone when he heard the word bones. He listened intently.

Angry Rae nodded. "I've met Mare." She then faced Bash and asked, "Beatrice Bones? Who's that?" After Nice Bash reminded her, Angry Rae then said, "I thought she was all made-up."

Nice Bash exclaimed, "How can you say that?" Tiny dropped his bone and looked at the boy as he continued, "She wrote a *real* book. It's a *true* story about a werewolf marrying a woman named Rose who I think is really Beatrice and they had a werewolf son. How can it be *made-up*?"

Tiny now looked at Angry Rae when she asked, "Are you listening to yourself?"

Nice Bash sighed. Then Tiny sighed. Shaking his head, Nice Bash said, "I know you're a skeptic, but I'm not. So, I reread some stuff and realized that Beatrice Bones is from this area and I was right. Mare knows her."

"Really? And you believe her?"

"Of course. Why would she lie to me?" Nice Bash's shoulders slumped. "Now comes the confusing part. When I started asking about Beatrice Bones, Jen interrupted the conversation and talked in a really strange way and insisted on changing the conversation to Rosemary's Apple Pie."

Nice Bash sounded stressed to Tiny. Tiny was also stressed. Looking at the apple pie that Angry Rae had on her lap, Tiny licked his lips. It was so close, yet so far away.

"And then, Aunt Rae, Matt was there and he gestured for me to leave. I think he kicked me out." After sighing, Nice Bash added, "It's really too bad because it felt like Mare would've told me more. In the end, all she could say was that Beatrice's son is long gone and the grandson wants no part of this. I wonder, though, if the grandson is still around here."

"Maybe," Angry Rae began, "this is a sign that you should drop all of this and eat some pie."

Tiny gnawed on his dog bone while dreaming of the pie and looked at Nice Bash who was pulling his bottom lip really, really hard. Nice Bash then leaned to one side and removed his phone from his back pocket.

"Aunt Rae, I never checked in with my mom. Do you want to talk to her?"

Angry Rae pursed her lips together. "Nah. I'm good."

"What should I do if she asks to speak with you?"

"Tell her I'm not here."

"But you are here. Do you want me to lie to my own mother?"

Angry Rae swiftly rose to her feet and Tiny lifted his head. "I'm going to the bathroom." Tiny nodded. "I'll be back in however long your phone conversation takes."

Tiny's head hovered over the apple pie and he salivated. Angry Rae picked up the pie and suddenly took off with it, racing into the north park office. Tiny groaned. Nice Bash chuckled, however, as he dialed the number. Only he didn't call his mother.

CHAPTER TWENTY EIGHT

Stone was astounded. In the short time that he followed Tom around the trails, this guy picked up three different women. And he didn't seem to have a type. No, this guy went after anything with a giggle.

As Stone hunkered down behind an evergreen tree, he watched in awe, again, as Tom picked up another unsuspecting woman. His fourth one and she was a brunette. Unlike the others, though, the brunette wasn't falling for any of Tom's lines. And with every failed attempt, Tom became more embarrassed and more angry. This worried Stone. In his experience of running a bar, when the guys became angry and embarrassed, that was a lethal combination. Guys couldn't handle those two emotions at the same time. They always exploded.

"Whatcha doin' there?"

Stone jumped at the voice behind him. When he looked over his shoulder, he was surprised to see Prissy again. She was also hunkered down in the same position as he was. They were both on one knee.

She peered through the branches. "Are you a birder too?"

"No," Stone whispered. "I was…just…looking at the needles."

"Oh." Prissy smiled. "They are fascinating, aren't they? You know, evergreen trees are the backbone of our forests. And these needles are so much more than just pretty. They capture sunlight, inhale carbon dioxide and exhale oxygen, providing the tree with food and giving us air to breathe." She sighed in wonderment. "I absolutely love these trees in this forest. They're like my friends. Whenever I die, I hope this is my heaven."

"Yeah," Stone said while squinting beyond the needles. Tom and the brunette just parted ways and they both looked upset. Stone quickly stood and said to Prissy, "Thanks for the information. Well, I gotta go. I'll see you later, Prissy."

"What?" Prissy looked confused and then an understanding rushed over her expression. "Oh, I see. You read my nametag. That's how you know my name. I'm not used to people doing that. Good for you, camper." She saluted him.

Now Stone was confused. "No," he said, "we've met already."

"We have?"

Stone narrowed his eyes at her. "Yesterday and again this morning, not too long ago."

Prissy had a blank look on her face. "Of course, we have."

Stone gestured to her shirt. "You don't even have a nametag."

Baffled, Prissy looked at her shirt pocket. "Well, I don't understand. I always wear a nametag. It's part of the uniform."

Feeling a little sorry for her, Stone suggested, "Maybe it fell off?"

Nodding absentmindedly, Prissy smiled. "Possibly." She suddenly brightened. "Well, it was a pleasure meeting you, I mean, seeing you…camper."

Stone could tell she forgot his name, so he helped her. "It's Stone."

"Yes, I know." Prissy awkwardly saluted. "I'll see you around."

As Stone watched Prissy march around the tree and onto the trail, he wondered about her mental well-being. Maybe she just needed a vacation? He needed a vacation. First, however, he had to save the crumpled body person from being murdered. He quickly stepped onto the trail and hustled after Tom.

■   ■   ■

Bash listened to the ringing on the other end of the line and prayed for her to pick up. "Please, please, please," he said aloud and Tiny whimpered. "It's okay." Bash petted Tiny's belly. "She'll answer her phone."

As if on cue, the line connected and Bash heard Sally say, "Hey, dimples, how is the cutest twelve-year old in the whole wide world today? I miss your face!"

Feeling his cheeks warm, Bash smiled from ear to ear. "Hi, Sally. It's good to hear from you. Listen, I don't have a lot of time and I need your help."

"Just a sec, hon, there's a guy leftover from last night. I almost dragged his whole ass out of here, but half of it is still in the door. He just needs one more strong kick. I'll be right back."

Sally must've set her phone down because Bash heard her heels fade as they clicked across the floor. Then he heard the distant jingle of a door, a few grunts, a man's voice holler something unintelligible, another jingle of a door and then the heel-clicking again. Finally, Sally returned. "Okay, dimples, what can I do for you?"

"I need you to research some people for me. I'd do it myself, but I don't have internet access from where I am."

"Are you trapped in an underground bunker? They're not that hard to escape, hon. I've done it three times."

"No, Sally, I'm camping with my aunt at Fun Warriors Ranch in the Ma'iingan Bluff area-"

Sally interrupted with a whoop before saying, "That's where Stone is. Are you all having a party without me?"

"No, I'm tracking a werewolf. So, it's kind of a party for me, but not for my aunt."

"Werewolf? Are you talking about The Ma'iingan Bluff Werewolf?"

Bash beamed. "Yes! Have you heard of it?"

"Of course, when I was a kid. It was a great story for sleepovers. Gosh, it's been a long time since I've heard about it. How exciting! Let me find a pen." Sally suddenly barked in laughter. "For goodness sakes, I forgot I have a pen right here in my bra. Oh, lordy. So, you say you need me to research some people? What are their names?"

"The first one is Beatrice Bones. The other names will be harder to research because I don't know who they are."

"Well, hon, that will make it difficult. I'm going to need a little more info than that."

"I'm trying to find the names of the son and grandson of Beatrice Bones. I'm really trying to find the grandson because I think he'll talk to me about Beatrice Bones. She's the author of the book titled *The Simply Complicated Werewolf.* She lives in this area. That's all I know."

"And you think she can help you track The Ma'iingan Bluff Werewolf?"

"Yes, especially since she was married to him."

"Really? So, then why do you need the name of her grandson? Just find her."

Bash sighed. "I can't. She's a recluse and refuses to talk about this. I was hoping to find her grandson and talk to him about anything he could tell me about her and her life with a werewolf husband. I thought it would be a start. The problem is I don't have much time. We're only staying here until Friday morning. Can you help me?"

"Well, I'm supposed to be doing inventory for Stone." Sally abruptly laughed. "Which is worse than getting kicked in the nuts by a mule. You can count on me to drop all my responsibilities and get cracking on this. I'll be in touch shortly, dimples."

Bash smiled wistfully. "Thanks. And may I just say that I wish you were here with me. I could really use a sidekick."

CHAPTER TWENTY NINE

When Rae returned to Bash and Tiny, she was biting a fingernail. "I ran into Jen and she just said something very odd to me."

Bash reclined with his head resting on Tiny's back. He caught her eye. "What odd thing did she say?"

"She suggested that since you're bored, I should take you to the waterpark that's two hours away. Then she told me all about the hotel that's adjacent to it and said that you would be happier there."

"You're joking."

Standing over Bash, Rae shook her head. "Other than talking about the werewolf, did you say something else to Mare that offended all of them?" Just then, Rae heard Travis call her name. There he was again, stomping across the grassy area toward her and still holding his little Tiny. Behind him trailed Tonya, Chuck and Kimmy. He stopped and waved her over to meet them. She rolled her eyes at Bash before joining the team, wondering about the subject of this impromptu conference.

"Rae," Travis spoke as he whipped a handkerchief out of his breast pocket and spread it on the ground with his one free hand. "I'm relinquishing your duty as The Team-Building Committee." He then gently set his Tiny on the handkerchief and stood, facing the team.

"Oh, thank god." Tonya's lips stretched into an impertinent grin, which didn't make Rae feel very special.

Ignoring Tonya's comment, Rae studied Travis in his pressed shirt and dress shorts. She asked him, "Who's going to be the committee then?"

Tonya stood a little straighter as Travis smiled at her and said, "I am." Tonya immediately slouched and Travis continued, "And, as the committee, I've decided that our next team-building activity is right now." Everyone groaned. "And what wonderful activity do I have planned, you ask?" Nobody asked. "We are going to build a pyramid with our bodies."

Chuck looked up from the ground. "Like a cheerleader's pyramid? With five people? Will that even work? I think we need six people, at least."

Travis stuck his two fingers in his mouth and whistled at Bash. When Bash looked at him, Travis yelled at him to hurry up. "Now, we have six."

Bash and Tiny happened to be studying the apple pie at that moment. Upon being beckoned, Bash jumped up. Quickly. Too quickly. He stumbled and his left foot landed in the pie. Shaking his head, he yelled, "Sorry, Aunt Rae. Another one bites the dust." He wiped his shoe on the grass and, as soon as Bash joined the group, Travis directed everyone into position. He, Chuck and Tonya were the base, kneeling on all fours. Kimmy refused to be on the top, so she and Bash cemented the middle level, also on all fours. It was now up to Rae to climb to the top of Kimmy's and Bash's backs. It was awkward, to say the least. Not exactly liking to touch people willingly, she had to grip Kimmy and Bash in questionable places in order to keep her balance. And every time she stepped on someone, Travis always yelped, even if she wasn't near him. Finally, she reached the wobbly top and, as their pyramid swayed, Tiny trotted over. He stood in front of them, licking the apple pie off his lips and watching them.

Travis, sounding strained, gave Rae an order. "Try standing up, Rae."

"What?" Rae couldn't believe her ears. "Are you nuts?"

Tonya agreed with her. "Don't make her stand up. Rae, get down."

Travis, still sounding strained, managed to yell, "Don't give up, Rae! We are a team! Stand up for all of us! Stand up for team-building! And love!"

Rae asked, "Love?"

Travis shouted, "For better or for worse!"

Rae wobbled, grabbed a hold of Bash's hair and said to Travis, "What are you talking about?"

"I'm talking about work, love and commitment, Rae! Come on, now! Stop dawdling and stand!"

Chuck yelled too, "You can do it, Rae! We got you!"

Rae put her foot on Bash's back and felt very unsteady. "Guys, I don't know about this. I don't want to hurt anyone."

Bash assured her with a strained voice. "I'm fine, Aunt Rae. Just hurry."

Placing her foot on Kimmy's back, Rae now squatted. She slowly rose to a hunched position with her rear end in the air and her hands still touching the backs beneath her.

"Are you standing?" Tonya's voice wavered.

"Not quite. Almost." Rae's balance was off. Actually, the whole pyramid's balance was off. When she looked up, the world swung from left to right to left again.

Kimmy softly said, "My back hurts."

Rae then made a decision. And that decision was to end this. By standing. Her hands released their grip and she stood straight up. "I'm standing! I'm standing! We did it!"

While Rae cheered, Tiny howled along with her in excitement. He stood on his two hind legs and jumped. When the Great Shepherd came down, it was with a crash. On top of the pyramid. All six bodies spilled over each other, knocking heads, bending elbows and straining hamstrings. Each pyramid member suffered an injury from having an eye poked to possibly breaking a toe. And as they remained motionless on the ground, some moaning and some cursing, Rae gently asked Travis, "Can we *please* have the afternoon off?"

· · ·

Travis was uncharacteristically generous. He not only gave Rae and her coworkers the afternoon off, but also the rest of the day. His only order was to have everyone reconvene at the campsite in the evening and the team breathed a big sigh of relief in unison. Kimmy even cried, although that could have been partly because someone kneed her in the eye during the pyramid collapse. After picking up his Tiny, Travis left the team, limping his way toward the wooded path.

Rae held her scuffed elbow as she watched his departure. As soon as he was out of earshot, she said to the group, "Hey, does anyone want to go to the beach?"

Massaging the back of his thigh, Chuck glanced at Kimmy. She covered her left eye with the palm of her hand, but looked at Tonya with her other eye. Tonya gave both of them the smallest head shake and Chuck then replied to Rae, "Um, no, I'm going to do something else."

"Yeah, me too," Kimmy meekly said while scanning the ground with her uncovered eye.

Tonya did not say a word. She turned and hobbled off toward the north park office.

Before Chuck and Kimmy left the scene, however, Rae stopped them. "What's going on?" Neither answered, but both wore guilty expressions. "Come on, guys," Rae continued, "I saw you three talking earlier and I have a sneaky suspicion that you were talking about me. So, just tell me what I did to offend you."

Chuck's words spilled out of his mouth. "You didn't do anything."

Bash innocently asked, "Did *I* do something?"

Shaking his head vigorously, Chuck replied, "Oh, no, Bash. You're awesome."

Rae raised her eyebrows and pointed to herself. "And I'm not awesome?"

"Well," Kimmy said while wringing her hands, "you're awesome, but also Travis's favorite, which makes you *not* awesome."

Rae's shoulders dropped and she heard Tiny softly groan next to her. She mumbled, "I don't know why you think that." Although Rae knew why. In the two months that she worked for Travis, he told her twice that she was a straight-talking, no-nonsense, sarcastic kindred spirit. And both times she was secretly flattered, which was hard to finally admit. That admittance made her feel like the black goo that formed inside the bathroom faucet.

Kimmy explained in further detail. "We think that way because you were chosen to be The Team-Building Committee, even though you're the new member of this team. It doesn't make sense."

Chuck shrugged. "It really should have been Tonya."

A spark ignited deep inside Rae's gut. She felt the burn as she spat, "I can't help that. It's not my fault that Travis chose me over her. That shouldn't affect my awesomeness." Heat intensified behind her slate-colored eyes, causing her to blink rapidly. "What are we? Twelve years old?" She answered her own question. "No, and you know what? I don't care." She shrugged, trying to keep her composure. "I'm going to the beach. You do you and I'll do me." Facing Bash, she asked him with a shaky voice, "Do you want to go to the beach with me?"

Bash smiled. "Of course, Aunt Rae. I'll go anywhere with you anytime."

Her nephew instantly cooled her hot emotions and she gratefully nodded to him. Stroking Tiny's head, Rae asked her dog, "Will you come to the beach with me?"

Tiny answered by licking her and wagging his tail. This pleased Rae and she began rubbing her hands all over his back. Curiously, the angry hurt that escalated inside of Rae now floated down to a level field of calming silk sheets. Rae heard of pet therapy, but never believed that it was a thing until now. A minute passed and she mentally stayed in doggy La La Land. As Rae slowly ran her fingers through the fur on his back, making trails, she kept her eyes on Tiny and eventually asked Bash, "Are they gone?"

"Yes, Aunt Rae. They left, and may I make a suggestion?" Rae stopped petting Tiny and looked at Bash as he continued. "If you want to fit in with them, you can't yell at them. Even when they are acting my age."

Rae straightened to her full height and wiped her hands on the sides of her shorts. While giving him a perturbed look, she said, "Maybe I don't want to fit in with them anymore?"

"Of course, you do. People naturally want to fit in, including you. So, next time, just keep your cool and try to put yourself in their shoes. That's what my mom always says to Emma." He shrugged. "It works. Sometimes."

"Look, Bash-"

"Don't worry. I'll help you, Aunt Rae. I'll help you find your calmer side."

"My calmer side?" Rae frowned. "I am calm. And I don't need any help."

"You're never calm. Look at your bitten fingernails, if you don't believe me." Bash warmly smiled. "Everyone needs help, Aunt Rae. You're helping Travis find his kinder side and I'll help you find your more relatable side."

"Now I need to be more relatable?"

"We'll start our personality development lessons later. Right now, we have a more pressing matter." He didn't wait for her to close her shocked mouth and added, "We need our swimsuits, if we're still going to the beach."

At first, Rae was indignant and determined to redirect the conversation back to the personality development lessons, but, at the mention of the beach, the lake flashed through her mind. It beckoned her to come. For her mental well-being, she needed to put her sore feelings aside and tend to her sore elbow by swimming in the medicinal lake water. Rae sighed and then studied her nephew's face with the swollen lip. As her eyes scanned the rest of his body, she noticed a stained t-shirt, faded nylon shorts and two scraped knees. "Well, we could either swim in our clothes or walk back to our campsite to change."

"And then walk *all the way* back here to the beach? How about if we buy some swimsuits at the north park office store? They have a nice selection."

Rae raised her eyebrows. "I don't have that kind of cash."

Bash then raised his eyebrows and Rae noticed a bruise forming underneath his right one, just above the eyelid. He said, "Well, I don't have full ability in my knees to walk back to our campsite in the south part of the campground and then walk *all the way* back to the beach in the north part."

"Then let's just swim in our clothes."

"Then I won't have any dry clothes to change back into."

"You didn't pack any clothes?"

"Just a pair of underwear." Bash shrugged and then winced. His right hand flew to his left shoulder and it remained there while he explained, "I didn't have a lot of room in my backpack for a lot of clothes."

"I see." Rae shook her head. "Clothes weren't as important as library books and garlic."

Now rubbing his left shoulder, Bash added, "And a utility flashlight, tarot cards, headlamp-"

"I'll be right back," Rae interrupted and entered the north park office store. Tonya stood at the counter and they made brief eye-contact before Rae diverted her line of sight. Without another Tonya thought, she quickly found the two cheapest swimsuits, the two cheapest beach towels and approached the counter to pay when she spied instant ice packs. After grabbing a generic pack of twenty-five, she paid, using her emergency charge card. Although Jen was at the cash register, when it was Rae's turn to pay, Jen motioned for a teenage girl to take over and then left the store, which Rae thought added to the strangeness of the day. Although, she was also a little relieved. Rae didn't want to have to tell Jen that the third apple pie she gave to them for free had also been destroyed. Upon leaving, one last grab for her cellphone was accomplished and Rae was on her way with her nephew and dog.

Any curious thoughts about Jen's behavior eventually vanished as Rae, who walked, and Bash, who shambled, followed the trail to the beach. Rae's eyes filled with concern whenever she looked at Bash, carrying his library books and gingerly walking with swollen knees. Not to mention that his bruised eye was darkening. Wishing to relieve Bash from all of his pain, Rae said to him while opening the box of ice packs, "I'm sorry you're hurt." Tiny moaned in agreement.

"It's okay, Aunt Rae. It wasn't your idea. Besides, you didn't know that the whole pyramid would land on me. Or, at least, that's what it felt like."

Rae crunched an ice pack, activating it to instantly cool. She handed it to him and he held it to his right eye. "I think I was the one who landed on you," she said. "Well, no matter. We'll just relax the rest of the day at the beach, okay? We'll do nothing, but cool off in the water. It'll be nice." She threw her arm around his left shoulder and squeezed him into her for a sideways hug. He yelped and she took out another ice pack, crunching it for him. Tiny shook his head at her, rolling his eyes.

The rest of the walk was quiet and the three of them eventually arrived at the beach restrooms that had adjacent dressing rooms. She and Bash entered their appropriate stations to change into their swimsuits while Tiny remained outside. Once the task of squirming into her one-piece was finished, she emerged with her folded clothes tucked underneath her arm, allowing her free hand to clutch the towel. Surprisingly, Bash was the faster one to change and already found a spot on the sand for the three of them to stretch out and relax. However, it didn't take long for Rae and Bash to abandon the towels and wade into the healing waters of Wolves Lake. Although Wolves Lake wasn't known for having the ability to cure one of bruised knees or a swollen elbow, Rae needed to believe that it could at the moment. Especially for Bash. They now both floated on their backs, allowing the cold water to act as a great ice-pack for their injuries. Every once in a while, Rae heard her nephew give a hum of contentment and then laugh, which made Rae feel better.

A few times, Tiny sploshed into the shallower water where they floated. He'd sniff their heads, sneeze, and then return to the towels draped on top of the sand. And that was where he stayed, looking across the lake and panting. Rae smiled at him, knowing that his head sniffs were his way of checking on them. This routine continued, except there would be floating intermissions involving a game of fetch with Tiny in the water. Mostly, however, it was very restful. And very pleasant, especially with her favorite genre of music being played over the sound system for all beach-goers to enjoy. At the moment, Rae softly sang along to "Sugar, Sugar" by The Archies, curing her elbow pain entirely. However, in true Rae fashion, even though the afternoon was nice, it was not absent of a couple strange events. And the first strange event involved Zalen, of course.

Rae saw him scurrying across the beach, looking every which way, but forward. He then spotted her soaking in the lake and hurried over to her. As he stood on the backshore, he cupped his hands around his mouth, calling to her, "Have you seen a guy with dreadlocks named Matt?"

"I know Matt," Rae answered while shaking her head, "but I haven't seen him. Why?"

Zalen only nodded and backed away from her. "No reason. See you around."

He scurried off toward the west family campsite and Rae turned her head just in time to see Matt entering the scene from the north. Rae thought about calling to Zalen to redirect his pursuit, but he was nearly out of sight. She instead took a deep breath and completely submerged herself underwater.

The second strange event occurred around five o'clock. Bash smelled hotdogs at the beach hut, causing hunger pains to awaken in the three of them. Rae bought two hotdogs for Bash and herself, as well as three for Tiny, who practically swallowed them whole. At the same time. That wasn't the eventful part though. The eventful part came when Travis's little Tiny showed up unannounced. The little dog trotted toward them like a prince with his head held high and he regally sat next to Tiny. Rae suddenly had two Tinys. One big and one small. And they both stared at her with their tongues sticking out of their mouths.

Rae turned her gaze from the Tinys to her surroundings, waiting for Travis to appear. He didn't and little Tiny stayed with them for a couple of minutes before yipping once at big Tiny. Then the little dog popped up and scampered away. Rae watched as little Tiny's four white stick legs fluttered across the grass toward the RV campsite. Rae stood, ready to chase after the apparent lost dog when she saw Travis suddenly appear. He bent down, scooping his Tiny into his arms. Travis didn't see Rae as he turned and limped into the RV campsite.

CHAPTER THIRTY

It was nice to see his little namesake, but it was also nice to see little Tiny go. After all, Tiny preferred having Angry Rae and Nice Bash all to himself. He loved it when the three of them were together.

Angry Rae suddenly left.

Miffed, Tiny stood to go after her, but Nice Bash stopped him. "Tiny, stay. She's probably just using the bathroom." As Tiny circled his lounging spot in the sand a few times, he finally decided to sit next to Nice Bash again, who held his phone near his mouth. He was speaking into it and Tiny could hear every word of the conversation.

"Hi, Sally, did you find out anything?"

Tiny wagged his tail when he heard Sally's voice say, "I found one very interesting fact about Beatrice Bones."

Nice Bash smiled at Tiny who licked his lips in anticipation. "Really? What is it?"

"Nothing."

Nice Bash draped himself over Tiny and, feeling the boy's distress, Tiny's tail dropped on the sand, making a thud sound. Nice Bash asked Sally, "How is that interesting?"

"Because she's an author. I mean it's strange to find nothing on anyone these days, especially an author with all the social media crap. Everyone wants to be noticed somehow, am I right?"

Tiny nodded and Nice Bash agreed. "You're right. That is interesting."

"So, dimples, I'm thinking it's a pen name. If so, I'm at a dead end. I then started researching Ma'iingan Bluff and any personal accounts about seeing werewolves. Again, I strike out. The stories that I read were clearly written by lunatics. So, out of desperation, I look at the website of Fun Warriors Ranch and guess what?"

Nice Bash pulled on his lip again. "What?"

"I started to get a strange feeling. Call it intuition or call it gin withdrawal. Regardless, whenever I feel this way, I know something is off."

"What did you find?"

"I found some interesting history. For instance, this campground opened thirty years ago in 1995. It's a family business owned by three people. And these three people don't mention their last name, only their first names, Mary, Jennifer and Matt, which are the most common first names ever."

"Actually, it's *Mare*, Jen and Matt. I've met them. Did you say that this campground is a *family* business? As in, Jen, Matt *and* Mare are family?"

"Yes and listen to this. There is no real information about them on the website, which isn't the norm, Bash. Like I said, people want to be noticed, especially business owners. I should know because I owned my cleaning business and I was all about marketing to get my name out there. Anyway, business owners want their customers to know a little bit about them. It's good business. I even looked on other websites about family-owned campgrounds and there's always a page about the family. It might not be a lot of information, but there's always some proud piece of information. You see where I'm going with this?"

In deep thought, Nice Bash slowly massaged behind Tiny's ears. "Jen, Matt and Mare want to stay as private as possible."

"Like they're hiding something. And, if so, what are they hiding?"

"I don't know."

"Well, what do you know about them?"

"Just that they run this campground. And Jen and Matt are mother and son and-" Nice Bash stopped talking. He wrapped his arm around Tiny's thick neck and hugged him. Suddenly, Nice Bash gasped and looked Tiny in the eyes. "Wait a minute. They are *mother* and *son*. Beatrice was married to a werewolf who left her and their son. What if Jen is Beatrice and her werewolf husband abandoned her and Matt? Jen's husband passed his curse onto his son, which makes Matt, The Ma'iingan Bluff Werewolf. I suspected that right away! I was right, after all, Sally!"

Sally spoke with excitement in her voice. "Good for you, hon! Now, what are you going to do?"

"I have a plan already in place, Sally. Want to hear it?" A smile slowly stretched across Nice Bash's face as Tiny's tail sprung up and began to flap back and forth, back and forth, in uncontrollable excitement.

. . .

Rae followed Travis as he unknowingly led her to the silver monstrosity parked in the RV campground. As he entered it, she fumed. With her hands on her hips and a scowl on her face, she spit on the ground. More upset with herself for not putting this puzzle of betrayal together, she now stood in front of the RV door and began counting to ten. She needed to calm down before confronting her boss. She made it to number two and pounded on the door with her fist.

Travis swung the door open in mid-pounding and Rae tipped forward. After bracing herself from falling through the doorway, she stood firmly on her two feet and ferociously scolded him with a low, booming voice. "Travis! How dare you!" She raised her arms and shook her fists in anger.

Travis shifted his eyes from side to side, as he placed a finger to his lips. He whispered, "Quiet down, Vin Diesel, and come in already. I don't want anyone else to see me."

Frustrated, she inhaled deeply and caught a whiff of freshly made buttery popcorn. She squeaked. "You have a popcorn maker in there?" Her low, booming voice returned. "How dare you!"

Travis reached with his hand and pinched her lips together. "Stop talking like that. It's not right. You sound like an angry little goblin."

Rae swatted his hand from her mouth. "You should be ashamed of yourself."

"Yeah, yeah, yeah."

"Don't yeah-yeah me. Camping was your idea."

"It was a terrible idea."

"I know! But you wouldn't listen to me!"

"I'm a bad listener."

"Travis, come on. Why would you deceive us like this?"

"Deceive who? That's a bit dramatic, don't you think?"

In her lowest of booming voices, Rae rumbled, "No!"

"Okay, okay." Travis sighed. "I got it. You're feeling left out. Do you want some popcorn?"

"I'm telling everyone. Right now. You're done for." Rae turned on her heels and took one step when she felt a large hand land on her shoulder, preventing her from leaving.

"Rae."

Turning around again, Rae met The Torch's gaze with newfound courage. She raised her chin, narrowed her eyes and crossed her arms. He peered down at her and she noticed that his eyes were a light brown with flecks of green. And they were bloodshot. Then she noticed that his frown lines deepened within the last day. He was still clean-shaven, however. What a curious, annoying man. "Well?" she testily asked.

"I can fix this, Rae." Travis pulled out his wallet from his back pocket and flipped it open. "How much do you want?"

Rae opened her mouth in shock. She had never seen so many one hundred dollar bills in one person's wallet. Rae stammered, "I d-don't want an-any of your money." She leaned a little closer to him as he flashed through the cash. "How much do you have?"

"I brought along two grand."

Clearing her throat, Rae confessed, "I only brought ten. Dollars. Well, actually eight."

Travis stopped leafing through his bills and he looked at her. "What about an emergency? You should always have extra cash in case of an emergency."

Rae nodded. "That's why I grabbed a five on my way out."

"Oh, Rae." Travis shook his head in pity and dealt her five one hundred dollar bills. "Take this."

Rae brought her hands to the sides of her head in disbelief. "No, Travis, I'm not taking your bribe."

"Pfft. It's not a bribe. The paid week off that I'm giving you is a bribe. Think of this money offer as a bonus." Travis waved the money at her. "You deserve it." Placing her hands on her hips, she shook her head. He continued, "I forced you to be The Team Building Committee." He took her hand in his. "I forced you to teach me how to be kind and messy in order to save my marriage." He placed the money in her palm. "You deserve this payment. So, take it as my way of saying sorry for dragging you into my problems." He closed her fingers around the cash. "That's right, Rae. Take it and no one has to know about this or your paid week off."

Confused, Rae asked, "What?"

"We don't have to tell the others about this. You don't owe them any explanation. It's not like you're close with any of them anyway."

Rae bit her bottom lip. "Well, I-"

"Use the money for yourself."

Squinting in thought, Rae began, "But, Travis, that would-"

"Go to a resort with a lap pool."

Oooo, a lap pool, Rae thought. She then shook her head.

"Or go to my hairdresser. He can do wonders."

Rae sighed and regained her ethics. "Hell no. I'm not taking your bribe, Travis."

"I keep telling you that it's not a bribe."

"Yes, it is. You don't want me to tell the team that you double-crossed them by staying in this luxurious hotel on wheels. So, you're bribing me with money to keep my mouth shut." Shaking her head, she added, "I can't be bribed, Travis."

"Does that mean you don't want the paid week off either?"

"I didn't say that." She pulled her hand away and purposely dropped the money. "I just don't want the money. That feels much more wrong than the paid week off."

Travis laughed while bending to pick up his Tiny who appeared behind him. "Take the money, Rae, and use it or don't use it. Or buy Bash a new piece of paranormal equipment or invest in toothbrushes for large dogs." He shrugged. "Whatever."

As he backed into the RV, Rae fell to her knees, quickly gathering the bills, and threw his cash back at him. He closed the door just in time for the bills to hit it. She helplessly watched the five Benjamin Franklins drift to the ground and she remained there. On her knees. On the grass. And she thought about what he said. Did she deserve it? Of course, she did. Did he force his problems on her? Affirmative. Was she close with her team? Absolutely not. Could she use the money for herself? And for Bash? Tiny? With pursed lips and a furrowed brow, she collected the five hundred dollars and shoved them in her back pocket.

CHAPTER THIRTY ONE

Stone found himself in the RV campsite. He followed the park ranger named Tom who just entered one of the RVs belonging to the redhead. She waited for him under the awning. Now, as Stone slowly walked by the vehicle, he heard squeals and moans. When the RV began to rock back and forth, Stone quickened his pace, thinking that Tom didn't waste any time.

Stone found refuge at a lonely picnic table perched in the middle of the RV park. As he rested on the faded seat board, the lonely picnic table creaked. Stone gently patted the top surface. "Sorry, old friend," he softly said to the table. "Hopefully, I won't stay here long." He shifted his seat and felt the table tip a little. As he tried to slide on the seat to a more balanced spot, he heard Rae's loud voice scolding her boss's name. The picnic table remained unbalanced as Stone turned his head to spy a silver RV that was as long as a blue whale and tall as the Space Needle. He saw the back of Rachel as she faced Travis who stood in the doorway. She gesticulated wildly and Travis said something to make her squeak.

Off in the distance, someone at a nearby RV started playing music on a speaker, which made it difficult to hear what Rae said to Travis. However, Stone knew Rae's body language pretty well and, right now, her body language was filled with profanities. Her stance was wide with both of her feet firmly planted on the ground. She leaned a little forward and her chin was up as she crossed her arms. He, on the other hand, looked relaxed. His stance was of a typical male who stood in line at a concession stand, waiting for his order. He put all of his weight on one leg and bent his other leg at the knee, lifting his toe. And Travis didn't even look at Rae. Instead, his attention was on his wallet that he now opened. The next series of events happened very quickly.

Travis produced a load of cash. Rae leaned forward. He tried to hand it to her. Rae's hands clasped the sides of her head. Travis waved the cash at her. She shook her head and placed her hands on her hips. Travis grabbed her hand and forcibly placed the money in her palm, closing her fingers around the bills. He held it in her hand and then Rae dropped the cash. Travis laughed and bent to pick up his little white dog. He turned his back and Rae rushed to pick up the money to throw at him. She wasn't fast enough and the bills met a closed door before falling to the ground.

Just then, Stone's attention shifted to Tom as he strutted by Stone. Tom seemed very at ease as he hummed a happy melody. Then Tom saw Rae and abruptly stopped. He turned on his heels and briskly walked past Stone again, heading in the opposite direction of Rae.

Conflicted, Stone wanted to rush to Rae and help her with whatever happened. He also felt compelled to follow Tom. After all, Tom was, more than likely, the crumpled body in his vision. He could sense it. Or, rather, his uneasy stomach could sense it and he knew he had to follow his nauseous gut.

Sighing, he patted the lonely picnic table, bidding it farewell, and then slid off the seat board. As he trailed after Tom, Stone glanced over his shoulder at Rae who was now picking up the cash with a tormented look on her face and stuffing it in her back pocket.

■　■　■

Night had fallen, but Bash had a manic buzz keeping him awake. His three library books sprawled in front of him on the picnic table as he worked by the light of a lantern. He wrote down every piece of relevant information in his trusty red spiral notebook while the others sat around the campfire, eating s'mores. He wasn't interested in the melted marshmallows, however. He was only interested in The Ma'iingan Bluff Werewolf.

He heard Travis ask someone, "What is that kid doing?"

Aunt Rae replied with an edge to her tone, "He's growing his mind by reading about very interesting things."

Travis called to Bash, "Hey, what are you reading about over there?"

Bash turned to face Travis and answered, "Werewolves that live in this area."

Travis held his Tiny on his lap and lovingly stroked the little dog's head. He asked Aunt Rae, "Werewolves help his mind grow? *Werewolves* are *interesting*?"

Aunt Rae uncapped her water bottle. "I think the real question is whether or not werewolves are as interesting as RVs."

Travis narrowed his eyes on her. "Well, you have five hundred answers for that."

Chuck sniffed the air. "I smell steak." He sniffed again. "And sauteed garlic. And fried onions." Leaning toward Travis, Chuck said, "I think it's you."

Tonya sounded upset. "Travis, how did you have steak for dinner? The closest restaurant is an hour away, but it's a bar, not a steak joint." Bash noticed that she had a nice purple goose egg on her forehead.

Kimmy shook her head and Bash saw that she had a black eye, just like he did. Only hers was blacker. She said to Tonya, "He didn't leave. His car was here the whole time. I know because so was I."

Bash looked at Travis. He had one bare foot elevated on another chair and his second toe was taped to this third toe. A smug smile appeared on his face. "I didn't have a steak dinner. I had a brat with onions from the beach hut."

Perplexed, Chuck looked at Travis. "Brats? The beach hut only serves hot dogs."

"Okay, Chuck," Travis said nonchalantly, "then I ate a hot dog. It's the same thing."

"Actually," Chuck casually addressed Travis, "brats and hot dogs are very different."

Travis testily rolled his eyes. "Whatever, Chuck."

"Hey," Aunt Rae scolded him, "be *nice*. Remember?"

Travis laughed. "Why be nice when there are more important characteristics to behold, like integrity."

Aunt Rae took a deep breath before saying, "You want to go? Let's go."

Travis hissed, "I'm ready when you are."

"For Pete's sake." Tonya sounded exasperated. "I swear, Rae, you like drama. Now, stop making a mountain out of whatever molehill you and Travis are bickering over."

Aunt Rae's eyes flashed and she turned to Tonya. "Excuse me?" Her heated tone was hotter than the campfire. "What did you just say to-"

Bash interrupted her. "Hey, Aunt Rae, remember the shoes. Think about their shoes."

Chuck spoke to Rae, "What shoes?"

Aunt Rae took another deep breath and locked eyes with Travis for a moment. When she looked away, he grinned and said, "Let's change the subject."

Tonya replied, "Yes, thank the good Lord. I'm tired of listening to this gibberish. I'd rather circle back and talk about the werewolf."

Bash didn't need any more of an invitation. "Okay!" He enthusiastically said, "It's actually werewolves and I think there's a family of them who live here. I'm pretty sure they run the place." There were some snickers and snorts from Travis, but Bash ignored them. After swiping his library books and red spiral notebook off the table, he joined them at the campfire. Tiny was at his side as Bash began his werewolf presentation.

CHAPTER THIRTY TWO

For the next fifteen minutes, Bash gave a wonderful disquisition regarding the history of Ma'iingan Bluff, beginning with its settlement by the Chippewa tribe. He spoke of the first sighting of The Ma'iingan Bluff Werewolf and showed photographs of the creature in the book. With voice inflections and exaggerated arm gestures, Bash told the group about how these beasts can shapeshift, eat hearts and livers of animals, particularly deer, and are really gentle by nature.

"What?" Travis interrupted Bash. "Did you say they're gentle?"

"Oh, yes. And often misunderstood." He picked up his red spiral notebook and turned to his outline. "I read that they are just as scared of us as we are of them. So, they try to push us away by howling at night, showing their fangs, acting like they're possessed by a demon and other stuff. But it's all in an attempt to keep themselves safe from us."

"So," Kimmy said, "they're not trying to eat us, they just want us to leave. That way, they can be free and live peacefully." She sighed. "I get that. I'd give anything to be free."

Bash nodded. "Exactly."

Kimmy added, "From my in-laws."

Chuck asked, "I know that last night's werewolf hunt was kind of a bust, but have you found any evidence of The Ma'iingan Bluff

Werewolf?" He tried crossing his leg, but winced in pain and vigorously rubbed his hamstring.

Bash nodded enthusiastically. "I found two deer carcasses that had their hearts and livers missing. One was near this campsite and the other one was near the beach in the woods. Nothing else on the deer had been touched." Bash glanced at his aunt who was biting her fingernails. He then addressed Travis, Tonya and Kimmy. "And, last night during the werewolf hunt, we had something very strange happen."

Travis held up his hand. "Was it that you were actually on a werewolf hunt? Because that is very strange."

Chuck tried leaning forward in his chair and winced again while reaching for his lower back. "Are you talking about the bell, Bash?"

Tonya shoved the last bite of a s'more into her mouth. With her mouth full, she asked, "What bell, dare I ask?"

Bash could hardly contain his excitement. "We heard a bell toll around three-thirty."

Chuck nodded. "It sounded like a dinner bell from an old western movie."

Tonya chuckled. "That's ridiculous. We're not on a ranch."

"But there is a dinner bell hanging on the porch at the south park office. I saw it. It's near the door." Kimmy widened her eyes. "Could it have been that one?"

Tonya looked annoyed. "Who would've rung it at three-thirty in the morning? The office is closed at that time. We're the only campers in this section, other than Rae's cohorts, Zigzag and Strain."

Aunt Rae corrected Tonya. "Their names are Zalen and Stone."

Sounding exasperated, Tonya continued, "My point is there's no one here who would've rung it."

Kimmy, on the other hand, seemed very interested. "And why did they ring it?"

"And then there were those two whooshes of wind, right, Bash?" Chuck prodded Bash with a head nod.

Bash said to everyone, "It was a sudden gush that happened *twice*."

"And the ground shook. Both times," Chuck added.

"Well," Travis spoke in a monotone voice, "it doesn't sound all that fascinating."

Dumbfounded, Bash said, "With all due respect, how can you say that?"

Travis shrugged. "It just sounds like a bell moved in a strong wind."

Bash argued, "The bell tolled first. Then the ground shook. Then a rush of air blew past us. Then the ground shook again and another rush of air." Bash's face shone brightly in the campfire light. "It was all very thrilling! Two whooshes of air mean two Ma'iingan Bluff Werewolves!"

Silence followed momentarily before Travis taunted, "Well, I guess I had to be there."

Bash widened his eyes as a thought struck. "Well, you can. We can do it again tonight."

Kimmy meekly raised her hand. "Me too? I'd really like to go this time."

"Sure!" Bash exclaimed and Tiny raised his head, looking around the area. Then he flicked his ear and rested his head on Bash's feet again. "The more, the merrier! Right, Aunt Rae?" He faced his aunt. To his surprise, she quickly guzzled the rest of the water.

Chuck now sat on the edge of his seat. "This is great! Maybe we can cover more ground with all of us hunting, you know?" Aunt Rae started coughing to the point where she gagged. Over and over. Uncontrollably. And Chuck continued, "We can be in teams."

Aunt Rae now raised her head and looked at Bash. Streams of tears ran down her cheeks and she wiped her nose with the back of her hand. "What have you done?"

Travis shook his head, ignoring Aunt Rae. "You can count me out. I need my beauty sleep." He kissed his Tiny's little head.

Tonya also opted out. "I don't believe in that stuff. It all sounds sacrilegious. I'd rather just say my prayers tonight and count my blessings."

Travis scoffed, "Because you think you have blessings?"

Bash blinked in surprise at Travis's rude remark as Aunt Rae said with a twinkle in her eye, "Now, Travis, that wasn't being *kind,* remember?"

Bash double-blinked in surprise at his aunt's insincere scolding and whispered to her, "You're forgetting about the shoes."

Tonya sprung from her seat, glaring at Travis. "It wasn't kind! But I'm glad you said it because you just made up my mind! I received a job offer to a real shitty place with a long shitty commute and no shitty benefits! And I'm taking it! Because *anything* will be better than working for *you.* Consider this my notice! Effective immediately!" Her voice then dropped a couple of octaves as she said, "And you can go to hell!" Tonya then gestured at Chuck and Kimmy. "Well?" Her normal tone returned with the usual terseness. "Are you two going to join me like we talked about or what?"

When they didn't answer, Travis asked them, "What does she mean?"

Kimmy looked at the ground and Chuck cleared his throat. "Tonya said that she can get us jobs at her new position, so that we could all leave. You. We could all leave you. At the same time." He cleared his throat again and looked at Aunt Rae. "That's what we were talking about earlier when you saw us."

Bash looked at Aunt Rae who appeared hurt. He saw her eyes beginning to glisten as she remained silent, seeming to be lost in her own thoughts and nibbling on a new fingernail.

Tonya replied, "Oh, please, Rae. Don't look so freaking sad. You and Travis are tight. You're like his short clone."

Aunt Rae started gagging again and Travis asked the others, "You staged a coup d'etat behind my back?"

"I think it's more that they're just leaving," Bash explained to Travis. "They're not trying to violently take over your business." Bash nodded to the others. "Right, guys?"

There was silence.

And then Travis exploded.

In laughter.

He laughed so loud that he stopped Aunt Rae from gagging. He laughed so hard that he knocked his little Tiny off his lap. He laughed so long that Tonya eventually sat down on her chair again, crossing her arms and one leg. When he finally exhausted himself and regained his composure, he said to the group. "Everyone has a breaking point. Am I right?" Then he gathered his Tiny in his arms, gently slid his hurt foot into the slider and steadied himself on his two feet.

As he hobbled onto the gravel path, trying to keep his weight off the broken toe, Kimmy asked him, "Where are you going?"

"Crazy," he answered. "Wanna come along?" When she didn't reply, Travis called over his shoulder. "I'm not accepting any resignations tonight. Maybe tomorrow morning, but not tonight. I'll be back later. Don't wait up."

The group was still. For many minutes. Feeling uncomfortable, Bash didn't know what to do. He tried to catch his aunt's eye, but she was in the process of biting her sixth fingernail. Bash feared that she would soon begin biting her toenails.

"Aunt Rae," he began and that seemed to snap her out of her fog.

She abruptly stood, placing her hands on her hips. "How dare you call me his *short* clone!"

Bash was soon on his feet, standing next to her and softly saying, "Keep calm, Aunt Rae. Be relata-"

With her hands on her hips, Tonya also stood and interrupted Bash, "Well, you are his short clone. You're just like him, after all, with the same sarcastic personality."

"That doesn't make me his short *clone*!" Aunt Rae suddenly clasped her hands around her mouth. Through her fingers, she asked, "Does it?"

Tonya then addressed Chuck and Kimmy, "Why didn't you guys stand up with me? That's what we said we were going to do."

Kimmy quietly said to Tonya, "I like my job. I don't want to leave it." When Chuck agreed with Kimmy, Tonya deflated into her chair.

This puzzled Bash and he asked Chuck and Kimmy, "Why do you like your jobs?"

Chuck answered first. "Are you kidding? I love web design. And Travis allows me to listen to my music. Not to mention, I have great clients and I like everyone who's sitting here with me right now. It's unusual to like the people who you work with. And, even though Travis can be hard, I am well-paid and have good benefits, compared to other places. Plus, I can walk to work and that saves me a lot of money on gas."

Kimmy offered, "I don't mind Travis. I think he's kinda funny. And, putting myself in his shoes-"

Bash shot his aunt a look. "Did you hear that, Aunt Rae?"

Kimmy continued, "I think he's been subjected to a lot of ridicule for being gay. That might explain why he's so guarded and tough on the outside. My heart goes out to him." She paused and then quickly said, "Oh, and I like my job too. I like my cubicle corner where I sometimes take naps. After lunch. All the time." Brightening, she smiled at Aunt Rae. "And I really like you, even if you're Travis's favorite. You bring a lot to the team."

When Chuck agreed, Aunt Rae's gloom lifted and she raised her arms in triumph. "Thank you! That's all I needed to hear! I like you guys too." She then playfully punched Tonya in the shoulder. "And you. I like you, Tonya, even if you don't like me."

Bash gave her a nod of approval, but Tonya raised her lip, muttering, "Bleh."

Aunt Rae then surprised Bash by pulling Tonya to her and hugging her. After the embrace, Tonya resembled someone who was flattened by a drum roller. Revived, Aunt Rae gleefully ordered everyone to stand, including Bash and Tiny. They all formed a circle and she stuck her hand in the center of it. "Okay, guys, who cares if we can't succeed at any of the team-building activities? We *are* a team. And we are a *good* one. So, let's put our hands together and, on the count of three, we'll yell *go team!*"

Everyone put their hands (and one paw) on top of each other's, except for Tonya. They waited for her. And waited. Each one wearing a hopeful and dopey expression. Finally, Chuck said, "Travis didn't accept your resignation. You're still part of the team."

With a loud exasperated sigh, Tonya placed her hand on top of the others and asked, "Isn't there something better we can say? *Go team* is *so* generic."

Aunt Rae furrowed her eyebrows. "Seriously?"

Kimmy shrugged. "I guess, in a way, it is. How about if we say *let's go?*"

"Or," Chuck smiled, "let's all say *we got this*. Yeah?"

Tonya shook her head. "I'm not feeling it."

Aunt Rae pulled her hand back and the others followed. As they bantered back and forth about what to say, Bash and Tiny exchanged glances, both rolling their eyes. Bash took the moment to check his phone's battery, which was half-charged, and then called his mom, who still sounded ill. He was about to return to the picnic table to continue his research when he heard the sound of gravel crunching. He spun around in time to see an unfamiliar vintage red Corvette with thick black tires pull up to their campsite. With his hands, he shielded his eyes from the bright headlights. As soon as the driver turned off the engine, he heard the car door open and saw a thin figure emerge. This person walked around to the front of the sports car and stepped into the beam of light. Bash's eyes adjusted and he finally realized that it was Sally, wearing a lime green wig styled in a sleek angled bob and t-shirt with a picture of a werewolf on it. She smiled at Bash, saying, "Hey, dimples, did I miss anything?"

Thrilled to see his sidekick, Bash exclaimed, "Nope, you're just in time!"

■　　■　　■

One minute ago, Stone and Zalen sat around their campfire, plotting the next move in saving the unnamed body from becoming a crumpled one, and the next minute, a familiar red Corvette unexpectedly drove by, instantly changing their conversation. "That's Sally!" Stone blurted as he pointed after the vintage gem. Zalen remained calm, which puzzled Stone as he stood and asked, "Did you hear me? That's Sally!"

Now Zalen stood, rocking back on his heels. He smiled, of course. "How nice. I had a *feeling* that she would come eventually."

Stone swiped his baseball cap off his head and he messed up his hair in frustration. "This isn't nice! She's supposed to be managing my bar!" He slapped his cap back onto his head and quickly marched down the gravel road to Rachel's campsite with Zalen in tow.

There Sally was. In her black disco pants and combat boots. Stone and Sally stood cap to wig, with him giving her his sternest look. He demanded, "What are you doing here? You're supposed to be watching The Rail."

Sally grabbed his cheeks and squeezed to make his lips pucker. "Stop the squawking. I called my sister and she's in charge until I get back." She released his face. "Don't worry. When we ran our cleaning business, she did most of the work. I was really the eye-candy." Sally then planted a big kiss on him. "The Rail is in very good hands." She patted his cheek and winked. "But my hands are better."

After she turned an about-face, Sally lunged for Bash and wrapped him in her arms. While she squeezed the life out of him, Stone beelined to Rachel and asked her, "Do you know what's going on at all? Do you know why Sally is here? Did I miss something?"

Biting her thumbnail, Rachel replied, "Well, it looks like Bash and Sally have been in cahoots and she came to hunt down a werewolf with my nephew." Stone groaned and Rachel continued, "I'm sorry for not keeping a tighter leash on Bash."

Stone nodded. "And I'm sorry for Sally. Period."

Zalen approached and stood between Rachel and Stone. With a bigger smile on his face, he said, "Now, it's a party. I mean, I don't really party, but, if I did party, it would look like this."

After Sally released Bash, all the introductions were made between her and the other three from Rachel's office. Chuck became instantly enamored with Sally and even Kimmy seemed more relaxed around her. The only one still scowling was Tonya and, as Bash talked about the reason behind Sally's arrival, she excused herself from the group, saying, "I don't want to be a part of this."

"Are you sure, sweetie?" Sally asked Tonya. "Staking out a werewolf sounds exciting and who doesn't want a little excitement in their life?"

Tonya didn't answer. She just covered her ears with her hands on her way to the tent.

Stone nudged Rachel. "You're seriously okay with Bash and Sally werewolf-hunting tonight?"

Bash answered before Rachel could. "She should be. We did the same thing last night."

Stone opened his mouth in shock and Rachel said, "Werewolves don't exist, Stone, so I wasn't worried about really meeting one. I just wanted to make sure a bear didn't eat him."

Bash added, "Besides, Chuck was with us, so there were three of us out there, hunting a werewolf. Or, I really should say werewolves."

Stone opened his mouth again in more shock as he addressed Rachel. "Three of you were in danger?" He then pivoted to Bash. "What do you mean by *werewolves*?"

Bash answered matter-of-factly, "There are two for sure. Sally and I are going to get proof of them tonight."

Stone incredulously asked, "How?"

Sally replied first, "By staking them out. Haven't we been over this?"

Chuck surprised Stone by adding, "With Bash's equipment. He has some cool stuff."

Kimmy eagerly joined in the conversation. "We're all going. Well, except for Tonya. She's in the tent. And our boss isn't going either." Kimmy then looked into the darkness. "He's somewhere."

Stone asked Rachel, "Is this for real? You're all going to stake out a werewolf?"

He heard Bash correct him. "Werewolves."

Stone fixed his eyes on Rachel. She spit out a piece of thumbnail, sighed and reluctantly nodded. As Rachel began to explain the reasons behind her involvement, Stone's first vision rushed at him. He saw the moon, the trees, and the crumpled body all at once. Then he saw the two beasts. Were they bears? Were they wolves? He gulped. Were they werewolves? Was the crumpled body a victim of a werewolf attack? He gulped again. Was the crumpled body someone from the team? Chuck? Or Travis? The idea almost knocked the air out of him and he felt the ground moving, like someone pulled the carpet from beneath him. He grabbed Rachel by her arms and held onto her. As he steadied himself, he lowered his face to hers. "Don't go out there. Understand?" He saw the fear in her eyes and immediately relaxed his grip. Straightening, he realized that everyone stared at him with puzzled expressions. "Sorry," he said to the group. "I just don't want anyone to get hurt."

With concern in his voice, Bash spoke to Stone. "Well, just come with us then."

Stone looked at Rachel who now seemed highly irritated. She rolled her eyes and said, "Hey, frenzy, try to stay hinged. There are no werewolves, so we'll be fine. The sooner we do this, the sooner we'll be done."

Zalen agreed. "I *feel* we need to do this."

Nodding like a bobblehead on a bumpy road, Sally added, "I also *feel* we need to do this. And I haven't felt anything this strong since the last time I was with this hunk and he shoved a straw up my-"

Rachel interrupted, "Sally! Watch what you say in front of Bash!"

"What?" Sally shrugged. "I was going to say nose." She offensively crossed her arms. "It hurt. I mean, he was cute and all, but very clumsy."

Refraining from commenting on Sally's story, Stone faced Bash and those hopeful blue eyes. *What a kid,* he thought. *Maybe I'm supposed to do this, after all? Maybe this is how I save the person in my vision?* After taking a deep breath, Stone said, "I guess I'll have to."

CHAPTER THIRTY THREE

Elation described Bash's feelings at the moment. Pure elation. He now had a werewolf gang. And as they all formed around the picnic table, Bash spread out the map of the campground and assigned teams to stake out a specific area. Next, he told them the plan. Aunt Rae, Stone and Zalen were assigned to the woods where Bash found the second dead deer victim by the beach. Chuck and Kimmy were going to investigate the long trail that led from their campsite to the north park office. And Sally, Tiny and Bash would set up home base at the south park office. Well, outside of it. On another picnic table. With all of his paranormal equipment.

Aunt Rae shook her head. "If you have all of the equipment, what are we supposed to use?"

"Your phones," Bash replied. "Take a picture and then text me. I'll come running."

Sally corrected him. "We'll come running."

Chuck asked, "But whenever I text, my messages aren't delivered. Should we call each other instead?"

Bash replied, "Only if we have to. We really shouldn't be making any noise. It'll scare The Ma'iingan Bluff Werewolf. I mean werewolves."

Chuck raised his hand. "And if we should scare the werewolves and they come after us, is there anything that we can do to protect ourselves?"

"Shoot them."

"No, Aunt Rae, shooting them won't do anything unless you have silver bullets. Werewolves are pretty much indestructible." Bash then addressed Chuck. "Your only chance is to play dead."

Kimmy clapped her hands in excitement. "Oh, this sounds so fun. Can we start now or is there more stuff you want to say?"

Bash shook his head. "We can't start now. The best time for any paranormal activity is between three and four in the morning."

Zalen checked his watch. "Well, let's see then. It's just after ten now. When should we reconvene?"

"I think at two-ten would be good. That will give you guys enough time to walk to your spots and get situated before three o'clock. Does that work for everyone?" When the team agreed, Bash smiled and said, "Okay, guys, let's get some shut-eye and be ready for the witching hour."

Sally corrected Bash again. "I think you mean the *werewolfing* hour." They high-fived and, as she turned and walked to her Corvette, she said over her shoulder, "I'll be sleeping in my car, if anyone needs me before then."

While the others dispersed, Bash watched his aunt and Stone. They stared at each other, but he couldn't tell what they were thinking. Finally, she spoke first. "What's wrong?"

He clenched his jaw while saying, "Nothing. Just soaking it all in."

Aunt Rae narrowed her eyes. "You clenched your jaw. That means you're lying. Talk to me already."

Stone shook his head. "I don't lie to you."

"Oh, please, you're lying right now." Aunt Rae placed her hands on her hips. "You have a wall, Stone. And I don't like it. If you can't trust me, then we have nothing." With that, Bash watched her turn and she entered the tent.

Bash then looked at Stone who sighed, shaking his head. He quietly said to Stone, "You should just tell her that you like her. I think it's time."

"I would, Bash, but I don't know how."

With an understanding nod, Bash said, "Maybe there's nothing to know? Maybe you just need to say it?"

. . .

Two-ten came quickly and Rae, still in her street clothes, was in line to be the last to leave the tent. After the others filed out, she approached the screen door and heard Tonya say, "You guys are really going to sit out there, hoping to see a werewolf?"

Rae shrugged. "Werewolves don't exist, so I'm just helping my nephew have some fun. Good night, Tonya." Tonya didn't reply and Rae glanced at Travis's spot, which was empty.

Tonya spoke again, "He never came back."

"Well, don't be worried. I'm pretty sure that he's-"

"I'm not worried, Rae. I decided to *really* quit and I'm leaving in the morning. So, *I* don't work for *him* anymore." Tonya's voice wavered as she laid her head on her pillow, covering her face with her sleeping bag and sniffling. "Goodbye, Rae."

Rae froze. Standing inside the tent and wrapped in darkness, she couldn't find the right words for this awkward moment. In the end, she decided to give any wisdom that she found on the surface of her brain. "I'm sorry to hear that." Albeit, it wasn't good wisdom and Rae, feeling like an invisible weight squashed the conversation, left the tent.

As she joined the group around the picnic table, Rae glanced at the cars. She saw her little blue coupe, Sally's Corvette and, thankfully, Travis's Mercedes. So, he hadn't completely abandoned the ship, after all.

Rae had to put the thoughts of her absent boss in her back pocket, along with his bribe money, as she was met with another umbrella from Zalen. This one had a long, aluminum shaft with red and white striped fabric panels. "Just in case," he told her as she rolled her eyes. Turning her attention to Bash, she listened to the same instructions that her excited nephew bestowed upon them earlier with an important reminder.

"Play dead," Bash began, "if you happen to be lucky enough to be in the presence of a werewolf. Okay? Werewolves typically eat at the witching hour. They may mistake you for a deer. If they do, they'll eat you. Possibly. The best thing that you can do is not move one muscle." Bash then passed out string necklaces with one small garlic clove tied to each. "I didn't have enough bulbs for all of us, so I had to split them up."

With all of them armed with their root vegetable jewelry, they all parted to their designated area with their designated partner. Or partners, in Rae's case. And neither of them spoke to her for the whole duration.

As their lengthy, silent walk ended, Rae found herself in the woods again, near the beach. Her olfactory senses appreciated the garlic lofting around her as she still faintly smelled the dead deer, even though it had been removed. She checked the time on her phone. It was quarter to three and she sighed. "I don't get it," she said aloud. "Why can't you just talk to me?"

"Oh, I'm sorry, Rae. I didn't know you wanted to talk. What should we talk about?"

Stone shook his head. "Zalen, she's talking to me, not you."

"Oh, that makes more sense. Anyone want a butterscotch candy?"

All three sat on the ground in the forest with the striped umbrella resting lengthwise in front of them. On the left was Stone, shining his cellphone flashlight on the ground, and Rae was on the right, holding her cellphone flashlight and sweeping the beam around her. Zalen perched himself in the middle of them with no phone, just a flashlight in his lap and a handful of butterscotch candies. He shook his hand in an enticing manner. "Butterscotch calms the nerves," he said. "I have more in my pocket."

Both Rae and Stone declined. Then they started talking to each other at the same time.

"Rachel, I'm sorry, but it's hard to tell you the truth about-"

"Stone, ever since high school, you have-"

"My problem." Stone took a butterscotch, quickly unwrapped its gold foil and shoved it in his mouth. "I'm afraid that you'll never speak to me again-"

"Built a brick wall around yourself." Rae then took a butterscotch that Zalen unwrapped and popped it into her mouth. "I need to break it down, for us-"

"And then I'll-"

"Or else I'll-"

"Die." They both ended this overlapping conversation with the same word and they both directed their beams of light at each other when they realized that they said the same word.

Stone reached across Zalen's lap for her hand. "I don't want you to die, Rachel."

Rae's heart swelled. "I don't want you to die either, Stone." She then reached across Zalen's lap and grasped Stone's hand. The light of the full moon shone brightly in their warm gaze and they smiled at each other while sucking on a butterscotch candy.

Zalen set his hand on top of theirs. "Isn't this nice? We should do this more often."

Unfortunately, this amorous moment ended as slow, careful footsteps quietly crunched towards them.

CHAPTER THIRTY FOUR

Bash, Sally and Tiny positioned themselves at a central picnic table within twenty yards of the south park office. Sitting in the middle of the bench with Sally on his left, Bash showed her the trusted paranormal equipment. Tiny rested next to Sally on the ground and busied himself by licking his front paws.

Talking to Sally about his equipment was as pleasing as hitting a grand slam for Bash, especially since he never even made it to first base in his entire baseball career during one distant summer. And Sally was the best teammate he could've had. She not only intently listened, but also asked appropriate questions at the appropriate times. It was nice, having an engaged participant who didn't yell at him for not keeping his eye on the ball.

When the tutorial finished, the three of them sat at the picnic table, facing the porch of the south park office. "So, dimples," Sally whispered while foraging inside her bra. She then presented two sticks of gum and offered one to Bash, who politely declined. After unwrapping both and pushing them into her mouth, she continued, "Back in my mechanic days, I watched a documentary called *Once Bitten, Twice Scratched*. Fittingly, it was about werewolves."

"Was it good?"

Sally nodded and asked, "So, you're not interested in my mechanic days?"

"Are we sitting in the middle of a garage?"

"Good point. The documentary was interesting. It was about this guy who had a friend who had another friend who was bitten once and scratched twice by a werewolf before turning into one. He could then shapeshift into a human and back into a werewolf, but the more he shapeshifted, the more he'd lose his human qualities. Eventually, he stayed a werewolf forever."

Bash set down his thermal camera on the table and gave his full attention to Sally. "Really? I knew werewolves could shapeshift, but I never knew that they could potentially stay a werewolf for eternity." He quickly snatched his red spiral notebook and pencil to make note of this new, inspiring information in the light of his utility flashlight, horizontally placed on the table.

Sally blew a small bubble with her gum and then sucked it back into her mouth. "So, you said that there are two Ma'iingan Bluff werewolves?"

While writing, Bash replied, "Yes. One of them is Matt and I thought the other one was Park Ranger Tom, but I think I'm wrong. Or I could be right."

"Who's that?"

"This really tall park ranger who hit on Aunt Rae. She described him as a predator." Bash shrugged. "He kind of fits the description. He's tall and looks strong."

"Or," Sally said after snapping her gum, "the other Ma'iingan Bluff werewolf could be Jen's husband."

Bash's pencil strokes stopped at the mark. He looked at her. "How so?"

"Doesn't it make sense?" Sally snapped her gum again. "You said Jen's husband was a werewolf who passed his curse onto his son, Matt. And you said that Jen's husband abandoned them. Then you think that Jen runs this campground to keep her son's secret hidden from the public. Well, why can't she do that for her husband too?"

"But he's not anywhere around here. I mean, I see Matt all over this place, but there is no other man that looks like he would be Jen's husband."

"Well, he wouldn't be a man anymore."

"You think that Jen's husband shapeshifted too many times and now he's a permanent werewolf?"

"Not just a permanent werewolf. He's The Permanent *Ma'iingan Bluff* Werewolf."

Bash thought about that for a second or two before strumming through his notebook. As he reread his outline, he stumbled upon a forgotten notation. "Something doesn't add up." Shaking his head at himself, he muttered, "I can't believe I missed this."

"Missed what?" Sally snapped her gum again. "What did you miss?"

"1977. Beatrice Bones wrote *The Simply Complicated Werewolf* in 1977. That was forty-seven years ago."

"If you say so, dimples. My mental math is forever soaked in gin."

"Jen told my aunt and me that she was twenty-two when she had her son, Matt. Matt is thirty-three, which means Jen is fifty-five. So, she was born in 1969 and couldn't have written a book at age eight."

"She told you that she was fifty-five? Maybe she's really sixty-five? Maybe she was born in 1959. Would that work?"

"She didn't lie about her age."

A wry smile slowly spread across Sally's face. "All women do."

"She would be sixty-five then." Bash shook his head. "Nah, she looks younger than that, like fifty."

The wry smile returned as Sally said, "That's my age."

Pulling on his lip, Bash softly said, "I don't think Jen is Beatrice anymore. And, if Jen isn't Beatrice, then Matt or her husband probably isn't a werewolf. And, then the question is, who rang the bell?"

Bash heard a series of gum snaps before Sally asked, "What bell?"

"Do you see that dinner bell hanging on the porch?" Bash directed the beam of the utility flashlight at the object in question.

"Yes, dimples, what about it?"

"Last night, while we were on our werewolf stake-out, someone rang it at approximately three thirty-one-ish. Right after the bell rang, a strong wind blew past us, twice, like two very large animals ran by. I thought it was Matt and Park Ranger Tom in werewolf form, and then I thought Jen rang it as a signal for them to change back into human form. But now I don't know anymore."

Sally didn't respond right away. While seeming to be in thought, her hand reached for Tiny and she caressed the back of his neck. Finally, she nodded and asked, "Are you sure it was *that* bell on *that* porch that rang?"

This question surprised Bash. He had no doubt because it was the only bell around this area. "Well," he began, "yes, I'm sure. There aren't any other bells around here." Confused, he asked her, "Why do you ask?"

Sally's eyes fixed on the bell. "That looks like the cast iron dinner bell that my grandma had on her farm. She would ring it when the food was ready and on the table." She swung her arm around Bash and hugged him closer to her. With a lowered voice, she said, "What if Jen is somehow connected to all of this and she did ring that bell to signal it's time for their *dinner.* If that's the case, then we're sitting here, right in the way of The Ma'iingan Bluff Werewolf."

"You mean," Bash corrected, "The Ma'iingan Bluff *Werewolves.*"

Tiny abruptly whined and stood on all fours. His ears pointed straight up and his tail stuck out behind him. He craned his neck and stared at the darkness behind him.

Looking at his equipment for thermal images or needle spikes, Bash saw nothing and anxiously asked Tiny, "What is it? Do you see something?"

Raising his nose in the air, Tiny huffed and quickly turned to face the porch. Bash watched as Tiny anxiously pawed at the ground before turning around in a full circle. As Bash reached to calm Tiny, the Great Shepherd gave a low, throaty growl and, without any notice, shot into the woods behind the south park office.

. . .

The little hairs on the back of Stone's neck were on their ends. He looked at Rachel who stared back at him. She had no fear in her eyes, just curiosity. Zalen's eyes, however, overflowed with horror as he carefully unwrapped another butterscotch candy. The crinkly foil was deafening in this quiet moment and Stone released Rachel's hand to stop Zalen from making the noise.

The world around them hushed.

Stone searched the area for the beast, but he saw only the trees and bushes. However, deep in the shadow of the forest, a darker shape emerged. And then another. They were both creeping closer, although they weren't being quiet about it. They were actually very loud. And they weren't creeping at all. The shapes were both upright and clumped through the brush, weaving between the trunks and shining their flashlights at the ground.

As the two shapes drew near, Stone glimpsed red spiky hair in the moonlight and then he heard Rachel call out to them, "Hey, guys, we're over here."

Chuck arrived first and crouched down. "We've been looking for you. We had an interesting development."

Kimmy now stood behind Chuck and said, "We were investigating that trail when we saw what looked like Bigfoot. With a limp."

Chuck cut her off. "We followed it into the woods to take a picture of it and-"

Kimmy interrupted, "It was a deer."

Rachel asked them, "You mistook a deer for Bigfoot?"

"No," Chuck said, "we lost Bigfoot and then found a deer. But then we heard what sounded like a small dog yipping and we saw Bigfoot carrying someone's dog."

Kimmy continued, "So, we followed Bigfoot and the dog all the way to the RV campground."

Chuck grinned. "Only, it wasn't Bigfoot."

Rachel sighed. "It was Travis."

"Yes," Kimmy replied, "and we watched him go into a big RV."

As Stone listened, the hairs standing up on the back of his neck never relaxed. He kept looking over his shoulder, like something beckoned him to come, but he could see nothing.

Chuck begged Rachel. "Come on, Rae. We need you to confront Travis with us. That bastard has been staying in the comfort of an RV this whole time!"

When Rachel didn't respond, Kimmy held her hands in prayer form and pleaded. "Please come with-"

"I can't," Rachel interrupted. "I have to stay here with Stone and Zalen."

Stone felt doom approaching behind him, although no one was near him. He didn't know what was happening to him, but he knew one thing was for certain. "Rachel, you need to go with them." Stone rose to his feet. "I'll stay."

Upon standing, Rachel gave him a questionable look. "What? Why?"

Stone glanced at Zalen who still sat on the ground, unwrapping the last of his butterscotch candy. Remembering her words about building a wall around him, Stone knew it was time to break down that barrier. He looked directly into her eyes and said, "I *feel* that I have to stay."

Rachel shook her head. "You *feel*? Like in the same way that Zalen *feels*?"

Stone exhaled. "Yes. I can feel things, just like Zalen."

Zalen added, "Only he's way better at it than I am."

For a moment, Rachel didn't speak. She only stared at him intently under the moonlight. Then she took his hand in hers and slowly said, "Okay. Well. Cool. You said that you feel that you have to stay?"

"Yes."

"But you're not sure why?"

Stone shrugged. "Not right now."

"Should I stay with you?"

"No."

"No? Are you absolutely, positively sure?"

Shaking his head, Stone calmly said, "No, I feel you have to go."

Then Zalen stood, extending the striped umbrella to Rachel and smiling. "Here, take this. It might rain."

There was another pause and then Rachel nodded at Zalen before facing Stone again. "Okay. I'll go, but then I'll-"

"Meet me back at the campsite." Stone spoke warmly, "We'll talk more then."

"We will?" Rachel's gray eyes filled with worry and hope. "You'll tell me what's going on?"

Stone nodded. "I'll tell you everything." He raised her hand to his lips and kissed her smooth skin. "No more secrets." Then he let her go.

CHAPTER THIRTY FIVE

No more secrets. Stone's words tumbled inside Rae's head like a team of acrobats in a Las Vegas show. Not that she kept many secrets in general. At the moment, however, she kept a big one. It involved Travis and a bribe and her unsuspecting coworkers.

Gulping continuously, Rae followed Chuck and Kimmy out of the woods and into the RV campsite. All of the vehicles were dark, except for Travis's silver monstrosity. It had an interior light on. As the three of them marched closer to the mansion on wheels, the folded money in her back pocket felt like a large hot piece of coal that weighed two elephants. *I shouldn't have picked up the lousy cash*, Rae thought. *I shouldn't have allowed myself to be bribed. I should've just let it all sit there and blow away. Or I should've given it to a food pantry or donated it to a hospital for children or pets or misguided graphic designers with horrible bosses or-*

Chuck interrupted her thoughts when he said, "He's been glamping all along. Without us, his team. What a schmuck."

"Yeah." Rae feigned her allegiance. *I wonder if the schmuck will have my back and not mention the bribe and money offer?* She then held her breath until she stood at the foot of Travis's door. After slowly releasing the air that filled her lungs, Rae raised her striped umbrella and used the handle to forcefully knock. There was no sound from within the camper and she breathed a little easier, thinking she might escape from being exposed as someone who accepted dirty deeds. Unfortunately, she heard both a grumble and a whimper on the other side of the door before the knob turned.

When the door swung open, the look on Travis's face startled her. In his eyes, she could see his heart breaking into itty-bitty pieces as a waterfall of tears poured down his face. Not to mention, all the snot running down and into his mouth. To say he was an ugly crier would be too weak of a description. Rae gagged a little.

"Y-Y-Yeah, R-R-Rae?" He sobbed. "Did you want s-s-something?"

Pushing the snot image out of her mind, Rae reminded herself of why she was here and cleared her throat. "Yes, Travis, I want to know why you're glamping behind *everyone's* back."

He cried some more while sipping a Sky High. He then blubbered, "*Not everyone's* b-b-back. And w-w-what do you want me to say? I'm a b-b-bastard."

Chuck, who wore a curious expression, asked, "What do you mean by *not everyone's* back?"

Kimmy leaned her head into the RV. "Do I smell cookies?"

"Yes." Through his weeping, Travis continued, "I'm making ch-ch-chocolate ch-ch-chip cookies."

Licking her lips, Kimmy inquired, "At this hour?"

Travis wiped his teary eyes with his hands and composed himself. Sort of. "It's wh-what I do when I'm up-upset. I was making my fourth-th batch when I ran out of sugar." His stutter dissolved a little as his voice strengthened. "I was going to drive to the grocery s-store and get some sugar, but thought a w-walk might be better for me. My little Tiny was asleep, s-so I went by myself. I was on the trail and got lost." His voice weakened and the tears returned. "I was s-s-so alone and s-s-scared." He hiccupped. "So alone." He hiccupped again. "So scared."

Kimmy reached for him and patted his arm. "Oh, how frightening. Travis, in times like those, you have to remind yourself that you're not alone. You're never alone. You have us."

Nodding, Travis drank some more coffee. After a few gulps, his composure returned as he nodded and said, "And, more importantly, I have my little Tiny. He's the one that found me tonight." Travis half-smiled. "All of a sudden, my brave little Tiny came to me out of nowhere. Yipping and squealing." He gave them a loving look. "He showed me how to get back. My little Tiny is my savior."

Anger boiled in Rae like a pot of hot lava. In an instant, she forgot about the bribe. In an instant, the five hundred dollars wasn't enough compensation for Travis's lack of team consideration. Was she a bad person for taking the cash in the first place? Yep. But Travis was worse. "How dare you?" Raising her pointer finger at him, she scolded, "You made us come on the camping trip under the *facade* of team-building and you had the nerve to stay in this sweet contraption the whole time. Shame on you!"

Chuck asked Rae, "What do you mean by *facade*?"

Rae continued to reprimand Travis. "That wasn't part of our deal!"

Kimmy raised her hand and asked, "What do you mean by *our* deal?"

Rae heard her coworkers' questions, but she couldn't bring herself to look at them in their eyes. Instead, she allowed her shoulders, full of tension and shame, to tighten even more than usual. She gestured to Travis and asked him, "Should I tell them or do you want to reveal the real reason why we're camping?"

Travis raised the Sky High cup to his mouth and shook it for any remaining drops of coffee. There were none and he sniffed. "You can."

With an air of bruised dignity, Rae unfolded the story of how this team-building camping trip was born. She told Chuck and Kimmy everything. Almost step by step. Starting with how his son, Mort, broke the pool filter with his two hands. She moved on to how Travis wanted a break from parenting and how it was Seth's idea for him to go camping. Rae added how Seth wanted Travis to find his messier side and inner kindness or else the marriage was over. The team-building was, more or less, a side note.

Kimmy asked Rae, "He was supposed to change in three days? That's impossible."

If Travis was offended, it didn't sound like it. This surprised Rae as he calmly explained to Chuck and Kimmy. "I had the messier side down. I'd smear dirt on my face, take a selfie, send it to him, and then wash my face." He nodded at Rae. "She was supposed to teach me how to be kind."

Chuck looked at Rae. "You failed."

Rae bit her fingernail. "Well, none of this was my idea."

Chuck commented, "But you went along with it."

Rae sheepishly said, "I didn't know what to do."

"So." Kimmy redirected the conversation back to Travis. "Why are you so upset?"

At first, Travis remained silent. Then, while looking at his feet, he confessed, "Seth figured out what I was doing. He noticed that I withdrew money from our savings to rent this sweet contraption, as Rae called it. He put it together that I was ditching you guys and staying in here most of the time, therefore not finding my messier or kinder side."

"You rented this?" Rae asked him.

"Yes, Rae." He gave her a quizzical look. "You don't think I'd *buy* one of these, do you?" Travis scoffed before continuing, "If this camping trip has taught me anything, it's that I *really* hate camping, even in an RV." He shook his head. "Never again."

Kimmy smiled as she softly applauded, like a spectator at a gulf match. "Good for you, Travis. You learned one thing, at least."

"Hold on a second," Chuck said to Kimmy. "I think you're missing the bigger picture. Both Travis and Rae partnered to put us through hell for no good reason. Those activities meant nothing. This whole team-building was really about Travis all along." He turned to Rae. "Why didn't you tell us?"

"Well, I didn't think." Rae's mouth dried up faster than one drop of water in the desert. "I mean, I guess it's because I thought I could really build a better team and help Travis all at the same time."

Travis nodded while adding, "She really was trying to please everyone. In fact, she didn't know about my glamping until this afternoon, after she discovered me here. A more important fact is she was going to tell you guys until I paid her to keep it to herself. In her defense, her heart was in the right place until she saw the five hundred dollars."

Horrified, Rae shrieked. "That's no defense!"

Chuck's mouth fell open and Kimmy squeaked. She then asked Rae, "He paid you five hundred bucks to not tell us? And you took the bribe?"

Shaking her head, Rae opened her mouth to speak, but all of the words in her mind evaporated. She then heard Travis say, "It wasn't a bribe. It was a bonus. I actually bribed her by giving her a paid week off anytime she wanted it."

Chuck's voice was flat and cold as he spoke to her. "Tonya's right. You really are Travis's short clone." A lump formed in Rae's throat, preventing her from responding, and Chuck continued, "I guess we're really not a team."

Kimmy gently touched Chuck's shoulder, "Come on, let's go. I've heard enough."

As the two disappeared into the darkness, Rae glared at Travis. She swallowed that lump and said with a shaky voice, "What do you have to say for yourself?"

Travis stared at her for a full half minute before mumbling, "I'm sorner."

"Stop it. What kind of a man can't even say the words thanks or sorry?"

Abashedly, Travis muttered, "I'm truly sorb."

"No, you're not. But I'll tell you what you are. You are a very selfish man. And a selfish man will never be a good leader. A selfish man will never have a team. A selfish man will never be a good husband or a good father. Seriously, Travis, if you continue this way, you will always be scared and you will always be alone."

Looking straight in her eyes, Travis said, "I'm already alone and scared. Seth left me."

Rae pursed his lips together. "Well, that's on you. Not me. You. All of this is on you. So, what are you going to do about it? Accept it? Or fix it?" Without waiting for a response, she reached into her back pocket for the wad of cash and threw the bills at him. "You can have all of that back." Rae then turned and walked on her shaky legs out of the RV campsite. She, too, heard enough.

Now, on the trail in the woods, she used her cellphone flashlight to guide the way back to camp. With a scowl, she glanced at the time. Through blurred eyes from hot tears, she read that it was almost three. If she, Bash and Tiny left now, they could be home by six. Rae blinked her tears away. Maybe Tonya wasn't the only one quitting the team after this wayward camping debacle?

■　　■　　■

Tiny hit the jackpot. That scrumptious odor returned and, after following it, he found a small wooden shed deep in the woods that smelled awfully good. The door was ajar and he jumped up to push it open with his two paws. He entered, leading with his nose, and was instantly swarmed by flies. Ignoring the pests, he instead focused on what the moonlit glow illuminated for him. And it was a glorious sight indeed! Hanging from the ceiling, as well as lying on the ground, was deer carcass after deer carcass. He barked a few times out of merriment and that was when Nice Bash and Sally joined him.

"This stench brings back memories of my honeymoon. We called it quits after two days."

"Whoa," said Nice Bash as coughed. He held two objects in his hands. Tiny recognized the one object that Nice Bash called a utility flashlight. As the boy raised the light and swooped it around the room, Tiny's tongue dropped out of his mouth. His stomach growled.

Nice Bash asked, "What is this place, guys?"

"It looks to me like someone hunts deer." Sally also held a beam of light. "How many are there?"

Nice Bash quickly moved his light around the area. "It looks like six are hanging and four are on the ground." Studying the other object in his other hand, he said, "That's strange." Tiny sniffed the screen of it as Nice Bash continued, "My thermal camera just stopped working."

Sally examined one of the hanging ones. "It's been somewhat disemboweled."

Nice Bash asked, "Only the liver and heart are missing, right?"

"Right. And, usually, a hunter takes out all the organs."

Tiny raised his nose and smelled fresh meat toward the back. As he advanced two steps in that direction, Nice Bash stopped him. Tiny whined and the boy comforted him by placing his hand on top of Tiny's head. He spoke to Sally. "Do you know what this means?"

"I sure do." Sally directed her beam at Bash. "Whoever did this isn't a regular hunter."

Just then, Nice Bash's cellphone rang. He answered and Tiny heard Angry Rae's voice on the other end. They spoke briefly, Nice Bash then groaned before disconnecting. Looking at Sally and Tiny, he uttered, "Apparently, we're leaving. Now." Tiny whined and Nice Bash petted his head. "I know, Tiny, I'm upset too." He looked at the time on his cellphone. "It's almost three. If we hurry, we can be back at the south park office and maybe pick up on something with the rest of my paranormal equipment before we leave. Or, at least, see if anyone rings that bell."

Although Tiny didn't want to leave this oasis of available meat, he would follow the boy anywhere. He lifted one paw to walk toward the door when the battery on Nice Bash's phone instantly drained, as well as his utility flashlight. Tiny turned toward Sally who still held a strong beam of light. Until it flickered. Then dulled. Then nothing. All three were now in complete darkness, except for the rays of moonlight seeping through the cracks between the wood siding.

A few long seconds passed and Tiny's eyes adjusted. He heard Sally's voice break the silence when she asked, "Did you say you counted ten deer carcasses?"

Tiny straightened his ears. He heard a soft step behind him.

Nice Bash replied, "Yeah, why?"

"How many were hanging?"

"Six."

Tiny turned his body and faced the back of the shed.

"Not seven? Dimples, are you sure?"

Tiny saw it. With one step, he positioned himself in front of Nice Bash to protect him from the standing figure. And this standing figure was tall. It kept creeping closer to them by stepping in between the dead deer carcasses. Tiny anxiously pranced and raised his nose, sniffing the fresh meat that was in the white box held by the tall figure.

CHAPTER THIRTY SIX

Stone and Zalen walked through the woods. As Stone took the lead, Zalen obediently followed, never saying a word. Even when Stone backtracked or switched directions impulsively, Zalen remained a loyal, quiet companion.

Allowing his sensations to guide him, Stone stopped when all of the feelings were at their peak. He knew he was close to facing his vision. Shivering from his tingling forearms, he closed his eyes from the severe head pain and rubbed the little hairs on the back of his neck. That was the only time Zalen intervened by placing his hand on Stone's shoulder and saying, "Take some deep breaths, my friend. You control them. They don't control you."

Stone listened to Zalen's advice and began breathing deeply through his nose, releasing the air slowly through his mouth. The sensations softened. When he opened his eyes, he was met with two very tall trees greeting him like two British soldiers in front of the King's castle. No, that wasn't right. They looked more like two identical monoliths, strong and erect, as the moon shone brightly above them. He instantly knew that he was in the right place.

He turned toward Zalen. "What time is it?"

Zalen quietly replied, "It's almost three."

"This is it," Stone said to Zalen. "Something is supposed to happen here." He returned his focus to the trees, as if they called to him, and that was when he saw the crumpled body on the ground. Only it hadn't been there a second before.

. . .

Rae disconnected with Bash and walked as fast as she could to catch Chuck and Kimmy. She needed to explain to them that she was not Travis's short clone! If anything, she was a victim of peer pressure. Or boss pressure. Couldn't they understand that? They worked with Travis a lot longer than she had. They should know how manipulative their boss could be. That was why Kimmy practically swallowed herself during the Monday morning meetings and why Chuck sweated so much all the time. They obviously felt bullied by him too.

Rae caught a glimpse of them and their flashlights as they left the woods ahead of her. She watched their beams bob along the gravel road and she quickened her pace. Then, curiously, they turned off their flashlights. Rae now jogged through the trees, using the umbrella to crash through bushes, and, as she spilled onto the gravel road, her cellphone flashlight failed. She stopped walking, trying to bring her phone back to life, but it refused. That was when she heard Chuck's voice ahead of her whisper, "Rae, don't move."

CHAPTER THIRTY SEVEN

As Stone stared at the crumpled body lying on its side, confusion came in a tidal wave. This body had broad shoulders and long legs, but it didn't feel like the body from his vision. Stone studied the scene before him and, for the first time, he noticed a Stetson hat resting behind the head, off to the side.

Zalen asked Stone, "What is it, Stone? What do you see?"

Perplexed, Stone gestured to the body and then looked at Zalen. "It's a crumpled body, Zalen."

"Where?"

Stone furrowed his eyebrows. "Between the two trees." When he returned his attention to the crumpled body, it was gone.

Zalen spoke gently, "I don't see anything, Stone."

"Neither do I now." Stone stepped toward the spot of where the body rested just a few seconds ago. He flashed his cellphone light on the ground and noticed that the dirt in that area looked like it had been disturbed. His attention shifted to another part of the ground. Feeling an invisible pull, he knelt down and started brushing the loose dirt aside with his hands. His fingers soon found a small object.

Zalen asked, "Is that a red lollipop? Like in your vision?"

Upon standing, Stone shook his head. "No, it's a nametag."

As he turned it over to read the name Prissy Willis, he heard a bright, friendly voice say behind him, "Hey, that's mine."

Stone flinched at her sudden appearance. *Holy shit,* he said to himself. *This all makes sense now.* He took a deep breath and faced Zalen, handing the nametag to him and calmly saying, "Take this and go find Bash at the south park office. Stay with him and tell Sally to call the police. There's been a murder."

"Murder?" Prissy looked shocked. "Who was murdered?"

While taking the nametag, Zalen talked over Prissy. "What about Rae?"

"I'll call her and tell her to meet you guys there. When the police come, I'll need you to bring them to me."

"Wait a second, campers," Prissy spoke quickly. "Once you give me my nametag, I'll just radio in some help."

Again, Zalen spoke over Prissy's words, completely ignoring her. "So, you're staying here. Are you sure, Stone?"

Stone nodded. "Go, Zalen. And hurry."

■　■　■

With the help of the moonlight, Bash could see better in the dark now. He crouched a little to be at Tiny's eye level. Squinting into the darkness at the back of the shed, he saw the white styrofoam cooler in the grips of someone's hand. Standing up, he now knew who was in the shed with them.

Bash spoke with a serene, jovial tone, even though he felt like he was starring in his very own horror movie. "Hey, Sally, I'd like you to meet Matt."

Matt stepped closer to him, causing stripes of light to illuminate parts of his shirt and face. He wasn't smiling. "You shouldn't be here, little bro."

Sally now moved to the other side of Bash while saying to Matt, "We're just having some stupid fun. We're leaving. Have a nice night."

She placed her hand on Bash's shoulder to turn him around, but he refused. "Wait, Sally. We're close to a break-through here. I can feel it."

Tiny growled again and Sally said to Bash, "I think we overstayed our welcome."

"One question," Bash said to Matt as Sally pulled on his arm. "Who's the heart and liver for? You? Or your dad? Tom?"

Sally stopped pulling on his arm and Tiny turned around, facing the door. When he started to whine, Bash broke his gaze from the back of the shed to the entrance. There, in the threshold, stood Jen and Mare. The stars' effulgence illuminated the women fully, giving Bash a glimpse of this serious situation. It wasn't the fear in Jen's eyes that disturbed him; it was the gleam of the sawed-off rifle in Mare's hands that put Bash on edge.

CHAPTER THIRTY EIGHT

Stone stood face-to-face with Prissy, whose eyes pleaded with him more than ever. She seemed both hurt and bewildered as she said, "I don't know what's happening. What murder? Who was murdered? I would know if something like that happened. This is my forest, my campground, my home. I wouldn't have let anything bad happen like that."

Stone's forearms were on fire, but he tried to maintain a calm demeanor. "I read that, sometimes, a traumatic event can make people forget certain things that happened to them. They can't or don't want to face reality."

"Traumatic event? Like murder? Are you suggesting that I killed someone?"

"I need you to listen." Stone rubbed his temples as they pounded both sides of his head. "Prissy, I need you to remember what you did today."

Prissy wrung her hands. "I…I don't understand why you're asking me to do this. I don't understand why you're here." Her voice cracked. "Why didn't you just give me my nametag?"

"You don't remember what you did today, do you?" When she finally shook her head, Stone asked, "Do you remember me?"

Prissy stopped wringing her hands and let them fall to her side. She searched his face under the moonlight and finally asked, "Have we met?"

"A few times," he gently replied. "My name is Stone." When she shook her head at him, he continued, "You never could remember me, even if a short time passed between our meetings."

She cleared her voice, but a despairing waver was still there when she softly asked, "What is wrong with me?"

Stone smiled at her. "Nothing." He dissuaded himself from reaching for her hand. It would've been a futile gesture. "Prissy," he softly began, "what is the last thing you remember?"

"Walking around here." She looked at Stone with tears in her eyes. "Why didn't you give my nametag to me?"

"Who was walking with you?"

Silence followed. Then he heard Prissy swallow before saying, "I…I don't remember."

"Try."

In a panic state, she looked around the woods. "I…I remember the trees." Prissy shook her head in frustration. "I love my job, but something's off. This isn't right." After feeling for her badge, she faced him and pleaded, "Please give me my nametag."

A tightening wrapped itself around Stone's chest. He desperately wanted to look away from the lost look on her pale face, but knew it was his duty to tell her. After taking a deep breath and releasing it, he asked, "Were you walking around here at night or during the day?"

Prissy stared at him with an aching, quizzical expression on her face. At first, she shrugged and couldn't speak. Then, her eyes drifted to the spot between the two tall trees and a small light of awareness swept over her face. As she opened her mouth to speak, Tom stepped *through* Prissy, carrying a shovel.

■　■　■

Rae felt a large presence behind her, breathing its hot breath on the back of her neck. Staring straight into Chuck's wide, horrified eyes, Rae knew that she was in grave danger. Both Chuck and Kimmy were on the gravel path, just a few steps ahead of her and both were frozen in fear. As Rae slowly turned her head to the side, a strong whoosh of air blew past her, almost knocking her over. She turned completely around with the umbrella raised like a baseball bat, ready to beat up any form of animal, but nothing was there.

She squinted into the blackness and heard Kimmy ask, "What was that?"

Chuck replied with trepidation, "I don't know. It was tall. Black. A black bear maybe?"

Kimmy's voice shook. "It just flew by. Where did it go?"

Chuck replied again, sounding more anxious. "I don't know. It took off somewhere. What do we do? Call animal 911?"

Rae finally exhaled, not realizing that she held her breath. Then she turned to face Chuck who was shrouded in darkness. "It's called animal control, but bears are around here all the time. Would animal control even do anything?" She shrugged awkwardly due to her body trembling.

Kimmy raised her hand and whispered, "I think we should go back to camp, pack up and get out of here."

Rae faced Kimmy as the moon's brilliance shone down on her worried face and she nodded. "You guys do that. I need to get Bash, Sally and Tiny first. And Stone. And Zalen." She paused. "My god, that's a lot of people."

Chuck said, "I'll help you, Rae." She looked at him in the darkness and couldn't see his face, but she felt his kind heart as he continued, "Who do you want me to get?"

"I'll help too, Rae." Kimmy smiled. "Maybe we can get Bash, Sally and Tiny?"

Kimmy now stood next to Rae. Like herself, Kimmy's features were clear as day. Rae then looked at Chuck who stood four paces away. He seemed to be standing in some shade, which didn't make sense to her. They all stood in the middle of the gravel path. The trees lined the road. None were hovering over Chuck, but something was causing a veil to shade him. Rae squinted. And as her eyes searched the area above her kind-hearted coworker, she quickly noticed the two glowing red eyes behind him.

The deepest, most spine-chilling reverberation filled the darkness around Chuck. It resonated through Rae's chest. Her body wouldn't move. It couldn't move. She could only watch the black shape move closer to Chuck, raising its arms and baring its fangs. Her brain finally acknowledged the frightening animal. *Animal?* She shook her head, knowing that it was time to face the facts. This was no animal. This was The Ma'iingan Bluff Werewolf. And as she locked eyes with the beast, it lifted its head up, arched its back and howled the way only a true beast could howl. The echo rang over the trees and into the night.

Bash. That was Rae's flash of a thought. *Play dead.* She shook her head. *That's not going to work.* With all her courage in her small frame, she lifted her red and white striped umbrella like Babe Ruth at home plate, steadied it high in the air and then accidentally dropped the damn thing.

CHAPTER THIRTY NINE

Tiny growled at Mare and Jen, pointing his tail straight up. He barked once at them as a warning. Then he growled again to make a point.

Nice Bash placed his hand on Tiny's head to quiet him as Sally said, "Look, we were just having some fun-"

Nice Bash interrupted her, "We know your secret."

Sally spoke over Nice Bash, "We don't know anything. I'm just a drunk and he's just a kid."

Tiny heard Matt approach from the back and now stood directly behind the boy. Turning himself completely around, Tiny pranced on his two front paws, readying himself to jump. Matt was not bothered by Tiny's intimidation tactics and said, "We're running out of time. What should we do?"

Tiny felt that a threat was coming. Fast. He stood on his two hind legs and lunged for Matt. However, Matt raised his free hand and Tiny sensed that he was outmatched. As he landed, now on all fours, Nice Bash caressed Tiny's side while calmly saying to him, "It's okay, Tiny. They're nice people. They won't hurt us." The boy then looked at Mare. "Will you?"

Mare stared at Nice Bash for a moment and then finally lowered the barrel, just a smidge. Without warning, she smiled at him. "No, we won't hurt you, but we can't let you leave either."

Sally asked, "Why not? We won't say anything to anyone. As far as you're concerned, your secret is safe with us. What secret, am I right? We won't ask any questions and you can let us go. I'll go on your website and give this place five stars. And I'll tell you what. Next year, let's meet for a drink and laugh at this whole situation. Yeah?"

Jen said to Mare, "I warned you not to talk to Bash. I knew he'd figure this all out. Why didn't you listen?"

Tiny began prancing in agitation again and Sally quickly said, "Please, he's just an eleven-year old boy."

Barely holding Tiny in place, Nice Bash corrected her. "I'm twelve, Sally."

"Well." Sally sounded nervous. "His voice is still moderately high, so his balls haven't dropped. My point is he's young and has his whole life ahead of him. Keep me, but let him go."

Shaking his head, Nice Bash said, "First, I won't go without you, Sally. Second, I think my high voice has nothing to do with my anatom-."

A distant hungry howl silenced the conversation. Everyone in the shed was still. Even Tiny. His ears stiffened, pointing to the ceiling, and he listened to a long wail as it decrescendoed before completely fading away.

"Mom!" Matt shouted. "We have to go. Now!"

Waving her arm for Matt to hurry, Jen stepped aside as he ran out the door, still carrying the cooler. Tiny whined, causing Jen to remain in the doorway. She looked at him and then at Nice Bash. She stared at the boy for a brief moment before saying to Mare, "Don't let them go." And with that, Jen hustled after her son.

"Don't worry." Mare raised the rifle while securing her grip. She leveled the barrel with the other and said, "I won't."

.   .   .

With the shovel swung over his shoulder, Tom held a flashlight in his hand and directed the beam at Stone. "What are you doing here? Are you a camper? Are you lost?"

Prissy appeared next to Stone now. "Oh my gosh. I remember everything."

Confused at Tom's sudden appearance, Stone stumbled at hiding his reaction, but managed to reply, "I…I'm just walking."

Nodding, Prissy said, "Yes, we were walking. A couple of nights ago."

Tom asked Stone, "Out here? At this hour?"

Prissy now appeared on the other side of Stone. "Yes," she said, "at this hour, which was strange. It wasn't his shift. But he found me. I was doing rounds, making sure everything was good. And he showed up out of the blue. He never did that before."

Tom snapped his fingers. "Hey, are you okay? Did you drink too much or something?"

Stone slowly nodded at Tom while listening to Prissy. He asked her, "It wasn't *his* shift? Who were you with?"

"Excuse me?" Tom tilted his head to the side. "I don't understand."

"He wanted to know why I wrote him up." Prissy faced Stone. "I told him it was for misconduct with a female camper. It was his second offense."

Stone focused on Tom while whispering to her, "I need a name."

"What?" Tom looked around the area. "Is someone else here?"

Closing her eyes, Prissy continued, "He got mad. He begged me not to do it, but I had to." She started speaking quickly. "It was part of my job as his superintendent. He was so angry. Deranged. He told me that I was a horrible boss and was out to ruin his life. His anger scared me. I ran. And then he ran after me." Prissy began a woeful cry, instantly breaking Stone's heart.

As perspiration covered Stone's face from sorrow and anger, he heard Tom's voice, distant and muffled. He asked Stone, "Are you okay, sir?"

Prissy spoke while weeping. "He pushed me down." She then pointed to the area between the trees. "Here. He pushed me down here and I remember losing my hat." Breathing heavily through her sobbing, Prissy removed her Stetson hat that she still wore. Stone sucked in air at the sight of the bloody gouge on the side of her head and she innocently said to him, "I think Tom killed me."

Shock radiated throughout Stone's body as he stared into Tom's darkened face. Anger turned to rage and all patience circled this murderous drain, emptying out of him. With a rough edge in his voice, he demanded of Tom, "Where is Prissy?"

"What?" Tom frowned. "Prissy who?"

"The park ranger. Don't play dumb. Where is she?" Stone pointed to the area between the trees. "Is she here?"

"Prissy quit. She just left without any notice. Did you know her?"

"No, I didn't." Prissy sobbed. "I wouldn't. I loved this job. I loved these woods and everything about these woods."

Stone shook. "No, she didn't. She loved this job." He glanced at the ground, at the shovel and then at Prissy. "Why are you back?"

Tom was as stiff as a soldier. "I'm just doing my rounds. Who are you?"

"No, he's not," whispered Prissy. "He's looking for something."

Stone asked him, "What are you looking for?" Tom was silent, but Stone continued, "Are you going to move her body? Are you going to dig a deeper grave? What, Tom? What are you up to?" Tom stood completely still and completely quiet. Stone asked, "Did you come to check over your work? Or did you forget something?" Tom shifted the weight from one leg to the other, signaling to Stone that he made Tom react to what he said. Narrowing his eyes, Stone wondered aloud, "What did you forget?"

"I don't know what you're talking about." Tom's voice was low and dry.

Prissy abruptly gasped. "He forgot my nametag!"

Stone softly said, "Of course. It was your nametag."

Her hand covered her heart. "It would be the only thing on me that identified who I was."

Stone looked at Prissy. Her once solid appearance changed to a transparent figure. She turned into a true ghost right before his very eyes. Her hand lowered to her side and a look of understanding and acceptance shrouded her facial expression. She said to Stone, "I'm okay, camper. Thank you for helping me."

Stone wasn't okay, however. He was enraged as he said to Tom, "You killed her just because she knew you were a fucking predator."

By then, however, Tom dropped his flashlight and the moon's bright rays acted as the center light on a wicked stage, casting its terrifying beam on the shovel. Taking a step forward, Tom scowled as he raised his arm and the shape of the blade appeared against the moon, similar to the scythe in Stone's vision. It hung threateningly over Stone's skull and instinct took hold of Stone's body as he reached for the handle. When the struggle began, a sudden bone-chilling howl ripped through the atmosphere, causing both he and Tom to lose their grips and the shovel fell to the ground.

CHAPTER FORTY

Rae heard the thud of her umbrella hitting the gravel road and time instantly eased, as if they all were dancers in a slow-motion choreographed scene. It began with Kimmy screaming, which led to Chuck turning around and falling onto his back. Then, as the beast loomed over Chuck, licking his lips and salivating, Tonya flew into view like an undetectable military aircraft. Rae opened her mouth to scream alongside Kimmy as Tonya picked up the umbrella, swinging it at the beast. In Rae's eyes, Tonya turned into her knight in shining armor as her co-worker yelled over and over, "If the bear is black, fight back! If the bear is black, fight back!"

Most of her swings missed, but she managed to connect three times before the umbrella broke. The werewolf then used its strong teeth to snatch it from Tonya, throwing it far into the woods with a flick of its head. Raising his nose in the air, the beast motioned with it, as if it told someone to come. Then, out of the darkness of the trees came another werewolf, nearly the same size as the other. It also had red eyes against the blackest of fur. It also had sharp claws that extended twelve inches, at least. And it also had very, very pointy fangs. *My god,* Rae thought as she started to shake, *there are two Ma'iingan Bluff Werewolves.*

Tonya, however, didn't shake. She now stood in front of Chuck, looking at the beasts in silent wonderment. "Holy shit," she muttered aloud. Tonya backed into Chuck who backed into Kimmy who then backed into Rae. As they all stood on the side of the road, one huddled behind the other with Tonya at the frontline, the werewolves stepped into the middle of the road, growling a cacophony of throaty croaks.

Strangely sounding at peace, Tonya then spoke to the team, or so Rae thought until she really listened to her words. "Get thee behind me, Satan," Tonya said bravely to the werewolves. "Thou are an offense unto me, for thou savourest not the things that be of God, but those that be of men."

The werewolves curiously paused. A new hope flooded Rae as she first thought the werewolves suddenly found God, but as they slowly stretched their necks like boxers before a good fight, the new hope succumbed to wretched dread. Rae closed her eyes and she thought of Bash. If she had to be the meal in order to keep her nephew alive tonight, then so be it. And, as she concentrated hard on his gray blue eyes and sweet soft smile that she would never see again, she prepared herself for her own death.

A different sound, however, filled her ears. It wasn't the sound of crunching bones as she suspected. It was the sound of an engine increasing speed. Finding some courage, Rae opened one eye and peeked down the gravel path from where the sound of the engine grew louder and louder. Two headlights abruptly appeared on an RV and behind the wheel of this silver monstrosity was Travis with his Tiny strapped to his chest. Even from where Rae stood, she could see the whites of Tiny's eyes as Travis increased his vehicle to lightning speed and slammed his RV into both werewolves.

·   ·   ·

The howl ended and Stone recovered first, diving on top of Tom. A full-blown fight ensued. They were both matched physically, taking turns at being the close victor before being overthrown by the other. Stone knew he was in the fight for his life, but his effort tired.

And Tom, fueled by insanity at this point, ended up on top, gripping Stone's throat and squeezing.

Prissy remained standing behind Tom. No longer crying, her eyes were as fierce as a tiger's as she said, "Don't give up, camper. You don't let him win." She began fading. "You win this fight for me."

Stone clawed at Tom's hands as they tightened. He was losing and even Prissy's encouraging words couldn't help him. As his legs tried to frantically buck Tom off his chest, his body began panicking from lack of air and his heels ended up kicking across the dirt. Stone wasn't surviving and he knew he wasn't going to survive. Unless a miracle happened. Or something like a miracle happened.

And something like that did happen.

It wasn't a strike of lightning, but it was a spectral object, hurling down from the heavens. Stone saw flashes of silver, red and white accompanied with the sound of flapping. It quickly struck Tom on his head and Stone felt Tom's grasp weaken. Taking advantage of this fortunate turn of events, Stone threaded his arms through Tom's and grabbed Tom's ears. He pulled, twisted and yanked those ears down, pushing Tom onto his side. Scrambling to his feet, Stone spied the object that saved his life and he picked it up, readying it above his head for another fight. Only, the object flopped open and Stone immediately recognized it as the umbrella that Zalen gave to Rachel. It was clearly broken. And that scared him more than Tom who was now standing opposite him with his sleeves rolled up and raised fists.

Suddenly, Prissy appeared next to Stone, screaming, "Go to Mare!" Stone froze until Prissy flew through him and wailed, *"Run, Stone, run!"*

CHAPTER FORTY ONE

Bash pulled on his lip as he watched Mare, blocking their only exit. For an old lady, she had a good grip on the rifle. It was strong and unwavering as her fingers curled around the barrel and the handle. The barrel had been cut down to about sixteen inches, Bash thought. His eyes followed the metal tube's smooth underside, which acted like a path leading to Mare's knobby-knuckled grip. Every now and again, she would turn her wrist and look at her watch. After she checked it for the sixth time, Bash casually asked, "What are you waiting for?'

Mare didn't say anything, however, and Sally began talking. "Bash, did I ever tell you about the time I accidentally dated a criminal?" Bash didn't have a chance to answer as she continued, "His name was Jimmy Jamison. Or so he told me. It probably wasn't his real name. Anyway, he had a sawed-off rifle that he never used. So, I asked him why he sawed off the barrel and then never used it. And do you know what he said?"

There was a longer pause, giving Bash the idea that she wanted a reply this time. "No, I don't." Bash held onto Tiny's collar. "Unless he said it was to make it easier to hide it under his coat."

"Exactly. Jimmy told me that's the reason why people do that. It's for making it easier to hide the gun. It's not for accuracy or even velocity. It actually sprays the pellets out in a less controlled fashion, which then causes more injury to the shooter."

Mare chuckled. "If you think that I'm scared to shoot this gun in fear of hurting my eighty-year old ass, you should think again."

Bash heard Sally say, "Oh, I'm sure you wouldn't waste another breath. I just wonder how you're going to pull the trigger when you don't have one."

Moving his eyes down to the trigger, Bash gasped. Sally was right and Bash didn't catch it. The clue was in the manner of how Mare gripped the gun. One hand held the barrel and the other held the handle. Her finger didn't loop the trigger because there was none.

Lowering her rifle, Mare sighed. "You have a good eye, lady. Even in the dark." She flung the fake rifle to the ground. "I wasn't going to keep you two hostage forever. I just needed to keep you until it was all over."

Bash quickly asked, "Until what was all over?"

"The feeding," Mare answered. "Every night, we leave out a cooler for my husband and my son. It's filled with the hearts and livers of deer."

Bash groaned and smacked his head. "*Your* husband." He placed his hands on his hips, like Aunt Rae always did. "*You're* Beatrice Bones, aren't you? Not Jen. Not some other person. It's you. You wrote the book." He shook his head at himself. "I was so close. I knew the dates didn't add up."

"Yes, Bash." Mare glanced at the time again. "I am Beatrice Bones, but that's not my real name. It's Rosemary."

"Wait a minute," Bash said. "As in Rosemary's Apple Pies? Are you that Rosemary?"

"Yep, but I go by Mare, which is short for Mary, which is short for Rosemary." Bash smacked his forehead and Mare continued, "I'm originally from Reedsburg, just thirty minutes away. Once people in my hometown found out I used a pen name and wrote that book about my werewolf husband, they thought I was nuts."

Bash asked, "Didn't you have proof of your husband being a werewolf?"

"Of course." Mare now found a stool near the doorway and slowly lowered her bottom onto it. "I had pictures and videos. But people don't want to see the truth. Their minds can't handle it. They come up with other reasons for what they're seeing. Instead of admitting that they see a werewolf, they instead say they see bears or people in costumes or even Bigfoot because it helps them sleep at night."

"Mare," Bash wondered aloud, "why did you write the book in the first place?"

"Money," Mare quickly answered. "I thought it was a fascinating subject and would be the next best seller. The money would have helped me provide for my son. God only knew my husband wasn't going to provide us with anything anymore, so I had to. But it didn't turn out that way. People can be cruel, you know. Even the ones who you thought were friends. They can say mean things and try to take your loved ones from you."

Sally spoke from the darkness. "Like your son. Did you move out here then?"

"Of course. I knew my husband was here. I'd watch him come to these woods, these bluffs, and shapeshift into that magnificent creature. My son and I settled in Sauk Prairie where no one knew I wrote that book. But, just to be careful, I slightly altered my name and opened a bakery, which people really seemed to like my pies. Before I knew it, I made a good living."

Incredulous, Bash said, "So, you're four people. You're Rose, the woman you wrote about in *The Simply Complicated Werewolf*; you're Rosemary, the pie maker; you're Mare, the campground boss; and you're Beatrice Bones, the writer." Bash nodded. "You're amazing."

"And you're a bright kid." Mare smiled. "Now, as I was saying." She massaged her elbow and continued, "My son, Jack, and I opened this place with the money I made from my pie business. We thought it would be a great way to make more money while living near my husband. Jack then met Jen and they fell madly in love. She didn't care one iota about him being a werewolf. Jen was like me. We were both mesmerized by it. But, then, she and I both saw what was happening to Jack. We knew it was a matter of time before he shapeshifted permanently into a werewolf, which he did. We tried to stop his shapeshifting, but, once you start, you can't stop. Anyways, that's what he always said. And when it happened, Matt was twelve years old, which was my son's age when I wrote the book and almost lost him." Mare stopped talking and briefly glanced at Bash. She then continued, "By then, Jen, Matt and I ran this campground like clockwork. The two campgrounds were manageable and the south area, where you're camping, was off-limits. It's our home for us and for my husband and for my son."

Sally said, "I don't understand. Why didn't you just leave it as the forest instead of making it look like an old, beat-up campground?"

"We didn't. This old section was the original campground of a place long ago. It was already beat up. We kept it this way to deter campers from wanting to be here, since we live here with my husband and my son. We needed seclusion and wanted to be alone. But we also needed money. So, we built the two nice campgrounds on the north and west side, but left the south looking like it was under construction."

"So, then," Bash asked, "why did you let us camp here?"

Mare scoffed. "That Travis character wouldn't take no for an answer. He waved his fat wallet at me and threatened to call the BBB. I couldn't have anyone looking into this."

Bash understood now. "He can be demanding."

Mare nodded. "And emotional. He started to cry. Over the phone. Big sobs. It reminded me of how my husband cried on the night I confronted him about being a werewolf. I guess I just pitied Travis and gave in." Mare shrugged. "That's it. That's the whole story."

The words poured out of Bash's mouth without much control, but he needed to know. "Is Matt a werewolf too?"

Mare didn't bat an eye at him and, instead, glanced at her watch. "It'll be any minute now."

Sally reached for Bash and clutched his forearm. "Then what will happen?"

"You need to just listen."

Bash asked, "For the bell? Who rings it? Does Matt ring it and then shapeshift?"

Sally tightened her grip on Bash's arm. "We have close friends and family out there. Are they in danger?"

Bash's heart thumped in his chest. He forgot about The Ma'iingan Bluff Werewolf gang. Tiny must've felt the tension in Bash rise because he now stood next to Bash with his ears pointing to the ceiling.

Mare calmly replied, "We trained my husband and son to only eat the hearts and livers of deer that we supply for them. Then they go peacefully. Usually."

Bash gulped. "Usually? That doesn't sound very good."

Mare caught his eye in the darkness. "We've been doing this for many years. I'm confident in saying that they won't harm your friends and family. Most likely."

Sally said to Mare, "What you're doing is a risk. Can't you see that? Your husband and son are beasts. Unpredictable and-"

Sounding angry, Mare scolded Sally. "Oh, you don't know anything. They are my husband and my son and they are gentle creatures! For the most part." She shifted in her seat and continued speaking to Sally. "Do you have a husband? Or a son?"

"Never had time for that nonsense, but-"

"Then you don't understand the love a woman has for them. The love that *I* have for them. They are kind. They are loving. And I thought I lost them. Forever. And I grieved. For some time. First, my husband. Then my son. And then I wanted to stop grieving, and the only way I could was to be with them. Here. In the woods, far from civilization. So, with the help of Jen and Matt, we built this campground to be near them. My son's wife, my grandson and me.

To help them. A woman, who is a wife and a mother, never stops providing for her family. That's what I've been doing. Providing."

A silence fell and Tiny leaned into Bash as Sally still held his arm. Without shifting his gaze from Mare, Bash stroked Tiny's head while contemplating. He found himself in a scary, yet astonishing, situation. He was so close to succeeding at this endeavor. In a tentative, hopeful voice, he asked Mare, "Can I see the werewolves? Just one? It doesn't matter which one."

Mare shook her head. "No, you really don't want to see them… or them to see you."

Bash's shoulders dropped. "Please?"

He heard Mare sigh before saying, "Bash, I can't. Don't you understand? They'll kill you. Probably."

■　■　■

The RV skidded to a stop. Rae's eyes frantically searched the darkness for the beasts, but only saw invading darkness. After a few tense seconds, Travis ran around the bent front bumper toward the group, still huddled together. Tiny happily panted as Travis quickly asked Rae, "Did I hit 'em?" He didn't wait for a response, though. Instead, he took the lead and herded everyone into his RV.

They all quickly found seats as Travis slid behind the wheel. Trying to start the engine, he talked to them, sounding winded. "I followed you, Rae. And when I saw that huge bear come up behind you, I ran back to the RV, as fast as I could. My plan was to drive over here and save you guys." The engine didn't turn over and, with shaky hands, he turned the key again. "I never ran so fast. I didn't think I was that coordinated. But I didn't stop. I didn't want to let my team down." The engine stuttered a few times, but never engaged. He swore and stepped on the gas. The engine cleared its throat, but that was all. Travis strained to look over his shoulder and said, "Don't worry. It'll start. The bears can't get us in here. We're safe now."

"Those weren't bears," Kimmy corrected as she rocked back and forth in a corner by the table. "Right, Chuck?"

Chuck crouched in the way back, pale and visibly trembling. "Those were werewolves."

Travis shook his head in disbelief. "Those weren't werewolves. They were bears."

"They were demons, conjured up by Bash and his tarot cards." With wide eyes, Tonya sat next to Rae on the couch. "All of his so-called readings came true. I picked the Two of Swords, which meant I was stuck between a rock and hard place, and I was. These past two days, I was deciding whether or not to quit my job for another." Tonya pointed at Kimmy. "You picked the Seven of Swords, which meant you kept a deep dark secret, and you did have one. You almost took out Tom with your car, but you forgave yourself, like the card said to do. Then Chuck picked the Tower card, which had something to do with losing his life." Tonya looked at Chuck and continued, "And you were almost eaten by a hellhound." Facing Rae, she said, "Your card was the Lovers card and, clearly, you and Stone are in love with each other. And you, Travis." Tonya uttered, "You drew the Four of Cups, which meant you're an unmotivated jerk." She scanned the group. "See? All the cards we picked were accurate."

Chuck nodded. "And, not to mention, we all picked the Death card and the Three of Pentacles."

Kimmy meekly added, "We all worked together as a team to evade death. How curious."

"Holy shit," Rae solemnly spoke. "Do you know what this means?" When no one replied, she said, "We actually succeeded at a team-building activity." When her meaning was understood by the team, they all started to chuckle, one by one. The release in each one grew and, soon, they were doubled over in laughter. Rae leaned toward Tonya, practically falling on her, and gave her the tightest hug her arms would offer. And, this time, Tonya returned the hug with the same strength. Then, the others joined that hug with Travis's wide wingspan enveloping everyone.

After a moment, Rae released herself from all of her newfound friends. While wiping away her tears, Rae said to the group, "Guys, I beg of you. Don't tell Bash that the cards were right." Rae then gasped, covering her mouth with her hands. "Speaking of Bash." Rae looked around the cabin at the others. "We can't tell him about the werewolves either. Please, promise me that we'll keep this to ourselves. I can't have Bash obsess over this. He'll never stop."

Chuck asked, "Do you think the werewolves are dead?"

Rae shrugged. "I don't know. I'm not a werewolf doctor and I'm not going out there to check."

Kimmy reminded the group. "Bash said that the only way to really kill a werewolf is to shoot it with a silver bullet."

Rae wondered, "Does a silver RV count?"

Without warning, the door of the RV ripped off its hinges and a long hairy arm with sharp claws reached into the cabin, swiping the air. Travis screamed at the top of his lungs. It was an ear-splitting high note that could have shattered the entire crystal city under Antarctica. Surprisingly, the werewolves didn't enter. Instead, Rae heard a rhythmic gallop as the werewolves retreated. Rae didn't understand the turn of events until she heard a distant bell, clanging three times. And, as the others breathed a sigh of relief at what felt like a successful escape, Rae stood, realizing that Stone and Bash were still out there. Somewhere. Her heart fell to her feet. Reaching for Travis, she grasped the collar of his pressed shirt and ordered, "Follow those werewolves!"

CHAPTER FORTY TWO

Stone ran as fast as he could. Holding his cellphone in his hand, he had no light to guide him around the trees and bushes. He solely relied on Prissy's help as she appeared at every turn, directing him to the south park office.

Finally, Stone burst out of the woods onto the grassy area. Using his last bit of strength, he pushed his body to its absolute maximum, feeling the burn inside his thighs. The pounding behind Stone alerted him of Tom's advancing feet. He tried to push himself more when, ahead of him, he saw Matt and Jen on the front porch.

Stone tried to scream, but the air left his lungs and the words were not audible. Matt and Jen didn't hear him. They weren't looking at him at all, but hunched over a cooler, absorbed in something else. Stone's legs buckled and he fell to the ground. As he lay on his side, his broad shoulders heaving and his long legs useless, he desperately looked at Matt and Jen. He yearned for them when his eyes saw a white, wispy figure, standing by the hanging bell. It was Prissy and her ghostly hand reached for the string, pulling it three times. Clang! Clang! Clang!

That familiar sound startled Stone. He recognized it as the same clanging in his vision. Rolling onto his back, he raised himself onto his elbows, just in time for Tom to throw a strong right hook across Stone's jaw. Pain radiated through his head. Tom grabbed him by the collar and pulled his arm back with his fist positioned for another strike. His murderous eyes were crazed and froth rained from his mouth. And, as Stone's sentience began to dissolve from the first punch, he lost the fight in keeping his eyes open, as well as the fight against Tom. His head tipped back in defeat. He thought of Rachel and her birthday. And he finally thought of a great gift to give to her. Helpless, the darkness of unconsciousness set in and Stone felt a strong whoosh of air rush past him followed by another. Heavy blackness overcame Stone, but he still felt Tom being ripped from him and he still heard Tom release a scream, distant and dripping with finality.

Stone lay motionless on the grass. He managed a grateful half-smile for interrupted boxing matches and for being saved by the bell. He then saw Prissy in his mind's eye. She smiled, touched the brim of her Stetson hat and turned, marching in the other direction toward a group of white trees. They were tall, breath-taking and comforting. Knowing Prissy was in a good place, her own heaven, Stone allowed himself to pass out. Cold.

∎   ∎   ∎

Bash heard the far-off clanging and he remembered Zalen's words, *'Therefore, never send to know for whom the bell tolls'*. Bash wondered. Who was the bell tolling for? Stone? His aunt? Tiny whined and Bash pulled him closer. "Don't worry. Everything's fine. Right, Mare?"

Mare replied softly, "Yes."

Bash asked her, "What time is it?"

"It's after three. It'll just be a few more minutes."

Sally's hand dropped from Bash's arm to clasp his hand and they stood together in silence. As a child, whenever he was frightened, his mom would tell him to think of something that made him happy and then count. Count to any number. It didn't matter.

Just count. So, even though he didn't feel super scared, but scared enough, Bash thought of his family. He thought of his mom and dad, Emma, Henry and Meg. A scream startled him and his eyes shot toward Mare. Her eyes were already on him and she gave him a reassuring smile in the moonlight. Bash started to count as he then thought of Aunt Rae, Stone and Zalen and their secret handshake. A dragging sound caught Bash's attention, as well as Tiny's. It was outside the shed. The Great Shepherd whined and Mare quickly, forcefully shushed him. Bash heard the tearing of fabric and the breaking of bones. His eyes widened in horror and he opened his mouth to speak, but Sally's hand covered it before he uttered a sound. Sally softly hummed in his ear and, closing his eyes, Bash continued his counting while concentrating on Tiny and Sally, who stood faithfully on either side of him. Blocking out the sounds of animals devouring their prey, he counted and counted, even through the spine-chilling nearby howls of The Ma'iingan Bluff Werewolves after they ate.

Then there was silence.

"Okay," Mare whispered. "It's over. You can go home now under one condition."

Bash softly asked, "What's that?"

With an imploring voice, Mare said, "Promise me that we'll keep this to ourselves. Understand? Don't tell anyone about what I said or what you heard. For your well-being, as well as for my husband's and my son's. I know you can understand that. So, please, promise me that you'll keep my family's curse a secret. Please."

Mare's face filled with a mixture of hope and fear. The sound of bones breaking echoed through Bash's ears. He nodded. "I promise."

Mare audibly exhaled, as if she had been holding her breath for years. Bash then thought, *maybe she has?* He watched her as she laboriously stepped through the doorway. Her legs bowed from the many years of walking on them. And, when the moon's rays cascaded onto her flannel nightgown and wrinkled face, Bash saw the loving warmth in her eyes. She gave him a sly wink while gesturing for them to leave and saying, "Now, go and don't ever come back here again."

ONE LAST THING

When Stone regained consciousness, he said her name. Rachel. Time magically slowed, allowing all of her stresses of werewolves and death and park rangers and bribes to melt like cheese on toast. And as she cradled his head in her arms, Stone began talking about visions, ghosts and psychic abilities, which surprised Rae because it all made sense to her now. His stone wall. His icy, cool stare. His distance. At that moment, Rae heard Bash's words echo through her mind. *Put yourself in his shoes.* She did. She felt his loneliness. She felt his confusion. She felt his pain. There was only one thing to do and that was to lower her lips onto his. He then smiled at her and she knew, no matter what, she would be with him.

The momentum of the early morning accelerated after that. It involved unnerving talks about Tom and Prissy, followed by immediate action to call the police. It involved more talks about ice packs, bears and clearing out the two campsites as quickly as possible. It involved secret looks between her team whenever the word *bears* was mentioned. And where was Zalen? More talks. More guesses. More concerns and then Zalen appeared at the campsite, thank goodness. He was lost and then found. Weren't they all? Another talk about driving arrangements. After all, Kimmy's car was forever stuck between two trees and Stone was still dazed. No matter, Kimmy would drive Rae's car, Rae would take Stone and Zalen home. Meanwhile, Sally offered to drive Bash to Polk and Travis would drop off Tonya and Chuck at the north park office where their cars were parked. But what about Tiny? There was really only one solution.

"Travis, don't drive all herky and jerky."

"I'll be very careful with your dog, Rae. He'll like riding home in the RV. I have a large couch that he can stretch out on."

"I'll be following you the whole way."

"I know, Rae. Now, let's stop wasting time. I really hate camping. I hope you plan a better team-building retreat next time." He grinned and Rae refrained from punching him.

They left then. The whole team. A train of cars, led by the silver monstrosity with a bent front bumper, maneuvered around the trees and vacant campsites without any regard to the speed limit. They all seemed to drive as fast as they could, even Rae. Stones on the gravel path shot in every direction from the fast-rotating tires as Rae stepped on the accelerator. When she turned the bend, Rae cast a glance toward the south park office in all of its rustic splendor. There, on the porch, stood Mare, Jen and Matt. Rae didn't wave, but kept her eyes on the road, relieved to go and to never come back. And, as she left Fun Warriors Ranch, she shuddered as a bell tolled faintly behind her.

■　　■　　■

It was Friday. Stone hung a sign on the entrance door to The Rail. It read *Closed.* However, the bar wasn't empty. A small gathering of people were there, wearing party hats. A nearby cake was displayed on a central table as music blared over the sound system. Someone lowered the music and the group assembled around the cake with Rachel standing at the head of the table. Bash joined her on one side and Tiny on the other. The rest of the circle was filled in by Chuck, Sally, Kimmy, Tonya, Zalen, Travis, Mort, Seth, Stone and, of course, the little Bichon Frise who happily sat next to the Great Shepherd.

A chorus of voices sang and Rachel listened graciously to the off-key rendition of the traditional birthday song. When it ended, Rachel simply said, "You are all such wonderful friends." As she picked up the knife to cut the cake, Travis stopped her and Seth handed her an envelope with the words *Well-deserved* written on it.

Seth then spoke, "He came home a changed man. Whatever you said to him made more of an impact than anything his therapist has said over these past ten years."

Travis wiped Mort's messy mouth with his bare thumb. "Oh, please. It's been twelve."

Chuck raised his hand and asked Travis, "Does this mean you're nice now?"

Travis snapped. "Shut up, Chuck." He then turned to Rachel again, raising his glass of wine and saying, "Anyway, Rae, there is something that I need to say to you for saving our marriage *and* for being a great Team-Building Committee. It's two humble words." He winked. "Thank you." Travis then nodded to her. "Well, open the damn card."

Rachel obeyed and squeaked when the five one hundred bills fell out of the card. With a look of shock on her face, she shook her head. "I can't take this."

Tonya disagreed. "Take it, Rae. He put you through hell."

"And all of you." Rachel immediately handed her one of the bills. "I'll share."

"He already paid us," Chuck said.

"Yeah." Kimmy enthusiastically nodded. "We're all good."

Bash nudged his aunt in the shoulder. "I'll happily take two hundred and fifty."

Travis scoffed. "What does a twelve-year old need two hundred fifty dollars for?"

Bash quickly answered, "Night vision binoculars. They only cost seven grand."

Rachel smacked her forehead and Travis laughed while saying, "You need a job, kid."

Chuck asked Bash, "What are you planning to do with those?"

Bash's blue eyes brightened as he replied, "Catch a squonk."

"Oooo," said Kimmy. "Sounds exciting."

Snapping her fingers at Bash, Sally said, "I've heard of them."

Tiny whined and looked at Rachel whose wide eyes were already on Stone. He shrugged and casually took her by the arm. Leading her to the bar, he reached behind the counter and found the small red gift bag. He handed it to her with a grin.

Rachel searched inside the bag for the contents and pulled out a pair of fuzzy socks with a design of a sloth on them. Not one fuzzy sock, but a pair. She bubbled in laughter and then wrapped her arms around him. "I love them," she said with even rosier cheeks than before. Her eyes teared as she searched his face. "And I love you, Stonehenge."

Stone caught his breath. He wasn't expecting that. And then he kicked himself for not buying her fuzzy sloth socks sooner. A mental slap brought him quickly back to the current situation and he blurted, "I love you, Stingray. I always have and I always will."

Rachel brushed her lips against his cheek before picking up the remote control to raise the volume of the music. A familiar tune filled The Rail and he smiled as Rachel's fingers interlaced with his. She led him to the middle of the floor to dance. While standing face to face, he lifted her hand and kissed her soft skin. And, then this time, when he lowered her hand, he didn't let go. As they bounced along to the beat, his smile widened as she sang along to "Lollipop" by the Chordettes, convincing Stone that his vision came full circle in *the end.*

THE END

ACKNOWLEDGEMENTS AND THANKS

I would like to give a special thank you to Black Rose Writing for offering a traditional contract in regard to publishing my book. I would also like to thank Kathie Giorgio for her editing expertise. Furthermore, I desperately need to thank all of my family and friends for their many, many words of encouragement. In particular (but in no particular order), my mom and dad, Brian, Ella, Hugh, Evan, Brooklyn, Annie Roonie, Chris, Kris, Kellie, Kelli, Kelly, Katie, Katie, the other Katie, Steve and Deb, Lynn, cousin Renee, Abbie, Hayley, Tamma and Cassandra, my number one fan. Last, but not least, a final warm thank you to my new friends in Hortonville: The Cedar Cliff Book Club. I'll see you soon!

ABOUT THE AUTHOR

Growing up, BW Hoff always had to dig the trench around her family's tent when camping. Nowadays, BW rarely camps. In fact, she doesn't camp at all. She would rather have all her teeth pulled. Living in the Midwest with her family, BW Hoff enjoys playing board games, touring haunted locations, and taking family vacations when they have the time and money. When she's not writing, BW works in the education field with many good people. Fortunately, none of them are anything like the antagonist, Travis, in her *Rae Greyson Mysteries.*

BW HOFF
A RAE GREYSON MYSTERY
THE SHRILL
OF IT ALL

NOTE FROM BW HOFF

Word-of-mouth is crucial for any author to succeed. If you enjoyed *Where Wolves Wait*, please leave a review online—anywhere you are able. Even if it's just a sentence or two. It would make all the difference and would be very much appreciated.

Thanks!
BW Hoff

We hope you enjoyed reading this title from:

www.blackrosewriting.com

Subscribe to our mailing list – *The Rosevine* – and receive **FREE** books, daily
deals, and stay current with news about upcoming
releases and our hottest authors.
Scan the QR code below to sign up.

Already a subscriber? Please accept a sincere thank you for being a fan of
Black Rose Writing authors.

View other Black Rose Writing titles at
www.blackrosewriting.com/books and use promo code
PRINT to receive a **20% discount** when purchasing.